THE ISLAND
WHERE TIME STANDS STILL

*

Gregory Sallust, perhaps the most famous of Mr. Wheatley's heroes, is shipwrecked on an island in the South Seas, and finds himself in a lost community of Chinese, ruled by descendants of the ancient Imperial House. When the throne suddenly becomes vacant, an expedition sets out to find the true heir. Its members include Gregory himself and the lady A-lu-te, as intriguingly lovely as her name; their search leads ten thousand miles across the Pacific into the remotest regions of inland China. Death in horrible forms and treachery follow them as closely as their shadows. Here we have fast-moving, high adventure, with that tingle of the spine which tells us that this is vintage Wheatley, the master at his most skilful.

D1514393

Dennis Wheatley

The Island Where Time Stands Still

ARROW BOOKS

ARROW BOOKS LTD
3 Fitzroy Square, London W1

AN IMPRINT OF THE HUTCHINSON GROUP

London Melbourne Sydney Auckland
Wellington Johannesburg Cape Town
and agencies throughout the world

✲

First published by
Hutchinson & Co (*Publishers*) Ltd 1954
Arrow edition 1961
Second impression 1964
Third impression 1965
New edition 1971

*Made and printed in Great Britain
by The Anchor Press Ltd.,
Tiptree, Essex*

ISBN 0 09 005470 9

CONTENTS

My dear Dennis,

I must admit that you have grounds for complaint; although, to me, it seems hardly credible that eight years should have slipped by since I last provided you with material for a book. I am all the more touched to hear that still, after all this time, a week seldom passes without some of your readers writing to ask what has happened to me.

In self-defence, I would point out that you could have satisfied their kind interest at least to the extent of relating my activities up to the end of World War II; but you chose to terminate your account of them in December 1941. Moreover, you left your readers under the impression that Erika's husband had been liquidated by Grauber. Had Erika and I been less mentally exhausted after our nightmare crossing of Lake Constance, we should have realized that none of the Nazis in the boat was armed; and that, as we learned later, the shot we heard was fired from a Swiss patrol boat in an unsuccessful endeavour to prevent Grauber and his pals getting back to Germany.

I think it rather a pity that you have not yet described for your readers how von Osterberg really met his death, my final round with Grauber, and those unforgettable last hours with Hitler in the bunker. But perhaps you are right about the public being temporarily surfeited with tales of how we got the better of the Nazis, and that they would arouse much greater interest after a lapse of a few more years, which would give them almost an historical flavour.

As far as my activities since the war are concerned, it is true that I have been on a number of secret missions; but to give an account of any of them in detail would involve disclosing information which a foreign power would be very glad to have; so there can be no question of publishing these for the time being. However, although few people know it, I was recently written off as dead for the best part of a year. During that time I became involved in what might almost be termed a private enterprise of a 'kill or be killed' nature; and, rather than disappoint your readers altogether, I am sending you my notes about it.

The Pacific is a big place; the Chinese are a strange people; but love and greed don't vary much the world over, do they? You know how my mind works well enough by now for me to be confident that you will give a fair picture of my reactions during these strange events which nearly cost me my reason and did cost a lot of other people their lives. More power to your elbow.

Yours ever,

Gregory Sallust

P.S.

I still have a little of the Pol Roger '28 you sent me in return for my last batch of notes, and it is now so good I'm keeping it for very special occasions. This time I rather favour Louis Roederer '45, preferably in magnums, if you can find me some.

G.

P.P.S.

I am hoping to be back in England shortly, and that will definitely be an occasion for us to knock off a bottle or two of the '28.

G.

PROLOGUE

'IN THE MIDST OF LIFE'

'T H I S,' thought Gregory Sallust, 'is It!'

Another huge wave loomed above him like the side of a cliff, curled over, broke in a seething cascade of foam, and submerged him as though he was a rag doll drawn under the torrent of a mill-race.

He had been in many a tight corner before, and courage, quick wits, endurance, audacity, or some combination of them, had always saved him ; but now, as hundreds of tons of water forced him fathoms deep into awful smothering blackness, he knew that even had he possessed the nine lives of a cat he would still be food for fishes long before morning. He was in the middle of the Pacific, a piece of human flotsam at the mercy of a raging tempest, and he had no chance whatever of being picked up.

At ten o'clock that night Sir Pellinore Gwaine-Cust's yacht had struck a submerged coral-reef. It had ripped a great hole in her bottom, and within ten minutes they had known that nothing could save her. As, with flooded engine rooms, she wallowed in the trough of huge seas they had striven to get out the boats. The big launch had hardly touched the water when it was caught up and smashed like an egg-shell against the ship's side. By then the yacht had been well down at the bows, so some of them had floated off on a cork raft from the fo'c'sle. Before they could distribute their weight evenly it had capsized and pinned several of them beneath it. Gregory was flung clear, caught on a wave crest and, in a matter of seconds, carried out of sight of his still-struggling companions. The moon was not yet up, only starlight lit the storm-tossed waters, as he struck out in a wild endeavour to rejoin them. His efforts proved unavailing. Above the booming of the hurricane he caught a single despairing cry, then his last contact with the two beings he loved best in the world was broken.

As he came gasping to the surface he thought for a second of the appalling swiftness with which calamity had overwhelmed them. When they had gone in to dinner at half-past eight the sea had been calm and the sky cloudless. Sir Pellinore's eight guests might then justifiably have counted themselves among the luckiest people on earth. Between them they had an unusual degree of charm, intelligence, wit and beauty ; all of them had a sufficiency of money, and the leisure to accept the elderly Baronet's invitation to accompany him on a trip around the world. Despite his magnificent physique he had at last begun to feel his age, and his doctor had prescribed a year of sunshine. He was one of the few Englishmen left who could still afford to keep a two thousand ton yacht and delighted to entertain in it lavishly.

With a French chef in the galley, the cellar of a life-long connoisseur, and every comfort that money could provide, they had cruised in leisurely manner through the Mediterranean, the Red Sea and the Indian Ocean. Every few days they had stopped for a night or two in one port after another, to go ashore, to meet old friends and make new ones, to entertain or be entertained by diplomats and celebrities. From Singapore they had gone down to Java, then up to Borneo and round by the Celebes through the countless islands of the South Seas to Tahiti. Thence, they had turned north for the two thousand odd mile run to Hawaii. It was on the third night out that the typhoon had caught them.

All unsuspecting they had assembled in the lounge, the men wearing dinner jackets, the women with light furs over shoulders left bare by their evening dresses. Even half way through dinner, when it had suddenly become obvious that they were in for a stormy night, only little Zenobia Walshingham and the lovely golden-haired Barbara Harland-Woolf had elected to retire to their cabins. The others had finished the meal and returned to the lounge for coffee and liqueurs. Arthur Walshingham had been setting up the backgammon board for his nightly game with Myra Blandish, when the ship struck. The shock sent every movable thing flying across the lounge, yet none of them had panicked. Who could, with Sir Pellinore calmly apologizing to them for his yacht having behaved in such a 'demned inconsiderate manner'? He had apologized to them again as she was going down, advising the women to wrap up warmly and the men to see that their flasks were full of brandy.

That had been half an hour—no, barely ten minutes—ago. And now, that grand old man, the pretty women and the battle-tested younger men he loved to have about him, his Captain, his faithful servants and his crew were all drowned or drowning.

Gregory closed his eyes, but not from fear of the next mountain of water that was rushing upon him. It was due to agony of spirit at the thought that somewhere not far off in the semi-darkness his beloved Erika must be choking out her life. His last glimpse of her had been as the raft turned over. She had been trying to calm the terrors of a young stewardess. Her arm had been round the girl's shoulders. Both of them were fair, and as the last distress rocket sent up from the yacht burst a hundred feet up its glare had lit their mingled hair as it streamed out behind them, like a yellow pennant in the tearing wind.

It was Pellinore who had been sending up the rockets. He had pretended that he was coming on the raft, but at the last moment pushed it off; yelling that some of his 'fellers' were still trying to launch a boat on the port side. Had there been time for thought, they might have known that the instinct of a man who for fifty years had worn a V.C. on all ceremonial occasions would never permit him to abandon his own ship while there was a living soul aboard her. Gregory loved the old boy like a father, and groaned again at the thought that for him too there could be no escape.

The rockets were no more likely to bring help in that vast waste than the lighting of a tallow dip; neither were the S.O.S.s frantically tapped out up to the last on the wireless. The only shipping route to the north of Tahiti ran north-east to San

Francisco, and their course to Hawaii being north-west had already carried them hundreds of miles away from it. The nearest land was the widely-scattered Manihiki Islands, but they were little more than coral atolls; many were uninhabited and even the largest were places at which ancient trading vessels called only once or twice a year.

Again Gregory was sucked down, down, down, until he felt as if his lungs must burst, and it was only after moments of excruciating agony that his life-jacket brought him back to the surface. Thrusting himself up, he gazed desperately round for the masts of the sinking yacht but they had disappeared. While under water he had been so whirled about that he had lost all sense of direction and with it, now that the yacht was gone, any hope of fighting his way back to the place where he had last seen Erika.

Realizing the futility of battling further against the wind-whipped waves, he ceased his struggles, and soon found that it was now easier to keep his head above water. For a while, like a bobbing cork, he was rushed at express speed up steep dark slopes, temporarily smothered in the white surf at their summits, then tobogganed down glassy inclines into further great water valleys. Now and then he let out a shout, but no answer came from the surrounding gloom, and the only sign of the wreck he sighted was a floating oar.

It was soon after he had seized upon it that he became aware that the storm was easing. The fact brought home to him how accursedly unfortunate they had been. The yacht, well found and capably handled as she was, could easily have ridden out the cyclone; or, had she struck the rock while the sea was calm, it should have been possible to keep her afloat until her radio brought help. It was the combination of the two menaces occurring simultaneously which had resulted in such swift and irretrievable disaster.

But the dying down of the wind brought him no comfort. He had lost the woman he loved, the old friend to whom he owed so much, and those other friends who had made such a gay and gallant company. He knew, too, that only the instinct of self-preservation had caused him to grab the oar. In those desolate waters the added support it gave him could only prolong the

14

agony. It meant only the difference of an hour or so before he also must perish.

Although the wave crests were no longer breaking with their former fury, freshets of spray continued to dash themselves against his face, and he was still swallowing a lot of water. It made him feel sick and giddy. His eyes were sore, his body ached from the strain to which it had been put and he felt incredibly weary.

In an effort to keep his mind off Erika he tried to conjure up scenes from his life before he met her. Memories of other women drifted into his mental vision. Sabine, the beautiful Hungarian, as he had first seen her at the casino at Deauville; lovely, laughing Phyllis, with whom he had taken a stolen holiday up the Rhine; wicked little black-eyed Minette, who had so nearly caused his death in China, during the first secret industrial investigation that he had carried out for Sir Pellinore. His thoughts turned to his closest men friends, then to other people—just faces, to many of which he could not put a name. Some were those of old enemies, others of girls with whom he had had only casual flirtations; a few of desperate idealistic loves which had tormented him in youth. One was sweet seventeen, with golden cork-screw curls, blue eyes and a big floppy hat bedecked with corn-flowers. He had adored her all one summer, living through the weeks only for Sundays to come again, when he would see her walking sedately with her parents after Church; but he had never even spoken to her. At that time he had been a Cadet in H.M.S. *Worcester*. The thought carried him back still further, to childhood days.

He was thinking of the wall-paper in his day-nursery when the oar slipped from his grasp. The effort needed to recover it brought him back with a jerk to the grim present. It occurred to him then that to recall episodes from one's past life was said to be usual with people on the point of drowning—and that he was drowning.

In sudden revolt he began to kick out vigorously. He was still in the prime of life. It could hold many joys and interests for him yet. He did not want to die. Somehow he must win through, as he had so often won through before. If he could only keep afloat long enough, some unforeseeable twist of fate would surely save him.

Moderating his movements in order to husband his strength, he kept his chin well up and endeavoured to breast each wave he met without taking in more water. It was not easy; and a fresh surge of despair at the thought that he would never again see Erika took the heart out of his new bid for survival. None the less, an inherent conviction that one should never surrender to an enemy or adverse circumstance kept him going until it seemed to him that he had spent a lifetime gliding up long watery slopes and sliding down their far sides.

The water was not cold, but its constant pressure had the effect of gradually numbing his limbs. His neck began to ache intolerably from the strain of keeping it rigid. From time to time he could no longer prevent his chin falling on his chest and, with his head rolling a little, his face slipping under water. Again his thoughts drifted to the past; the night he had drunk Stefan Kuporovitch under the table at Kandalaksk; the final bout in his year's-long duel with Gruppenführer Grauber; the beach at Dunkirk, from which he had watched the British Army taken off in little boats; his old henchman Rudd describing in graphic cockney how he had won a darts match at the local in Gloucester Road; his first assignment as a journalist. Then a succession of long-forgotten scenes from his youth floated before his mental vision.

He was thinking of the two great mulberry trees in his grandfather's garden when, unnoticed this time, the oar again slipped from his grasp. Above him the Southern Cross and a myriad of other stars shone with serene indifference. All effort spent, and now buoyed up only by his life-jacket he lapsed into unconsciousness, becoming no more than an inert speck on the bosom of the mighty ocean.

1

THE CAGE

IT was some fishermen collecting the catch from their lobster pots who came upon Gregory's body the following morning. Had he remained conscious a little longer he might have seen against the star-spangled sky the dark bulk of the island towards which the aftermath of the hurricane had carried him, for its volcanic cliffs rose sheer and high from a narrow strip of beach. Luckily for him it was not upon the beach that he had been washed up, otherwise he might have remained there unnoticed until the birds had picked his carcass clean. A wave had thrown him into a shallow pool on the barrier reef, between which and the shore lay a half-mile-wide stretch of placid water. The lobster pots were on the lagoon side of the reef and could be reached only in a small boat which had to be manœuvred through a narrow channel from the sea. It was while the little boat was nosing its way through that one of the men in it caught sight of Gregory's head and shoulders protruding from the pool.

Scrambling across the rocks, they bent above him in a chattering group. At first they thought him dead, but after a brief examination the eldest among them declared that his spirit still inhabited his body; so they took him to the larger vessel which had brought them to the outer side of the reef, and set about endeavouring to revive him.

Their methods were primitive but effective. Having stripped him naked they threw him face down across the low gunwale with his head hanging over the side; then they proceeded to pummel and slap him all over. The treatment restored his circulation and caused him to spew up much of the water he had swallowed; but when his mind began dimly to grope for its surroundings again, it was for a long time conscious only of his body as one universal ache. This was hardly surprising as, apart from the rawness of his internal membranes caused by the salt water, he had suffered severely from having been thrown up on the reef. Two of his ribs had been broken, the back of his skull fractured and in a score of places he had been terribly bruised.

When his rescuers heard his breath whistling regularly between his teeth, and saw his shoulder muscles twitching from his retching, they pulled him inboard, laid him on the bottom boards in the stern, threw his clothes over him in a heap to protect him from the sun, and went about their own business. Staring upwards, Gregory took in the fact that the one of their number they had left behind to tend the tiller looked like a Chinaman, then he again lapsed into unconsciousness.

When next he came to, he was lying on a mat bed with a light cotton covering over him. As he opened his eyes there was a slight stir beside him. Another Chinese face bent over his and he was given a few mouthfuls of a pleasant-tasting drink; but no sooner had he moved his head than an excruciating twinge shot through it and his senses once more ebbed away in a wave of pain.

For most of the four days that followed he was either in a drug-induced sleep or delirious; but during his few lucid intervals he gathered that he was in a small, clean, sparsely furnished room that had a vaguely oriental atmosphere.

When his thoughts at length became intermittently coherent, actual memories of his immediate past began to mingle with frightful nightmares, in which he was again upon the sinking yacht or struggling in turbulent seas. At first he could not bring himself to believe that these were anything other than appalling dreams. Yet as his mind became clearer it demanded to know how otherwise he could be where he was and physically in such a shocking state.

Eventually he rallied his strength enough to question the man who was looking after him, but the oriental spoke no English. Having spent the best part of a year in China in the early nineteen-thirties, Gregory had learned to speak 'pidgin' fairly fluently and picked up a smattering of 'Mandarin'. With an effort he managed to recall a few words of the latter, but they proved insufficient to make himself understood.

The attempt had taken a lot out of him, so he abandoned it and drifted off to sleep. When he woke there was another Chinaman sitting on the chair beside his bed, whose face he recalled having seen several times while he was semi-delirious. This one was better dressed; his blouse was of blue silk and he wore a round silk skull-cap. He appeared to be about forty years of age and his grave face was that of an educated man. Hoping for better luck, Gregory addressed him.

He immediately stood up, bowed ceremoniously, and said with a lisp but in good English, 'This person is Ho-Ping. He has the honour to be your doctor. It has been his difficult privilege to restrain your spirit from joining those of your distinguished ancestors. Informed by the menial who attends you that your excellent mind has regained its clarity, this one hastened to bring you reassurance regarding your condition. The danger of your honourable spirit leaving your admirably proportioned body is now passed; but the meagre talents of this unworthy practitioner will require the co-operation of your obviously sensible self if the numerous injuries inflicted on you by evil chance are to be quickly healed. It is deferentially prescribed that you should refrain from exerting your muscles for some time to come, and that for the present you should talk very little.'[1]

Gregory thanked him, introduced himself, and, in a half-cracked husky voice, asked the things he most urgently wanted to know.

In reply Dr. Ping confirmed that his patient was on a Pacific island and had been rescued from its barrier reef when three parts drowned; but he had heard nothing of any recent

[1] The pronoun 'I' is rarely used by the Chinese, as to do so is considered outrageously immodest. It is also customary for them to belittle self in almost every sentence, and to use most involved methods of expressing their meaning. Even 'pidgin' is far from easy to understand by those unaccustomed to it, and the better-educated Chinese who speak correct English rarely succeed in overcoming a marked lisp. Any attempt to give a literal rendering of the dialogue spoken by the Chinese characters in this story would therefore be most tiresome for the reader. In consequence it has seemed preferable to give only, where possible, a Chinese flavour to their speech, while interpreting their expressions into our vernacular.

wreck, and he was quite certain that no other survivors, or bodies, from it had been washed up.

'What is the name of this island?' Gregory inquired.

Dr. Ping hesitated a second, then he said, 'It is not very large, and it is of no importance whatever. In fact, it is rightly considered unworthy of being named, except on large-scale nautical charts. On those it is referred to as Leper Settlement Number Six.'

Refraining from comment on this depressing piece of information, Gregory croaked, 'Is it one of a large group?'

'Very large.' Ho-Ping's pleasant face broke into a placid smile. 'The Manihikis are spread over an area greater than that of France and Germany together ; but they are few in number, and so widely scattered that most of them are further from their nearest neighbours than London is from the coast of France. To reach any other land from here it would be necessary to cross about one hundred and forty miles of ocean.'

'In that case, as I was the only person to be washed up here, it seems certain that no one else could possibly have survived the wreck.'

The smile left Dr. Ping's face as though it had been wiped off with a towel. He bowed again. 'It is to be feared that your discerning statement is unquestionably correct. And now, please, permit the observation that further talking may retard recovery.'

Gregory replied with a slow nod, and as the doctor left him turned over with his face towards the wall. He knew the worst now. His nightmare fears were only too well founded. His beloved Erika was dead. So too were gallant old Pellinore and all the rest. He had other friends in England and scattered up and down the world, but weighed in the balance against this terrible double blow they hardly counted. He felt as if his heart had been ripped out of his body. Life could never be the same again. After prolonged and agonized thought he decided that he now had nothing worth living for, so he did not want to recover. He would rather die.

But he did not die. His lack of the will to live slowed up his recovery, but his lean, sinewy body, deep lungs and strong heart mended him physically despite his mental wounds. For days on end he lay doing nothing, refusing to amuse himself with the puzzles and Chinese picture books that Ho-Ping brought him, and politely declining the doctor's offers to teach him Ma-jong or play chess. Yet at length the time came when he had to face the fact that he was quite well enough to get up.

Reluctantly, one afternoon, he allowed the doctor to lead him from his room and make him comfortable in a chair that the servant, whose name he now knew to be Chung, had placed just outside the door for him. His utter lack of interest had so far stifled any desire to find out about his surroundings; so he knew only from casual glances through his window that the building in which he lived must be high up on the side of a valley, as nothing could be seen from it except a steep, barren cliff, topped with sun-scorched undergrowth, about half a mile away.

Now he could see the whole panorama, and he was considerably surprised by it. Below him lay a land-locked harbour partly fringed with palms, but evidently deep enough to take an ocean-going tramp, as on one side of it there was a hundred-yard-long wharf, with cranes for unloading and a row of warehouses. Tied up to the wharf there was a grey-painted vessel that looked like an obsolete destroyer from which the guns had been removed; while near-by were moored a number of Chinese junks, one of which had a dragon's-head prow and was elaborately painted and gilded. At first he could not make out how the shipping had got into the port, as from the angle at which he was looking down he could see no entrance to it, but the departure of a junk disclosed that it was through a narrow canyon between two towering cliffs, which concealed the basin from the sea.

It occurred to Gregory at once what a perfect place it would be for a pirates' lair; and it might well have been used for that purpose in the days when the buccaneers, having been driven from the Spanish Main, had taken to roving the South Seas.

Turning his head he glanced at the building behind him, and saw that it was a long, one-storied, flat-roofed block, of which his own room made about one-twelfth part. It looked strictly utilitarian, being built of concrete slabs that had been white-washed over, and it had been erected on a wide flat ledge of rock that jutted out from the cliff face. Twenty feet from where Gregory was sitting the cliff dropped sheer away, and a few yards behind the building it reared upwards with almost equal steepness; but higher up some trees had found enough earth to take root in, and as they grew outwards at an angle the foliage of the branches of the largest gave to the building some shade from the sun.

After a moment he noticed that at each end of the terrace there was an eight-foot-high wire mesh fence, which gave the impression that the place was a prison compound; so he said to the doctor: 'What is the idea of having your sanatorium in a cage? Don't you allow your patients to go out?'

The Chinaman shrugged. 'This is not in the ordinary sense a sanatorium. It is more in the nature of an institution in which we can suitably entertain—er, immigrants.'

'Really!' Gregory raised his eyebrows. 'Since you say the island is a small one, it seems rather surprising that you should have immigrants in sufficient numbers to need a special clearance station for them.'

'Immigrants is, perhaps, hardly the right word. From time to time other vessels have been lost off our coast. This building was erected to accommodate their survivors.'

'It doesn't look as if it could hold very many.'

'Because you were severely injured, alone and your clothes indicated that you were a person of quality, you were put in one of the cubicles; but the greater part of the building consists of a large dormitory-mess room with bunks for thirty, and it is most unusual for ships with crews exceeding that number to enter these waters. Happily, too, so little shipping of any kind comes into this vicinity that wrecks are very infrequent, but it is convenient to have a place like this in which to put up such castaways as are driven on to our shores.'

'I still don't see the reason for making it a prisoners' cage,' Gregory persisted.

Dr. Ping made a deprecatory gesture. 'As soon as we can, we ship those whom fate selects as its occupants to San Francisco; but the steamer that plies between here and there is at our disposal only once in every four or five months. Experience

22

has taught us that our uninvited guests are apt to become rest-less should their departure be delayed for more than a few weeks, and we do not consider it desirable that they should roam the island at will. The electrified fence restrains any temptation they may feel to do so.'

When the doctor had bowed himself away, Gregory suddenly realized that, after a lapse of weeks, his normally active brain had again begun to function. It was asking all sorts of questions, some of which had been simmering in his sub-conscious for days past and others resulting from his emergence on to the terrace that afternoon.

Anyone washed up on a South Sea island would, on coming to, normally have expected to find themselves being cared for by natives in a palm-leaf hut, or, if particularly fortunate, in a white man's missionary station. How did it come about that he was being looked after by Chinese?

He knew, of course, that on nearly every island of any size hard-working and thrifty Chinese traders had established them-selves as store-keepers, but they did not run free hostels for shipwrecked mariners, and had little in common with cultured Ho-Ping.

And there was much more to it than that. The fact that all castaways were brought as a matter of routine to this hostel staffed by Chinese indicated that they controlled the whole island. The junks, and particularly the gorgeously decorated one, moored down in the intriguingly secret harbour could be taken as further evidence in support of such a supposition. Yet Gregory, who rather prided himself on his general knowledge, felt sure that China did not own any islands in the middle of the Pacific.

Again, why these precautions against uninvited visitors get-ting to know anything about the place? He had made no comment on Dr. Ping's statement that the wire fence was electrified, but it was that more than anything else which had galvanized his own brain out of its inertia. What was going on here that either the suave doctor, or some bigger shot who employed him, was taking such drastic precautions to hide?

It occurred to him that as the place was a leper settlement their object might be to prevent rash and ignorant seamen going

23

among the lepers and contracting their disease. But he knew that leprosy can be caught only through long and intimate association with the afflicted; so that did not seem a really adequate answer.

During the days that followed he continued at odd intervals to puzzle over the matter while gazing down at the port. Often for hours at a stretch, particularly during the midday heat, it was deserted, and such activity as he did see there told him nothing. With one exception, it was limited to the occasional arrival or departure of some of the junks, which obviously constituted a fishing fleet and were entirely manned by Chinamen.

The exception occurred on the third day after he had left his room, by which time he had recovered the use of his legs sufficiently to walk up and down the terrace. Down an avenue of palms that led inland from the harbour appeared a palanquin borne on the shoulders of eight trotting men. As it came closer he could see the sun shining on its brilliantly lacquered roof, and gaily embroidered silk curtains. When it was set down on the waterfront the curtains parted and three people got out. Two were small boys who appeared to be between eight and ten years of age. Both were richly dressed in traditional Chinese costumes and wore round hats with turned-up brims. The third was a woman in a plain blue blouse and black trousers, and evidently their amah.

They were received most deferentially by an important-looking personage whom, from the fact that he directed all activities in the port, Gregory rightly assumed to be the Harbour-Master. He had been accompanied from the small building which was evidently his office by two men dressed in clothes of somewhat better quality than those worn by the ordinary coolies who manned the junks, and they also bowed deeply to the children.

The bearers of the palanquin picked it up and set off at a trot, leaving the little group about the two boys the only people to be seen in the vicinity. With the Harbour-Master leading, and the amah bringing up the rear, they walked along the deserted wharf towards the beautiful dragon-prowed junk, which was moored at its far end.

24

The hillside from which Gregory was watching was on the opposite side of the harbour and he was over a quarter of a mile away ; but in the clear atmosphere he felt certain that his eyes could not have deceived him about what followed, although it happened very swiftly.

When the party was half-way along the wharf a door opened in one of the warehouses they had just passed, a man thrust his head out and—evidently in a low voice, as the amah was the only one to turn round—called something to her. Halting uncertainly she hesitated for a moment, then on his beckoning urgently to her, she walked back to join him. When they had exchanged a few sentences he took her by the arm, pulled her into the dark interior of the shed and quickly closed its door.

Unsuspecting of what had happened, the remainder of the party walked on. When they reached the dragon-prowed junk the Harbour-Master's two companions disappeared behind it, to emerge a moment later in a small gaily-coloured sampan. The two boys had watched the operation with keen interest, and it was only when they started down the steps to which the sampan had been brought that they missed their nurse. As they turned to the Harbour-Master it was evident from their gestures that they were questioning him about her disappearance, but apparently his answers satisfied them as they allowed themselves to be bowed into the boat without her. One of the men in it hoisted its brightly-coloured sail, and after a single tack it disappeared through the narrow cleft in the cliffs that Gregory knew must lead to the sea. Meanwhile the pompous-looking Harbour-Master, mopping the perspiration from his red face with a handkerchief, had walked back to his office and re-entered it, leaving the harbour once more deserted.

For a while Gregory ruminated on possible explanations for what he had seen. The most likely seemed to be that the man who had pulled the amah into the shed was a frustrated lover. Perhaps her duties made it impossible for her to meet him in the evenings, or she did not like him enough to do so, and he had seized on this opportunity to get her to himself for an hour or two, counting on her influence with her charges being sufficient to restrain them from giving away to her employer that she had left them during the afternoon. In any case,

Gregory felt, it was no business of his and, somnolent from the heat, he soon afterwards dropped off to sleep.

When he woke the harbour was still deserted, and soon afterwards he went into his room ; so he did not see the amah come out of the shed or the two boys return from their afternoon's sailing trip, and he thought no more of the matter. Neither did he connect it with the fact that Ho-Ping did not come in as usual to see him that evening, nor that on the following day both the doctor and Chung were unusually abrupt in manner and seemed either to have quarrelled or been upset by something.

After he had been out of bed for a little over a fortnight he slowly became conscious that to his grief there was now added another cause for depression, in that he was virtually a prisoner. It was not that he had ever been a devotee of violent exercise. On the contrary, in normal circumstances he would have been quite content to lounge about on a sunny terrace for a week or two without thought of leaving it ; but the fact that he could not do so if he wanted to had begun to rile him.

He still had no inclination whatever to get back to England and pick up again the threads of his shattered life. In fact he dreaded the ordeal, but he recognized now that there could be no escape from his having to do so sometime ; and, irked by his subconscious sense of captivity, he tackled Ho-Ping on how soon he was likely to be able to leave.

The doctor told him that as the steamer had left the port only a few weeks before his arrival, it was hardly to be expected that it would return, take on its cargo, and be ready to sail again in less than three months.

Gregory accepted the information with a shrug. 'That's all right by me. I'm in no hurry to get home.' But after a moment he added, 'All the same, I trust you don't expect me to remain cooped up here all that time.'

'It would be distressing for us both should you fail to reconcile yourself to doing so,' Dr. Ping answered placidly.

'Oh come! All I wish to do is to go for a walk now and again, and see something of the island.'

'That is understandable, but most regretfully out of the question.'

'Why?' inquired Gregory with a frown.

'It is preferred that our guests should not mingle with our people.'

'What harm do you suppose that I could possibly do them?'

'None. None whatever; but we are great observers of custom in this place and it would be contrary to custom; so I am afraid you must abide by it.'

'Now look here,' Gregory said firmly. 'If I were a trader who might corrupt your islanders by selling them unmatured whisky, I could understand your point of view. Even if I were a lusty young fo'c'sle hand who was likely to start a riot by seducing one of the village maidens, there might be something to it. But I have neither the means nor desire to create trouble of any kind.'

'That is self-evident,' Ho-Ping hastened to assure him. 'Indeed, it was apparent from the first that you are a most superior person. It is for that reason I have honoured myself by seeking your company with more frequency than my medical duties demanded. Although you are now fully recovered, with your permission, I shall continue to devote such of my time as I can to you in the hope that my visits may help a little to alleviate your boredom.'

Gregory smiled. 'Thanks, Doctor. You have been very kind to me. I think, this offer too, of yours might be the means of overcoming our difficulty. Whatever the objections to my leaving the compound on my own, there can surely be none to my going for an occasional walk in your company.'

'Ah, if that were only possible, how pleasant it would be.' The doctor shook his head sadly. 'But most unfortunately I suffer from a weak heart, and all unnecessary exertion is forbidden to me.'

Since Dr. Ping walked up the zigzag path in the steep cliff-face on his daily visits and had never appeared to be unduly affected when he reached the terrace, Gregory felt quite certain that he was lying. However, apart from politely commiserating with the doctor on his disability, he forbore to comment. Neither did he suggest that he should be accompanied on walks by Chung, or someone else, in order to ensure his good behaviour. It had been made unmistakably clear that whatever he might say, he was not going to be allowed out of the cage.

That did not worry him particularly, as he still lacked sufficient interest in things to care whether he left it or not. But during the week that followed he could not help wondering from time to time what could be going on in the island that its inhabitants were so anxious to prevent strangers from finding out.

One morning, soon after dawn, he woke with the same question in mind. Having pondered it for some ten minutes he decided to get up and investigate ; so he dressed and went out on to the terrace. Below him the harbour lay veiled in mist and one great rocky promontory still threw a heavy shadow, but soon the mounting sun would glare down into every corner of it through another long tropical day.

As far as Gregory knew, no one except himself and Chung lived in the block, but he thought he would first make certain of that. A few days earlier he had taken a cursory look at the empty cubicles and at the big dormitory. Now he tiptoed through the latter to the far end of the building, where the kitchen quarters were situated. Long practice had enabled him to move as silently as a cat, and a swift examination showed him that the door to the galley was not locked. Very gently he eased it open and looked in. With a domestic economy typical of the East, Chung, being a servant, had no room of his own, but lay sleeping soundly on a mat that he had unrolled along the floor. Through a gauze screen door on the far side of the galley Gregory could see the scullery, and a window in its wall. As that wall formed the far end of the block it was clear that there were no other rooms further on, and no one else sleeping in it.

Soundlessly, Gregory re-closed the door, tiptoed back the way he had come, and again went out on to the terrace. Advancing to its edge, he peered over. It dropped sheer for about twenty feet, then came a much narrower terrace barely two yards wide. Along its outer edge ran the high wire-mesh fence ; so even if he had been able to scramble down to the lower ledge he would still have been inside the cage.

Turning, he walked quietly round to the back of the block, but he had already guessed what he would find. As he expected

28

the fence was there too, barring the way to any prospect of climbing the last fifty feet of cliff. Unbroken, except for the gate at the north end of the terrace, it entirely surrounded the building.

Being methodical by habit Gregory next made a careful examination of the gate. He was now not at all surprised to find that its lock would defy anyone not equipped with a cracksman's kit; and his knowledge of electrical fences was sufficient to tell him that without proper implements it would be impossible to cut off or short circuit the current, as it was laid on from a generating plant housed in a small concrete structure outside the compound.

Nothing of the least importance hung on the result of his reconnaisance, so he felt little disappointment at having failed to find an easy way out of his prison. For some time past he had recognized that the real prison in which he was confined lay not in any fence, but in his own mind. Freedom to explore the island could not break down the barriers of sorrow that now walled him in from the joys of life, and with the grim thought that it did not really matter to him how he spent the next three months—or the next ten years—he went back to bed.

It was therefore very probable that but for a false move by Dr. Ping, Gregory's mental indifference to the world about him would have led to his resigning himself to remaining in the cage until the steamer could take him to San Francisco. As it was, soon after the doctor arrived that afternoon he came out to Gregory and said with an asperity quite unusual in him:

'Honoured Sir. Chung tells me that when getting up this morning, he saw you through the window of the kitchen making close examination of the gate in the fence. Already I have courteously intimated to you that it is contrary to our custom to allow our guests outside this cage. I have now to inform you that any attempt to get out is definitely forbidden. Moreover, it would be highly dangerous, as the fence carries an electric charge strong enough to inflict serious injury.'

Something of Gregory's old belligerence stirred within him. The muscles of his lean face tightened, and he said, 'If I wanted to get out of this place I should get out. It would take more than an electric fence to stop me.'

Ho-Ping bowed. 'That may be true. Therefore I must ask you to give me your word that you will not try to escape, but accept the very mild form of captivity imposed, for as long as you must remain here.'

'What if I refuse?'

'That would imply an intention on your part to assault Chung with the object of gaining possession of the gate key which he carries, or to steal it while he is asleep. As a precaution against either I should be compelled to place guards over you.'

Gregory's firm chin jutted out aggressively, and he retorted with sudden sharpness, 'I don't know what you are trying to hide, and I don't care. But I have committed no crime and you have no right whatever to hold me as a prisoner. I will give you no undertaking of any kind, and you can do as you damn well please.'

'I find your attitude both regrettable and unbecoming,' the doctor remarked. Then he added as he turned away, 'You will have only yourself to blame for the additional restrictions placed on your liberty.'

The 'additional restrictions' arrived an hour later in the form of three stalwart men all dressed similarly and carrying long staves. They wore broad-brimmed straw hats, belts and gaiters of brown leather, their blue trousers were embroidered both back and front with a large complicated Chinese character in red, and it seemed obvious that they were part of the local police force. After depositing in the dormitory the bundles they carried, two of them made themselves comfortable with Chung in his kitchen, while the third went and squatted by the gate. At intervals of two hours they relieved one another of gate guard. Then, as a further precaution against Gregory's attempting to get away, shortly after sundown all three of them came to his cabin and, having salaamed politely, locked him in. It was little more than a gesture, as the door was a flimsy one and egress through the window prevented only by a permanently fixed wire mosquito screen ; but had he forced either he would have had to risk attracting the attention of the guards by the sound of his breaking out.

At the time he was just finishing his evening meal. When he had toyed for a few minutes longer with the highly-spiced contents of the dozen or more little bowls that Chung had brought him, he pushed the tray away and, for the first time since he had arrived in the island, began deliberately to set his wits to work.

In the past there had been occasions when his life, and sometimes more than his life, had depended on his regaining his freedom. Now, there was no more to be gained than the satisfaction of an idle curiosity. But, quite unconsciously and in blissful ignorance of the type of man with whom he was dealing, Ho-Ping had, most ill-advisedly, provoked him with a challenge. Gregory had always been a lone wolf. He did not take kindly to any form of discipline. He had never allowed anyone to dictate to him, and he was much too accustomed to doing what he pleased to start submitting to that sort of thing now.

Presently the door was unlocked by one of the guards for Chung to retrieve the dishes, and Gregory smiled at the elderly Chinaman. Dr. Ping's fears that he might attack his servant were quite unfounded. He might have stolen the key to the gate while the man was sleeping, but he would never have used brute force on anyone who had cared for him kindly while ill. All the same he realized that having had a watch set on him was going to make it much more difficult to get hold of the key by any means, and now even that would be only half the battle ; for, having got it, how would he be able to evade the vigilance of his guards in order to use it unchallenged?

Sleeping on this problem brought no answer to it, and next morning he paced the terrace with considerably more vigour than usual. Taking long strides, his arms hanging loosely and his head thrust slightly forward, he walked quickly up and down while his mind worked with equal swiftness. A dozen embryo plans started to take shape in it but he rejected them all, either because of the difficulty of purloining the key from Chung in daylight, or because at night he was locked in his cubicle and could think of no way of getting out unheard and

31

unseen ; or, again, because he felt that in view of what he owed to Ho-Ping, decency dictated that he should rule out any plan entailing violence against the doctor's henchmen. Nevertheless, long before midday he had hit on an idea, and during the heat of the afternoon, while all but one of his guards was sleeping, he made a preliminary investigation which satisfied him that the first stage of his plan was practical.

That night, after he had been locked in, he gave the guard and Chung a couple of hours to settle down. At the end of that time he removed the curtains from his window, tore them into strips, knotted them together to form a rope, and in one end of it wrapped and tied securely a heavy stone that he had brought in from the terrace. He then stood on a chair and set to work on the ceiling. His examination of it during the afternoon had shown him that it was only a flimsy affair of sun-baked mud on a foundation of thin, split bamboo canes strung together with string. Within half an hour he had torn an oval hole in it as wide as his shoulders. Taking his stone-weighted rope in one hand, he scrambled through the hole out on to the roof.

Cautiously now he crawled to its front edge and peered over. The starlight was just sufficient for him to make out the line of the fence beyond the kitchen end of the building and the dark splodge of a figure squatting near the gate. As he expected, a watch was being kept by night as well as by day, in case he managed to get out of his cubicle unheard and attempted to pick the lock. But he had no intention of trying. For his purpose all that mattered was that the man was sufficiently far away to be out of ear-shot. It seemed probable that he was dozing ; in any case it was unlikely that he would look up to the roof unless his attention was attracted by sounds of movement on it.

Turning away, Gregory crawled to the back of the roof, then stood up beneath the overhanging tree that gave it partial shade from the midday sun. Its lowest branch was about four feet above his head, so well out of his reach. Holding his home-made rope near its weighted end, he whirled the weight round and round then threw it up into the foliage. The cotton-wrapped stone failed to find a lodgement but he deftly caught it as

32

it fell back, and tried again. Like the spider watched by Robert the Bruce, success required patience. Sometimes the stone caught but came away at a sharp tug, more often it just fell back at once; but at last it twisted twice round a medium-sized branch and Gregory was able to pull the branch down until with his left hand he could clutch its nearest twigs. Letting go the rope, he seized another handful, then risked a little jump and grabbed the branch itself. Praying that it would not snap, he jumped again and clung on higher up. As the bough gave under the strain his toes scraped the roof but the branch did not snap and it was now taking most of his weight. With a final heave he got a grip on the main bough, then hand over hand swung himself along it until he passed over the electrified fence; but he gave it only a glance as he sought for further good holds, and cautiously lowered himself to the cleft in the rocks from which the tree was growing.

That afternoon he had spent some time memorizing the face of the fifty-foot cliff at the back of his prison. It was fairly steep but frequently broken by cracks and ledges on which grew scrub, and in some cases smaller trees of the same kind as the one down which he had just clambered. After a brief rest he set out up the route he had planned to take, and found it comparatively easy going. Ten minutes later he was standing on the top of the cliff, a free man again.

Sadly he realized that his freedom did not really mean much to him. Perhaps that was partly because his escape had been so easy, and partly because, unlike his escapes in the past, there had been no threat of death to spur him to it. In fact he had every intention of returning to his prison before dawn by the way he had left it. He would not even have bothered to outwit Ho-Ping, but for his resentment at being arbitrarily confined, and a vague temptation to derive cynical amusement from the doctor's face next day, when he learned that during a midnight prowl his prisoner had discovered the secret of the island.

That he would discover it, Gregory felt confident; as, if a cage was necessary to prevent ordinary castaways stumbling upon it during the course of a casual walk, it must obviously be something very easy to find out. But at that moment he might well have turned back, had he had any idea of the chain of strange and murderous events into which the knowledge of that secret was going to lead him.

2

THE SECRET OF THE ISLAND

T H E top of the cliff formed a small plateau which sloped gently away on its landward side. In that direction Gregory could see a sprinkling of lights down in a valley bottom that appeared to be about a mile off, but he knew that lights seen at night could make the judgment of distances very deceptive. The ground was uneven and the starlight only just sufficient for him to make out the potholes and scattered rocks ahead ; so he went forward cautiously. When he had covered a few hundred yards the rocks gave place to large tussocks of coarse, sharp grass and stunted undergrowth ; then the occasional trees became more frequent until their tops merged into a screen that hid the valley.

Now he would have given a great deal for a torch and knee-high boots, as he knew that this tropical semi-jungle might well harbour snakes or other poisonous reptiles. A light would have driven them from his path, but in the dark he might step on one at any moment and his legs were highly vulnerable. Ho-Ping had lent him a Chinese robe for sitting about in, but apart from that the only clothes he had were the evening things in which he had been washed ashore. His dinner jacket suit had been mended and pressed with such skill by Chung that it looked almost as good as new, and over it to conceal his white

34

shirt he was wearing the robe; but patent shoes and silk socks were the last things he would have chosen for a midnight walk across the island.

As he advanced, parakeets that he disturbed screeched in the tree-tops, and occasionally there came an ominous rustle in the undergrowth; but after ten minutes' nerve-racking progress, greatly to his relief he emerged from the trees on to a strip of cultivated land. From it he could see again the lights down in the valley, and that he was now separated from them only by a series of terraces on which sugar-cane and other crops were growing. Soon he came upon a path and followed it down from terrace to terrace until the land flattened out and he found himself in a vegetable garden behind one of the houses from which the lights were shining.

Against the background of the starry sky he could see that the village consisted of a hundred or more scattered buildings, most of which were bungalows. With two exceptions the roofs of all of them gracefully turned up at the corners in the Chinese style. The exceptions were much larger than the rest and had the appearance of modern factories. They stood some way from the nearest houses and, Gregory guessed, on a road which led round the hill he had descended to the port.

To minimize the risk of running into anybody, he made his way through a series of vegetable plots until he had passed the back of the last bungalow, then headed for the open space between it and the factories. As he expected, he struck a road, and looking along it could see the entrance to the village. For some time past the lights in the houses had been going out and the street was now lit only by a faint glow. On the still air he could catch the strains of thin Chinese music, but he could see no movement and it was evident that the village was settling down for the night.

Turning away, he walked along the road to the nearest factory, and approached it cautiously. It was in complete darkness and there was no one about. Reason had already told him that there could be nothing worth concealing about the life of a Chinese village; so it was much more likely that the factories held the key to the secret that Dr. Ping was so anxious to protect.

The approach to the building told Gregory nothing. There were the usual heaps of refuse, bits of rusted obsolete machinery, and stacks of wood for making cases lying about, but no indication at all of the type of goods the factory turned out. Going up to the windows he peered through them, but the darkness made it impossible for him to get even an idea of what the place was like inside. For a moment he considered breaking in, but quickly abandoned the idea, as to have found a light switch and turned it on might have brought a night watchman on the scene; and having no torch, it would be pointless to grope about in the darkness.

As he worked his way round the back he stumbled into a rubbish heap which, from the sharp crackling sound beneath his feet, seemed to consist mainly of potsherds. Then, on the far side of the factory, facing the road, he came upon a row of large concrete bunkers. Some were empty but others held several tons of slightly slimy whitish stuff. It weighed heavy in the hand as he took some up to examine it, but he had no idea what it could be.

Hoping for better luck at the other factory he crossed the road. It was somewhat smaller but its surroundings were much the same and it also had a row of storage bunkers. In them, instead of the whitish substance Gregory found neatly piled slabs and blocks of stone. In the starlight it was impossible to tell their colours but he could see that they ranged from light to dark and the feel of them showed them to be of different textures. Most of these pieces of stone were much too small to have been used for monumental masons' work; so still puzzled, he began to ferret about for some clue to what was made out of them.

Presently, near the back of the building, he discovered a big pile of fine stone chippings, from which it seemed reasonable to infer that the blocks were cut into small statues, or something of that kind. As he let a handful of the chips run through his fingers an idea came to him. Hurrying back across the road he went to the refuse heap behind the other factory and picked up some of the potsherds. Seen closer to, all of them showed a glaze, and the curves of some implied that they had formed part of graceful bowls or vases.

With rising excitement, Gregory rummaged among the pile until he found other, more solid, irregular pieces. Picking up one of the largest he looked at it with a faintly cynical smile. Its paleness suggested that its colour was yellow, and it was a rider on a headless horse from which the lower parts of the legs had also been smashed off. In shape it was unmistakably the greater part of a T'ang horseman. Such figures, he knew, had been made to be placed in the graves of the Chinese upper classes between the seventh and tenth centuries A.D. Now, according to their quality, they fetched in London, Paris or New York anything from thirty to three hundred pounds a pair.

Carelessly he threw the broken figure back on the heap. It had let him into Dr. Ping's secret. The whitish substance in one set of bunkers was china clay, the others held pieces of uncut onyx, jade, soap-stone and malachite. The two factories were employed solely on turning out fake Chinese antiques, and the pile of debris by which he was standing was formed from rejects which had been cracked or broken during the process of firing.

The reason for secrecy was clear enough now. Obviously the two factories were capable of turning out many thousands of pounds' worth of fakes a year ; and, no doubt, whoever ran the place had an under-cover organization that distributed them to unscrupulous antique dealers in the principal cities of Europe and America at an enormous profit. But if it once leaked out that such fakes were being made in large numbers, every genuine piece would at once become suspect, and the bottom drop out of the market.

Having accomplished his self-imposed mission, he decided that there was no point in wandering aimlessly about the island in the dark, so he might as well return to his room and go to bed ; but he was most averse to risking a second walk through the jungle on the hill-side. In consequence, he set out along the road away from the village, with the idea that on reaching the harbour he would be able to take the track leading up to the cage, and work his way round outside it to the tree by means of which he meant to get in again.

The road curved round the base of the hill, and after about

a mile entered the avenue of palms down which, some days previously, he had seen the bearers come trotting with the palanquin containing the two boys. During his walk the moon had risen, so that now, looking down the avenue, he could see the port quite clearly and the great barrier of cliff that concealed it from the sea. In the opposite direction the avenue rose fairly steeply until it breasted a ridge of high ground half a mile away. It was the moon having come up that decided Gregory to change his mind about returning to the cage at once. Now that he could see something of the country he thought he might as well walk up the avenue and find out what it was like on the far side of the slope.

At the crest a new surprise awaited him. He had thought that beyond it he might see the roofs of a single large mansion, for it was reasonable to suppose that the richly-clad children came from a big home, which was probably also that of the owner of the factories. But this scene that lay before him was infinitely more intriguing than anything he had expected.

The avenue ran steeply down again into a broad shallow valley. In it were several small lakes and patches of woodland, while scattered amongst them were a score or more of beautiful Chinese buildings and a tall, many-storied pagoda. With the moonlight glinting on the still waters and the tiled roofs, and an occasional light twinkling here and there, it was like a scene from fairyland. As Gregory gazed down upon it he caught his breath in wonder and delight.

The only thing he had ever seen to compare with it was the Forbidden City of Pekin ; for that, although termed a city, had really been a vast garden the high walls of which enclosed many artificial lakes, temples, pagodas, and innumerable courtyards and pavilions. This had no walls, and its buildings were fewer and much smaller, but that in no way detracted from its beauty. And its existence was surely another, even more jealously-guarded, secret ; for no rumour had ever penetrated the outer world that on an island in mid-Pacific, charted only as Leper Settlement Number Six, the patient, gifted Chinese had erected in miniature another Forbidden City.

Slowly he walked forward down the avenue until he came abreast of the nearest building. It looked like a large private house and was in darkness. So was the next he passed, a quarter of a mile further on, and now that it was after midnight he felt that there was little risk of his running into any of the inhabitants of this lovely valley.

The assumption was premature. Before he had covered another hundred yards he caught the swift patter of running feet. Just in time to escape being seen he managed to dodge behind a clump of bamboos at the roadside. Out from a side turning, barely twenty feet off, dashed a coolie pulling a hooded rickshaw. Swerving round the corner he raced on down the hill towards a cluster of the largest buildings, which stood in the centre of the valley.

This narrow shave made Gregory realize that he was being careless, and that if he continued along the main avenue he was much more likely to meet people who were still about; so he turned off down the lane from which the rickshaw had emerged. Soon he came upon another house, set well back in its own grounds; then the lane continued on for some distance at a gentle incline through a grove of palms, to emerge half a mile lower down the valley on the shore of one of the lakes. At that point the lake narrowed in a wasp-waist and was spanned by a graceful bridge which rose above it almost in a semi-circle. It was as Gregory paused for a moment on the summit of the arch that he first saw through the trees on the opposite shore a house with a light shining from it.

As he descended the curve of the bridge he was suddenly tempted, by the sight of the light, to get a glimpse of the room from which it came. No walls or fences enclosed the grounds in which any of the houses stood, so he had only to turn off the track and walk through the garden. Taking advantage of the groups of shrubs for cover he moved silently forward until he could get a full view of the building. It had an upper gallery and a double-tiered pagoda roof, the lower projecting over a veranda which was approached by a flight of shallow steps flanked by two stone dragons. The light came from a pair of french windows covered with delicate lattice-work, and a wire-gauze screen against insects.

From where Gregory was standing he could make out little of the interior of the room, but he hesitated to go nearer, as the moon was now well up and its light so strong that had he advanced into the open anyone looking out would have been certain to see him. While pondering the matter he noticed a little way off an ornamental tree with low twisted branches, and it struck him that by climbing up into them he would get a better view. In one swift dart he covered the few yards to it, then scaled the gnarled trunk and perched himself in its fork.

Now, although the lattice-work still made it impossible to get a clear view of the room, he could form a fair impression of it, and its furnishings seemed a queer mixture of East and West. To one side there was a large lacquer cabinet on which sat a gilded Buddha, the far wall was almost hidden by shelves of books, in a corner stood a large radiogram, and in the foreground a woman lay reading on a Chinese day-bed under a hideous but efficient chromium electric light standard. He could not tell if the woman was old or young; only that she had thick black hair and was wearing a pale-coloured wrap which left exposed her small bare feet.

He had been looking at the woman for some moments when he suddenly became aware that he was not the only person watching her. Up on the veranda there had been a movement in the deep shadow cast by the overhanging roof. Straining his eyes, Gregory made out a crouching figure about ten feet from the french windows. Stealthily the figure moved again, halving the distance and now becoming clearly revealed in the soft glow radiating through the lattice-work. It was that of a man, and he was obviously up to no good.

Gregory wondered what he ought to do. To intervene would mean disclosing his own presence, and, while he had committed no crime, he did not want to have to admit that he had been snooping. It occurred to him that he could give a loud shout which would probably scare the man into running away—and would anyhow put the woman on her guard—then bolt for it himself. But such a course was all against his instincts. Besides, there was always the possibility that the man was the woman's lover. Perhaps she had been waiting up for him, and he was approaching her room so stealthily only to preserve their secret. Should that be so Gregory was the last person to wish to spoil their fun, and perhaps bring tragedy upon them.

He was still debating the matter with himself, when the man acted. Springing up, he tore open the gauze-covered doorway and rushed into the room. The woman's startled cry was strangled almost instantly by his throwing a cloth over her head. Next moment he had picked her up in his arms and come running out of the house. The violence with which he handled the woman placed it beyond doubt that this was no abduction, to play a passive part in which the lady had secretly consented in advance ; and as he reached the top of the steps Gregory got his first proper view of him. He was a big, heavy-limbed man and, judging by his clothes, an ordinary coolie. In the bright moonlight his bared teeth, flashing eyes, and coarse features contorted with excitement, looked like a mask of evil.

Gregory dropped from his perch in the tree. As he did so he used an unprintable and peculiarly blasphemous Italian oath. Few prospects could have annoyed him more than that of becoming involved in a fight with a hulking coolie over a woman totally unknown to him. In his youth he had more than once slapped other men's faces for making rude remarks about girls whom he knew perfectly well were no better than they should be ; but that sort of thing had long gone out of fashion and he had since learned to adopt a less quixotic attitude where questions of chivalry were concerned. Now, willy-nilly, he felt he had no option. It was just one of those things which however dangerous and unpleasant could not be shirked. Having instantly made up his mind to that, had he been St. George in person he could not have gone more swiftly to the rescue of this, possibly hideous, damsel in distress.

His unexpected appearance had the effect of temporarily depriving the coolie of his wits. Halting dead in his tracks, he stood for a moment boggling at the figure racing towards him. His expression was one of mingled hate and fear. Suddenly recovering himself, he swung round to the left, threw the woman over his shoulder, and dashed for the nearest cover.

The man's reaction came too late. Burdened with the woman's weight he now had no chance of gaining a sufficient lead to throw off his pursuer among the dark undergrowth ahead. Gregory swerved and ran all out to intercept him, failed to do so only by a bare three paces, and was hard on his heels as he crashed through a screen of tall pampas grass.

On its far side there was an ornamental stream. Unaware of its presence the coolie proved unequal to the hazard. His belated leap landed him with one foot in the water. The woman was flung from his grasp as he pitched face down across the farther bank. Gregory, coming after, was warned of the trap by the other's fall. With the spring of a panther he landed on the coolie's back.

Few people would have had much chance against Gregory after that. At one time or another he had been mixed up in a score of rough-houses, and when it came to serious fighting he regarded the Queensberry rules as of only academic interest. In his view, whether attacking or attacked, the object of the operation was to render one's opponent helpless as speedily as possible, thus minimizing the risk of severe injury to oneself. His favourite weapon was a champagne bottle, and failing that a heavy marlinspike ; but even unarmed he was a formidable antagonist, as he had no scruples about holds or using his knees and feet.

Now that he had secured the initial advantage he seized the coolie's ear with his left hand and clenching his right fist aimed a terrific blow at the small of the man's back. Had it landed as intended on his kidneys that would have been the end of the matter, but he was exceptionally strong and agile. At that instant he hunched his great shoulders in a violent effort to throw Gregory off. The movement only partially succeeded but saved him from the worst effects of the blow. It thudded on solid flesh just above his right buttock.

Before Gregory could strike again, the man had staggered to his feet, dragging his attacker up behind him. Clenching his teeth he wrenched free his ear, gave a gasp of pain and swung round. As he did so Gregory slogged him hard below the ribs ; then, as he half doubled up, dealt him a left upper cut under the chin. Reeling away the coolie tripped and fell, but rolling over came up on his knees half turned away. In a second attempt to finish him, Gregory rushed in and aimed a swift kick at the side of his head. By throwing himself backwards the man

dodged the kick, and managed to grab Gregory's ankle, bringing him down.

For a moment they were in a tangled heap on the ground.
With his free foot Gregory kicked out again. His heel caught
the coolie on the adam's apple. Giving an agonized gulp, he let
go the ankle he was clutching and they rolled apart. Next
minute they had staggered to their feet with barely two yards
separating them.

Both were panting from their exertions. As they fought to
get their breath they stood with heads thrust forward, eyeing
one another warily. Now, for the first time, Gregory felt concern about the outcome of the conflict. The coolie was by far
the bigger man and overtopped his five foot ten by several
inches. Moreover the half-naked arms that protruded from his
robe were as long and sinewy as those of a gorilla. Gregory's
ribs had mended well, but he knew that if he once let those
arms close round them he would be finished.

3

THE PRICE OF CURIOSITY

So far Gregory's desperate encounter with the coolie had not
lasted much more than a minute. During it no sound had
broken the stillness of the moonlight garden except their gasps,
the thud of their falls and a curious malevolent hissing that
the coolie was making as he glared at his attacker. Suddenly the
night was pierced by a high-pitched scream. The breath had
been driven out of the body of the woman by the violence of
her fall, but now she had got it back, freed her head from the

cloth in which it was muffled, and let out a shriek fit to raise the dead.

At that very second the coolie was in the act of launching himself forward. His long arms were outstretched to seize Gregory, but her wailing cry caused him to bungle the attempt. That sudden, unexpected, screech in his rear made him half turn his head. The moon was shining straight on his face, and Gregory saw the ferocious hatred in his gleaming eyes instantly give way to fear of capture. Taking advantage of his momentary hesitation, Gregory swiftly side-stepped and, as the man rushed in, tripped him.

Just for a moment, as the coolie pitched forward, their bodies brushed together. Gregory's right fist shot out and landed heavily behind his enemy's ear. Already off balance, the man lurched sideways and crashed to the ground. Instantly, Gregory was upon him. Grabbing his left wrist he wrenched his arm behind his back and gave it a violent jerk. He heard the bone snap. The woman was still screaming, and now the coolie's screams were added to hers.

In spite of the pain he was in, the man still struggled desperately. Squirming round, he managed to get to his knees, thrust out his good arm and grab Gregory by the throat. His grip was like a vice. Tearing at the coolie's hand with both his own, Gregory strove to break the grip ; but could not. His eyes began to bulge, the blood beat in his ears. Suddenly he ceased pulling away, threw himself against the man and kneed him in the groin. The stroke had not much weight behind it, but enough. The strangle-hold loosened for a moment and he was able to jerk his head free.

Cries in answer to those of the woman were now coming from the house. Somewhere in it a gong was being loudly banged. With its reverberations and the shouts was mingled the patter of running footsteps. Both men struggled to their feet. The coolie's left are dangled uselessly by his side, and now that his grip had been broken his last hope of revenging himself was gone. Flight once more took first place in his mind. Swerving away, he dashed towards the thicker bushes. In a second Gregory was after him. Flinging himself at the man's knees in a rugby tackle, he brought him down.

The struggle lasted only a few moments longer. Half a dozen people in various states of attire burst upon the scene. Several men grabbed both Gregory and the coolie, pulled them apart and hauled them to their feet. One, who from the glance Gregory caught of him looked much older than the rest, sought to reassure the woman, although she had already ceased screaming and showed no signs of hysteria. Another very fat woman, wheezing loudly from having had to run, joined them belatedly and added her shrill, excited inquiries to the general clamour.

Raising his voice, the elderly man uttered several staccato sentences. At once silence fell, and as he turned away a short procession formed, the two women falling in behind him and the others leading the two captives after them in the direction of the house. They did not enter it by the french window but took a path leading through the shrubbery to the side of the house facing away from the lake, which was evidently its main entrance. After mounting a flight of steps, they passed through big sliding lattice-work doors into a spacious hall that was richly furnished, entirely in the Chinese manner.

It was well but softly lit, and for the first time Gregory could get a good look at the people with whom he had to deal. A glance was enough to show that all the men were servants— with the exception of the one who had given the orders, and he was obviously the master of the house. He was old, tall and very thin. He wore no pigtail, but had a long sparse grey beard, and thin drooping moustache. The robe he was wearing had a plum-coloured ground on which were embroidered, in gold thread and many-hued silks, a gorgeous array of dragons, butterflies and improbable flowers. On the top of his round skull-cap was a large button, which proclaimed him to be a Mandarin.

As he seated himself in a high-backed, carved ebony chair the woman whom the coolie had attempted to carry off went and stood beside him. Gregory could see now that she was still a girl, and he judged her to be about twenty-two. She had a broad forehead, bright intelligent eyes and a firm chin. As she sought to tidy her ruffled hair he noticed that she wore it swept up in a high double wave that formed a dark halo, making her golden-tinted face pale by contrast, and that it was cut short at the back. Her eyebrows were thin and tapering, her mouth full. Her features, although oriental, were not flattened. Both she and the old man had prominent noses set between high cheek-bones, which suggested that they were Manchus of noble blood. The fat, older woman did not resemble either of them, and from her nervous, hen-like manner Gregory rightly assumed that she was the girl's duenna.

The Mandarin asked the girl a question, to which she replied volubly, pointing several times at the coolie. He stood with hanging head between the men who held him, making no attempt to defend himself. When questioned he babbled something, then threw himself on his knees. At an order from the Mandarin he was pulled to his feet and led away.

Gregory was standing between two of the servants, but they were no longer actually holding him ; so, knowing the value of making a good impression, he swiftly untied the girdle of the loose robe he was wearing and slipped it off. It had become soiled and torn while he was struggling on the ground, so in it he had looked like a tatterdemalion of dubious origin ; but now, in his dinner-jacket suit, he stood revealed as a white man of the upper class.

The girl's face showed her surprise and lit up with a sudden smile, but that of the old man remained impassive, as he asked in English:

'Who are you?'

Gregory bowed. 'My name, Honoured Sir, is Sallust. I am a British subject, and the unhappy survivor of a wreck.'

'How comes it that you are in my garden?'

'I was taking a midnight walk. On the roadside there is no indication that this delightful domain is private. As a humble lover of beauty I felt compelled to enter it, so that I could better admire the most artistic manner in which the trees and shrubberies are set out.'

Evidently the owner of the garden did not understand this in its entirety, as he gave a questioning look at the girl. She quickly supplied an interpretation of the words that puzzled him, upon which he nodded gravely and said to Gregory:

'You wear the ceremonial dress of a Western Barbarian, but

46

you speak the words of a civilized man. Do you know the Chinese tongue?'

'Your Excellency's fluency in English puts my ignorance to shame. My knowledge of *mandarin* is limited to a few phrases.'

'My own English is poor but perhaps adequate, and my daughter understands it better than myself. We shall continue to use it.' With a wave of his hand the old gentleman added, 'Please seat yourself.' Then he gave an order to the servants in Chinese.

When they had trotted from the room, the Mandarin said that his name was Sze Hsüan, and introduced his daughter as the lady A-lu-te. With downcast eyes she then thanked Gregory for having saved her from being carried off, and asked him to enlighten them further about himself.

Seeing no reason to conceal the truth, he gave an abbreviated version of the wreck and of his treatment since he had been washed up on the island. The old man knew Dr. Ping, and all about the cage. Regarding Gregory thoughtfully, he said:

'In confining you Ho-Ping acted rightly. He obeyed an order of long standing. I marvel only that you escaped without injury from the fence—or was it that you used force upon the guard?'

Gregory had no intention of giving away his escape route in case he wished to use it again, so he lied smoothly. 'In my own country I have had the good fortune to win many athletic events. I got out of my room by making a hole in the ceiling. From the roof, unseen by the guard, I took a running leap, cleared the fence at the back of the building, and landed on the cliff-face.'

'You took a great risk. Few men could accomplish such a feat. But few men could have made to bite the dust that big coolie. To converse with a cultured man who is also brave is elevating to both heart and mind.'

As Gregory acknowledged the compliment a servant brought in tea. It was served ceremoniously in tiny cups by A-lu-te, first to Gregory then to her father.

After commenting politely on the exceptionally fine aroma of the brew, Gregory held up the fragile cup and inquired, 'Are these originals, or may I congratulate you on having succeeded in producing such treasures in your factory?'

The Mandarin's eyelids dropped a fraction lower. 'So you have found out about our industries. That is to be regretted.'

'Honoured Sir,' Gregory smiled. 'Had I not taken occasion to admit it, you would certainly have suspected that I might have done so. In any case you must know that on my midnight walk I could not help being amazed at finding a great civilization flourishing on what is believed to be an almost uninhabited Pacific Island. What is one secret more or less when it forms only part of a far greater secret. The manner in which you deal with me will not be influenced by my knowledge of your commercial activities.'

Again the girl had to make clear for her father the more involved portions of this longer speech ; then he said, 'Your discourse shows wisdom. But your future does not lie in my hands.'

'Then may I be permitted to know in whose hands it does lie?' Gregory asked.

'In that of the Council of State. To it authority in such matters has been delegated by the Son of Heaven.'

Gregory knew that in the old days when the Chinese were ruled by an Emperor they never used his title or spoke of him by name as long as he was alive ; instead they referred to him by flowery pseudonyms of which 'Son of Heaven' was their favourite. Yet for over forty years now China had been a Republic. Could it be that the authority of which Sze Hsüan spoke had been delegated all that time ago, and that this Chinese colony, protected from molestation by the fact that its existence was secret, continued to observe the Imperial decrees of a long since vanished regime ; or did he refer to someone on the island whom they had made its ruler? In the hope of solving the point Gregory put an apparently irrelevant question.

'Dr. Ping told me, Excellency, that this island is charted as Leper Settlement Number Six ; but it is obvious that your beautiful buildings could not have been erected by lepers, and I have seen no signs of that terrible scourge in any of its inhabitants. Have you succeeded in stamping it out?'

'We were not called on to do so,' came the quiet reply. 'This was one of several leper settlements started by the Portuguese Fathers long years ago. Already it had ceased to be one when we came. To have renamed it would have been to arouse the curiosity of the inquisitive. In our circumstances it was preferable to let sleeping dogs sleep.'

That gave Gregory the lead he was seeking, and he said, 'Inquisitiveness in the affairs of others is rightly stigmatized as a mark of ill-breeding; yet I would not be human were I not tempted to inquire the origin of the rich community now established here.'

The Mandarin did not understand English nearly as well as he spoke it, and again his daughter had to help him out. When she had done so, choosing his phrases carefully he said with a faint smile:

'That is understandable. As your eyes have discovered so much, why should I not enlighten you regarding our brief history? We are the survivors of the old China—of all that was best in China during the long centuries before the Western Barbarians came to pervert our people. First the Missionaries, then the Concessionaires with the soldiers at their backs. They taught the young to reject the precepts for the conduct of life. To think only of self. To forget their ancestors. They undermined authority. That was in the time of your Queen Victoria. In the new century the poison they had put in the pot caused it to over-boil. In 1908, with the death of the Great Empress Mother, Yehonala, the last protecting rock of our traditions was swept away. The Emperor was still a small child. After a time of dissension comes open rebellion. A Republic is proclaimed. In 1912 the Emperor abdicates, but remains in Pekin as guest of his own country. China's more recent history you will know. Upstart War Lords tear the land between them. They ravish it. The Bolshevik agents add to its disruption. The Japanese seize great portions of it. The World War brings further calamities. The defeat of Japan gives the Russians their opportunity. Chiang-Kai-Shek is driven out to Formosa. Anarchy is the food of Communism. With its triumph there follows the final abolition of the virtuous life.'

The old man paused for a moment, then went on. 'After the death of the Great Empress Mother, my honoured father and a circle of his friends foresee much of these happenings. They weep from knowing that the old China is doomed. There are seven of them. All are of high descent and having great wealth. They wish to preserve the ancient teachings. They wish their children should be brought up in a state of right-mindedness. For this they see that they must leave China. Wise men do not act rashly. Years pass. They send their fortunes to London, New York, Buenos Aires, Amsterdam. In their houses they gather learned men and great artists. By 1913 the boy Emperor has abdicated. He came of a junior line. His education is in the hands of a Western Barbarian. For these reasons the heads of the Seven Families reject his suzerainty. The posthumous son of the Emperor Tung-chih is thirty-eight and in all ways suitable. He is chosen to rule over us. In the years many remote places have been inspected. The choice falls on this island.'

Again the Mandarin paused, and this time supped up another tiny bowl of tea before continuing. 'Those who demand everything end with nothing. This island is too near the equator to grow mulberry trees for silk-worms. We must import our China clay. The hills hold no stone worthy to be carved. A greater matter weighed the choice. It had to be a territory owned by a small power. Thus only could we barter money for special rights. By secret treaty we bought from the Portuguese a lease of a thousand years less one. The treaty makes us subjects of Portugal but our own masters in the island. They surrendered the right to tax, to involve in war, to inspect, to govern. In 1913 the son of Tung-chih and the Seven Families leave China very quietly. With them they take their scholars and artists. Also from their estates in the interior many servants who have not been corrupted by Christianity or the Socialism of the revolutionary Dr. Sun-yat-sen. Here, while the Barbarians of the West seek to destroy one another in their first Great War, we build a small old China in a new land. We can grow rice, many vegetables and many fruits. We have the secrets of China's ancient industries. These give us a larger revenue than we need. We observe the ancient rites. We conduct ourselves in accordance with the teachings of the Great Sage. We have no ambitions. Only to live graciously, and to perpetuate a way of life that long experience has shown leads to

50

the well-being of the spirit. In that we are successful, while the outer world is disrupted by irresponsible men seeking power through innovations. Here we live like a placid stream—ever unruffled yet ever renewed. We have learned the wisdom of making Time stand still.'

Gregory had listened to the old man with intense interest. Knowing the patience, the wisdom, and the devotion to tradition of the high-caste Chinese, he found nothing the least improbable in this account of the carefully planned salvaging of their ancient civilization. Smiling, he said:

'Please allow me to offer my congratulations, Excellency. In this age of instability and disillusion it is a remarkable achievement to have created a Utopian State. I could almost believe that I have arrived in Shangri-la.'

Sze Hsüan did not understand the allusion, but his daughter did, and said a little sharply, 'Apart from its building, Sir, you will find little in this island which resembles the imaginary country described in Mr. James Hilton's beautiful book. Here we have not learned the way to retain youth and beauty beyond its normal span, or to prolong our lives until we feel a desire to cast off our bodies for good. We are subject to all normal ills, vices and temptations. I do not question my honoured father's contention that here there is better opportunity to follow the path of virtue than in the outer world, but do not let that lead you to suppose that we have achieved a state near perfection. The population is normally law-abiding, but occasionally criminals emerge from it. This very night, but for your fortunate presence and gallant intervention, I should have fallen a victim to one who has certainly not benefited from the ancient teachings.'

It was the first time that lady A-lu-te had addressed Gregory directly, and he bowed. 'Madam, I am not surprised at what you tell me, for I was not serious in my suggestion that any group of human beings could have entirely eliminated all baser instincts. But I should be interested to hear what lay behind that man's attack upon you?'

Her eyes widened. 'There can be but one. His labour must have brought him to the vicinity of the house. Probably for days he has watched me in secret. In any case, having looked

51

upon me, his lust must have got the better of his reason. I owe it to you that I was not raped and left strangled among the bamboo breaks.'

'Then your peril was more desperate and immediate than I imagined. What punishment will be inflicted on him?'

'People who commit minor breaches of the law here are warned, and if that proves insufficient fines are imposed on them. For murder and *lèse-majesté* the penalty is death. But experience has shown that it is futile to attempt either to reform habitual criminals or to cure criminal lunatics ; so we do not go to the trouble and expense of providing for their confinement. This man falls into the last category. Such as he are injected daily for three months with a drug which destroys memory. Those who have had it are no longer plagued by their phobia ; they do not remember their crimes and feel no urge to repeat them.'

'What happens to them then?' Gregory inquired.

'They are put to work in the fields, or on other simple tasks.'

'That is certainly an economical way to protect society.'

'It is also merciful. They retain the enjoyment of their normal senses, but live only from hour to hour. They do not even realize that any punishment has been inflicted on them. You see, the loss of memory entails the loss of individuality ; so they feel no craving for their former position or possessions, or to be reunited with those whom they may have loved.'

Gregory sighed. 'I lost those dearest to me in the wreck from which I am the sole survivor. I wish that I had died with them ; so what you tell me makes me inclined to envy that poor brute who attacked you. I have a prejudice against committing suicide, but to escape the years of loneliness ahead of me I would be quite willing to undergo this course of injections.'

A-lu-te's face showed shocked surprise ; but her father, who had managed to follow the gist of the conversation, said quietly, 'It is fortunate that your mind should be so disposed. The Council will decree it for you tomorrow. For them, I see no alternative.'

'But this is horrible!' the girl exclaimed. 'Honoured father, can you not——'

He cut her short with a gesture. 'The gratitude of individuals must not prejudice safety of the State. Our secrets are uncovered. If known to the world we are ruined.'

'Of course, that is true,' Gregory admitted slowly. 'And I have no right to expect you to trust me. I see now that having left the cage means that you dare not now allow me ever to leave the island.'

'That we must keep you here is obvious.' A-lu-te's voice was high and excited. 'But to destroy your mind, that is quite another thing. The thought appals me. It is by the mind that all educated people live. You are clearly a person of considerable mental attainments. However great your grief it will pass. That you should be willing to submit to this shows that you are temporarily unbalanced. Somehow it must be prevented.'

Her father shook his head. 'My child ; this thing does not lie with you or me. He must remain. That is agreed. It is also agreed that time will heal his grief. What then if he succeeds to become stowaway? Only by taking his memory of all things past have we guarantee that he remains. The first duty of the Council is protection for our secrets. They will decree it. Of this I am certain.'

Angrily, A-lu-te broke into a torrent of Chinese. For a full minute her words poured out in a tone of violent argument. Then, in a single sharp sentence her father cut her short. A brief silence ensued ; after it, she turned to Gregory and said in English:

'My honoured father graciously permits me far more liberty of speech than is usually allowed to women here. But now he has forbidden me to speak further on this matter. He and I both owe you a great debt. His sense of duty as a member of the Council makes it impossible for him to attempt to repay it, and most unhappily I am powerless to do so.'

'I am sure you have done everything you can,' Gregory smiled. 'But please don't worry. My life no longer holds any interest for me, and the thought of having my memory blacked out does not distress me in the least.'

Meanwhile Sze Hsüan was tinkling a small bronze bell. One of the men servants whom Gregory had already decided was the Number-one Boy appeared. The Mandarin gave him some order, then rose from his chair. Gregory exchanged bows with him, with the lady A-lu-te, and with the duenna, who had remained a silent spectator of the scene; then the servant led him from the reception hall to a bedroom, provided him with things for the remainder of the night, and left him.

Although it was now close on two in the morning his brain was far too active for him to go to sleep at once, and he lay for a long time thinking over his extraordinary situation. No guard had been placed over him, but the reason for that was obvious. It was pointless to leave the house when there was no way of escape from the island. To stow away, as Sze Hsüan had suggested he might attempt to do later if left in full possession of his faculties, was impossible as the steamer that served the port was not due back for two months or more. During so long a time he could not possibly evade capture. The problem of concealing his identity while obtaining food from a population whose language he could not speak would have been utterly insoluble. Expert escaper as he was, he doubted if he could remain uncaught for a week if he had to make nightly raids on people's larders, and, since the island must be quite a small one, the odds were that search parties sent out to find him would round him up long before that.

But he considered the possibilities of escape only from habit. He felt no urge whatever to attempt it. The lady A-lu-te had been right when she had said that his mind was temporarily unbalanced. Otherwise he would have faced death rather than tamely accept the idea of being deprived of his personality. As it was he regarded the prospect rather favourably. For the past weeks he had known a misery of which he had never believed himself capable. The thought that he would never see Erika again had encircled his heart with an icy chill which was comparable only to Dante's 'Seventh Circle of Hell'. To the continuance of such suffering it seemed to him infinitely preferable that his mind should be made a vacuum. On that thought he dropped asleep.

Soon after dawn he was woken and served with an excellent 'first rice'; then the Number-one Boy indicated that he should get up, and, when he had dressed again in his dinner-jacket suit, led him out to the front entrance of the house. Sze Hsüan was waiting there and gravely wished him good morning, then mounted into a richly-appointed palanquin with eight bearers. Gregory, meanwhile, was escorted to a rickshaw drawn by a single coolie. A-lu-te was nowhere to be seen but the slight movement of a bead curtain that veiled one of the windows made him wonder if she was watching from behind it. The palanquin bearers set off at a trot and the rickshaw followed.

As they proceeded at a swift pace along the road on the far side of the lake, Gregory marvelled at the beauty of the valley even more than he had the previous night. Then, in the moon-light, everything had appeared grey, silvery or black ; now, under a sun still low in the sky, an infinite variety of soft colours blended to enhance the scene. Although it was evident that the Council met early to avoid the great heat of the mid-day hours, there were very few people about. Speculating on the reason, Gregory decided that it was probably because all markets and utilitarian activities were deliberately excluded from the valley in which the aristocracy lived. The only build-ings they passed were large private houses, none of the land was being farmed and there were no meadows with livestock grazing in them. Apparently the valley had once been dense tropical jungle, but since brought by immense labour under control and converted with consummate artistry into an un-broken succession of glades, orchards and gardens.

After about a mile they entered the avenue of palms and turned inland along it. Ahead now lay the most massive build-ings, including the tall pagoda. From the position of the sun Gregory saw that they were heading north ; and, now he was aware of the reason for the similarity of the lay-out to that of the Imperial City, he felt sure that the palace in which the Emperor gave audience must be a triple-roofed building straight ahead. In old China it was traditional for a superior always to be seated with his back to the north when he received an inferior. One of the many pseudonyms by which people referred to the Emperor had been *Nan Mien,* meaning 'The Face which is turned towards the South'. Pekin itself is backed by a semi-circle of mountains to the north, while through the plain to the south passes the great trunk road, leading through gate after gate in the city, courtyard after courtyard of the palace, to end only at the steps of the Imperial Throne.

Gregory's guess, that here on a miniature scale the old sym-
bolism would have been copied, proved correct. After passing
through three handsome gates with roofs like inverted sickle
moons they entered a spacious courtyard crowded with people.
Before the main door in its far side the palanquin was set down
and Sze Hsüan got out. He was received with deference by a
number of men wearing the same uniforms as those who had
done guard duty in the cage, spoke briefly to their officer, then
passed into the palace. The officer came over to Gregory,
bowed, and said in English:

'You will please follow me.'

Beyond the huge outer door, across a lofty entrance hall,
there was another, made of scrolled bronze-work having great
flowers inlaid with mother of pearl; but the officer took Gregory into a small side room and told him to wait there.

It was almost bare of furniture, but its walls were panelled
with hand-embroidered silk depicting scenes from Chinese life,
and for about twenty minutes Gregory amused himself admiring the superb needlework. The officer then came for him,
led him through a further door and back into a second hall
where a number of officials were evidently waiting to transact
their business. They glanced curiously at him as he was conducted past them towards what appeared to be a blank wall;
but the officer touched a hidden spring in it, a panel slid back,
and he stepped through the opening into a far more magnificent
hall than either of the others.

A glance showed him that by a side entrance he had been
brought to the Throne Room. At its far end there was a dais
on which stood a golden throne formed from an intricate lotus
design, the stems of the flowers being studded with pearls and
the flowers themselves made of bright blue lapis lazuli.

The throne was unoccupied, but on a stool a little to its right
sat Sze Hsüan. Below the dais on either side were ranged three
other stools, on each of which sat a Mandarin. They varied in
age from a young man in his early twenties to a venerable grey-
beard with a creased, monkey-like face, who might well have
been over eighty. Gregory at once decided that the six Mandarins, together with old Sze Hsüan, each represented one of
the Seven Families who had originally colonized the island,

and that, from his place on the dais, the latter filled the function of Prime Minister. Squatting on the floor at low tables, with ink, brushes and paper scrolls were a number of clerks taking records of the proceedings.

The officer led Gregory forward to within about twenty paces of the throne, made a low obeisance and stepped back from him. He also bowed, then stood quietly waiting while the members of the Council regarded him with impassive faces.

Sze Hsüan addressed his fellow members in Chinese, speaking at some length. When he had done, no attempt was made to translate what he had said for Gregory's benefit. Instead complete silence was observed while seven young women came in single file round from behind the throne, each carrying an opium pipe on a velvet cushion which they presented to their respective masters. Gregory knew then that he was not to be asked anything about himself, or whether he had anything to say. The Council had already heard all they wanted to know about his case, and the production of the opium pipes was a ritual symbol that it only remained for them to consider the matter before passing judgment. As he expected, the pipes were lit, but, after each Mandarin had taken a puff or two, laid aside.

Starting with the eldest, three of them spoke briefly, and it seemed obvious that they were in accord. Then, just as the fourth had begun to give his opinion, Gregory heard a sudden commotion behind him.

Turning, he saw that a side door had been flung open and that the lady A-lu-te had entered by it. Running as swiftly as if she were pursued and in fear of her life, she crossed the great chamber. Within a few feet of the throne she extended her arms and flung herself flat on the floor before it. No one moved or spoke. Now motionless and silent she continued to lie there as if the violence with which she had thrown herself down had knocked her out.

Over a minute elapsed before her father slowly rose to his feet. Stepping down from the dais he took up a position beside her and briefly addressed his fellow Mandarins. It seemed evident that he had temporarily relinquished his status as a member of the Council, and was asking permission for her to speak. One by one they nodded in assent. He said something to her; then, at last, she raised her head from the floor, sat back on her heels and spoke for several minutes.

When she had done, Sze Hsüan turned to Gregory and said, 'The gratitude of my daughter is deep. She makes a proposal to the Council. I also feel gratitude. I support it. To accept or reject is for them. But first you must consent. She shall tell you of it.'

Before looking round at Gregory, A-lu-te made three obeisances to the Council, then she said quickly, 'I have offered to go surety for you. It would mean your becoming my bondsman. If I am to be responsible for you they will require that you should take an oath of service to me, as a safe-guard against your living idly and perhaps becoming a focus for unrest amongst the people. You will also have to swear not to make any attempt to leave the island. Should you do so, or become a cause of trouble here, I shall be called on to pay the forfeit. They will order for me the course of injections which you would otherwise start tonight. Are you willing to allow me to save you in this way, if they agree to it?'

Slowly, Gregory shook his head, 'Madam, it is most generous of you; but I have already made up my mind to accept the fate decreed for me. Since tragedy robbed me of all I held dear, my future is completely barren. To think at all has become a torture, and this treatment offers the equivalent of sleep. Perhaps I might even find a new happiness of a simple kind working in the fields. In any case I would rather accept mental obliteration than continue to suffer the mental torment with which I have been afflicted since being washed up here.'

'You are not competent to judge for yourself!' she exclaimed angrily. 'No state of mind lasts indefinitely. Faced with this in a few months or a year, you would agree to anything rather than consent to the destruction of your personality.'

For a moment he wondered if she was not right, and that he had allowed despair temporarily to cloud his reason. Yet he felt so terribly tired. All he craved was peace; so he shook his head again.

'It is not that I would object to serving you, or that I want to leave the island. It is just that my life is now such a burden to me that I've no heart left to go on.'

'Please!' she pleaded. 'Please let me save you from yourself. If later on you still feel the same, no doubt it could be arranged to cancel the arrangement, and for you to have the treatment.'

He shrugged. 'In the meantime I should suffer greatly ; so I stand to gain nothing by postponing it.'

There was a moment's silence, then Sze Hsüan addressed Gregory. 'My daughter has shown generosity. For you she offers to imperil her mind. To us it is a worthless thing ; but for her it is her greatest treasure. To refuse her is to act with grave discourtesy.'

It was a typically Chinese point of view, and one which had not occurred to Gregory. Suddenly he realized that if he stuck to his decision A-lu-te must suffer a most shaming loss of 'face' among her own people. Publicly to insult someone who was evidently taking a desperate step in the belief that it would save him from his own folly was entirely contrary to his nature. And, after all, she had said that if in a few months' time he felt the same the arrangement could be cancelled. He saw now that, in the circumstances, it was up to him to save her from the ignominy to which she had exposed herself by her act. With a wry smile he bowed to her, and said:

'Madam, I am ashamed that my sorrow should have made me forget my manners. I gratefully accept your generous offer.'

A-lu-te gave a sigh of relief and her father, reverting to Chinese, asked the consent of the Council to the arrangement. The young concubines with the opium pipes appeared again. Each of the six Mandarins took a ceremonial puff then laid the pipes aside. In turn they gave their opinion. Only the very old monkey-faced man appeared to be against acceptance, but his opposition was overcome by the others. A-lu-te expressed her thanks and rose to her feet.

Sze Hsüan then told Gregory to kneel in front of her. Concealing his indifference, he did so. Laying his hands on hers, as ordered, he repeated a simple oath dictated to him, by which he bound himself to serve her in all things according to her commands, and not to attempt to leave the island. When the brief ceremony was over they both bowed to the Council, Sze Hsüan resumed his seat on the dais, and the officer led them out of the great hall by a side door.

In the sunny courtyard several palanquins and scores of bearers were waiting. A-lu-te led the way to one with pale green silk curtains, got into it, and told Gregory to walk beside her. At her order the bearers lifted it and set off at a walking pace. She had left the curtains of the palanquin undrawn, and as they passed through the gate he said:

'I'm afraid you must think very badly of me for having shown reluctance to agree to your proposal; but you may be right and I am not yet quite normal. Anyway, I can assure you that I am sane enough to feel deep appreciation of the kind heart that impelled you to make it.'

She smiled, but her voice held a slightly ironical note as she replied. 'I can claim no credit for my conduct. It was simply that I wished to have you for a slave.'

This calm confession took him completely by surprise, yet his equally ironical retort came swiftly. 'I thought the Chinese had given up slave-owning long ago; but if you are still living in the dark-ages here, I hope I'll make you a good one.'

'There are many degrees of slavery,' she said lightly. 'It is my wish that yours should be as little irksome to you as possible. Is there any particular work for which you have a preference?'

'You are most considerate, but I detest all work. It just happens that I was born lazy.'

'Before very long you would get tired of doing nothing. Besides, for some time to come it is important that you should have an occupation to take your mind off your bereavement.'

He glanced at her with new respect. 'Yes; there is something in that. All right, set me to work at anything you like, providing it has nothing to do with a machine. I detest getting my hands oily or greasy.'

'Do you know anything about gardening?'

'Not much; and nothing about gardening in the tropics. But I like growing things. Since the war ended I have had a house in the country; and whenever I've been at home in England I have taken a great interest in my garden.'

60

'Then you shall keep yourself healthy by working in mine. But I have another, quite different, occupation already planned for you, and I hope you may derive some pleasure from it.'

'What is it?' he asked a shade suspiciously.

'It is to talk to me.' She turned towards him on her cushions and he saw that the irises of her almond-shaped eyes had flecks of gold in them, as she went on with sudden bitterness: 'I hate it here! For the old ones it is well enough. They have succeeded in putting time back to where they would have it be. To live a life of decorum in comfort and security is all that they desire. But for me this island is a gilded cage. From it I can see no hope of physical escape, but at least my mind is free. With books, and periodicals, and my radio, I have learned English well enough to understand it perfectly ; so I can follow all the great events that happen in the outer world, and even form a vague idea of their setting. But never to have travelled is a great handicap. There are still a thousand things I want to know. The young men of our Seven Families go to the great universities in America and Europe, but my opportunities to talk with them are comparatively few. With you I look forward to conversing without interruption every day. The variety of subjects on which I wish to be informed is infinite, and as an educated Englishman I feel sure that you have a wide knowledge of the world. Will you act as my magic carpet and carry me with your words across the great oceans to the sights I long to see?'

Gregory now understood a lot that had been puzzling him about this young woman, and he said at once, 'It so happens that I have travelled in many countries ; so I am better qualified than most people to do as you ask. It will be a pleasure to tell you all I can about anything you want to know.'

He was still speaking when they caught the first sounds of confused shouting behind them. Glancing back down the half mile of the avenue of palms they had covered while talking, he saw that a commotion had broken out in front of the palace. People were running in all directions and some of them were throwing themselves on the ground. Bad news travels fast, and when next Gregory looked round a runner was speeding towards them. The bearers of the palanquin heard his shouts.

Without orders they halted, set their burden down, and broke into a loud wailing. As the man raced past, still yelling, A-lu-te stared at Gregory, her mouth half open, her eyes distended.

'What is it?' he asked impatiently. 'What the devil's the matter?'

'The Emperor!' she gasped. 'The Emperor! The runner was crying out that he has just been found dead.'

4

THE VACANT THRONE

I T transpired that the Emperor had been stung on the tongue by a wasp during the night, and had choked to death before he could summon help. As he was a man of only thirty-two and in excellent health his death came as a totally unexpected blow to his people. Except for those who had important duties, everyone abandoned work and shut themselves up to mourn his loss.

To this the lady A-lu-te was no exception. When they reached her home she gave orders to the Number-one Boy that Gregory was to be accommodated in a small pavilion in the garden. Then, having asked him not to leave the vicinity of the house, she went to her room and did not emerge from it for the next seventy-two hours.

In consequence it was not until three days later that Gregory learned of the crisis that the Emperor's death had brought about in the affairs of the island; but during this time he picked up quite a lot about the pattern of life led there.

Ho-Ping was his informant, as it was part of the doctor's duty to find out how Gregory had escaped from the cage; and he paid him two visits with that object. Thinking it to be just possible that there might come a time when he was put in the cage again, Gregory exercised his usual learyness in such matters and refrained from disclosing the truth. The lowest branches of the overhanging tree were so obviously out of reach from the roof of the building that no one had thought of it as a possible means of escape, and he stuck to his story that he had jumped from the roof to the cliff face. In vain the doctor argued that for any ordinary man such a leap was impossible. Gregory maintained that his athletic prowess made him an exception; so after a second attempt to get at the truth, there the doctor had to leave it.

On both occasions, after a dead-lock had been reached on the subject, they had talked for a while of other things; and, now that Gregory's attachment to the Hsüan household had been sanctioned, Ho-Ping no longer showed any disinclination to answer his questions frankly.

He learned that conditions on the island were an interesting blend of the old and new. As Sze Hsüan had told him, the object of its colonization had been to preserve a society in which the Confucian tradition could be maintained; but it was observed only as a spiritual guide to the right conduct of life.

Women enjoyed a much greater freedom than they had in the old China, although the degree of liberty they were allowed was still at the individual discretion of their fathers or husbands. It had always been considered the first duty of Chinese women to preserve their attractions, so that they might continue until well on into middle age to delight their husbands, and they were particularly proud of their beautiful hands and figures; so, to this end, it had become traditional that apart from cooking, which was regarded as an art, none but the wives of coolies should ever do any menial work. This gave them ample leisure to beautify themselves and enjoy a very full social life, mainly composed of family celebrations. But there was no dancing at these functions, there were no cinemas on the island, and only the immediate relatives of the Mandarins were allowed to own radio sets.

As the most satisfactory means ever devised for protecting marriage, the ancient institution of concubinage had been retained, but with regulations that safe-guarded the interests of the girls concerned. For each month that a concubine spent in a man's household he had to bank in her name a sum sufficient to keep her in modest circumstances for six months. She was free to leave him whenever she chose, and if it was to marry—as most of them did—she was allowed to draw the money as her dowry. If she failed to marry before her attractions faded the money was paid out in the form of a pension to support her in honourable retirement. The man who took her had to keep her for a minimum of three months. At any time after that he could dismiss her, but he remained responsible for the upbringing of her child, should she have conceived one while living with him temporarily ; and, of course, for that of any children born to her during their association should it—as more often than not proved the case—turn out to be a long one.

There were no brothels, and no large harems in which numbers of idle, frustrated women languished in gilded captivity. Any man, married or single, could take a concubine, but the coolies were permitted to maintain only one, the artisans and petty officials two, the professional class and members of the Seven Families three, and the Mandarins themselves four. The Emperor was catered for by a modification of old Imperial custom. In China, at an appropriate age, the heir presumptive had been given a harem of two or three dozen young women of good family. In due course—the only qualification being that the girl should be of pure Manchu blood—he raised one or more of them to the rank of wife, while the rest remained concubines. Here, each of the Seven Families provided him with a concubine, and from them he chose one to be his future Empress.

There was no poverty in the island, as life had been organized to become as nearly as possible self-supporting. The staple foods were rice and fish, but a great variety of fruits and vegetables were grown, there were several large poultry farms, a dairy herd, and in the forests along the north coast a small army of pigs was preserved to provide meat. The revenue from the export of faked antiques far more than sufficed to pay for imports, the principal of which were raw materials and oil to run the electric power plants. From the surplus came the salaries of the official and professional classes, all of whom ranked as Civil Servants. The Mandarins received no salaries, but all of them possessed large private fortunes and each contributed one-fifth of his income to the treasury of the Emperor ; apart from which there were no taxes.

Imports, other than necessities, were restricted in order to maintain a balanced budget. In 1913, when the emigration had taken place, motor cars were still only very rarely to be seen in China, so here they had been permanently ruled out as redundant ; but many labour-saving devices had been adopted, refrigerators were installed in all the better-class houses, and electric stoves for cooking. Perfumes, which from the earliest times have rejoiced the hearts of Chinese women of all classes, silks and tea were the only luxuries imported in any quantity ; but the privileged families were allowed to send for books, wine, gramophone records and other special items that they desired.

Spirits, tobacco and coffee were prohibited to all as a wasteful expenditure, but the time-honoured pleasures of smoking opium and chewing nuts were allowed, although the former was rationed as a restraint on individual excess.

All children received a primary education, but as the girls often married at the age of fifteen they left school when ten years old to learn household duties from their female relatives at home. At that age, too, the boys were separated into three groups for further attendance at schools which taught mainly agriculture, crafts and the higher learning respectively. At thirteen a few, who at the first showed special intelligence, were transferred to whichever seemed the most suitable of the other schools, while the remainder were put to light work out of doors. At fifteen the majority of boys at the school of crafts went into the factories, but the brightest amongst them were transferred to the school of higher learning. Education there continued until seventeen, after which its pupils mostly became junior officials, except for a minority who showed promise in the arts. These were then absorbed into a special school which, up to that age, was exclusively reserved for the children of the Seven Families ; and only original students at this Mandarin school were later sent abroad to complete their education at American or European universities.

Gregory smiled to himself as he thought how scathing the comments of the Socialists of the Western World, who championed equality for all whatever the cost, would be on such a social system. Clearly it was based on the archaic conception of a privileged aristocracy, which still denied opportunities for intellectual development to women and reserved to itself both the best jobs and all functions of government.

Since the Emperor appeared to be little more than a figurehead it was virtually an oligarchy; although unlike the ancient ones of evil reputation, in which a few rich men ground the faces of the poor, here an Emperor was supported by them and they alone paid any taxes. That, he realized, was made possible only by the fine revenue derived from the faking of antiques, but it said much for the good sense and high-mindedness of the Mandarins that they devoted these profits to the welfare of the people instead of piling up further riches for themselves. There was, too, equal opportunity for all boys to acquire a higher education, if they showed themselves worthy of it, and they could aspire to occupy the highest positions in the State, with the one exception of a seat on its governing Council.

When he asked Ho-Ping if the system really worked, or if at times there had not been agitations by the people for a share in the government, the doctor assured him that there had never been anything of the kind. The prohibition of wireless and the literature of the outer world, except to the members of the Seven Families, ensured the exclusion of ideas which might lead to discontent; and as far as the women were concerned he felt certain that, with few exceptions, they were far happier living protected lives in their homes than they could possibly have been if reared to work in the factories or to compete with men for specialized jobs. He added that as, until the advent of revolutionary doctrines, the old civilization of China had remained fundamentally unchanged for several thousand years, and that this was in all essentials a continuation of it—provided the secrets of the island could be kept—he saw no reason why it should suffer disruption in any foreseeable future.

Gregory picked upon the mention of the island's secrets to get in a sly dig at the doctor by inquiring if he thought the faking of antiques, for sale at prices greatly in excess of their real value, was in keeping with the Confucian tradition ; but Ho-Ping was not to be caught. Smiling blandly, he replied:

'Different races have different ideas about what constitutes beauty, but such ideas are not constant, and again in each race differ in different centuries. It so happens that in the present era cultured people in the West see beauty in many objects which were made in old China only for their usefulness, or for religious purposes ; the age of these objects plays no part whatever in this. The Western connoisseur concerns himself with the age of these objects only because he believes that certain shapes, colours, textures and glazes could have been produced in no other. It is our good fortune that we hold the secrets of producing from uncut stone and unbaked clay these particular attributes which he so greatly admires. If we offered them to him cheaply and for what they are, he would either refuse to buy them, or imagine a difference that does not exist and continue to hanker after originals. As it is he pays a price out of all proportion to the intrinsic value of the object, but he gets a thing that his particular sense of beauty has urged him to acquire and rejoices in its possession. I see no cause for shame in making money by satisfying such desires.'

This specious argument entirely ignored the question of integrity on the sellers' part ; but Gregory let it pass because he was inclined to agree that if a buyer could not tell the difference between a genuine antique and a fake he suffered no great hardship, and that in such transactions dealers were certainly fair game. The thought prompted him to inquire the means used to dispose of the goods.

'That side of the business is entirely in the hands of the Seven Families,' Ho-Ping replied. 'As I have told you, no one but their male members is ever allowed to visit the cities of the outer world. That is because it is only with them we can rest assured that our secrets are safe. Several of them live abroad for a term of years while running depots we have established in such places as Hong Kong, Hanoi, Singapore, Suez and San Francisco. From these our goods are filtered through to the great cities of Europe and America.

'But sometimes we make use of our young men when they go overseas to complete their education. As you may have guessed from the fact that I speak fluent English, I am of the Mandarin caste. I took my degree at Cambridge. While there I was provided with ample money, so it did not appear at all strange that I should form a valuable collection of jade scent bottles. Before going down to become a medical student at Guy's, I gave out that I had overspent myself and disposed of my collection at a handsome figure to a London dealer.'

Dr. Ping laughed happily at the recollection, and Gregory laughed too ; but it was one of the very few occasions during those days that even a pretence of mirth stirred in him. His meals were brought to him regularly, but he had no visitors other than Ho-Ping. Apart from the servants, he saw no one except Sze Hsüan, and that only once. The Mandarin had just arrived back in his palanquin—presumably from a meeting of the Council of State—and was accompanied by a younger, larger and much fatter edition of himself, whom Gregory later learned was his brother and heir, Kâo Hsüan. Both of them were wearing the full Chinese mourning of unrelieved white, and walked to the house in silence with their hands buried in the sleeves of their robes and their eyes cast down. Gregory chanced to see them only because one of his periodical strolls in the grounds had brought him round to the front entrance ; but most of the time he sat doing nothing on the small veranda of his garden house, so, apart from the change of scene, his routine differed little from the life he had led while in the cage.

On the fourth afternoon A-lu-te and the plump, fussy, middle-aged lady whom Gregory had seen on the night of his arrival came out and joined him. A-lu-te introduced her companion as Madame Pan-chieh, and added:

'You will see a great deal of her, as it is customary here for an older woman to be present whenever a young one of my birth receives a man or goes to a party to which men are invited. She is my father's second senior concubine; the others employ themselves in running the house. I chose her for my companion because, although stupid, she had a kindly and placid disposition. She does not understand English, so you need not fear to offend her should you feel like criticizing some of the customs that make life in this island so narrow and wearisome.'

Gregory smiled at Madame Pan-chieh and installed her comfortably in a bamboo chair. She was indeed a placid woman, and he soon found that she was content to sit sewing for hours at a stretch, simply preserving the conventions by her presence, but otherwise intruding upon them no more than a piece of furniture. When all three of them were settled, he said to A-lu-te:

'I gather that the death of the Emperor has been a great blow to you all, and I should like to offer you my condolences upon it.'

She nodded. 'Thank you. I suppose you have heard the details?'

'No; since I saw you last I have spoken only to Dr. Ho-Ping, and he did no more than confirm what I had already heard—that death was due to a wasp sting on the tongue.'

'There is not very much to tell. My uncle Kâo Hsüan was the gentleman-in-waiting on that night. He saw the Emperor to his room a little after eleven o'clock, presented his opium pipe to him, and left him. A half-bitten preserved apricot was found on the floor, so evidently he helped himself to one from a bowl of crystallized fruit at his beside during the night, and the wasp was lurking in it. His custom was to ring for his valet at about six o'clock, but occasionally he slept late, so it did not occur to the man that anything might be wrong until half-past seven. Not daring to enter the bedchamber without having been summoned, he sent for my uncle to take that responsibility. At about eight they knocked on the door and receiving no answer, went in. Just inside lay the Emperor, dead. Apparently he had made an effort to reach it, but had collapsed before he could do so.'

'A wasp sting takes effect pretty quickly,' Gregory remarked, 'but all the same it seems a little surprising that he should not have had time to summon help.'

'Although not an opium addict, he was at times given to smoking several pipes. It is thought that this may have been such an occasion, and that the effects of the drug had deprived him of the power to make any great effort.'

'How about his women, though? As he was quite a young-ish man I should have thought that he would always have had one of them with him, or anyhow in an adjoining chamber.'

'No; they occupy a different part of the palace, and with regard to them the custom of old China is observed. In the ante-chamber to the Emperor's bedroom there is a table on which lie seven jade tablets. One is inscribed with the name of the Empress; the others with those of the six concubines. On his way to retire he turns over the tablet bearing the name of the lady whose company he desires for the night. She is then carried to him wrapped up in a fleecy blanket. In old China that service was performed by one of the chief eunuchs, but here the horrible custom of making boys into eunuchs has been discontinued. Their functions are now performed by old concubines who have been either in the household of the previous Emperor or those of deceased Mandarins. But some-times the Emperor preferred to sleep alone, and it was so on the night of his death.'

'I take it the new, er—Son of Heaven, must still be a child; or at most a youth in his teens,' Gregory observed.

A-lu-te shook her dark head. 'No; it is that which doubles our misfortune. The Emperor had no heir. Tragedy has twice stricken within a few weeks. His sons were both drowned less than a month ago. They were beautiful little boys of seven and nine, and were taken one afternoon to enjoy a sail along the coast; but the boat overturned and their attendants were un-able to save them. It is only a few days ago that we went from full mourning into half mourning on their account.'

Gregory immediately recalled the two children he had seen down by the harbour. That had been within a day or two of his first leaving his room to sit out on the terrace, and he remem-bered now that on the following day Ho-Ping had given the impression that something had occurred which caused him considerable distress. On his describing the boys A-lu-te at once confirmed that they were the two little Princes.

'What happened to their attendants?' Gregory asked, curious to know the fate of the nurse who had allowed her charges to be taken sailing without her.

'Their usual attendants were not with them,' A-lu-te replied. 'Had they been it is unlikely that the tragedy would have occurred. The Emperor had issued an order that they were never to be taken outside the reef. The Imperial boatman knew that, and so did their amah. By some mischance the Imperial boatmen were not warned for duty that afternoon ; so rather than disappoint the children the Harbour-Master sent them out with two of his men. It was in the rough sea outside the reef that the boat overturned. The men managed to swim ashore, but as soon as the Harbour-Master learned what had happened he naturally had their heads cut off, in the hope that the immediate action he had taken would help to placate the Emperor.'

'And did it?'

'The Emperor was a just man. The Harbour-Master had sought only to save the children from disappointment, and he vowed that he had told his men not to take them out to the open sea ; so the Emperor did not hold him responsible for the tragedy.'

'What about the amah?'

'The real blame lies with her. Had she accompanied the children, as was her most positive duty, she would have prevented the boatmen from taking them beyond the reef. As it was, for some private purpose of her own she remained behind. When she appeared at the harbour to meet them the news that they had been drowned threw her into a frenzy of remorse. She snatched a knife from one of the Harbour-Master's people, ran off behind a hut, and before she could be stopped stabbed herself to death.'

As Gregory had seen a coolie half-persuade, half-pull the amah in through the doorway of one of the warehouses, he felt that in having lured the woman from her duty the man was as

71

much to blame as she was; but since he could not have given the vaguest description of the coolie there seemed nothing to be gained by mentioning the matter. After a moment, he asked:

'Will the Emperor be succeeded by a younger brother, or some more distant relative?'

'Neither. He was an only son; and, most unfortunately, the last of his line.'

'To whom will the throne go, then?'

A-lu-te shook her head. 'I have no idea. It lies with the Council of State to decide. The problem is an intensely worrying one for my father and his fellow Mandarins.'

'When a Monarch dies without an heir-apparent, it is usual for him to nominate his successor in his wiil. Didn't the Emperor leave even an indication of his wishes?'

'No. Until less than a month ago the succession was assured by his two healthy sons. As he was still quite young it was natural for him, and everyone else, to assume that he would make good their loss by begetting others; so no provision at all was made to meet a situation so unexpected as this.'

'How about the Empress? Could she not be made ruler?'

'Oh no; that is quite out of the question.'

'Why? The old Empress Dowager reigned in China for nearly as long as Queen Victoria reigned in England.'

'You are mistaken. The Great Empress Mother acted only as Regent for her son, and later for other members of the Imperial Family.'

'Whatever her status this one would have infinitely less power. She would be no more than a figurehead, and entirely in the hands of her Council.'

'They would never agree to that,' A-lu-te asserted. 'The fact that she is not of the Imperial blood rules her out absolutely.'

Gregory could see that A-lu-te was a prey to acute anxiety, and he guessed the reason. Giving her a shrewd glance he asked, 'Who are the two strongest personalities in the island?'

Without hesitation she replied, 'Ho-Ping's elder brother and my uncle, Kâo Hsüan. The one is already a Mandarin and the other, as my father's nearest male relative, will be when he dies. Both of them are extremely ambitious.'

'I see,' Gregory nodded. 'Then, since the Emperor has no legitimate successor, you are afraid that these two will fight it out between them, and that this island paradise is about to become a field of blood?'

5

THE IMPERIAL FAMILY

THIS question of the succession seemed to occupy A-lu-te's mind to the exclusion of nearly everything else, and when she came out to join Gregory in the garden the following afternoon she told him that the Council had held another long but unsatisfactory meeting. Ho-Ping's brother Tsai-Ping had pointed out that as the Council of State had always done the real governing in the name of an Emperor, there was no reason why it should not continue to do so without one.

To this the other Mandarins were strongly opposed; both because the creation of any form of Republic would have been entirely contrary to their cherished traditions, and because they feared that without an Emperor to wield permanent authority over them Tsai-Ping's ambitious nature might lead him into attempting to become a dictator. But the sudden extinction of their own branch of the Imperial Family had left them at their wits' end, as they could think of no male member of any other branch whom they would care to invite to ascend the throne.

'Surely,' Gregory remarked, 'if they wish to observe tradition, it is not a question of "caring". Provided the Prince who has the best claim is sound in mind they should accept him. Anyhow there must be some precedent to go on. How was the last Emperor selected?'

'He inherited the throne. His father and grandfather reigned before him. We have had three Emperors since the island was first colonized in 1913.'

'Well, how was his grandfather selected? In 1913 Pu-yi was still Emperor of China, and remained there until driven out in the nineteen-twenties; so the heads of your Seven Families must have created some precedent in selecting the Emperor they brought with them.'

A-lu-te looked at him gravely, and asked, 'How much do you know of the history of the Imperial Family?'

'Not very much; only that the Manchu dynasty dates back to the invasion of 1644, and that from about 1860 the Emperors were little more than puppets dominated by the old Dowager Empress.'

'Then for you to understand our situation I must tell you of the way in which her influence affected the succession. The Emperor Tao-kwang died in 1850. He had nine sons and was succeeded by the eldest, Hsien-feng. When the period of court mourning was over sixty girls, all of the noble Manchu families that form the eight Banner Corps, were summoned to the palace. From them the Empress Mother and the Chief Eunuch selected twenty-eight to form the harem of the young Emperor. Those chosen included two sisters, Sakota and Yehonala. The latter was classed only as a concubine of the third grade, but it was she who later became the Great Empress Mother. Sakota was a girl of exceptional beauty so Hsien-feng made her his Empress, but Yehonala fascinated him with her mind, and was soon assisting him with affairs of state; moreover she gave him a son, so he raised her also to the rank of Empress.

'In 1861, Hsien-feng died. Two older Princes attempted to seize power but with the help of her girlhood sweetheart, Jung Lu, who commanded one of the Banner Corps, Yehonala outwitted them. She had her little son, Tung-chih, proclaimed Emperor, with her sister and herself as co-Regents. As you may imagine, Yehonala made Sakota Regent with her only for appearances' sake; and from that day on, for very nearly half a century she imposed her will upon everyone who played a part in the government of the Empire.

'Perhaps business occupied so much of her time that she had

none left to give to her son. In any case, the boy gave all his affection to his aunt, and by the time he became of an age to rule he thoroughly disliked his mother. In 1872, when he had reached the age of seventeen, the two Empresses selected for him a number of women, and it was agreed between them that he should be allowed to decide for himself which he would have for first Imperial Consort. He chose a girl of fifteen named A-lu-te.'

Gregory looked up in surprise, and A-lu-te smiled at him. 'Yes, I am named after her. The reason for that will be plain to you in a minute; and, as you will see, she plays a very important part in this story.

'She was a girl of spirit and she disliked Yehonala as much as did her husband. Very soon the young couple were at daggers drawn with the Empress Mother, and she could no longer delay in making at least a show of handing power over to them. In China there is a saying "Who rides the tiger cannot dismount", and Yehonala realized her danger. Tung-chih and his little Empress were scarcely more than children, and totally inexperienced, whereas Yehonala was wise in the ways of the Court and by her charm and intellect kept nearly all its principal personages bound to her interests. For a year or so she let her son make a fool of himself; then, early in 1875, he caught smallpox and died.'

A certain inflection in A-lu-te's voice made Gregory turn and glance at her. She shrugged her slim shoulders.

'No one will now ever learn the truth about that. Tung-chih was a dissolute young man and had formed the habit of leaving the palace secretly at night to indulge in disreputable pleasures in the outer city. He had undermined his health by excessive dissipation and it is quite possible that he contracted the disease on one of those nocturnal forays. On the other hand, in old China there was a very unpleasant practice connected with the small rough towels, heated with steam, that it was customary to offer people for wiping their hands and faces whenever they entered theatres, restaurants or private houses. When it was desired to get rid of someone, these towels were first passed over the ulcerated face of a man who had smallpox.'

Gregory made a grimace. 'What a revolting idea!'

'Yes; but in the majority of cases effective; and a good way of evading the condemnation usually aroused by the more open methods of murder. I think my ancestors had little to learn in such matters from the Borgias. Of course, it may have been only malicious rumour which suggested that the Emperor was handed infected towels by the eunuchs on the orders of his mother. In any case, he died before he was twenty without an heir, but leaving A-lu-te about to have a baby.

'Yehonala needed no telling that if A-lu-te bore a son history might repeat itself. Should the child be proclaimed Emperor, A-lu-te would become Empress Mother, and perhaps Regent. A new era would begin. Yehonala's friends would be sent silken cords as an intimation that they could hang themselves, and her own days would be numbered. She had to strike down the young Empress or be struck down herself.'

A-lu-te paused a moment, then continued. 'The history books will tell you that Tung-chih's widow survived him by only a few days, then died of grief. That was the official statement issued by Yehonala, but it was not the truth. Realizing that so much hung on her pregnancy that it had become her death warrant, the young Empress fled from the palace secretly by night and sought sanctuary with my grandparents. They took her to a remote estate that they owned in the province of Sze-chuan. There she was delivered of a boy.'

Gregory's quick mind anticipated the sequel, and he murmured, 'That boy, born in 1875, would have been just forty in 1914. It was he whom your father and the other Mandarins brought here as their Emperor, and it was his grandson who has just died.'

As A-lu-te nodded, he went on: 'I see now how it was that when they decided to colonize this island they were faced with no problem in selecting an Emperor. Directly your father let his friends know that his parents had brought up Tung-chih's posthumous son in secret, the choice was obvious. No one could possibly dispute his claim as he was the only son of the late Emperor and Empress. But who did Yehonala put on the throne of China?'

'There were three claimants—the son of Prince Kung, who

was the eldest surviving uncle of Tung-chih ; the son of Prince Ch'un, another uncle who was known as the Seventh Prince because by birth he came sixth after Tung-chih ; and a nephew of Tung-chih's named Pu-lún. Only the last was strictly eligible, because it is traditional that the ancestral rites to a deceased Emperor must be performed by a member of a younger generation. But Yehonala was not the woman to allow a matter of ceremony to stand in the way of her ambitions. In China the law of primogeniture has never been observed, yet in this instance Prince Kung urged it in favour of his son's candidature, and Sakota, who was officially the senior Dowager Empress, supported him. But that would not have suited Yehonala, because the boy was already in his teens and it would have meant a short Regency. She favoured Prince Ch'un's boy because he was still a child, and at a midnight meeting, during which a terrible storm raged, she forced the Council to accept him. He was named Kuang-hsu.

'So it was that Yehonala's second joint Regency began ; but, as in the case of her own son, the little Emperor disliked her and gave his affection to the more gentle-natured Sakota. Other causes for quarrels developed between the Regents, and it may be that Yehonala began to fear that when Kuang-hsu grew up he would combine with her sister to bring about her downfall. It is at least significant that it was after eating some sweet cakes sent to her by Yehonala that Sakota suddenly fell ill and died.'

'It certainly seems that the Borgias had nothing on this old lady,' Gregory remarked with a grim smile. 'Anyhow, little A-lu-te showed very good sense in getting out of her clutches while she had the chance.'

A-lu-te nodded. 'Yes ; but you must not think of Yehonala as old then. She was still only about thirty-five, and it was not until many years later that her affectionate subjects gave her the nick-name of "The old Buddha".'

'Affectionate subjects?'

'The term implies "The Wise One", and she was greatly beloved by her people. You see, she was the champion of the old China. During four thousand years of isolation China had developed a great civilization. It was not until the last half of the century that the European powers began to force their way

77

into the country. Yehonala was still a young wife when the first clash occurred. Lord Elgin, with British, French, Russian and German troops, captured Pekin and sacked the beautiful Summer Palace. She never forgave them, and from then on for the next forty years, right up to the Boxer risings in 1900, there was constant friction with the "Foreign Devils". Yehonala fought a losing battle, but she fought it bravely and skilfully to protect what she believed to be the best interests of her people. That is why they loved her.'

'I take it she became sole Regent after Sakota's death?'

'Yes ; but once again she was unlucky in her choice of a child Emperor. Kuang-hsu was unhealthy in mind and body. As a youth he imbibed many Western ideas without properly understanding them. He detested the ceremonies it was his duty as Emperor to perform, and was morbid, shy and difficult to deal with.

'In 1889 he was given concubines, and Yehonala selected a niece of hers to be his wife ; but he proved impotent so begot no children. On his marriage Yehonala formally gave up the Regency, but she reserved for herself the right to appoint and remove public servants ; so the real power of government still remained in her hands. The young Emperor proved hopelessly incompetent. He attempted to introduce all sorts of reforms which threatened to disrupt the whole life of the country. For a few years things went from bad to worse, then Yehonala stepped in again. She arrested Kuang-hsu and his Empress and kept them as prisoners in the Ocean Terrace Pavilion of the Summer Palace. For a time she ruled through him. Then in 1898 she entered on her third official Regency. From then on, as the Great Empress Mother, she continued as supreme ruler to the day of her death.'

'Where does the young Emperor Pu-yi come in?'

'In 1908 Yehonala's health began to fail. Her death might have enabled the morbid and dangerous prisoner of the Ocean Terrace to regain his rights as Emperor, and she would obviously have been most averse to leaving China at his mercy. Perhaps it was coincidence, but he also fell ill, and he died just before her. On the day after his death she appointed little

Pu-yi as Emperor and his father as Regent, then she herself died.'

Gregory nodded. 'What an appalling story. But, unscrupulous as she was, Yehonala seems to have been the only strong character in it. Every one of the three Emperors she chose grew up either dissolute or unfit to govern. And if the Mandarins are determined to observe tradition it is from this decadent family that they must choose a ruler for this island. I don't wonder that they're worried.'

'Yes. The Imperial Family is now scattered. The only Princes who might be worthy are too old. The others have either become dissipated through living an idle life in exile, or so Westernized that they might prove a menace to the ancient customs which it is the Council's main object to preserve. How they will solve this problem I cannot think.'

Nevertheless, solve it they did, and in a most unexpected manner. Two mornings later A-lu-te came out to Gregory and, her gold-flecked eyes shining with excitement, exclaimed:

'I can scarcely believe it! Instead of an Emperor we are to have an Empress.'

Gregory smiled at her. 'I hope they have chosen you. I've seen nothing so far of the other ladies on the island, but I can hardly imagine that any of them are better suited to the job.'

'No, no!' she shook her head impatiently. 'It had to be someone of the Imperial blood; and anyway I wouldn't want to be. I'd prefer to remain free so that I can continue my studies.'

'It is because you are so well-informed that I think you would do well in the part,' he remarked. 'But come and sit down and tell me all about it.'

Madame Pan-chieh came bustling up behind her young mistress, and when the two ladies were seated A-lu-te went on with her news.

'They have chosen a Princess who lives in the United States and was baptized into the Christian church with the name of Josephine.'

'On the face of it she does not sound very suitable. What place does she occupy in the Imperial Family?'

'You may recall that when I was giving you its more recent

79

history the other day, I began with the Emperor Tao-kwang, who had nine sons. It was the eldest of them, Hsien-feng, who made Yehonala an Empress. The second son was Prince Kung, and it was his son that Yehonala passed over after her own son died, selecting instead the son of the Seventh Prince as the new Emperor. This Princess is the great-grand-daughter of the boy who was passed over.'

'Since the eldest branch came to an end a week ago with the death of the Empress A-lu-te's great-grandson, Prince Kung's then became the senior,' Gregory remarked, 'so at all events the selection of his descendant has legitimacy to recommend it. Do you know how old she is, or anything about her?'

'She is twenty, an only child, and lives with her widowed mother in San Francisco. It is said that she is very pretty but, poor thing, she is quite dumb.'

'Dumb-stupid or dumb-no-talkee?' Gregory inquired.

A-lu-te frowned at his levity. 'I mean that she suffers from a terrible affliction. She was born in Saigon and while still an infant caught diphtheria. The tracheotomy was done by a doctor who was not properly qualified. He bungled the operation and injured her vocal cords. As she could still cry and gurgle the damage was not discovered until she was of an age when she should have started to talk, and by then it was too late to do anything about it.'

'What a frightful thing! It seems extraordinary, though, that any member of the Imperial Family should have failed to secure the best surgeon available to operate on his daughter.'

'Her father was both head-strong and eccentric. When his branch of the family went into exile they settled in French Indo-China. There he met a very beautiful woman. She was of Manchu blood but had become a courtesan. He insisted on marrying her and his family were so outraged that they publicly disowned him. He accepted their repudiation, became a Christian and took the name of Joseph Août. It is said that he chose it as a pun on the month in which he was born and the fact he was of "august" descent; although he never afterwards used his title or traded on his imperial connections. Later he managed to raise the money to take his wife and child to America, but for the first few years of his marriage he was desperately poor. This is why when the baby went down in a diphtheria epidemic he had to take it to a local hospital where only a student was available at the time to do the operation.'

'I see,' said Gregory thoughtfully. 'Then her parents were not exactly patterns of virtue and filial obedience; but I suppose that is outweighed as far as the Council are concerned by her ancestry. All the same, I find it very surprising that your father and his friends should have decided to invite a dumb Princess to come and reign over them.'

'Her affliction makes it more likely that she will accept,' commented A-lu-te, and went on a shade acidly. 'Any normal girl who has the luck to live in the United States would be crazy to do so. I would give this island and everything in it to get there.'

'Perhaps; but quite apart from the girl being dumb, it astonishes me that the Mandarins should be prepared to kowtow to any young woman.'

'They are not, except as a formality. This is simply an expedient, and adopted only as a last resort rather than allow a situation to develop in which an open struggle for power would break out among them. The Princess is unmarried. If she accepts the throne it is intended that each of the Seven Families should put forward its most eligible bachelor, and that she should be asked to choose a husband from among them. Whoever she chooses will automatically become Emperor.'

'Isn't that rather a chancy way of choosing a ruler? She may quite well pick on the biggest fool or knave of the lot if he happens to be the most attractive physically.'

A-lu-te shrugged. 'You're right, of course. But I don't think that would make much difference in the long run. The Council would continue to do the real governing. The point is that they could regard her choice as in a sense a decree of fate; so they are willing to accept whoever she may choose. And by this means they hope to start a new dynasty; because, whoever she may take as her husband, through her their children will be of the Imperial Blood.'

'Has this decision definitely been taken?'

'Yes. Orders have been given to prepare the Imperial Yacht

for a voyage to San Francisco. It is the first time for years that it has been used for more than a local pleasure cruise, so it will take some days to make ready ; but as soon as it is, my Uncle Kâo is to leave in it and, it is hoped, bring the Princess and her mother back from America with him.'

'From what you have told me of Tsai-Ping I wonder at his agreeing to that. As they seem to be rivals in most things I should have thought he would have gone to pretty well any lengths to prevent your uncle getting such a marvellous free field with the girl before anyone else has even had the chance to meet her.'

'They could not become rivals in that sense, because both of them are already married.'

'I meant that the choice of your uncle to bring the girl and her mother here will give him a quite exceptional opportunity to get both of them under his influence during the voyage.'

'That is true,' she nodded, 'and I don't doubt Tsai-Ping would have much preferred that someone other than my uncle should be charged with this mission. But Uncle Kâo was such an obvious choice that Tsai-Ping would only have made himself look foolish had he stood out against it.'

'What special qualifications has your uncle for the job?'

'His knowledge of conditions in the outer world is far greater than that of any of the Mandarins, or of anyone else on the island. Until last year he was what I suppose you would call our Export Manager. During the past twenty-five years he has travelled in every continent, inspecting our depots abroad and assessing the value to us of old and new foreign markets. Without revealing the secret of the island, he has also kept in touch with numerous members of the old Imperial Family, among them the Princess Josephine's mother. Alone amongst us he knows her personally. In addition he will succeed my father as the head of one of the Seven Families. He is, too, a man of cheerful disposition and great charm ; so for this affair it would be difficult to conceive of a more suitable ambassador.'

Later in the week Gregory had an opportunity of judging Kâo Hsüan's personality for himself, as A-lu-te's uncle called one afternoon and came out to see her in the garden. The

Manchu nobility are generally well above average height and he was both tall and corpulent. Although his features proclaimed his relationship to Sze Hsüan he was the son of a different mother and very much younger, being only a little over fifty. His face was round and cherubic with a full, sensual mouth and thick black eyebrows like inverted sickle moons. Like most Chinese he had an excellent sense of humour, and was by nature a very jolly man.

He had already heard all about Gregory and spoke to him most pleasantly in excellent English. They were soon exchanging reminiscences about happy times they had enjoyed in various European capitals, and he said what a pleasure it was to have an educated foreigner to talk to in the island. He added that the journey he was about to make would deprive him of that pleasure for some weeks, but on his return he would greatly look forward to developing Gregory's acquaintance.

Although Kâo did not actually say so, Gregory gathered the impression that he regretted the days of his travels being over, was glad of the chance to go to America again and, like his niece, would have preferred to live there had not his duty to his family made that impossible.

A-lu-te listened to their conversation with eager interest, particularly when it touched on the United States; and presently with an earnestness that was only thinly disguised as jest, she asked her uncle to take her with him, launching her plea on the pretext that the Princess should have at least one lady-in-waiting in attendance for the voyage; but he laughed and shook his head.

'No, no, my dear. The Princess lives very quietly with her mother in a small apartment. It is quite pleasant, but so modest that it would embarrass them for another lady, who might afterwards describe it here, to see their home and learn that they fend for themselves with the help of only a daily maid. That is between ourselves, of course; for over their past a veil will be drawn so that they shall not suffer loss of face. It will be time enough when the Princess lands here for her to assume Imperial status. Then if you like her, and wish to give her your companionship, I have no doubt it could be arranged for you to become one of the new Emperor's concubines.'

'Thank you ; but I have no wish to be anybody's concubine.'

'Then you should marry. It is against nature that a pretty young woman like yourself should spend the best years of her life without a husband. With all respect to my honourable brother, I think he acts selfishly in refusing to arrange a marriage for you.'

'On the contrary, Uncle Kâo!' A-lu-te threw up her firm chin. 'I can never be sufficiently grateful to him for refraining. I have no desire at all to marry—as yet.'

'Ah well!' The big man shrugged good naturedly. 'The time will come. But that in itself is a sufficient reason why I could not take you with me to San Francisco. The Council would never permit it. As you know, it is an axiom with them that no women should ever be allowed to leave the island, lest contamination with the ways of the outer world should unfit her for making a contented wife on her return.'

It was later on the same day that Gregory met Tsai-Ping. An hour or so after Kâo Hsüan had gone, Ho-Ping arrived and asked A-lu-te's permission to take Gregory to call on his brother. None too graciously, she gave it, and Gregory set off with the doctor. Two rickshaws carried them swiftly round the lake, then along half-a-mile of by-road to the Ping mansion, where the Mandarin was waiting to receive them.

He was about the same age as Kâo Hsüan and nearly as tall, but much thinner. His face was long, thin, and pale for a Chinaman's, and he wore old-fashioned steel-rimmed spectacles. After apologizing for his English, which was only just sufficient for him to make himself understood, he told Gregory that he had attended the University of Bonn and asked if he spoke German. As Gregory spoke it like a native they were able to converse fluently in that language ; but, all the same, very little spontaneous warmth animated their conversation.

Gregory was still too occupied with his own morbid thoughts to care much about the sort of impression he made, and constrained himself to be polite only out of consideration for Ho-Ping ; while the Mandarin, being of the cold intellectual type, unlike the jolly Kâo Hsüan, proved incapable of drawing him out. He decided that Tsai-Ping had asked to meet him only in order to form some idea whether he could be written off as a nonentity, or might as a member of the Hsüan household prove an asset to Kâo's political aspirations.

After bowing to one another over numerous tiny fragile cups of tea, and some desultory talk about German literature and international affairs, Gregory excused himself, and was sent home in Ho-Ping's spare rickshaw.

When the burial of the late Emperor had taken place, and Kâo Hsüan had departed in the small warship which had been converted to serve as the Imperial Yacht, the life of the island settled down to normal; but for Gregory it meant entering on a new existence.

A-lu-te's plan, that he should keep himself fit by working in the garden, met with only partial success. Work for the sake of exercise had never had the faintest appeal to him. To induce him to exert himself physically he had to be tempted by the prospect of some definite achievement. Once embarked on digging a swimming pool, building a wall, creating a new rock garden, or planting twenty thousand bulbs to transform a glade into a fairyland in spring, he would have laboured cheerfully from dawn to dusk for days on end; but according to Chinese standards the Hsüan garden was perfection already, and needed none of these things.

In consequence he never did more than potter in it; removing the heads from flowering shrubs on which the blossom had gone over, pruning dead branches from trees, and cutting flowers for the house. He took a mild interest in watching the growth of the plants that the real gardeners tended, but his continued indifference to everything about him robbed him of the initiative to ask the gardeners' names or even make an effort to identify them individually by memorizing the differences in their features.

His physical lassitude caused A-lu-te little concern as, from the beginning, it had been the possibility of exploring his mind which had intrigued her. In the gratification of this urge she spent never less than two hours a day, and often double that time, with him. During their sessions she displayed an insatiable curiosity about every aspect of life in the outer world; but he did not find her endless succession of questions at all trying. One was quite enough to set him off for half an hour or more, almost as though he was a penny-in-the-slot machine. She had only to mention such words as 'divorce', 'caviare', 'guillotine', 'rhododendron', 'whisky'. Her reading, wide as it was, had left her with only vague ideas about scores of such things, and he found that it took his mind off his own gloomy thoughts to describe and discourse upon them in a leisurely manner.

As far as Europe was concerned she could not have hoped for a better instructor. He told her of Paris in spring and the Riviera in winter; of the Margit's Insel at Budapest in high summer, and the gathering of the vintage on the Rhine in autumn; of the Acropolis at Athens in blazing sunshine and the Winter Palace near Leningrad under snow; of the Blue Grotto at Capri, of salmon fishing in Scotland, of the night life of Vienna, of Windsor, of the Escorial, of the Vatican, and of scores of other places.

Upon the United States, which was her greatest interest, she found him disappointing, as, except for short spells in transit, he had stayed only in New York, Washington and Florida; but he had travelled many thousands of miles in aircraft, in liners, in trains and in automobiles, none of which she had even seen. He knew far more than she did about ancient civilizations and modern warfare. His knowledge of science was sketchy, but he knew his way about most of the great picture galleries, had read or seen performed most of the finest plays from those of Aristophanes to Christopher Fry, comprehended the principles upon which architecture had developed, and was quite a passable cook.

About all these subjects, and many more, he gave his views with the same lucidity as if they had already been inscribed on a gramophone record, but the one thing that A-lu-te could not persuade him to talk about was himself. It was not that he was now making a deliberate effort to forget his past. On the contrary, he continued to nurse his grief much as one tends to play with an aching tooth; but he felt greatly averse to saying anything about Erika to someone who had never known her.

At the beginning of his acquaintance with A-lu-te he had

quite naturally assumed that she was a typical product of her class in the island; but he soon found that was very far from being the case. In having reached the age of twenty-two unmarried she was unique, and only unusual circumstances had resulted in her doing so.

Her father had suffered the greatest misfortune that can befall a Chinaman, as he had had eight daughters but no son, and he had to resign himself to the thought that after his death a son-in-law would perform the ancestral rites on his behalf. For all his daughters he had arranged suitable marriages while they were still infants, and A-lu-te's sisters had duly been married on reaching the age of fifteen, but her fiancé had died a few months before she was to become his wife. Even so, according to custom in old China, that made her a widow and precluded her from ever marrying anyone. But in the island this harsh restriction upon girls who had met with such ill-fortune had been abrogated to twenty-seven months mourning; so by the time A-lu-te had become eligible again to be contracted in marriage she was over seventeen.

During her two years' semi-seclusion she had amused herself by learning English and reading books about the world beyond the ocean; and, as she was unusually intelligent, her father had been so impressed with the knowledge she acquired that he had agreed to let her continue her studies for a further year. At eighteen her will and reasoning powers had developed to such an extent that she had the temerity to argue when he began seriously to press her on the subject of marriage. For another year the battle had gone on, and, at the end of it, old Sze Hsüan had come to accept the fact that even if Heaven had denied him a son it had sent him a daughter who could fill a son's place in all but the manner of the ancestral rites. Her mother had died when she was still a child; so he had made her the head of his household and now secretly hoped that she would never marry.

As Gregory soon gathered, the prospects of her doing so were becoming increasingly slender. It was not that she lacked physical attractions. She had a tall, willowy figure and moved gracefully. Her black hair was glossy and abundant, her eyes lively with intelligence, and her teeth two even rows of dazzling ivory. But by Chinese standards she was no longer a girl, and her mental attainments made her relatively so much older than she in fact was, that to her contemporaries she appeared to be verging on middle-age.

In due course Gregory met her sisters, their husbands and a number of other young people who came to the house. The women were most decorative and charming, but childlike and obviously just a little frightened that they might make fools of themselves while conversing with the learned A-lu-te. The men clearly respected her but never attempted to be in the least flirtatious, and it seemed as if they did not even think of her as a pretty young woman. Cynically, Gregory reflected that her simple laughter-loving sisters were far happier than ever she could be, and it was the very fact that she had developed her brain which debarred her from the full enjoyment of life. By eating of the fruit of the Tree of Knowledge she had acquired a discontent with the carefree existence of the island, and was no longer suited to become the wife of one of its nobility.

Most of the men visitors could speak English fairly fluently, or had a smattering of it and could speak French or German well ; so Gregory was able to talk freely with them ; but none of the women spoke anything but Chinese. In consequence, from constantly hearing the latter tongue, the little 'Mandarin' he had picked up as a young man soon came back to him, and he began to practise speaking it again with A-lu-te as his teacher.

The days passed pleasantly enough, and it was for him as though he now lived in a world that was not quite real. Something seemed to have died in him with Erika, and he simply accepted the routine that had been set for him without thinking about it. As the island was only eight degrees south of the Equator, the change in its seasons was scarcely perceptible. The hours of sunrise and sunset varied little, and all the year round cool night breezes refreshed it, keeping its climate pleasant apart from the blistering heat of midday, during which everyone slept. Almost the only indication of the changing seasons was the growth of crops and some variety in the flowers that from year's end to year's end made the gardens gay.

Gradually he came to know all the Mandarins and principal

officials of the island. On account of his extensive travels and wide general knowledge, they enjoyed talking to him. He showed no desire whatever to leave the island and at times expressed admiration for the way in which it was administered ; so they began to regard him almost as one of themselves and treated him in the most friendly manner.

The wreck had occurred early in March and it was mid-June when, one morning as Gregory was tying up a Bougainvillaea along a trellis, A-lu-te came running out of the house to tell him that a wireless message had been received from Kâo Hsüan. The yacht was approaching home waters and would dock that evening.

Elaborate arrangements had already been made for the reception of the Princess. Practically the whole population of the island was to welcome her as she stepped ashore, and the members of the Seven Families, arrayed in their most gorgeous garments, were to be presented to her by Kâo Hsüan. The Pings, the Wongs, the Sungs and the rest had entered on a cheerful rivalry for the distinction of presenting the most splendid turn-out, and every woman among them would wear her finest jewels for the occasion.

Having told Gregory the exciting news, A-lu-te hurried back indoors to superintend the final preparations of her father's household ; but, some ten minutes later, she came out again. He was still arranging the brilliant-hued creeper and as she called to him he noticed that her voice had lost its cheerfulness. Turning he saw that her walk was no longer quick and buoyant, and that she had a set frown on her face.

'What's wrong?' he inquired.

'Another runner has just arrived from the palace,' she replied, still frowning. 'The first was dispatched to let us know at once that the yacht would reach port this evening ; but he had only half my Uncle Kâo's message. The Princess is not on board.'

He shrugged. 'You did say yourself that if you lived in the United States nothing on earth would induce you to take the job ; and, after all, there was always a possibility that young Josephine might refuse it.'

'What I said was not meant to be taken seriously,' A-lu-te replied with an indignant expression. 'Had I been of her lineage

I should have felt compelled to accept from a sense of duty; and the possibility that after a few years here she might hanker to return to America has no bearing on the matter. How could any girl who had this island described to her for the first time, and was offered its sovereignty, possibly resist the glamour of becoming the central figure in such a fairy-tale—above all one who is dumb and, apparently, has been leading more or less the life of a Cinderella? It never even occurred to anyone here that she would refuse. I consider it most extraordinary.'

That evening it transpired that the Princess had not refused. She had never been asked. But for Kâo Hsüan to communicate with the island from the mainland would have given its existence away; so he had had to wait until he got back there to make his report. It was brief and, up to a point, perfectly straightforward, but, after that, it suddenly developed into a problem wrapped in mystery.

Soon after his arrival in San Francisco he had gone to call on the Princess's mother, but, with the procrastination typical of an Oriental, he had done no more on that occasion than assure himself that the two ladies were in good health. On taking his leave he had said that he would wait upon her again in a few days' time. He had then gone to a soothsayer to find out the earliest date upon which it would be propitious to carry out the object of his mission. The soothsayer had told him five days hence. On the fifth day he had gone to the apartment again but found only the daily woman in occupation, and that she was greatly upset. Apparently on the previous day Madame Août had been knocked down by a car, seriously injured and taken to hospital. As soon as Josephine had learned of the accident she had hurried to her mother's bedside. Her failure to return had been put down to her having either remained at the hospital or spent the night with friends. But enquiries next morning elicited the fact that Madame Août had died without regaining consciousness and that on being told, the grief-stricken girl had accepted sympathetic ministrations for only half an hour. She had then insisted on leaving the hospital and from that moment she had completely disappeared.

Kâo had then hoped that after suffering a temporary aberration from grief she would reappear to attend her mother's funeral; but she did not do so, and he had spent the next fortnight using his utmost endeavours to find out what had become of her. He had traced as many of the Août's acquaintances as he could and questioned them, sought the help of the police, and spent a considerable sum consulting every soothsayer in San Francisco's Chinatown, all to no avail. Josephine Août had vanished utterly, and there was not even the suggestion of a clue to her movements after she left the hospital. Feeling now that the odds were on an excess of grief having caused the Princess to take her own life in some secluded spot where her body had not yet been discovered, and knowing how puzzled and anxious the Council would become if he delayed his return overlong, Kâo had then decided that he had better come back and report the sad failure of his mission.

As was to be expected, his news resulted in another wave of pessimistic speculation sweeping through the Seven Families. For the best part of two months the decision of the Mandarins, that the Princess should be sent for to choose an Emperor from one of their families, had seemed an inspired solution to the problem with which they were faced. Now they were back where they had started, and they murmured despondently that, unless some other way of selecting an Emperor could be agreed, they would be subjected to all the evils resulting from intrigue, bribery, and finally a *coup d'état* by which one of their number would arbitrarily seize power over them.

But the Council proved unwilling to give up without a struggle the idea which had met with such universal approbation. Several of its members argued that since there was no proof of the Princess's death there was a very good chance that she was still alive. The majority agreed, and a decision was taken that everything that money could do should be done in an effort to trace her. Kâo Hsüan was ordered to return to San Francisco, and at the Mandarin Tsai-Ping's request it was agreed that he should go too.

It was on the second morning after Kâo's return that A-lu-te told Gregory of this new decision. In the course of the day he saw little of her, and during such brief conversations as they had she seemed unusually preoccupied. It was after dark, and he was contemplating turning in, when she again came, with

91

Madame Pan-chieh panting along behind her, across the garden to his little pavilion.

'They have agreed! I have got my way!' she cried, her voice vibrant with excitement, as soon as she saw him stir among the shadows.

He had as usual at this hour been thinking of Erika. Bringing his thoughts back reluctantly to the present he asked with a shade of annoyance, 'What are you talking about?'

'I'm going to San Francisco! I'm going with Uncle Kâo!' Her white teeth flashed and her words came tumbling out. 'When he went before they were counting on the Princess's mother to come back with her. Now, if we can find her, she will be alone. At least, there'll be no woman with her suitable to act as her companion on the voyage. The Council had to agree that it would not be right for her to travel in a ship with only men. It's true! It's true! I've got my way, and I'm going to America.'

'I'm so glad,' Gregory smiled, now fully roused from his morbid musings. 'I know how much this means to you, and I'm delighted that you have managed to pull it off.' Then, after a moment, he added politely, 'What I shall do while you are away I can't think. I shall miss you tremendously.'

'Oh no, you won't!' She gave a sudden laugh.

'I assure you that I shall,' he insisted.

'No!' she laughed again. 'I have my own theory about what has happened to the Princess Josephine. She may be dead or out of her mind; but she could equally well have been kidnapped by either the Nationalists or the Communists to be used as a pawn in their game. If I am right, getting her back is going to be a very dangerous undertaking. I have done my utmost to re-animate in you the vital spark that went out when you lost your wife, and I've failed. But I am determined to do it yet, and for a man of your type the one thing that might bring it back is danger. I have the Council's consent to take you with me!'

6

LURED BY LOVE OR VICTIM OF LUST?

GREGORY hardly knew whether to feel pleased or sorry at this surprising announcement. For him, even more than for the majority of its inhabitants, the island was a place where Time stood still. They were protected by their isolation from having their lives disrupted into contrasting periods by wars, changes of government, unemployment, or even voluntary removals to new localities and taking holidays abroad ; but he was in addition immune from any personal happenings which would have made a landmark in his life. He had no worries concerning love, health or money, no ambition to satisfy, no problems to solve. One day followed another with the same placid routine and he was content to have things so. A return to the outer world meant encountering innumerable sights and sounds which would inevitably remind him of his loss. On the other hand he admitted to himself that in recent weeks, while not in A-lu-te's company, he had been vaguely conscious of an increasing sense of boredom.

However, his first definite reaction was amazement that the Council should even have considered trusting him to keep their secrets while participating in such a mission ; and he said so to A-lu-te.

She shrugged. 'You underrate them as psychologists. Now that they have had an opportunity to get to know you they have a high regard for you. They have formed the opinion that you are a man of integrity, so would not betray us wantonly.'

'Within certain limits I am.' The furrows round the corners of Gregory's mouth deepened in a cynical smile, as he added, 'But it would be rash for anyone who had done me an ill turn to bank on that.'

'I can well believe you,' she retorted promptly. 'Still, it was argued that we had given you no cause to regard us as enemies, and that you had nothing to gain by telling anyone our secrets.'

'Once in the United States, what is to stop my refusing to return?'

'Nothing; except your oath of service to me, and the fact that I have gone surety for you. Such a possibility was, of course, considered; but it was felt that even should you decide to barter your conscience for your liberty there would still be no incentive for you to disclose that life in this island differs from that in any other on which you might have been washed up.'

Gregory smiled again, but this time with no trace of cynicism, as he said, 'I am much touched by the faith you place in me not to run away; but for your own protection I think you ought to insist on an assurance from the Council that they will not hold you responsible should some unforeseen circumstance separate us while we are away, and make it impossible for you to bring me back with you. I must say, though, I still find it astonishing that you should have succeeded in winning the Council's consent to take me on this mission.'

'My father tells me that when he put my proposals to them they at once saw the propriety of sending a lady to attend the Princess if she can be found, and agreed that no one could be more suitable than myself; but over the suggestion that you should accompany me there was much argument. It would, he thinks, have been turned down but for the strong support it received from Tsai-Ping.'

'Really!' Gregory raised his eyebrows. 'Of course, I am on excellent terms with his brother, but I know the Mandarin only slightly, and he seems a cold dried-up stick of a man. I had no idea that he had any special regard for me.'

'I don't think he has. But he put it to the others that Orientals, however wealthy, are always at a certain disadvantage when dealing with officials in white men's countries; and that as you are both intelligent and a person of some standing your help might prove very valuable during our inquiries.'

Thus it was that four days later Gregory sailed with A-lu-te, the jovial Kâo Hsüan and the taciturn Tsai-Ping in the converted destroyer for San Francisco. As Kâo was A-lu-te's uncle it had been decided that she need not be accompanied by a chaperon, but she took her personal maid to act as stewardess and the two men had their body servants with them.

Appearance had been sacrificed to comfort in the ship's conversion and a good job made of it. From her bridge aft she had been stripped of all gear to permit of the erection of a superstructure consisting of a double range of cabins, each facing a seven-foot-wide promenade deck that ran nearly the length of the ship. The boats were now stowed on the after end of the new upper deck formed by these cabins, and the remainder of it had been glassed in as a sun lounge with a service pantry; while below the main deck several of the original cabins had been gutted to form a large dining saloon.

On the first evening out Gregory found the dining saloon peopled by a considerably larger company than he had expected. The reason for this was that the ship's complement was sharply divided into two categories—those whose duties might necessitate their communicating with the outside world, all of whom were permitted to go ashore when the ship was in port, and those who were not. The latter were all simple seamen of the coolie caste, whereas the others—engineers, pursers and wireless operators, as well as navigating officers—had all been selected from the Mandarin families; so as social equals they messed with the passengers.

The Captain's name was Ah-moi Sung. In everything connected with the ship his word was, of course, law; and in all other matters he ranked equal to Kâo Hsüan, as both were heirs to Mandarins and, in the normal course of events, would inherit seats on the Council. He was a magnificent specimen of the Manchu aristocracy, being six feet four in height and broad in proportion, with handsome features and a friendly expression. Gregory had already met him several times and liked him for his cheerful open manner, but found his conversation limited, as his passion was the sea and he had few interests outside it; yet that, and the fact that he had been a sailor from the time he had been given his first fishing junk at the age of seventeen, made him an extremely capable commander.

Everyone in the saloon was aware that they were again bound for San Francisco and of the reason, so a subdued excitement prevailed. A score of theories were put forward to account for the disappearance of the Princess, but after a day or two the topic wore thin and the company settled down to contain its speculations in patience during the three thousand five hundred mile journey.

All the officers and others who messed in the saloon were, when off duty, equally free to use the two promenade decks and the upper deck sun lounge. In consequence, wherever A-lu-te sat as the only lady on board she found herself the centre of attraction. She was far from unsociable, and much too well-mannered to drive away the constantly renewed little circle of men which always surrounded her. But after two days, during which she had not had one moment to read, take a nap or carry on a private conversation, she began to find these long unvaried sessions of small-talk distinctly trying; so she asked the Captain if he could not provide her with some retreat to which when she felt inclined she could retire to enjoy the sun in privacy.

He at once obliged her by having awnings rigged up partially to screen-off the small semi-circular deck at the stern of the yacht, and with a divan, bamboo chairs and an array of large pot plants converted it into a pleasant little lounge. From then on she continued to use the public decks for some part of each day, but spent most of the time in her sanctum, inviting there those whom she chose to keep her company.

Her uncle having her good name in mind, at first stipulated that she should never entertain there less than two men at any time; but she insisted that Gregory must be counted an exception to this ruling. She urged that although a social equal he was technically her slave; and she wished to continue the routine they had observed at home, whereby he tutored her on many subjects concerning the outside world, and she gave him lessons in Chinese, to which it would be most boring for any third person to have to sit and listen.

After some discussion a compromise was reached, and it was agreed that A-lu-te's maid, or alternatively Kâo's man servant, should always sit at such times just outside the gap between the screens which formed the entrance to the little lounge, as the presence of one of them there would not be obtrusive but would satisfy convention.

On most occasions the maid, a modest young girl named Su-sen, performed this duty with admirable discretion ; but at times her other duties necessitated her being relieved by Kâo's man, P'ei, whom they thought an objectionable person. He was a middle-aged man with a lean and hungry look, which was not improved by a slight squint. Although there was nothing they could actually object to in his behaviour, he had a surly manner, and they soon realized that he considered the job he had been given a justification for spying upon them whenever he got the chance. As making love played no part in their curriculum they did not particularly mind, but all the same they found it vaguely annoying.

During the voyage they saw little of the Mandarin Tsai-Ping, except at meals, as he was a serious student of astronomy and spent most of his time either making abstruse calculations in his cabin, or at night watching the stars through a telescope. But the jovial Kâo had the right of entry to A-lu-te's lounge at any hour and often used it, whilst on most evenings Captain Ah-moi or some of his officers came there at her invitation ; so the time passed very pleasantly.

Except for two days during which they ran through the aftermath of a storm, the ocean was calm and the weather sunny. It was late in the afternoon of July the 1st when they sighted land, and by the evening they had passed between the two peninsulas—a bare nine furlongs apart—that form the Golden Gate into San Francisco's vast bay, which encloses five hundred and forty square miles of land-locked water. Directly ahead lay the great rock that forms Alcatraz Island, surmounted by its tall lighthouse and the grim prison in which the now almost legendary ex-King of the Chicago underworld, Al Capone, had long lain confined. Veering to starboard, they rounded the southern promontory and were directed to an anchorage opposite San Francisco City, which lay facing east upon its landward side.

On coming abreast of Fort Point they had run up the Portuguese flag, and in due course customs and immigration officials came aboard to examine their papers. Under their secret treaty with Portugal, the inhabitants of Leper Settlement Number Six had acquired the right to issue a limited number of passports each year, and these had the appearance of having emanated from a Portuguese Consular office on the island; so no difficulty was made about furnishing those of them who had passports with landing permits. It had been intended to provide Gregory with one of these passports but when the matter arose it transpired that before Sir Pellinore's yacht sank he had had the presence of mind to go to his cabin and slip his own into his breast pocket. Although stained from long immersion in the sea, it was still perfectly legible; so he was able to claim the status of a British subject.

While the formalities between the Captain and the Port Authorities were proceeding, A-lu-te could hardly contain her excitement. Leaning over the stern rail with Gregory she gazed wide-eyed at innumerable buildings of the city, which with its suburbs seemed to spread endlessly through several valleys and over half a dozen hills. In spite of her reading she was a little awed by the thought that in it there lived at least two hundred times more people than populated the whole island in which she had been brought up; and, after the quiet to which she was accustomed, she found the intense activity of the harbour with its hooting tugs, great churning ferries and roaring motor boats quite bewildering.

Gregory, having spent a day there in the early nineteen-thirties, was able to point out to her some of the most interesting features of the panorama—Telegraph Hill, below which, close to the waterfront, nestled San Francisco's Chinatown; the City Hall, made a focal point by its great dome which was higher than that of the Capitol in Washington; Nob Hill, on which stood the mansions of many Californian millionaires; the Twin Peaks, and to the south of them Mount Davidson which towered up nearly a thousand feet above sea level. Then, still further south, the wooded hills of San Mateo county, and to the west Goat Island—the principal home base in the Pacific of the United States Navy—and again, beyond it on the opposite shore, Oakland and its adjacent towns which together now covered almost as great an area as San Francisco itself.

As they surveyed the bay, the sun sank behind the hills of the city, and by the time the port officials were through, the scene had become a fairyland of a myriad twinkling lights beneath a sky still tinged with the purple afterglow of sunset. A-lu-te was madly keen to be taken ashore that evening, but her Uncle Kâo immediately opposed the idea and clinched the matter by reminding her that they were expecting their countryman Wu-ming Loo to join them; and that their absence on his arrival would be regarded by him as a grave breach of manners.

Mr. Wu-ming Loo, as Gregory was already aware, was Tsai-Ping's nephew by marriage and had succeeded Kâo Hsüan a little over a year before as Export Manager for the island's products. En-voyage a radio-telegram had been sent to him in New York to meet them on their arrival in San Francisco. Kâo had half-heartedly opposed the idea, on the grounds that Wu-ming could do nothing they could not do themselves, so it would be a waste of his valuable time to divert him from his proper business; but Tsai-Ping had overruled his colleague, declaring that the search for the lost Princess should take priority over all else, and that as his nephew had a more up-to-date knowledge of conditions in the United States than either of them his co-operation might prove of value.

When Wu-ming Loo came aboard from the water-taxi, Gregory saw at a glance that he was an extremely presentable man of about thirty-five. His dinner-jacket might have been built for him in Savile Row and he spoke English with the accent of a Bostonian who had been educated at Harvard. He was above medium height, of athletic build and had curiously wide-set eyes, but otherwise pleasing features.

Although he had lived abroad for some years, understudying Kâo in preparation to succeed him, he already knew all the members of the party except Gregory, and having swiftly assessed the degree of regard in which the Englishman was held among them he at once assumed an air of smooth cordiality towards him.

Wu-ming knew nothing of the Council's decision to offer the Princess Josephine the vacant throne, or of her disappearance following her mother's tragic death. He had met them only once, at a christening party given by a mutual acquaintance in San Francisco, so when told the purpose of the mission he could contribute no information of the circumstances in which they had lived; but he willingly offered his utmost assistance in the search for the Princess, and proposed that he should place himself and his car at their disposal the following day.

At nine o'clock next morning Kâo, Tsai-Ping, A-lu-te and Gregory went ashore in the ship's launch—which, when she was in a foreign port, was always manned by young Cadets who were all members of the Seven Families—and Wu-ming duly picked them up in a Cadillac near the dock gates. It had been decided that the investigation should start at the Août's home, which had been not in Chinatown but in a block of flats overlooking Golden Gate Park and just off Stanyan Street; so, Wu-ming drove them there.

The apartment proved to be one of the less expensive ones in the block, as it was at the back looking out on to a coke yard and consisted only of a narrow hall, one living-room, two bedrooms, bathroom and kitchen. Before sailing for home after his previous visit, Kâo had signed a banker's order for the rent to be paid until further notice, so unless the Princess had returned in the meantime they expected to find it just as he had left it.

The hall-porter of the block told them that Miss Août had not returned, and that no communication had been received either from or about her. He then produced the keys and took them up to the abandoned flat. As Kâo had visited Madam Août before the tragedy, and later made himself responsible for the rent, the porter raised no objection to their request that they should be allowed to search it thoroughly; stipulating only that they should remove nothing from it. He also gave them the address of the daily help who had done the rough work of the flat. It was then decided that Wu-ming should go there and, if he could find her, bring her back with him; as it was hoped that in a second questioning something might emerge which Kâo had failed to extract from her during his first inquiry.

Immediately the porter and Wu-ming had left them, the others set about searching systematically, A-lu-te taking Josephine's room, Kâo her mother's, Tsai-Ping the living room and Gregory the rest of the flat.

As the only objects likely to hold a clue were letters or

papers, Gregory soon covered the territory allotted to him and had nothing to show except a few old bills for provisions found in the kitchen. Returning to the living-room he saw that Tsai-Ping was going through the writing desk there. Kâo had said that he had already done so a few days after the tragedy, and that it contained nothing which could be helpful; but, in spite of that, the Mandarin was carefully scrutinizing each paper that he took from it. The majority were in Chinese, but some were in English; so he had made a separate pile of these, and as his knowledge of that language was limited he now asked Gregory to help him read them.

The contents of the desk disclosed that the two ladies had lived in extremely strained circumstances, being apparently entirely dependent upon a small allowance from a relative of Madame Août's who lived in Saigon and at times caused them acute anxiety by getting behindhand with his payments. Near poverty had obviously restricted their social life, but Tsai-Ping was making a careful note of all the addresses he found among the papers. As Kâo had said, none of these offered any obvious clue; so Gregory, being an experienced searcher, turned his attention to places in which the others were unlikely to look, on the off chance that more private papers of some kind might be hidden somewhere.

Beneath the rugs on the sitting-room floor there were no signs of a hiding place, and the walls were too solid to have been tampered with. There was nothing behind or under any of the drawers in the furniture or above the eye-line on the pelmet ledges of the two windows. Nothing had been pushed down the back of the sofa and there were no papers between the leaves of a shelf of books.

Tsai-Ping meanwhile had come upon a meticulously-kept account book recording household expenses, and was conscientiously going through it; so Gregory left him and, entering Josephine's room, asked A-lu-te if she had any luck. She shook her head.

'No, I've found nothing except a writing outfit with a few letters in it from a shop that sells fine needlework. Apparently the poor girl had to supplement their meagre income by making cushion-covers and that sort of thing.'

He nodded. 'Being dumb would have debarred her from most jobs and that is one of the few at which she could have made a little money.'

His glance roved round the room and came to rest on a large framed photograph of a middle-aged Chinaman in European dress that stood on a small table beside the bed. Murmuring, 'I suppose that would be her father,' he walked over, picked it up and undid the catch at the back of the frame. A dozen sheets of paper covered with Chinese writing tumbled out.

After a moment's swift scrutiny of a few of the sheets, A-lu-te said hesitantly, 'These are love letters. It . . . it doesn't seem right to read them.'

'You must,' Gregory insisted. 'To observe such scruples would render our search for the Princess a farce ; and, remember, she may be in grave trouble or danger.'

Sitting down on the bed A-lu-te spread out the sheets and put them in order according to their dates. When she had read them all, she looked up with tears in her eyes, and said:

'They are very beautiful, and come from a young man whose mind must be both delicate and cultured. But oh, how sad they make me for her.'

'Why?'

'Apparently he is a poor student and cannot possibly afford to marry until he gets through law school. Even then he would have little to offer her, and her mother was pressing her to marry a lecherous old merchant who is wealthy enough to keep her as a plaything, and of course, would ensure her mother a life of luxury as well. For that reason she dare not tell her mother about the young man. As it was, they could meet only occasionally, and if her mother had known that they were having an affair he would never have been allowed to come to the flat again.'

'That certainly was tough ; especially as most men would think twice before asking a dumb girl to be their wife, however beautiful she was. Having a young man with serious intentions must have meant more to her than it would have to most girls. What is his name?'

'He does not give it, but ends his letters with such phrases as

102

"He who lives only to prostrate himself again in the gentle light of his sweet silent Moon".'

'We must find him somehow. Does he give his address?'

'Yes; they are written from the law school at which he is studying.'

'How long ago were they written?'

'It is nearly eighteen months since he wrote the first two. Both of them are quite formal and he mentions in one of the later ones that he ceased writing only because he received no reply. Then this spring it appears that they met again and were alone together for a short time, during which they made a mutual declaration. From that point his letters give free reign to his feelings. But he dared not send them through the post for fear that her mother might see them. They evidently exchanged letters surreptitiously each time he called; but he had to restrain himself from coming here too frequently, otherwise her mother's suspicions might have been aroused. That's why there are only seven or eight letters altogether. The last one was written about a fortnight before she disappeared. None of them gives any hint of what may have become of her; but in the circumstances it seems very probable that either the shock of her mother's death, or the fact that she had become free to follow her own inclinations, sent her flying straight to the arms of her young man. They may even have decided to stake their love against the uncertainties of the future and got married there and then.'

'Her first impulse would obviously have been to go to him,' Gregory agreed thoughtfully, 'but I rather doubt if she did—or anyhow that she remained with him for more than an hour or two, whatever plans they may have made for the future. Remember they were both extremely hard up. If they had decided to get married, as you suggest, or even live together, they would have needed every cent they could raise. They could have set up house together here, or, if there were no objections to that, have sold the contents of the flat for two or three thousand dollars. Surely she would have come back, if only to collect her clothes and personal belongings?'

'She may have relatives in San Francisco that we don't know about. Perhaps she was afraid that on hearing of her mother's death they would insist on her going to live with them, and then assert their authority to marry her off to the rich old merchant. In Chinese families the men still have rights over their unmarried female relatives that far exceed anything of the kind among Americans or Europeans. Dread of some new restriction on her freedom may have decided them to disappear together while they had the chance.'

'That is a possibility. But suppose you are right; I see no reason why, after they had been married, she should not have returned to claim her property. She would have had nothing to fear from her relatives then.'

'Oh, but she would!' A-lu-te protested. 'Any sensitive girl would dread the recriminations she would have to face; particularly a Princess, after having made such a misalliance as to marry a penniless student. He would get into serious trouble too. Chinese marriage customs cannot be flouted with impunity. It is a grave offence to marry a girl without first having obtained the consent of her nearest male relative. It is even possible that his family might disown him, and it is certain that he would be ostracized in future by all respectable members of the Chinese community. Rather than submit to so much unpleasantness, most young couples would decide to sacrifice a small inheritance and leave at once for another city, in which they were known to no one.'

'You have overlooked the fact that he was a law student. Such a step would mean his having to abandon his hopes of getting a degree. Most students, too, are dependent upon their parents. It's hardly likely that he would be quite such a fool as to both wreck his future and carry a dumb wife off into the blue without knowing how he was going to feed her.'

'It is you who forget the fact that these two young people are in love. Admittedly the poor Princess's being dumb would prove an additional handicap, but any number of men have thrown away their careers for love's sake. And love is the greatest of all incentives to earn a living. To begin with, having each other, they would be content with very little; and he could easily get a job as a waiter, a clerk or a garage hand.'

Gregory shook his head. 'I'm still not convinced that your explanation is a plausible one. It doesn't account for her failure to claim her own things and her mother's. Even if she had good reasons for not returning personally she could have had them collected by a firm of furniture removers, or have sent instructions for them to be sold on her behalf. Besides, your theory that she was afraid that relatives might coerce her is the wildest speculation. Her father had cut himself off from his family and there is nothing whatever to suggest that any of Madam Août's family live in San Francisco. On the contrary, as far as we know her only relatives live in Saigon.'

'If you can produce any more plausible explanation I should like to hear it,' retorted A-lu-te a little sharply.

The old scar that drew up the outer end of Gregory's left eyebrow went white as his forehead contracted in a frown. 'The contents of those letters have given me one line of thought. It is far from being a pleasant one, but it is slightly more plausible than yours because it does account for all her belongings still being here. We know that she and her mother had very few friends, and that in losing her mother she lost her only legitimate protector. It could therefore be assumed by anyone who knew them that if she disappeared no one would start a hue and cry after her ; or at all events, not for several days, by which time any evidence concerning her last known movements would have become obscured, making it next to impossible to trace her.'

'Are you suggesting that she has been White Slaved?'

'More or less: I had in mind the old boy who was itching to pull her into bed with him. Naturally, as long as Mamma was around, marriage was the price, but once she was out of the way he may have taken a different view of things. Perhaps it sounds a bit melodramatic, but if he was rich enough what was to prevent him paying one of the Tongs to kidnap her?'

'I don't think he would have dared to. Although she was reduced to living very frugally she was a member of the Imperial Family, and she must have known that.'

'He may not have, in view of the way the late Mr. Joseph Août chose to hide his light under a bushel.'

'You may be certain that her mother would have told him.'

'Anyhow, the sort of thugs he would have employed would not have known who she was, and being dumb she could not have told them. That, too, would make it impossible to enlist help to escape, providing all writing materials were kept from her. Once she had been handed over to him in some snug hideout he might keep her there for years without anyone learning of her identity.'

'I feel sure that his inherent respect for her ancestry would have restrained him from behaving towards her as if she was a common tea-house girl.'

Again Gregory's lips twitched in a cynical smile. 'You were saying only a few minutes ago that some men will commit any folly for love. It is equally true that others, particularly old worn-out ones, will sometimes throw overboard the precepts of a lifetime, if by so doing they can possess a woman who has re-aroused their lust. As she had so far refused to marry him that might quite well have driven him to seize this opportunity of taking her by force. I only hope that I am completely wrong. Anyhow, we had better show the letters to the others, and see if they get any bright ideas from them.'

In the living-room they found Tsai-Ping still poring over the account book, while Kâo sat with folded hands in the most comfortable arm-chair, a bored expression on his chubby face. When A-lu-te produced Gregory's find, both men were galvanized into eager interest, and Kâo so far forgot his decorum as to snatch the letters before the Mandarin could take them from A-lu-te's extended hand. When both of them had read the letters, Tsai-Ping removed his steel-rimmed spectacles, blinked his weak eyes, and said in his awkward English:

'One thing letters have make clear. Our big fear is that perhaps very much about her mother's death grieving, the Princess make do herself away. These writings show very much that her mother's wish she oppose. Where no filial respect there no very much grief for death of parent. Princess no commit suicide. She is alive. Time come, we find her.'

7

DEATH WITHOUT WARNING

THE others agreed with the Mandarin's reasoning; then A-lu-te and Gregory gave their respective theories to account for the Princess's disappearance. Neither of the Chinamen could produce any third hypothesis, and both of them inclined to A-lu-te's as the most likely; but they had not been arguing the pros and cons for long when Wu-ming returned with the daily woman.

Her name was Lubsitch. She was of Lithuanian extraction, middle-aged, wooden-faced and of low intelligence. The Chinese treated her with patient courtesy and promised a generous reward if she could give them any fresh information worth working on, but she persisted that she had already told Mr. Kâo Hsüan all she knew about the Août household.

Wu-ming Loo did most of the questioning and, having told her of the love letters, asked her about visitors to the apartment; but she had come there only for two hours in the mornings, and declared that she had never answered the door to anyone except tradesmen and touts who were trying to sell things on the 'never-never' system. Neither of the ladies had ever told her anything about their private affairs and she had no idea at all who Josephine's two suitors might be; so, after pressing a five dollar bill into her moist palm, Wu-ming sent her about her business.

Since it now seemed that they could learn no more at the apartment, Wu-ming proposed that they should all lunch with him at his hotel, and over the meal discuss the next steps to be taken. A-lu-te begged to be excused, on the plea that she wished to buy some American clothes before appearing in such a public place, and asked Gregory to act as her escort until it was time for them to return to the ship. The others endeavoured to persuade her to change her mind, and Gregory told her that even in a creation by Dior or Balmain no Chinese woman looked so soigné and attractive as she did in her national costume; but she proved adamant. So at the entrance of the block of flats the party split up and, having secured a taxi, Gregory took her down to the city's smartest shopping centre.

From that hour onward A-lu-te gave little thought to the search for the Princess. A new world had opened to her and she threw herself into its delights with a reckless abandon engendered by her years of pent-up longing. Until they were actually launched among the luxury shops and great department stores, Gregory had never realized how utterly strange life in a big city would appear to her. From books, radio talks and magazines she knew a great deal about the United States in theory, but even the pictures of buildings, streets, homes, clothes and people had not prepared her for the bewildering crowds, the flashing-past of hundreds of cars and lorries, the ceaseless noise, and the desperate urgency that seemed to inspire every form of activity. Until that morning she had never driven in an automobile, been up in an elevator or heard a loudspeaker. To her the smell of the throngs hurrying along the pavements was both noticeable and surprisingly unpleasant, but her mind was largely distracted from it by amazement at the immense variety of goods displayed in the shop windows, and having frequently to ask Gregory the use of various articles that she had never previously seen.

She had come ashore with a wad of hundred dollar bills, and when Gregory saw the rate at which she was disposing of them he remonstrated with her; but she only laughed and assured him that if she spent as much every day for a month that would still not exhaust the sum that her father had placed at her disposal. Even so, it was only with the greatest difficulty that he dissuaded her from buying everything that took her fancy, on the plea that if only she would be a little patient she would almost certainly find things she liked better when they had had time to inspect the goods in other shops.

He was wearing a light suit of tussore that had been made up for him in the island and, knowing the scantiness of his wardrobe, as soon as she had satisfied her immediate craving for a collection of smart Western clothes she made him take her to the best men's shops, where she insisted on his acquiring a complete new outfit and being measured for several suits.

Her generosity did not end there either, as she bought expensive presents for her maid and all her friends aboard the yacht. Then, much to his surprise in view of her normally intellectual recreations, a mechanical bear in a toy shop having caught her eye she went in and bought it, and after it a dozen other playthings of a similar nature, emitting little squeals of childish delight as the assistant made them display their clockwork antics for her.

Only the closing of the shops put a temporary end to her spending, and although they had not eaten since breakfast it was not until they got back with their mountain of parcels to the yacht that either of them realized that they were at all tired or hungry.

Gregory had derived the same type of fun from their expedition as one gets from taking a child to the pantomime for the first time, and so absorbed had he been that not once during the day had he thought of Erika. It was not until he was getting into bed that night that she came into his mind as a graceful presence, rather than a reproach, and he felt now that she would be glad that the sights and sounds of the city had not re-aroused his useless longing for her.

However, it occurred to him that he ought to let others know of the tragedy that had overtaken Sir Pellinore's party, and of his own survival; so after breakfast the following morning he wrote to his solicitor in London, giving a full account of the yacht's sinking. He still felt no desire to take up the broken threads of his old life, and doubted if he would ever wish to do so, but as a precaution against his estate being dispersed in his absence he added that even should he not write again for many years his death was not to be presumed except on the production of irrefutable evidence.

By the time he had finished his letter, A-lu-te was impatiently waiting for him to accompany her ashore. She was dressed in some of her new clothes and, although he secretly felt that her head looked as if it did not belong to her body, he good-humouredly complimented her on her turn-out. Half an hour later it transpired that she was perfectly well aware of the unsatisfactory contrast, and had already decided to spend her morning in a beauty parlour. Having found one that was

109

obviously patronized by wealthy women she asked him to call for her later and take her to lunch at one of the big hotels; so he bought a number of papers and periodicals and whiled away the next few hours sitting on a bench in the park, bringing himself up to date with the international situation.

When he collected her at one o'clock he was pleasantly surprised. They had made no endeavour to disguise the fact that she was Chinese, but by clever make-up had made her skin appear whiter and her cheeks a delicate pink. They had also thinned her thick eyebrows and done her hair in a different style, so that she appeared quite Westernized and very attractive. Gregory teased her about the admiring glances she received as they went in to lunch, and she pretended that they embarrassed her, but he could tell from the brightness of her long almond-shaped eyes that the interest she had aroused filled her with delight. After the meal he took her to her first movie. She sat through it enthralled, and when they returned to the yacht she was much more anxious to tell the others about her exciting day than to hear the result of their inquiries about the Princess.

Actually they had only negative results to report. The law school from which the student had written was attended by more than a score of young Chinese, and now, during the long vacation, they were scattered; some doing temporary jobs in holiday resorts to earn their fees, others on walking tours or visits to Eastern cities; so it would only be possible to find and interview a few of them. The professor who had been left in charge of the college had no more than a nodding acquaintance with the Chinese students and the only hope he could render was to instruct the office to furnish a list of their home addresses.

The occupants of flats on the same landing as the Aoûts had been tactfully questioned, but could throw no fresh light on the two-months'-old mystery, or give any information which might help in identifying Josephine's elderly suitor.

The police Captain of the district had already forgotten the case, but got out the file on it to refresh his memory. Madame Août had been knocked down by a black Ford sedan at twelve-twenty, when crossing the road to re-enter her block of flats after doing her morning's shopping. The car had not stopped and they had failed to trace it, so no prosecution had ensued. The lady had been taken to the St. Ignatius hospital and died from her injuries shortly after admission. Her daughter had been reported as missing the following day, but there had been no suggestion of foul play in connection with the girl's disappearance, so no special effort had been made to find her. Her name and description had been passed to the Bureau of Missing Persons, but no information about her had been received.

The Captain had added that after this lapse of time it was now unlikely that any would come in. He then went on to say that thousands of people were reported missing each year, and by far the highest proportion of cases concerned young women. White-slaving accounted for only a very small proportion and most disappearances were carefully prepared beforehand. The commonest causes were secret love affairs with men who were already married, a desire to take up some career of which the parents disapproved, and revolt against restricted liberty, crowded conditions, or having to hand over the greater part of earnings to the head of the family. Since none of the latter circumstances fitted the case of Josephine Août, all the odds were that of her own free will she had gone to live with some man, probably in another city. Anyway, there was nothing further the police could do in the matter.

This series of culs-de-sac had been more or less anticipated and plans were already in hand for an attempt to break them down. The following morning an advertisement was to appear in the leading Californian papers offering a thousand dollars' reward for information which would lead to Josephine being found. All Madame Août's acquaintances and all the Chinese students at the law school who were still in San Francisco or its vicinity were to be interviewed.

A-lu-te listened to all this with ill-concealed impatience, then boldly tackled her uncle on a matter that she had been meditating for a good part of the afternoon. Lunching with Gregory at the Fairmont had inspired in her the wish to dine and dance there, but she had no chaperon and was rather doubtful if she would be allowed to go ashore at night without one.

Easy-going as Kâo was by nature, his reaction proved far from favourable, but Wu-ming Loo at once took up the cudgels on her behalf. He argued that when away from the island none of them continued to observe its customs, and that since the Council had given permission for A-lu-te to come to San Francisco it was only reasonable that while there she should be allowed to behave like an American girl.

Gregory had already noticed that since A-lu-te's return from her beauty treatment the young Chinaman could hardly keep his widely-spaced eyes off her, and that he was not disinterested in championing her cause he showed a moment later by saying to Kâo:

'Unfortunately I do not dance; but given your honourable permission I should be most happy to take the lady A-lu-te to dinner and a theatre tomorrow night, if she will allow me to do so.'

After brief consideration Kâo replied, 'As I am responsible to her father I do not think I can agree to that, or that she should go ashore at night accompanied only by Mr. Sallust. But I would raise no objection to her going if she were escorted by both of you.'

A-lu-te accepted this solution with delight, and Wu-ming with the best grace he could muster, while Gregory was secretly amused by the thought that he might soon have to play gooseberry.

As matters developed during the following week, it became clear that he was not to be called on to do so. Wu-ming made no secret of the fact that he had fallen in love with A-lu-te, but although she always treated him kindly, she could not altogether conceal that she preferred Gregory. About that Gregory was sorry, as he felt that the new life on which she had entered would entirely unfit her for a return to the island, and that when she had to do so there would be less chance than ever of her finding a suitable husband or settling down happily there. On the other hand, if only she could fall for Wu-ming, what could have been more suitable? As the Council had given her permission to go abroad they would certainly not oppose her remaining there if she married Wu-ming. Her unusual intelligence and passion for Western civilization would make her the perfect wife for the island's Export Manager. She would prove a great asset to him in his work, and he would be able to provide her with a life of elegance and culture in one after another of all the great cities she longed to see.

With this in mind Gregory did all he could to further Wu-ming's suit, but the Chinaman evidently believed the goodwill he displayed to be only feigned and, with little cause, soon began to show signs of the most bitter jealousy. Each evening they went to a cinema or play, then on to Marsalli's, the 365 Club, or one of the big hotels on Nob Hill to dine and dance. Gregory had always danced passably well and from their first evening out A-lu-te had taken to it like a duck to water. So keen on it had she become that she would rarely let a number pass, which meant that from ten o'clock till one in the morning, or later, Wu-ming spent the greater part of the time sitting morosely alone at their table.

Had Gregory in fact been his rival he would have been at a further disadvantage from A-lu-te's spending her days alone with the Englishman; and, believing him to be so, he began to make pretexts to neglect the business of searching for the Princess, so that he could accompany the two of them on their sightseeing expeditions and trips to the beaches.

Gregory would not have minded that if only the Chinaman had not shown his jealousy so openly, and on two occasions he even suggested to A-lu-te that she should go shopping or bathing alone with her smitten compatriot. But unfortunately for Wu-ming his lack of success with her had made him nervous, gloomy and tongue-tied whenever they were together, so she had come to regard him as a bore, and would not hear of the idea.

The situation was aggravated by her refusal when he asked her to spend a day alone with him on a trip down to Monterey Bay, and from that point a further deterioration in their relations followed. He was so dominated by his passion that he could not bring himself to stop going about with them, although she now made it plain that his presence was no longer welcome. His cringing desire to please brought out the very worst in her, and Gregory's attempts to pour oil on the troubled waters earned him only angry looks from both parties. In consequence he was by no means sorry when circumstances enabled him to put an end to the three of them being thrown together daily, at all events for a time.

They had been in San Francisco for over a fortnight when one morning after breakfast Tsai-Ping asked Gregory to step into his cabin. On the rare occasions when they were alone together they always spoke German, as that was the European tongue in which the Mandarin was most fluent. Having waved Gregory to a chair, he said in that language:

'Mr. Sallust, I am much worried by the lack of progress we make in our search for the Princess.'

Gregory knew that the advertisement had produced only two replies both of which had been try-outs to secure a share of the reward by supplying bogus information, and that nothing of any value had emerged from any other source; so he nodded sympathetically.

The Mandarin went on, 'I have myself interviewed all the Chinese students of the law school who can be traced and are spending their vacation within two-hundred miles or so of this city, and drawn a blank with all of them. More than two months must elapse before the vacation is over and the others will return. My colleagues are not proving as helpful as I could wish. Mr. Kâo Hsüan told me that he had contacted all Madame Août's acquaintances and tradespeople, yet learned nothing of value from them. Knowing his somewhat irresponsible disposition I felt entitled to doubt his perseverance in this matter; so I ordered my nephew to assist him. Perhaps between them they have fulfilled their assignment, but their conduct makes me inclined to doubt it. After the first week our friend Kâo no longer sought to disguise the boredom which afflicts him while making such inquiries. He takes a great delight in gambling and he makes no secret of the fact that for several nights past the dawn has found him still playing Faro with old cronies of his in the Chinese quarter. In consequence, he now spends most of each day in sleep. Young Wu-ming, as you must be aware, has found another and even more potent distraction, which renders him equally unhelpful in our quest.

'As far as possible I am now checking up on their results, but in certain cases my indifferent English proves a severe handicap, and to make sure that they have left no known activity of Madame Août's uninvestigated will take me a considerable time.'

As the earnest, bespectacled Chinaman paused, Gregory felt quite sorry for him, so he said: 'Perhaps I could be of help as your interpreter. If so I will tell the lady A-lu-te that I intend to place myself at your disposal.'

Tsai-Ping rose to his feet, and with his hands buried in the wide sleeves of his gown bowed from the waist. 'Since this affair is no concern of yours, your offer does you much credit ; but I will admit that it was not altogether unexpected. When I sponsored the lady A-lu-te's request that you should accompany us on this mission, I did so in the belief that we could count on your goodwill and that if we came up against difficulties it might prove a valuable asset to us. However, I had in mind something rather more than your acting as an interpreter.'

Gregory had begun to be intrigued, so he replied with a smile, 'If you will tell me what you wish to do, providing it is nothing against my conscience I will willingly attempt it.'

'I thank you.' Tsai-Ping bowed again. 'Although you have said little about yourself, it has become clear to us that you are a person of some consequence in your own country ; also that you have paid previous visits to the United States. That being so it is reasonable to assume that you must have made contact while here with at least a few people who are not altogether without influence. For us, as private individuals, the police will make no further move ; we are in no situation to invoke the help of Portuguese diplomats, or those who now misrepresent the Chinese people, and to employ private detectives would be to risk their learning something that might lead them to take a most unwelcome interest in affairs which we wish to keep secret. Do you think that, while continuing to respect the confidence we have placed in you to disclose nothing about our island, you could persuade friends of yours in the United States to exert sufficient pressure in official circles to have the Août case re-opened, and a nation-wide search instituted for this young woman who is of such importance to us?'

'I can promise nothing,' Gregory said slowly. 'But I used to be on very friendly terms with several Americans who have quite a bit of pull. If I'm to do any good it would mean my contacting them personally, though; so I'd have to go to Washington.'

The Mandarin's thin lips drew back in one of his rare smiles, as he murmured, 'Personal contacts in the capital itself were more than I dared to hope for, Mr. Sallust. I will have a seat booked for you on tomorrow's aircraft. Even should your mission prove a failure we shall still owe you our gratitude for this endeavour.'

Gregory had expected A-lu-te to show annoyance when he informed her that he would have to desert her, but when he told her the reason she took the matter quite philosophically, and said:

'Were I not convinced that the Princess is living happily somewhere with her young student, I would not have shown such indifference to the search for her and given myself up entirely to selfish pleasures. But, of course, it is of great importance to our people that she should be found, and knowing the Mandarin Tsai-Ping's persistent nature I felt certain that he would succeed in tracing her sooner or later. It has been my good fortune that he has not asked your help before, but now he has it is only right that I should endorse his request and wish you good fortune.'

'Thanks.' He smiled. 'I'm glad you feel that way about it,' although for the time being it will put an end to our jolly evenings, and I'm afraid you'll have to make do with Wu-ming as an escort if you want to go ashore. Anyhow, this is a lucky break for him, and as I've told you several times you may find him much more entertaining with me out of the way.'

She made a little grimace. 'Perhaps. But knowing the time I had to enjoy myself here was limited, I should have been a fool to sacrifice any of it to him as long as you were available.'

'That is a charming compliment.'

'You may take it as one if you wish; but it is simply that I am never bored in your company whereas I always am in his.

116

Still, rather than not bathe at all I shall let him take me to some of the beaches. How long do you expect to be away?'

'Probably only for a few days. I shall return here as soon as I have succeeded in getting an inquiry going, and as the inquiry is bound to take some time you've no need to fear that your stay in San Francisco is likely to end for quite a while yet.'

With this consolation A-lu-te, accompanied by Wu-ming who had suddenly become all smiles, saw him off at the airport the following morning.

In Washington Gregory spent three nights, and thoroughly enjoyed the change of again being in the society of people of his own kind. He had rather dreaded that, and had not intended to look up any old friends except those he would have to see in connection with his mission ; but he ran into a couple he knew within a few minutes of landing at the airport, and with typical American hospitality they carried him off to their home in Rock Creek Park instead of letting him go to an hotel. As they had never met Erika he said nothing of his loss, and told them only that for some months past he had been living on a South Sea island to which he intended to return. Then, from that evening onward, he found himself involved in a succession of parties which gave him no time to brood over the past.

On undertaking his mission he had realized at once that it was a matter for the F.B.I. ; but his work had never brought him into contact with any of its senior officials, so he intended to make his request through one or other of his war-time associates in the O.S.S. His first choice was that famous chief of the United States cloak and dagger men, Colonel Bill Donovan, but he found that the Colonel was not in Washington ; so he rang up the Secretary of State's brother, Alan Dulles, whom he had known when the American was directing underground operations in Germany from Switzerland.

Mr. Dulles gave him an appointment for next day and received him most cordially. Although Gregory did not actually say so he allowed it to be inferred that he was still acting as the confidential agent of very highly-placed persons in Britain ; so Mr. Dulles tactfully refrained from asking his reasons for wishing to have Josephine Août traced, and said that he would

117

take up the matter in the proper quarter. The following morning a note arrived for Gregory from the headquarters of the F.B.I., informing him that a Mr. Edgar C. Grace of their San Francisco office would be dealing with the matter in which he was interested; so after one more hectic evening in Washington he took a plane for the West.

The day after his return he called on Mr. Grace, who had the appearance of a mild middle-aged professor, but proved to be brisk and business-like. As soon as Gregory was seated he tapped a folder on his desk, and said:

'Mr. Sallust, this is the file on Josephine Août. Headquarters have instructed us to find her for you without prying into your personal affairs. That bars me from asking you any questions; but it would be to your own interest to put us wise about what's cooking as far as you can. The more we know about her background, the sooner we're likely to be able to hand you her present address.'

To this sound sense Gregory readily responded, giving particulars of Josephine's life as far as he knew it, and an account of the contents of the love letters found in her room. Then he gave the yacht as his address and returned to it.

With the sole exception of Wu-ming, everyone had been pleased to see him back, and now he could report that the F.B.I. had actually taken matters in hand on instructions from the highest level, they all showered him with compliments and thanks. As nothing further could be done but await the result of the F.B.I. inquiry, the passengers in the yacht quickly reverted to the life they had been leading before Gregory's trip to Washington.

During the week that followed A-lu-te, Gregory and Wu-ming spent many hours each day together, often hardly separating from the time they came out of their cabins in the morning until well after midnight, but the relations between them were no easier. As A-lu-te had treated Wu-ming with a little more consideration during Gregory's absence his return had the effect of still further increasing the Chinaman's hostility towards him. At length a point was reached where Wu-ming, goaded by his unhappy passion, so far forgot his upbringing as to be actually rude, upon which Gregory told A-lu-te that unless her compatriot was prepared to mend his manners he would not accompany them ashore again. Since that would have meant an end to their dinners and dancing A-lu-te flew into a fine rage, and so scarified Wu-ming with her tongue about his ungentlemanly behaviour that he positively grovelled. After that he managed to conceal his feelings by a smooth civility, but Gregory felt certain that beneath it his humiliation had aroused in him the sort of fanatical hatred of which only an Oriental is capable.

It was two days after this explosion that Gregory received a note from Edgar C. Grace, asking him to call. When he did so the F.B.I. chief said:

'Well, Mr. Sallust, you certainly gave my boys a hard nut to crack. But I've news for you, although I'm afraid it's not very good news. You'll know what a Tong is, of course?'

Gregory nodded. 'Yes; it's a Chinese secret society!'

'That's so. And some of them are so secret that the penalty exacted from a member who talks out of turn is death. Naturally those sort of rules make it difficult for us to keep abreast with their activities, and they are by no means always criminal ones at that. In their aspect as funeral clubs, benevolents, and that sort of thing they do quite a piece of good among their own people; so generally speaking, as long as they keep within reasonable limits we leave them alone. But we usually have enough stuff up our sleeves to crack down on them if necessary, and this may be such a time. Josephine Août was snatched within an hour of her mother's death on the orders of a gentleman named Quong-Yü, and he's the boss of the most powerful Tong in S.F.'s Chinatown.'

'It looks then as if he is the wealthy man who wanted to marry her?'

'Could be; but Quong has the pick of the girls in half a dozen tea houses. I'd say it's more likely that some other old boy paid him handsomely to pull this young Josephine in.'

'I take it you've no idea at all where she may be at present?'

'No; none. But I don't doubt Quong could tell us.'

'What's the drill now, then?'

Edgar C. Grace stubbed out the butt of a very black cigar, before replying. 'If you wish us to continue handling the matter, Mr. Sallust, we will. But the moment Quong learns that the F.B.I. is gunning for him he'll move heaven and earth to cover up. He'll fear we're out to pin a kidnapping charge on him, and that is now a very serious matter in this State; so maybe he'd outsmart us and we'd get nowhere. If he's got the girl himself in one of his houses, rather than risk us catching him with the goods he might kill her and feed her body to the sharks.'

Having paused to light a fresh cigar the F.B.I. chief went on: 'It's common knowledge that on the yacht in which you are living everyone else is Chinese. You may take it as certain that some of them will know Quong-Yü, or anyhow all about him. My advice is that this is where you let me toss the ball back to you. Get these Chinese friends of yours to make a date for you with Quong. Maybe they are as interested in this girl as you are, but that's not my affair. With or without you, they stand a much better chance of getting Quong to produce Josephine Août than I do. He has nothing to fear from them, and if he has handed her over to someone else all the odds are that he'll be perfectly willing to have her snatched again for a good sum down in cash.'

Gregory nodded. 'I'm sure that's sound advice, but there is just one snag we may come up against. Say he is the old boy referred to in the letters, then the fact that he was pressing the girl to marry him shows that he must have been pretty goofy about her. From that it follows that if he has got her he now regards her as the apple of his eye; so he wouldn't part with her for all the tea in China.'

'I doubt your premises, Mr. Sallust; but if they're right you've certainly got something there. Say it does pan out that way, we've still got a shot in the locker. As I've already told you, we always keep enough stuff on the Tong bosses to make things mighty unpleasant for them if we want to. If Quong refuses to give—denies all knowledge of the girl—just tell him you're a friend of mine and that if he continues to be uncommunicative I may have to take an interest in the use to which he is putting his lamp shop.'

'Thanks a lot, Mr. Grace,' Gregory grinned, as he stood up and shook hands. 'Your help has been invaluable.'

When he got back to the yacht he found the others all sitting on the after-deck waiting to hear the result of his interview. As soon as he had told them, Wu-ming said quickly, 'I know Mr. Quong-Yü, so you had better leave this business in my hands. I will telephone this afternoon and ask when it will be convenient for him to see me.'

Kâo raised a plump hand. 'Young man, you go too fast. I have known Quong-Yü for many years so I am much better fitted to come to an amicable understanding with him.'

'I at the interview must be,' Tsai-Ping announced quietly.

'Honourable One,' Kâo said, turning towards him. 'Permit me to observe that agreement is always easier to reach when each side is represented by only one person.'

'Whoever goes, I go also,' the Mandarin declared with a cold finality.

'I have no wish to butt in,' Gregory remarked. 'But surely you don't intend to offer Quong-Yü a whacking great ransom for the Princess when there is a good chance that you can frighten him into producing her for nothing. If he is to be threatened, though, as I am the only one among you who knows Mr. Edgar C. Grace only I can use threats effectively ; so you'll have to take me with you.'

'That is good sense,' A-lu-te commented. 'And as the Honourable One desires to accompany either my Uncle Kâo or Wu-ming, why should not all four of you go?'

As the bottom had already been knocked out of Kâo's proposition that matters could best be handled by a single negotiator, her proposal was agreed to, and Tsai-Ping asked Kâo to arrange a meeting for them with Quong-Yü that evening if possible.

All of them spent the afternoon in the city, but returned to the yacht at tea time to learn if Kâo had been successful. He was still absent and did not rejoin them till nearly eight o'clock. He then excused his lateness by saying that he had been unable to get Quong-Yü on the telephone until half-past seven ; and added that Quong could not see them that night, but would receive them the following afternoon between four and five o'clock.

Next morning, A-lu-te, Gregory and Wu-ming went ashore

together as usual, but with much reluctance the latter excused himself from bathing and lunching with the others on the plea that he had to try to catch up with his business affairs. Then at a quarter to four the whole party met at the dock, A-lu-te returned to the yacht and the four men set off together for Quong-Yü's.

They had no great distance to go, as San Francisco's Chinatown lies down near the waterfront, and they were walking up its main boulevard before Gregory realized that they had entered it. He had expected a warren of narrow twisting streets and noisome alleys, with cotton-clad celestials hawking vegetables on the pavements and furtively sidling into low doorways. In the past the quarter had presented just such a picture, but now it consisted of fine modern blocks. The shops differed little from those in other business districts, most of their signs being in English, and the great majority of its inhabitants were wearing American clothes. The only striking indication of its individuality was that the city council had tactfully adorned it with tall lamp-posts of Chinese design that had tops like small pagodas.

After walking a few hundred yards up Grant Avenue, they turned down a side street, then along a narrow canyon-like thoroughfare that was flanked on both sides by warehouses. Half way down it the road was blocked by a lorry, into which several crates of bananas at a time were being lowered by means of a big rope attached to a pulley. Kâo and Wu-ming were walking side by side down the middle of the street with Tsai-Ping and Gregory behind them. To pass the lorry they took to the narrow pavement and split up into single file, with Kâo leading and Tsai-Ping bringing up the rear. It was just as they had done so that Gregory noticed that his shoe-lace had come undone. Halting, he stooped down to tie it up, while Tsai-Ping walked on past him. Next moment there came a cry and a rending crash. A net full of the heavy crates had struck Tsai-Ping full on the head. Beneath them he was smashed to the ground.

As some of the crates burst, scattering their contents, Gregory threw himself backwards. In doing so he caught sight of a Chinaman framed in the opening three stories up in the ware-

122

house from the bananas were being lowered. The man was in the act of thrusting a long knife back beneath his jacket.

Instantly Gregory realized that the pulley rope had not snapped but had been cut deliberately. Hard on the thought, another flashed into his mind. But for his shoe-lace having come undone, it would have been himself instead of Tsai-Ping now lying dead in the gutter.

8

THE REAL CHINATOWN

GREGORY'S first impulse was to dart into the warehouse and attempt to seize the murderer, but he promptly checked it. .The man had already withdrawn from sight and he was three floors up. This could be no case of personal malice so he had obviously acted under instructions. He was probably the 'hatchet-man' of one of the Tongs. Anyhow, the other coolies would cover up for him and all say they could not remember who had been standing by the opening at the moment the rope parted. The deadly ambush must have been carefully planned and already the assassin would be making off by a pre-arranged escape route. Even if he could still be intercepted by a swift dash up the stairs, after only one brief glimpse it would be impossible to swear to his identity.

As Gregory ran forward to lend a hand in dragging the broken crates of bananas from on top of the Mandarin, another good reason occurred to him for refraining from any immediate attempt to pin the crime on its perpetrator. There seemed good grounds to suppose that he had been the intended victim. If so, and somebody was out to kill him, it would be to his advantage to continue to appear unaware that his life was threatened. Were he to proclaim his knowledge that the rope had been sliced through, it might be assumed that he had also tumbled to it that the murderous attack had been intended for himself. In that case any second attempt to bring about his death would be made by even more subtle means, so be more likely to succeed. Far better to say nothing, but make the utmost use of the warning he had been given, and hope by constant vigilance to foil an enemy made over-confident by believing him still ignorant of his danger.

Jabbering excitedly in a mixture of American and Chinese, the little crowd that had swiftly gathered uncovered Tsai-Ping's grotesquely twisted body. His cranium had been smashed like an egg-shell, and he must have died instantaneously. A policeman shouldered his way through the crush and began to take notes. A few minutes later an ambulance drove up to collect the corpse. Wu-ming, who appeared quite distraught by his uncle's death, went off with it. Kâo had already been questioned by the cop, and when Gregory's turn came he said nothing to upset the general assumption that their companion had been killed as the result of an accident. Then, on Kâo whispering to him that it would not now be seemly for them to pursue their intention of interviewing Quong-Yü, they returned in silence to the yacht.

A-lu-te was much surprised to see them back so soon, and when she heard the reason her eyes opened wide with shocked dismay; but for a woman to have made any comment or asked questions in such circumstances would have been a breach of good manners; so, bowing her head in a token of respectful grief, she at once retired to her cabin.

Within ten minutes the whole ship's company was absorbed in the rituals of formal mourning, and Gregory learned that for the next twenty-seven hours no meals would be served in the saloon, or any conversation be entered upon apart from necessary exchanges among the officers concerning the running of the ship. His own narrow escape from death being so recent he was by no means averse to an evening's solitude in which to think matters over quietly; and, having made himself comfortable in his cabin, he began to cogitate on a variety of factors which might have contributed to Tsai-Ping's body having been so suddenly deprived of its spirit.

Gregory had one fact only to go on which he regarded as entirely beyond dispute. It was that, although he had not actually seen the coolie cut the rope, the man had done so. One glance at its end, as it lay where it had fallen in the gutter, had confirmed that. It had not frayed and finally parted after long wear. A sharp blade had sliced through two of its strands ; only a part of the third was ragged and ravelled from having snapped under the strain. That partially severed end had been evidence enough on which to call in the homicide squad ; but, for what at the time had seemed good reasons, Gregory had refrained from pointing it out to the policeman.

He wondered now if they were good reasons. His decision to say nothing had been taken with the thought fresh in his mind that the attack had really been directed against himself. It had seemed so obvious that had he not stopped to tie up his shoe-lace the crates would have fallen on his head. But on calmer reflection he realised that there was no certainty about that. If he had walked on, the coolie, staring down from above to identify the man he had been posted there to kill, might have waited another few seconds before slashing the rope. Then, just as had happened, Tsai-Ping would have been the one to be struck down.

Gregory's thoughts turned to the unknown person on whose orders the coolie must have acted. If that person's identity were known it would make it very much easier to formulate a sound guess about whom he had planned to have murdered. Although it was pure speculation, for the part of 'villain off' the first candidate to spring to mind was Quong-Yü.

The Tong boss certainly had an obvious motive for preventing anyone from poking their nose into his affairs ; and, even more significant in this matter, professional killers in his service who were bound by oath to do his will. Yet it seemed to be going a little far to resort to murder before he had even been questioned. Again, did he even know what the visitors he expected were going to question him about?

Of course it was just possible that Kâo had told him over the telephone that they were searching for Josephine Août, and

125

that a Mr. Sallust had secured information from the F.B.I. that he, Quong, had snatched her ; but for Chinese like Kâo—brought up in tradition of circumlocution, prevarication, and a fundamental belief in postponing rather than facing issues—to have done so, seemed most unlikely.

If Kâo *had* spilled the beans, and Quong was holding Josephine in some hide-out for his own pleasure, he would certainly regard Gregory as his most dangerous enemy. Therefore, should his passion for Josephine have decided him to hold on to her at all costs, it was against Gregory that he would direct his killers.

But no! That did not make sense. Unless Quong was stark staring mad, Gregory was the one person whom he would not dare to attack. Gregory was linked with the F.B.I. If he died in mysterious circumstances, knowing that Quong had a reason for wishing him out of the way the Tong boss was the first person they would pull in ; and they would grill him until they had checked up on his every action for the past week. He would never be fool enough to take such a risk.

Perhaps then it really was Tsai-Ping whom Quong had planned to kill. But why? Against Kâo or Wu-ming, both of whom he knew, Quong might have had some old grudge ; but he had never met Tsai-Ping, and the Mandarin had never even spent a night in San Francisco.

Another thing—if Quong was endeavouring to stall off a hunt for Josephine, what point would there be in his killing one of the investigating party when three others would survive to continue the inquiry?

Yet if Quong had not organized the ambush, who had? Kâo and Wu-ming had both had the opportunity to do so ; and, as they had been walking side by side ahead of Gregory and Tsai-Ping, either could easily have ensured that the whole party took such turnings on the way to Quong-Yü's as would necessitate their passing the warehouse from which the bananas were being loaded. Quong, on the other hand, could not possibly have played any part in directing them down one particular street out of a choice of three or four ; and that very fact now seemed to eliminate him from the rôle of 'probable villain'.

Kâo and Tsai-Ping were undoubtedly antipathic personalities. Both were ambitious men, and, although it was never referred to openly, Gregory had learned from A-lu-te that in secret the two of them had been waging a bitter struggle for power to influence appointments in the island. Could Kâo, knowing San Francisco and its Tongs, have taken advantage of this visit to the city to arrange for the liquidation of his rival?

That was certainly a possibility. But the word 'rival' passing through Gregory's mind conjured up another thought. What of Wu-ming Loo? He too had a rival—not in the uncle whom he revered, but in the Englishman who had consistently come between him and the lady A-lu-te. Wu-ming also knew San Francisco and its Tongs. A Chinese of his wealth and influence would have known quite well how to set about securing the services of an assassin; and, on the excuse of catching up with his work, he had spent that morning alone in the city.

Visualizing the scene of the crime, Gregory endeavoured to live again those few terrifying moments. While doing so he sought for any detail that he had registered then which might since have escaped him. Kâo and Wu-ming had been walking down the narrow street a good dozen paces ahead of himself and Tsai-Ping. As the two former fell into Indian file and stepped on to the pavement to pass the lorry, he recalled now that he had noticed Wu-ming look upward. He had followed his glance and seen the rope net holding the crates of bananas slowly revolving a good thirty feet above the pavement. A moment later his shoe-lace coming undone had caused him to look down ; then, on reaching the pavement, he had stopped to tie it up, while Tsai-Ping walked past him to his death.

When about to pass a lorry that was being loaded from above anyone might have glanced upward ; so it was no proof of Wu-ming's guilt that he should have done so. Yet if a man had planted a murderous ambush there he would hardly be able to resist the temptation to assure himself that the trap was ready to be sprung. Perhaps, therefore, it was not altogether without significance that whereas Kâo had not looked up, Wu-ming had.

Considering the matter further it occurred to Gregory that

he had not so far given sufficient importance to the time factor. As the crates had been swinging some thirty feet above the ground, the assassin would have had to allow a couple of seconds for their fall. Had he intended to kill Tsai-Ping he would have waited until Gregory was beneath the crates before cutting the rope. As it was he must have timed the cutting for them to fall on Gregory, and seen too late that Tsai-Ping had stepped forward into his place.

Another small point emerged as Gregory was attempting to picture the scene as the murderer must have looked down upon it from above. To have picked out any one of the three China-men could not have been easy, as they were all wearing soft felt hats; but since his second day in San Francisco he had been wearing a panama. Its light-coloured straw and broad brim would have identified him beyond all doubt, making him the perfect target.

Later that night, before going to sleep, he went over the whole wicked business again, but could think of no other factor which might throw further light on it. There was, he knew, nothing concrete to go on except the fact that the coolie had deliberately cut the rope with intent to murder someone. Yet all his speculations led him to the belief that the 'someone' had been himself; and that it was Wu-ming, goaded into taking desperate measures by his insane jealousy, who had planned the attempt upon him.

It was not until the following evening that Gregory saw Wu-ming again, and when he did his belief was strengthened. The young man's usually impeccable clothes looked as if he had slept in them, his face was haggard and his widely-spaced eyes were dim from weeping. Kâo and A-lu-te, who were con-doling with him when Gregory came upon them in the upper-deck lounge, accepted as quite natural his hesitant explanation that his extreme grief was due to his having as a small boy cherished a deep affection for his uncle. But as Gregory had never seen him display the least trace of such a feeling towards Tsai-Ping, he thought it much more probable that his acute distress arose from a very different cause.

As ancestor worshippers, the Chinese regard patricide as the most appalling of all crimes, and next to it they rank the mur-

128

der of any other male relative of a senior generation. More-over, Wu-ming had been born and bred among an island population specially dedicated to preserve China's ancient traditions. If, therefore, even unintentionally, he had caused his uncle to be killed it was not grief which had reduced him to this parlous state, but terror and remorse.

That, in spite of the years he had spent among unbelievers, he was still dominated by Confucian ideas soon became apparent by the concern he showed about the proper disposal of his uncle's body. He had temporarily lodged it in San Francisco's most expensive mortician's parlour, where it was now in process of being embalmed. The purpose of his visit to the yacht that evening was to arrange for a suitable mortuary chapel to be fitted up on board; so that the Mandarin's remains could be conveyed in a fitting manner back to the island for burial.

Kâo at once agreed that the honourable spirit of Tsai-Ping would know no rest until his bones reposed beside those of his honourable father—who had been the original head of one of the Seven Families responsible for colonizing the island—and said that he would personally supervise the furnishing of a mortuary chapel. After a moment he added thoughtfully:

'So far the Council's decision to invite the Princess Josephine to become our Empress has resulted in nothing but disappointment and ill fortune. I am convinced that my instinct to abandon the project after her disappearance was a sound one. The Council's having overruled me and sent me back to renew the search for her has now deprived us of the wise and upright Tsai-Ping. Clearly the whole venture is subject to the most evil influences. Therefore I am most averse to tempting providence further. In fact, I feel that the wisest course would be for me to accept the Mandarin's death as an omen and bear his honourable remains home with a minimum of delay; then humbly submit to the Council that they should devise some other means of providing for the succession.'

Somewhat to Gregory's surprise this defeatist pronouncement by Kâo was immediately countered by excited protests from both A-lu-te and Wu-ming. It was the former who got in first.

'But Uncle!' she exclaimed. 'You cannot have forgotten what happened when the Council was faced with this problem before. It had got to its wits' end, and almost despaired of finding a solution until the proposal of making Josephine Empress was put forward. That happy way out of our trouble met with everyone's approval; and since we are now convinced that she is still alive how can we possibly return without her?'

—'I entirely agree!' Wu-ming cried with heat. 'To disappoint our countrymen with no better justification than the fear that some misfortune might come upon us while endeavouring to carry out their wishes would be shameful.'

Such plain speaking by a Chinaman was quite exceptional, as even in the smallest transactions of daily life it is their custom to go to almost any pains to save one another from loss of 'face'. It was inexcusable, even allowing for Wu-ming's overwrought state, and Gregory was not surprised to see Kâo's eyes go dark with anger at this open imputation of cowardice. But A-lu-te saved the situation by swiftly putting in:

'You must not allow your concern for *us* to prejudice your judgment, Uncle. Your proposal to sacrifice your own principles in order to carry us out of danger does you much honour, but we could not agree to it.'

The fat man eagerly seized upon the come-back she had given him, and nodded vigorously. 'You are right, my child. It was of you younger people that I was thinking.'

'Of course I realized that, Sir,' Wu-ming diplomatically completed the face-saving process. 'But however evil the influences we have to combat, we must see this matter through. We owe that now not only to ourselves but to the dead. You are all aware how conscientiously my honourable uncle devoted his energies to tracing the Princess, and how alone among us he concentrated his every thought upon that duty. Since his death I have been greatly oppressed by recalling how little aid I gave him, and I feel that to make good that neglect is a debt I owe to his spirit. While standing by his bier this morning I took an oath that I would not engage in any other undertaking until this mission with which the Council charged him and yourself is completed.'

Kâo bowed gravely. 'I should be grateful for your help; but

permit me to point out that as our Export Manager there must be many other matters requiring your attention.'

'There is nothing that cannot wait,' replied Wu-ming with a shrug. 'At banks in a dozen cities we have large credit balances, and many other considerable sums are due to us. If we made no further sales for a year the Council would still be in no danger of running short of funds. In fact, as a long-term policy, it would prove to our advantage to stop selling altogether for a while, as that would create a shortage of our products in the world's markets and later enable us to raise our prices. In any case my sense of guilt led me to take this oath to my uncle's spirit, so I must now abide by it.'

As Wu-ming ceased speaking, Gregory thought to himself, 'This oath that he has taken clinches matters. He would never have committed himself so deeply simply because he failed to give his uncle all the help he could. The sense of guilt he talks about is really fear that unless he does his utmost to atone for Tsai-Ping's murder the old boy's spirit will revenge itself upon him.'

Meanwhile A-lu-te was declaring with an earnestness that equalled Wu-ming's, 'I too, have reason to reproach myself. The novel delights of this American city led me to forget how much hangs upon the success of our mission. Instead of frittering away my time in vain amusements I should have been keeping a record of the inquiry and writing many of the letters in connection with it.'

'Oh come!' Gregory protested. 'You are being much too hard on yourself. Right up till the day before yesterday, when I received the F.B.I. report, you believed Josephine to be living happily with her boy-friend. No one could possibly blame you for feeling that there was no great urgency about tracing her, and in the meantime taking the opportunity to enjoy life here while you had the chance.'

She shook her head sadly. 'What I believed is no excuse. We know now that the Princess was kidnapped. All this time that poor dumb girl may have been suffering acutely both in mind and body; yet I—the person who was sent here specially to act as her friend and companion—have not lifted a finger to help her. Still worse, for my selfish ends I have monopolized

131

your time and a great deal of Mr. Wu-ming Loo's, when both of you should have been concentrating on the search.'

'If we had, we wouldn't have got anywhere. Before I went to Washington the inquiry had already reached a dead-end.'

'If we had all helped it might not have been necessary for you to go to Washington. One of us might have hit on a trail leading to Quong-Yü weeks ago. Had we done so the honourable Tsai-Ping would not have been on the spot where he lost his life yesterday.' She paused a moment, then added sharply, 'Why do you smile?'

'Forgive me. I was impious enough to find amusement in the fact that the Gods should have elected to strike down the worker of the party rather than one of us drones.' As Gregory told his bland lie he was careful to include Kâo as well as Wu-ming in his glance.

'I see nothing at all funny about that,' A-lu-te replied coldly. 'On the contrary, the Gods could have chosen no more serious way of reminding us of our duty. For myself, I applaud the oath that our companion Wu-ming has taken, and I now pledge my word that I will not concern myself with any other interest until we have freed the Princess and invited her to return with us.'

Greatly as Gregory was intrigued by the reactions of these Orientals to a crisis that one of them, unknown to the others, had brought about, he found the high sentiments that were being aired somewhat theatrical. But he could see that A-lu-te had been deeply moved and was very much in earnest so without a hint of mockery, he said:

'I am the lady A-lu-te's obedient servant, and whenever she desires the inquiry to be resumed she has only to tell me so.'

'In a case like this I think we ought to ignore the fact that we are in mourning, and resume it at once,' she replied with a rather dubious glance at her uncle.

He shook his head. 'For us to take up any worldly activity before we have received the honourable remains of Tsai-Ping on board would be most unfitting.'

'Now that Quong-Yü is expecting a visit from us I cannot help feeling that the sooner he is interviewed the better,' Wu-ming said with an uneasy frown. 'But if you feel, Sir, that my uncle's spirit would take offence should we fail to adhere strictly to the formalities, I must be ruled by your greater experience.'

'This seems to me a case in which you can eat your cake and have it too,' Gregory remarked. 'Since convention requires you to remain temporarily inactive why not observe it, and leave Quong to me. I am quite willing to tackle him on my own, and I see no reason why I should not get as much out of him as would any of you.'

'That is an excellent idea!' exclaimed A-lu-te; but the two Chinamen considered the suggestion in silence for a moment, until Wu-ming said:

'I see nothing against it; although I would have liked to hear for myself what Quong has to say.'

Kâo nodded. 'So would I.' But with a shrug of his broad shoulders, he went on, 'No matter. Let us accept it. I shall have to go ashore tomorrow morning to purchase funeral furnishings for the mortuary chapel. I will then ring up Quong-Yü and make an appointment with him for Mr. Sallust.'

'You are most kind; but I too shall be going ashore, so I can save you that trouble. The mention of your name when I ring up should be quite sufficient to ensure Quong-Yü's granting me an interview.'

Gregory's polite little speech displayed no trace of guile, or hint of the importance he attached to it; but, in view of his narrow escape the previous day, he had made up his mind that no one should know in advance the hour at which he meant to call on Quong, and so be given the opportunity to lay a second ambush for him.

He felt that if he was correct in his belief that Wu-ming had laid the first, the shock he had sustained from murdering his uncle by mistake was so severe that it would be a long time before he screwed up his courage again to hire an assassin. But one could not be certain of that, or even that Wu-ming was definitely the villain of the piece. It was just possible that Quong-Yü, having the full resources of the most powerful Tong in Chinatown at his command, might have laid three or four ambushes—one to cover each approach to his dwelling.

With this in mind Gregory gave very considerable thought

133

to measures for his own protection, and when the yacht's launch put him ashore the following day he went straight to the office of the F.B.I. After a short wait he was shown in to Mr. Edgar C. Grace, who listened attentively to all he had to say. Feeling that no useful purpose could be served by reporting Tsai-Ping's murder, Gregory refrained from mentioning it; but he told Mr. Grace that he intended to visit Quong-Yü, and that he had reason to suppose that on entering Chinatown his life might be in danger. He then suggested a means by which the risk he had to run could be minimized, providing Mr. Grace was willing to give him a little unorthodox co-operation.

The American cocked an eyebrow and asked with a friendly grin, 'Would you say doing as you wish would come under the phrase "render any reasonable assistance"?'

'I certainly would,' Gregory grinned back.

'Then if I refused I'd be going contrary to the terms of reference I received about you from Washington. And if I did that I might get my top taken off, mightn't I?'

'I'm afraid you might,' Gregory agreed solemnly. 'And that would be very hard, seeing how much you've helped me already.'

'Seems then I've no alternative but to go on, and fix this thing for you.'

'That's about it. Joking apart, though, I'd be awfully grateful if you will.'

'Sure I will. Come back around three o'clock and I'll have everything ready.'

As a result of this conversation, Gregory left the F.B.I. headquarters at a little before four o'clock dressed in the uniform of a Californian State policeman. His change of costume also changed his bearing as, habitually, he was inclined to walk with his head thrust forward, whereas now that he was again in a uniform he instinctively held himself erect. As a disguise it could hardly have been bettered; it had the additional advantage of enabling him to go to his meeting not only armed but actually displaying the fact that he had a gun, and, yet further, would, he hoped, solve for him the problem of how

134

to reach Quong-Yü without having made any appointment at all.

From the F.B.I. headquarters he took a taxi to the top end of Grant Avenue. On the way he acknowledged to himself that the precautions he had taken to prevent anyone recognizing him, or knowing the time he meant to call on Quong-Yü, were probably quite unnecessary ; but he was none the less glad that Mr. Grace had enabled him to take them, as he was far too old a bird to run risks when they were avoidable and, moreover, the very fact that he was disguised now gave him the initiative.

At the inland end of Grant Avenue he slipped a piece of chewing-gum into his mouth before paying off the taxi ; then, with the brisk and purposeful step of an American cop, he made his way into Chinatown. Mr. Grace had given him particulars of Quong-Yü's abode, and advised him that the most suitable of its numerous entrances to use would be one through a tailor's shop in Mimosa Street.

Gregory found the shop without difficulty. A bell tinkled as he pushed open its glass-panelled door, and a Chinaman came forward to its streaked and pitted counter, one end of which was piled high with bales of cloth.

'Evening, Chinky!' Gregory rolled the chewing gum round his tongue. 'Go tell the Boss I want a word with him—an' make it snappy.'

The Chinaman gave a bland smile. 'This one-man shop. Me boss, and pleased to make you very nice suit, very cheap too.'

'Can that! It's old man Quong I'm here to see.'

'You come wrong place then.'

'You heard me. Get moving.'

'You make big mistake. Mr. Quong-Yü, he——'

Gregory brought his fist down on the counter with a crash, leaned over it and thrust his face within a few inches of the unoffending tailor's. 'Listen you! Either you get inside and tell Quong-Yü I want to see him, or I'm pulling you in for obstruction.'

With a shrug the Chinaman drew back, then turned and shuffled off through a doorway at the rear of the shop. He was away for about ten minutes and when he reappeared he was followed by an older man.

The newcomer displayed a much more challenging manner, and asked coldly, 'What is your reason for wishing to see Mr. Quong-Yü?'

'That's my business,' retorted Gregory. 'An' unless you want trouble around here you'd best not keep me waiting.'

'You will not make trouble for very long, and unless you answer you get no further. It is not the custom of Mr. Quong-Yü to speak with Patrolmen. Any business he has with police he transact with Captain of the quarter.'

There was no rudeness in the man's tone but it held the quiet assurance of a superior fully confident of his ground addressing an inferior. Gregory saw that he must change his tactics; so, by the symbolical gesture of removing the gum from his mouth and flicking it into the street, he abandoned his role of tough cop as seen on the movies, and said in his normal voice:

'I'm sorry. Let's start again, shall we? My name is Sallust and I was coming here two evenings ago with Mr. Kâo Hsüan. If you tell Mr. Quong-Yü that I think he will see me.'

The elder of the two celestials gave him a long unwinking stare; then, without a word, he turned and disappeared through the door at the back of the shop. After an absence of nearly a quarter of an hour he returned, bowed and said with cold politeness:

'Mr. Quong-Yü consents to receive you. But first a small formality. Please to place your pistol on the counter. It will be given back to you when you leave.'

Gregory was not at all surprised by the request. In fact he had thought it highly probable that, should he fail to bluff his way straight to Quong-Yü, the Tong boss's guardians would insist on his giving up his weapon before allowing him to enter the presence of their chief. But now that he was inside the Tong headquarters he had much less fear of being attacked; so he surrendered his pistol to the tailor, and followed the other Chinaman out through the back of the premises.

Beyond the shop the place proved to be a positive rabbit warren of narrow twisting passages and short flights of stairs;

which made it apparent that although the exterior of the block had been modernized the interior had not. Its tortuous ways only dimly lit by hanging lanterns, dragon-scrolled sliding panels, entrances screened by bead curtains, and faintly spicy smell, all combined to give it a truly Oriental atmosphere. This was just the sort of thing Gregory had expected to find on first entering San Francisco's Chinatown, and it intrigued him to think that on passing through the tailor's shop he had stepped back fifty years in time to the real Chinatown, which had simply gone underground.

After some minutes his guide brought him to a small room panelled in pink silk, on which there was a faint design of tortoises by a river. Its only furniture consisted of two lacquered arm-chairs and a low table. There, having told him to wait, the man left him.

Sitting down he looked about him, admiring the colouring of the Kang-he vase that had been converted to a table-lamp, the pattern of the thick carpet and the effectiveness of the simple design of the tortoises on the silk panelling. It was only then that it struck him that the silk on one wall seemed to be a slightly different colour and consistency from that on the others. As he peered at it again, two of the large panels began to move noiselessly apart, leaving a wide gap between floor and ceiling.

Beyond the gap was another, much larger, room. At its far end on a low dais a man sat hunched up in a throne-like chair of elaborately carved ebony. At his feet a girl was crouching. She had the broad head and heart-shaped face of a Southern Chinese, and was very lovely, but probably not more than fifteen. Beside the big cushion on which she squatted cross-legged was a small lamp. In its flame, on a needle point, she was preparing a pellet of opium for her master, whom Gregory assumed to be Quong-Yü.

He was much older than Gregory had expected. His magnificent robe, gaily embroidered with dragons, peacocks and butterflies, hung in loose folds about his shrunken figure. His face was as wizened as a monkey's, and many of the grey hairs had evidently fallen out of his drooping moustache, as one side of it was longer than the other; but his blue silk cap was set at a jaunty angle on his bald head, his black eyes held a lively sparkle, and his voice betrayed no sign of senility as he called out in good English:

'Come forward and tell me what you wish to see me about.'

As Gregory stepped through the aperture he caught just the whisper of a hiss, resulting from the release of hydraulic pressure as the panels slid to behind him. It caused him to glance over his shoulder and he was amused to see that the silk had been specially treated in some manner which rendered it transparent when seen from the larger room; thus enabling Quong-Yü to have a good look at any visitors who were waiting to see him in the ante-room before admitting them to his presence.

Feeling now how unsuitable his Patrolman's uniform was for such an interview, Gregory bowed and said:

'Venerable one; no doubt you will be aware that when the honourable Kâo Hsüan proposed to pay his respects to you two evenings ago he intended to bring three friends with him. I was one of those friends.'

Quong-Yü shook his head. 'With Mr. Kâo Hsüan I have been acquainted for many years; but I know nothing of his recent activities.' Waving his ivory fan towards a low stool, he added, 'Please be seated, and continue.'

Accepting the invitation, Gregory said, 'Am I to understand that you are still unaware of the reason why Mr. Kâo Hsüan and his friends were anxious to have a talk with you?'

'Entirely,' came the bland reply. 'As they never arrived here why should you suppose me to be aware of it?'

'I thought perhaps that Mr. Kâo Hsüan might have dropped some hint of it while speaking to you on the telephone.'

'He said no more than that he wished to consult me about a matter in which only I could help him. Why did he fail to keep the appointment I gave him, and why does he now send you to me instead of coming himself?'

'You must have heard about the accident which occurred only just round the corner from here,' Gregory replied. 'A man was killed by the fall of some crates of bananas. The victim

138

was one of our companions, and he was struck down when we were on our way to see you. Naturally we were too upset to keep the appointment; and it is through being still occupied with the mourning rites for his compatriot that prevented Mr. Kâo Hsüan from coming here this evening.'

Quong-Yü nodded gravely, but his small dark eyes remained quite expressionless as he said, 'A most distressing occurrence; but I heard nothing of it. You see, at my age I find it wise to confine my thoughts to matters which interest me; so I have long forbidden my people to bother me with local gossip.'

Gregory felt certain that the old man was lying. It was just possible that he might not have heard about a genuine accident, but as a Tong boss it was his business to know of all the criminal activities which took place in his area; so it seemed most improbable that he had remained ignorant of a violent death almost on his own door-step. Evidently it was just because he knew it had been murder that he had decided to deny all knowledge of the affair. So shrewd a man would be quick to realize that the victim's companions might have their suspicions that it had not been an accident, and, if so, even suspect that one of his 'hatchet-men' had been the murderer; so to appear to know nothing whatever about the matter was clearly the best defence against possibly awkward questions.

As soon as Gregory had appeared the young girl had laid aside her opium pellet and turned her attention to making fresh tea. She now bent before Gregory, offering him a tiny egg-shell-thin cup of the new brew, thereby giving him time to develop his recent line of thought and wonder if Quong-Yü had actually given orders for the ambush at the request of Wu-ming. After all, if Wu-ming had paid anyone to do the job Quong was the most likely person to whom he would have gone. If so, Quong had lied again when implying that he knew nothing of Kâo Hsüan's companions, and he must be aware that he was now facing the man he had been paid to have killed. With a view to checking any idea that this might be a favourable opportunity for Quong to make good his part of such a bargain, Gregory said:

'I must apologize, Venerable one, for presenting myself to

you in these clothes; but friends of mine at Police head-quarters insisted on lending them to me.'

'It is an honourable uniform, if lowly,' remarked Quong-Yü, 'and it had certainly appeared strange to me that Mr. Kâo Hsüan should select an ordinary Patrolman as his ambassador. However, if your observation was intended to disclose your reason for adopting this form of dress, I fear my dull mind has failed to grasp it.'

'Forgive me!' Gregory hastened to answer the question he had incited. 'I should have told you that I had some reason to fear being killed in mistake for another on my way here, and it seemed much less likely that would happen if I wore this uniform.'

Far from appearing the least disconcerted at this thrust, the old man's face wrinkled into a wintry smile, and he murmured, 'I trust you will soon be free of this annoyance. In any case I cannot allow even an acquaintance to be killed on leaving my abode; so as an additional precaution you must permit me to provide you with an escort when you leave.'

Gregory smiled back. 'You are most kind; but I shall be quite safe without it. In half an hour's time, my friend at Police Headquarters will be waiting in his car just round the corner from the tailor's shop to collect me.'

Having made it clear that he was under police protection, Gregory accepted a second cup of tea from the flower-faced hand-maiden. In recent months he had become accustomed to discriminating between the finer varieties of Chinese tea; so, as he sipped the fragrant straw-coloured liquid, it was easy for him to frame a suitable compliment on its excellence.

Quong-Yü bowed. 'It is rare to find such delicate apprecia-tion of our national beverage in a Caucasian, and I am much flattered; although I feel sure you have enjoyed many better infusions with our mutual friend Mr. Kâo Hsüan.'

This apparently pointless dragging in of Kâo's name Gregory took to be a sign that he might now go ahead with the real business that had brought him there; so he said, 'None of them was superior to this; but the last time we drank tea together we were discussing the disappearance of Miss Josephine Août. It was about that we wished to consult you.'

The dark little eyes peeping out from between creased layers of flesh, like those of a tortoise, never wavered, and the reply came with unhurried promptness. 'The name you mention is vaguely familiar, but in what connection I cannot recall. I fear there is nothing I can tell you about this lady.'

Gregory knew well that he would never get anywhere unless he provided Quong-Yü with the means to save face; so he said diplomatically, 'It is not at all surprising that anyone with your Excellency's innumerable interests and responsibilities should have temporarily forgotten the details of a transaction which occurred some months ago. Permit me to recall the circumstances in which you took Miss Août, er—under your protection.'

'Women,' declared the aged Chinaman, 'are as numerous as the sands of the sea, and of as little value. If she had the right to claim the protection of the Tong you may be sure it was afforded her, but no record would have been kept of the matter.'

'This was hardly a case of that kind. Miss Août was not an inhabitant of Chinatown. She was of noble Manchu blood and lived with her mother in an apartment off Golden Gate Park. On the morning of May the 18th her mother was run down by a car and killed. That afternoon Miss Août disappeared, and it has proved impossible to trace her movements since. However, we know that a wealthy Chinese merchant wished to marry her and it was thought possible that, learning that she had lost her natural protector, he might have sought your good offices to secure her compliance.'

Gregory felt quite certain that everything he had so far said was already known to the Tong boss; but he counted on his final sentence jerking him out of his passivity, and he uttered it with an air of unchallengeable authority. 'Anyhow, the one thing we do know for certain is that you took charge of her. You see, the F.B.I. has proof of that.'

For a moment there was complete silence in the warm, dimly-lit room, then Quong-Yü said, 'I hope there is no suggestion that any of my people kidnapped this young woman?'

141

'I fear there may be'—Gregory twisted the screw a little—'unless you can clear them by recalling what has happened to her. Mr. Kâo Hsüan and his friends have a very special interest in Josephine Août. They have no desire at all to make trouble for your Tong, but they are determined to solve the mystery of her disappearance. If you cannot help them get her back, what alternative will they have but to ask the further help of the F.B.I.?'

'There have been riddles before now which even the F.B.I. has failed to solve,' remarked Quong-Yü with sudden acidity.

'True,' replied Gregory quietly. 'But should they believe that you are withholding information from them, they might cause you considerable inconvenience. I don't think I mentioned that the man who is coming to pick me up in—yes, in about a quarter of an hour's time—is not just a Police captain, but Mr. Edgar C. Grace, whose name is, I think, known to you.'

The loose folds of Quong-Yü's multi-coloured robe rustled as he suddenly sat forward in his big chair and asked, 'Who are you? What interest have you in all this?'

Gregory shrugged. 'I'm just an Englishman who has specialized in getting to the bottom of various odd affairs. At the moment I have nothing much to do, so I promised some Chinese friends of mine to help them find Josephine Août; then I took a trip to Washington and some people there ordered Mr. Edgar C. Grace to give me his assistance. I found that he was very well disposed towards you, but all the same he's got to produce the goods or answer for his failure to the boys on top. He is hoping that you will give me all the information that you can, otherwise in about ten minutes' time, instead of going off to enjoy a good dinner with me he may feel compelled to spend his evening looking into what goes on in that lamp shop of yours.'

Having fired his big broadside Gregory sat calmly waiting for results. They were not long in coming. Quong-Yü's wrinkled face remained expressionless, but he said a little wistfully, 'If only I could remember this Miss Août. Perhaps you could describe her to me?'

It was the final measure for face-saving, and Gregory had

deliberately left that door open by refraining from any mention of Josephine's affliction. Without the suggestion of a smile he said, 'She is now twenty years of age and reported to be very good-looking; but unfortunately, owing to a surgeon bungling an operation on her throat when she was a child, she is completely dumb.'

'Ah!' Quong-Yü gave a well-simulated sigh of relief. 'Now I recall this Miss Août and can tell you what happened to her. Does the name Lin Wân convey anything to you?'

'No; nothing.'

'It will to Mr. Kâo Hsüan and your other Chinese friends. Lin Wân comes of an old family and possesses great wealth. He is what you would call a Merchant Prince. It seems that he was in close touch with the Aoûts, for on the day of the mother's death he came to me and said that the daughter's now being alone in the world, and a girl of noble lineage, he wished to offer her his protection. I had that offer conveyed to her and she accepted it.'

'Might that perhaps be interpreted to mean that he has taken her as a wife or concubine?' Gregory asked.

Quong-Yü shook his head. 'Oh no. I feel sure that Mr. Lin Wân had no thought of marrying her; and, as you are doubtless aware, the lady's lineage was so exalted that it placed her above any thought of concubinage.'

Gregory smiled. 'In that case Mr. Lin Wân has fulfilled towards her the true functions of a protector. I am most grateful for the information you have given me. Now it remains only for Mr. Grace and myself to check up on these particulars. We should be able to do that before dinner this evening, if you will be good enough to give me Mr. Lin Wân's address.'

For a moment Quong-Yü remained silent, then he began to laugh. He laughed and laughed until the tears ran out of the slits that now concealed his eyes. His beautiful little handmaiden threw Gregory an angry look and lifting her aged master up in his big chair began gently to pat his back. At last from sheer exhaustion his laughter ceased and opening his eyes he wheezed:

'Check up if you wish—but it will not be this evening. The

great House of Lin is near Yen-an, and it is there that he will have taken the dumb Princess. To find her you must cross the Pacific, travel eight hundred miles up the Hwang Ho, and then by camel caravan right across northern China, almost to the wall beyond which lie only the deserts of Mongolia.'

9

THE BIG DECISION

O N the afternoon following Gregory's interview with Quong-Yü a council was called of those principally interested in the information he had obtained. It was held in the little stern lounge of the yacht, and while A-lu-te reclined gracefully on her divan, Kâo, Wu-ming and Captain A-moi sat round the table with Gregory. In eager silence they listened as he told them what had happened, and of his subsequent thoughts and inquiries.

At first he had been most disinclined to believe Quong-Yü's story that Josephine was now some seven thousand miles from San Francisco in an almost inaccessible part of Communist China, and thought it simply a skilful device for evading a check-up. But later he was forced to conclude that the old man had been telling the truth.

Among the qualities which had earned Quong-Yü his position as Tong boss, foresight was one of the most valuable. When acting in the matter of Miss Août, he had evidently realized that, sooner or later, a time might come when the importance of that young woman's family connections would lead to a police investigation. To protect himself from the possibility of a charge of having made away with her, or sold her for secret export by some illicit trafficker in women, he had had the shrewdness to extract from Lin Wân a receipt for her safe delivery; and this he produced for Gregory's inspection.

Gregory's knowledge of Chinese writing was sufficient only for him to make out the rough sense of the document, and it occurred to him that it might be a forgery; but Quong-Yü said that he was quite willing for Mr. Grace to have it examined, and that there were plenty of reputable merchants in San Francisco who would vouch for Lin Wân's signature; so that seemed to put its authenticity beyond doubt.

The old man had further strengthened the plausibility of his story by stating that Lin Wân was the owner of a fleet of cargo ships regularly calling at San Francisco; that every few years he visited the city in one of them himself; that he had arrived in the port some ten days before Madame Août's death; and that her daughter's disappearance was explained by the fact that she had embarked on Lin Wân's vessel that same night, then sailed in her with him for China three days later.

Over an excellent dinner, Gregory had discussed this new development very fully with Mr. Grace. They agreed that whether Josephine had gone willingly or unwillingly was still very much in doubt, and that the odds were all on Quong-Yü having been paid a considerable sum to kidnap her; but they knew that the chance of ever being able to bring that home to him was now extremely remote, and that, anyway, it had no bearing on what had happened to the girl afterwards.

The F.B.I. chief said that he knew Lin Wân by name as a wealthy Chinese ship owner, and would make inquiries about him; although he did not think it would get them very much further, as Quong would not have been fool enough to invent Lin Wân's visit to San Francisco, or forge his name on a receipt; so the explanation that Josephine had sailed with him to China could almost certainly be accepted as true.

In the morning Gregory had gone ashore, to learn that Mr. Grace had confirmed Lin Wân's presence in the port during mid-May, and that his ship had sailed on the 21st. Its destination had been given as Tsing-tao.[1] The American had then gone on to say:

'The reputation of this Lin Wân stands pretty high; so it looks to me less than ever like an into-bed snatch. It's my guess that there's a political angle to it. Communism hasn't taken the Chinese in at all the same way as it did the Russians. The Reds have bumped off thousands of reactionaries, but in the main they've let be their big industrialists. There's a good reason for that. The Chinese are a cynical lot, and most of them don't give a cuss what sort of government they have, provided they are allowed to live much as they always have done. It follows that the best chance Mao and his boys had of remaining permanently in the saddle was to keep the shops well supplied with the usual run of goods at reasonable prices; and the only way they could do that was to string along with the old merchant princes, like Lin Wân. That has suited Lin Wân and Co. a sight better than being sent to join their ancestors; and I doubt if they have even suffered much financially, as the squeeze the Reds take off them is probably no greater than they had to ante-up to a succession of War Lords in the old days.

'But there's no future to it; because it can only be a matter of time before the Communists will have infiltrated enough of their own people into China's big business to take it over. The king-pins can't be so dumb as not to realize that, so there's always a possibility that they'll gamble everything in a counter-revolution. If they ever do, their chances of success must largely depend on their ability to produce a rallying cry which will win for them immediate popular support.

'Now, what's to prevent this Août girl being used in just that way? Her social register stuff would render an appeal in her name ace high with all the conservative elements, and the fact of her being beautiful but dumb would gain her the sympathy of the romantic masses. You may think I'm crazy, but I'd hazard a guess that Lin Wân and his buddies figure to keep a

1 Since the establishment of the First Republic most Chinese place names have been altered—many more than once and some so drastically that they no longer have any resemblance to those they bore for many centuries. Therefore the better-known originals, as given in *The Times Atlas* of 1922, have been used throughout.

hold on their millions by running this dame for Queen of China.'

Gregory did not think Mr. Grace at all crazy; and that afternoon, after making a full report to the small company assembled in the stern deck lounge, he produced the F.B.I. chief's theory, then waited with much interest for reactions.

Kâo nodded solemnly. 'What your friend says about China is largely true. During the past half century the morality of the people has sadly deteriorated, but they are still so set in the ways of centuries that it must be many years before they are conditioned to the same unquestioning acceptance of Communism as the Russians. I think him right, too, in his contention that the continuance of the Communist regime is largely dependent on its ability to maintain a fair standard of living for the people; and I know that the majority of the men who for the past twenty years have run China's industry and commerce have suffered no molestation. Mr. Lin Wân is one of them, and I have no doubt that they would all like to see a counter-revolution, but I do not think he is the type of man who would play a leading part in one.'

'You know him, then,' said Gregory quickly.

'Oh yes. We first met many years ago, and have since run into one another in various cities. He is the head of a family that has long been greatly respected. In his own province, before the Communists came, his word was law; and even now it must still carry great weight. But he concerns himself only with commerce and has never shown any interest in politics.'

'Perhaps he was acting for some friends of his who happen to be more politically minded,' Gregory suggested. 'Knowing that he was coming to San Francisco they might have asked him to collect Josephine, and he could have agreed without knowing that they intended to use her in a conspiracy.'

Ah-moi shook his handsome head. 'I do not believe there is anything in this idea that the Princess is to be used for the figurehead in a revolution. During the past few weeks, in the Mariners' Club ashore, I have met several ships' officers recently arrived from China, and learned quite a lot from them about present conditions there. They all say that the Communists have used their propaganda most skilfully to discredit the old regime, so that all young people now believe it to have been an age of tyranny. Therefore, if in time there is a revolution, its object will be to throw the Communists out in favour of a Democratic Republic ; but the people would never accept a restoration of the Imperial House.'

'I entirely agree,' said Wu-ming. 'But since everything points to Quong-Yü's having told the truth about the Princess's having gone to China with Mr. Lin Wân, why should we not give credence to the rest of his story—that she was offered the protection of this powerful man and decided to accept it?'

'No!' A-lu-te raised herself on her divan. 'You forget that she was in love. I am sure she would never have left her young student willingly.'

Wu-ming gave her a bitter smile. 'Love can become an obsession with all of us at times, but occasionally a sudden change of circumstances is enough to smother it. Having been poor all her life and with no prospect of bettering her lot than by submitting to the old man who was pursuing her, she may have regarded the idea of sharing a two-roomed apartment with her student as bliss. But the third alternative presented to her by Mr. Lin Wân may have seemed even more attractive. It meant that she would go to China—a land of which she had no doubt often dreamed—and after all her years of living meanly in restricted quarters become instead an honoured guest, surrounded with every luxury and attention in a great mansion having many rooms and courts set amid beautiful gardens. This dazzling prospect so suddenly laid before her may have reduced her love for her student to little more than a sentimental regret at having to leave him behind.'

'There may not have been anything very sudden about it,' remarked Ah-moi. 'Perhaps Lin Wân was the rich man who wanted to marry her, and as the young one was too poor to do so, her mother's death meant for her loneliness as well as poverty. That thought may have proved the last straw causing her to succumb to a prolonged secret temptation to sell herself in order to obtain security and an easy life.'

Gregory sat forward. 'I think you are off the track there, Captain. Quong said that Lin Wân comes to San Francisco only at intervals of a few years, and this time he did not arrive

148

until ten days before Madame Août's death. That makes it very unlikely that he is the same rich merchant as the one referred to in the love letters Josephine received from her boy friend.'

'He may have seen and fallen in love with her on his last visit, when she would have been about seventeen,' put in Kâo, 'and have pressed his suit in letters to her mother ever since. The knowledge that he was coming here again in May to woo her in person would have been quite sufficient to account for the perturbation of the two young people as disclosed in the letters.'

Raising his eyebrows Gregory glanced across at the fat man. 'It surprises me, Sir, that you should support such a story. When you called on Madame Août a few days before her death, Lin Wân must have already been in San Francisco. If he had long cherished the hope of marrying her daughter his first act on arriving would have been to pay his respects to these ladies. Surely, had he done so, Madame Août would have been so agog at the prospect of making a fine marriage for her girl that she could not possibly have refrained from telling you about it.'

Kâo looked slightly foolish and muttered, 'Yes, I suppose you are right about that.'

Wu-ming had been striving to get a word in, and now he said, 'I think I can dispose of the question of the Princess's elderly suitor. This morning I went through the notes made by my late uncle on the Aoûts. As you know he spent many days questioning people who lived in the same block, and tracing all their acquaintances. By a process of elimination he had arrived at the conclusion that the rich merchant referred to in the letters must be one Tung-ho Ting, who owns a chain of Chinese restaurants with premises in most of the larger towns along the Pacific coast. My uncle had intended to seek an interview with Mr. Tung-ho Ting, but his death prevented that; so I propose to try to see this gentleman myself to-morrow. If I succeed I shall be greatly surprised should he not prove to be the man that Madame Août was pressing her daughter to accept.'

'Then for the moment let's assume he is,' Gregory suggested.

'That would clear Lin Wân of any suspicion of having personal designs on the girl. If Captain Ah-moi is right about the political motive being highly improbable, that leaves us with very little option but to accept Wu-ming's theory that, dazzled by the prospect of the sort of life to which her birth entitled her, she decided to abandon her boy friend and sailed willingly with Lin Wân.'

'I do not believe it!' exclaimed A-lu-te. 'Those letters show that she was as much in love with her student as he was with her; and no young girl who is desperately in love for the first time can be dazzled by material things. She would not have given him up had we offered her the throne of our island—no, not if she had been offered the throne of the world.'

Gregory grinned at her. 'I don't believe it either. There is a lot in what you say, but more to it than that. The time factor is the crux of the whole affair. She could not have had any opportunity to consider Lin Wân's offer in advance, before her mother's death, and be tempted by it, because he never made it. Had he done so it is a certainty that he would have called on the Aoûts to make it personally, then, when he learned of the mother's death, he would have gone to the girl himself and pressed her to accept it. But it is obvious that he hadn't even met them. Why otherwise should he have employed Quong as an intermediary? For some reason still unknown to us he wanted to get hold of Josephine. When he heard that her mother had been killed he had to work fast. Possibly he already knew enough about her private life to fear that old Tung-ho might beat him to it, or that she might clear out of town with her young lover. Anyhow, I've very little doubt that he went straight to Quong and paid him a packet to kidnap her before she had a chance to turn round. Quong says she was put aboard Lin Wân's vessel that same night, but it did not sail till three days later. If she was still a free agent why didn't she come ashore to attend her mother's funeral and collect her personal belongings from the flat? There can be only one answer to that. Lin Wân had got her under lock and key, and when she sailed for China it was as a prisoner.'

For a moment there was silence, then Kâo heaved a heavy

sigh and said, 'Alas, I fear you are right. We can only pray that no further ill has befallen this unfortunate Princess.'

'I see no reason why Lin Wân should wish to harm her,' Wu-ming replied. 'In fact, I still incline to the belief that she went with him willingly. There may be a quite simple explanation for her not having come ashore during the three days before the ship sailed. Her mother's death must have been a great shock to her. Perhaps she collapsed soon after she got on board and became so ill that she was unable to leave her bed for a week or more.'

Kâo nodded. 'Perhaps. In any case it seems that Fate has now finally placed her beyond our reach, and that for the second time I shall have the distressing task of reporting failure to the Council.'

'But Uncle!' cried A-lu-te in quick protest. 'How can you think of returning to report failure while there is still a chance that you might carry out your mission sucessfully?'

'Indeed, Sir,' Wu-ming swiftly gave her his support, 'the lady A-lu-te is right. We have every reason to believe that the Princess is alive, and I feel certain that my late uncle would have considered it our duty to continue the search until we find her.'

'It ill becomes a younger man to address an older on the subject of his duty,' Kâo retorted with sudden anger. 'Now that your uncle is dead, it is not only the headship of the mission which has devolved upon me but the responsibility for the safety of you all. Lin Wân lives near the city of Yen-an. that lies beyond the great bend of the Yellow River, in the distant province of Shansi. Such a journey is not to be lightly undertaken.'

Wu-ming bowed submissively. 'Pray pardon my rudeness, Sir ; it was unintentional. Yet had we learned that the Princess had gone to New York, or Europe, or for that matter Australia, we should have followed her without a second thought ; so why should we not follow her to China?'

'There is no comparison between the journeys you mention and one to the borders of Mongolia. The former could be accomplished openly and without difficulty or danger, whereas an attempt to penetrate several hundred miles into Communist

151

China without proper documents would expose us to many perils.'

'Permit me to disagree, Sir. Money has always been the golden key to all doors in China, and we have ample funds at our disposal. All the information I have received from my agents leads me to believe that, provided one can pay one's way, one can still travel in China very nearly as freely as one could in the old days.'

'Even then, young man, in the remoter parts the traveller had to risk being captured by bandits and held to ransom. Besides, however successful we might be in bribing our way through the country once we had landed, we should first have to get ashore. As we are in no position to secure visas, the only course open to us would be a secret landing from a small boat. To make that possible would entail the yacht approaching close in at night to a coast unknown to our officers. Navigation in such circumstances is highly dangerous. It would mean risking the ship and all in her.'

Ah-moi slowly shook his head. 'I don't think there would be any great difficulty in putting you ashore. Having lived abroad for so long, you have probably forgotten that one of the clays used in the manufacture of our most expensive products can be obtained only from China, and that every eighteen months or so we send our trading vessel to fetch a quantity of it. I have made many such voyages in her so I am well acquainted with the Yellow Sea ; and one of the estuaries along the marshy coast to the south of the Shantung Peninsula would not be at all a bad place to land you.'

Kâo frowned at him. 'We should still have to get there, and Chinese waters would prove a cauldron of troubles for people like ourselves. If we took the shortest route to the neighbourhood you suggest, it would mean passing almost within sight of Korea. The Americans may turn us back, or one of their young airmen bomb us in the belief that we are a Communist blockade runner. Should we approach it from the South, that would necessitate our passing through the area in which sporadic warfare is still being waged between Chiang Kai-shek's Navy based on Formosa and that of the Communists operating from the mainland. So either course would present grave dangers. Remember, too, that this vessel was originally a warship, and re-armed could be used as one again. Her design will swiftly attract attention wherever she appears, and if either the Nationalists or the Communists decided to seize her, our peculiar position debars us from appealing to any court for compensation or restitution.' Staring hard at Ah-moi, he added, 'You must agree, Captain, that I am right about all this?'

'To some extent, yes,' the big man replied thoughtfully, 'but I think you exaggerate the dangers from war or piracy. The former have greatly lessened since last year, and the answer to the latter, as Wu-ming has pointed out, is a plentiful supply of money. The course I should set would be too far north for interception from Formosa to be likely, and there is every reason to believe that the Captains of Chinese Communist gunboats are as susceptible to bribery as their Civil and Military colleagues ashore. But the sea is very big, you know, and provided we keep well away from the main ports the odds are against our running into trouble. Our trading vessel has always succeeded in evading unwelcome attentions by the simple expedient of at once altering course away from any smudge of smoke sighted on the horizon, and we should exercise the same precaution. Of course, in the event of our finding ourselves within sight and range of a patrol ship as dawn broke, and her Captain proving an unbribable fanatic, we might be compelled to hand over the yacht and all be sent to a concentration camp; but I think such a double misfortune most unlikely.'

Gregory had been watching Kâo's normally cheerful face become more and more glum, and he sympathized with him. From many years of good living in the great cities of Europe and the Americas he had become soft and self-indulgent. It was very natural that he should regard the proposed journey with dismay. His contention that an illicit landing in China could not be attempted without running into danger was obviously correct. Then, from the coast to Yen-an and back meant a journey of over a thousand miles by tedious waterways and camel caravan, with all its attendant discomforts, and no relief apart from sometimes sleeping at night in bug-infested inns.

And all this for what? By now the Princess might be dead or in some other part of China. If she were still in Yen-an Lin Wân might, for some reason of his own, be holding her prisoner and refuse to let her go. In that case it would prove a next to impossible task to rescue her, and take her all the way back to the coast without being overtaken by his retainers. Again, should she be there and free to decide her own future, if she was living in comfort and security why should she abandon her new home and friends for the uncertain prospects of going to live among strangers in a remote Pacific island?

Even as these thoughts were passing through Gregory's mind, Kâo summed the matter up by saying: 'In my opinion if we go to Yen-an our chances of bringing the Princess back with us are very slender. What we have to decide is if, for that slender chance, the Council would consider us justified in hazarding this ship, the liberty of its crew and possibly our own lives?'

Having no personal interest in placing the lost Princess on the throne of the island, Gregory was most averse to facing the dangers and discomforts of a journey through China ; but he felt that it was not for him to express an opinion, so he could only hope that Kâo's obviously sound arguments against this forlorn hope would be accepted by the others.

But Wu-ming replied at once, 'I took an oath by my uncle's corpse to abandon all other interests until this mission was completed ; so whatever you may decide yourself, Sir, I must now go to Yen-an.'

A-lu-te said more slowly, 'Although I did not realize what it might entail at the time, I pledged myself to help in that. I beg you, Uncle, to make it possible for me to keep my word.'

Kâo looked across at Ah-moi. 'I have listened to the views of these younger people only out of courtesy, and my position entitles me to ignore them. But you are my equal. Moreover, you are responsible for the safety of this ship and her crew. Be good enough to let me have your opinion.'

The Captain shrugged his great shoulders. 'My mind is quite clear upon the matter. No one but a fool would be optimistic enough to believe that he could take this ship into the China seas without a certain degree of danger. But I consider that the risks I should run are not sufficiently high to justify my refusing to do so in the circumstances. The instructions of the Council were that no effort should be spared to trace the Princess and offer her the throne. My duty as I see it is to do my utmost to assist you in carrying out the mission with which they entrusted you.'

'Very well,' replied Kâo abruptly. 'As soon as you have fuelled and provisioned the ship for the voyage, we will sail for China.'

There was no more to be said, and four days later the yacht re-passed the Golden Gate outward bound.

In the interval, strict mourning for Tsai-Ping was maintained; so A-lu-te reluctantly had to forgo any last opportunity to enjoy the high-spots of San Francisco, while Kâo and Wu-ming went ashore only in the afternoons on business. The latter succeeded in interviewing Mr. Tung-ho Ting, and the wealthy restaurant proprietor admitted to having sought Josephine's hand in marriage. He had been greatly shocked by Madam Août's death and distressed by her daughter's disappearance. But he could throw no light at all on the mystery; and his identification as Josephine's elderly suitor coming so belatedly did no more than clear up what had now become a side issue to it.

Unlike his Chinese companions, Gregory had felt himself free to spend most of his time in the city, and he made several shopping expeditions. Most of his purchases were books, gramophone records and toilet preparations which he had been asked to get by A-lu-te; but some were on his own account. Among them, as he had no faith whatever in Chinese medicine, was a stock of drugs which might prove useful if any of the party fell ill on the journey to Yen-an; and, as his belief that Wu-ming had planned to have him murdered was never far from his mind, a medium-sized automatic that he could carry in his hip pocket without its bulk being obvious. On the last night he again took Mr. Grace out to dinner and, after a thoroughly enjoyable evening, said good-bye to that capable and friendly ally.

In the morning of the day the yacht sailed, Tsai-Ping's embalmed body had been brought on board. It was received by the entire crew with much wailing, and letting off of fireworks to scare away evil spirits; then ceremoniously deposited in the newly prepared mortuary chapel, for which a cabin amidships, once the forward armoury of the ship, had been selected.

Gregory was somewhat surprised to find that although the Chinese believed in demons they did not, apparently, subscribe to the superstition that having a corpse on board brought ill luck. With the practical good sense characteristic of them, once the ceremony was over no one made any further pretence of grief. Within a few minutes they were chattering and laughing as usual, and by the time the ship left harbour it seemed that everyone on board, with the possible exception of Wu-ming, had forgotten that such a person as Tsai-Ping had ever existed.

This lack of concern about the dead Mandarin's possibly having the effect of a Jonah was a disappointment to Gregory, for he had planned to use it as a lever in an attempt to sabotage the journey to Yen-an. His idea had been that if Kâo could be provided with a face-saving excuse for calling at the island on their way across the Pacific the Council would be given all the information so far acquired about Josephine's disappearance and might decide against this forlorn hope of trying to get her back from Lin Wân. If the presence of the Mandarin's body had rendered the crew uneasy, to get rid of it as soon as possible by burial on the island would have served as such an excuse. As it was, after nursing this project until it had been proved baseless all Gregory could do on their first night at sea was to throw out the idea that before actually risking the ship in Chinese waters they should run down to the island and place the matter before the Council.

Kâo, presumably from a desire to erase from his companions' minds any impression that at their last conference he had shown luke-warmness about carrying out his mission, received the suggestion rather coldly, and without expressing an opinion asked that of Ah-moi.

The hefty Captain replied without hesitation. 'I have already set a course almost dead across the Pacific. San Francisco is on latitude 38° north and a falling-off to the south even to 33° north would bring us abreast of the southernmost tip of

156

Japan. As you know, our island lies approximately 8° south of the equator, so to call at it I should have to alter course in the direction of New Zealand. Such a detour, along two sides of a vast triangle, would add the best part of four thousand miles to our journey. Since the Council has declared so positively their wish to have the Princess for our future Empress, the sooner you can make your attempt either to lure her away from Lin Wân, or buy her freedom from him, the better. I do not feel we could reasonably justify a fortnight's delay in calling to secure what would almost certainly be a repetition of their instructions.'

That settled the matter without further argument, and Gregory resigned himself to the uninviting prospect that lay before them. He could easily have deserted ship while they were still in San Francisco, but A-lu-te had shown such implicit trust in his not doing so that he had banished the thought from his mind without even seriously considering it. Since his grievous loss he had been much more prone than formerly to regard himself as a plaything of Fate; and now, his far from whole-hearted attempt to get the hazardous expedition called off having failed, he began to feel distinctly intrigued about its outcome.

On the first day out they fell back quite naturally into the routine they had followed during their voyage to San Francisco; but A-lu-te and Gregory soon realized that the substitution in their party of Wu-ming for Tsai-Ping would make it difficult for them to resume fully the long uninterrupted sessions of companionable study they had previously enjoyed. The love-lorn Wu-ming now had no duties of any kind to engage him, and for A-lu-te to have excluded him on all but special occasions from her private stern lounge might easily have been interpreted as a wish to be with Gregory alone for reasons far removed from the improvement of her mind.

In consequence he had to be given, more or less, the freedom of her sanctuary; and while he appeared quite content to sit there for hours in silence, just gazing at her with his widely-spaced eyes while she discussed English gardens, Roman history, the First World War, and scores of other subjects with

Gregory, her unwelcome admirer's presence was a source of secret irritation to them both.

It was on the third morning after they had left San Francisco that a mild excitement occurred to provide a topic of conversation throughout the ship. The previous night a stowaway had been caught while stealing food from the pantry of the saloon. Ah-moi told them at lunch time that on being questioned the man had made the excuse usual in such cases when a ship was bound for China—he had been beset with a persistent urge to visit the graves of his ancestors and was too poor to pay for a passage.

A-lu-te asked what would be done with him, and the Captain replied, 'He has been sent below to earn his keep as a stoker.'

'Will you allow him to land when we reach China?' Gregory inquired.

Ah-moi shook his head. 'No ; and even if he had chosen some other ship in which to stow away he would not be permitted to do so. He would be detained until he could be put ashore once more at the port in which he had made his illegal embarkation. As it is, he will see neither China nor America again. During several weeks on board it is inevitable that he should learn from the crew something of our island. We cannot allow even second-hand talk of its existence to get about, so we have no option but to take him back with us.'

'This is by no means the first time such a case has occurred,' Kâo added. 'Chinamen in foreign ports always assume that a ship manned by Chinese is about to return to China ; so from time to time stowaways are discovered in our trading vessel. Our method of dealing with them is quite simple. On their arrival in the island they are given a course of the drug which you would have been given but for A-lu-te's intervention. Once it has blotted from their minds all memory of the past, they become quite content to spend the rest of their lives helping to man one of the junks in our fishing fleet.'

Gregory's first reaction to this was that to inflict on a man what amounted to a life sentence for a comparatively trivial offence seemed harsh in the extreme ; but on consideration he realized that if the Council of Mandarins were to protect their people from corruption, and their miniature State from outside interference, they had no alternative other than to silence dangerous tongues in this by no means inhuman manner ; so he dismissed the matter from his mind.

He had, in fact, entirely forgotten the existence of the stowaway when, three nights later, a chance encounter recalled it to him. The time was just after midnight ; A-lu-te, Kâo and Wu-ming had gone to their cabins, and one of the stewards was putting out the lights in the upper deck lounge as the last of the officers who had been chatting there left it ; but Gregory did not feel sleepy so he decided to stretch his legs for a while on the starboard promenade deck.

The officer of the watch, the quartermaster and the look-out were now the only people remaining above decks, and none of them was visible to Gregory. It was very quiet and the only sound that broke the stillness was the hissing of the water along the ship's sides as she ploughed her way steadily through the sea. There was no moon and drifting clouds made the usually bright starlight fitful and uncertain.

Gregory had made only two turns up and down when an iron doorway forward of the bridge swung open, a man staggered from it, lurched to the rail, and clung there. As the watch had just been changed Gregory assumed the man to be an engine-room hand who had come up for a breath of air before turning in, and for a moment thought he might only have imagined his unsteady gait owing to the uncertain light. But, as he continued his advance under the dark arch formed by the starboard side of the bridge, the man gave a loud groan, let go the rail and collapsed upon the deck. Stepping quickly up to him, Gregory said in Chinese:

'What's the matter? What's wrong with you?'

The man did not reply. He had fainted. Yet even as Gregory asked the question he saw the answer to it. A break in the clouds let the starlight through to reveal that the man was naked from the waist up and that his back was criss-crossed with angry weals, some of which were still bleeding. It was clear that within the past half-hour he had been most brutally beaten.

Stooping, Gregory grasped his shoulder, pulled him into a sitting position, then thrust his head down between his knees.

After a moment or two he groaned again and muttered in English with a touch of American accent:

'I can't! I can't! I'm not strong enough.'

While man-handling him Gregory had already observed that he was of slight build, not much more than five feet seven in height, and still probably in his early twenties. Having given him a minute to recover he said:

'I've never heard any of the hands speak English, so I take it you are the stowaway. What's your name?'

Without looking up, the youngster nodded. 'Yes, Sir. I am that unfortunate person; and my name is Foo Wang.'

'Who has been ill-treating you like this?'

'The chief stoker. He says that slowness in one holds up the whole gang. But I have not been used to manual labour. Towards the end of each watch my strength begins to fail, then he beats me.'

Unsteadily the boy got to his feet. Taking him by the arm, Gregory said, 'You'd better come to my cabin, and I'll do what I can for that back of yours.' Then he led him aft.

Having told Foo to wash the grime from his face and hands at the basin, Gregory went to the galley and dissolved a little cooking salt in warm water. Returning, he gently cleansed the stowaway's back with the solution, patted it dry, and anointed the weals with ointment; then he told him to sit down and asked him:

'Is it true that you smuggled yourself on board because you wanted to visit the graves of your ancestors?'

'Not my ancestors, Sir, but those of my parents. They were very poor and both of them died with many others in our village from a typhus epidemic, when I was quite young. As often happens in such cases, all the poorer victims of the epidemic were put in a row into a common grave, and that has always worried me. An American missionary took pity on me and later sent me to be educated in the United States. By great economy I have managed to save a little money. Enough to give my parents a respectable burial, but not enough also to pay for a passage back to China. That was my reason for stowing away.'

Having regard to the veneration for their parents which is

160

second nature to the Chinese, the account Foo Wang gave of himself was a highly plausible one, and the only thing which might have caused the least doubt about it was that he did not look like the child of poor parents. Now that he had cleaned himself up and could be seen under electric light, his appearance was much more pleasing than might have been expected. Although he was of modest height his limbs were well proportioned, his features delicate, his eyes intelligent and his hands well moulded. It then occurred to Gregory that it was probably these very attractions which had caused the missionary to single him out, and give him a far better chance in life than fell to the lot of the vast majority of Chinese orphans.

After a moment, Gregory asked, 'What led you to choose this ship?'

'Simply a belief that she was bound for China, Sir ; but oh, how I wish now that I had waited for some other.'

'Why? You could not have hoped to make so long a voyage without being discovered. In any ship you would have been made to work your passage ; and as stowaways are in no position to protest against harsh treatment, you might equally well have had the ill luck to find yourself at the mercy of a brutal taskmaster. You must have realized the risk you were running.'

'I did, Sir ; and it isn't that. There is something queer about this ship that I don't understand, and it frightens me. The crew are different from any Chinamen I have ever met, either among those who have travelled widely or others who have never before left China. They will say nothing of the part of China from which they or their families come. None of them either drinks or smokes. There is no radio in the fo'c'sle, and except for sending signals they do not appear to realize that any other use can be made of wireless. Their speech too is neither exactly dialect nor quite the sort of bastard Mandarin that most poor men use, but a mixture of both with many old-fashioned expressions thrown in. They seem quite happy, but everything about them is unusual and reminiscent of a past generation—even their clothes. At times during these last three days I have become quite terrified, from the feeling that I must be dead and am now a spirit doing penance in some strange other world. Talking to you, and your great kindness to me, has reassured me upon that. But tell me, I beg, are we really on our way to China?'

Gregory nodded, and, refraining from telling him that he was not to be allowed to land when they got there, said: 'In due course I expect you will learn why the crew differ quite a bit from any other Chinese seamen you have come across; but for the time being I think the fewer questions you ask them about themselves the better. Anyhow, while we are on our way to China you have no cause to be frightened of anything worse happening to you, than you have experienced up to now.'

'Thank you, Sir.' Foo stood up with the polite intention of showing that he did not wish to outstay his welcome, and added with a bow, 'Your assurance that we are really going to China is a great comfort, and will give me new courage to bear my present hard lot.'

As Gregory got to his feet, he said: 'Tell me, what was your job before you left San Francisco?'

Foo hesitated only a second, then replied, 'I was a clerk, Sir, in a surveyor's office.'

'Have you had experience in any other kind of work?'

'I am not a bad mechanic, and for a time I acted as chauffeur to an old lady who lived up on Nob Hill.'

'Anything else?'

'I have sometimes taken night work as a barman. People are kind enough to say that my Old Fashioneds are very good.'

Gregory smiled. 'You make my mouth water. But I'm afraid we couldn't find much use for a shaker of cocktails as, apart from carrying light wines, this is a dry ship. Bar-tending is not far off waiting, though; so I take it you could do that.'

Foo's pleasant young face suddenly lit up. 'Do . . . do you mean, Sir, that you will try to get me taken out of the stoke-hold?'

'I'm only a passenger, so I can promise nothing; but I'll see what I can do. Now off you go, and try to keep your chin up.'

With many expressions of gratitude Foo bowed himself away, and Gregory began to undress. As he did so, he felt that he had been rather rash to raise the young man's hopes at all, for he knew only too well the strange contradictions of the

162

Chinese character, which could make the same man the very essence of kindness about one thing and callous almost beyond belief about another; so good-natured as Captain Ah-moi appeared to be, his reactions to a request for Foo's transfer were quite unpredictable.

However, Gregory was determined to do his utmost, not only for Foo's sake but for his own. Since they had sailed from San Francisco, Wu-ming had shown him no open hostility, but he felt certain that it was only latent; and the curious sixth sense, which had often stood him in good stead, repeatedly warned him that at any time, driven to desperation by A-lu-te's obvious preference for his company, the China-man might make another attempt upon his life. The strain of living from day to day under such a menace was considerable, and he felt that it might at least be eased a little if he had someone like young Foo, who, bound to him by gratitude, could be relied on to act as watch-dog should he find that the lock on his cabin door had been tampered with, or have any other reason to think that Wu-ming meant to attack him while he slept.

Next morning, having waited patiently for a suitable oppor-tunity, he tackled the Captain and told him of his encounter with the stowaway. As he had feared might prove the case, Ah-moi appeared quite unmoved by Foo's sufferings at the hands of the chief stoker, and simply said that he never inter-fered with his petty officers provided they did not become slack.

Gregory was shrewd enough not to press the point, but skil-fully shifted the attack to another angle. He said, quite un-truthfully, that he had always previously travelled with a per-sonal servant, and on the trip to San Francisco had greatly missed having one. When they sailed again he had hoped that Tsai-Ping's man, Che-khi, might be given to him, but he had been taken over by Wu-ming; so he still had to brush his own clothes and perform other menial tasks unfitting for a gentle-man. As the stowaway was superfluous to the ship's company, and a type that could easily be trained to such duties, could he not have the use of him?

That put the matter on an entirely different footing. Ah-moi both liked Gregory and, in spite of his curiously anomalous position, regarded him as an equal. He at once apologized for his lack of thought in having allowed his passenger to suffer such inconvenience for so long, and promised to give orders for Foo to be put at his disposal.

After lunch the chief steward brought Foo, now dressed in a suit of white drills somewhat too large for him, along to Gregory's cabin. There, Gregory explained his new duties, and the beaming young man set about tidying his things with a will.

During the six days that followed, no event occurred to mar the serenity of the voyage. For hours each day, while A-lu-te talked with Gregory, played Mah-jong with Kâo, or flirted mildly with one or other of the officers, Wu-ming sat, making only an occasional contribution to the conversation, but all the time devouring her with a wide-eyed unwinking stare. By now she had got so used to his obsession for her that she was no longer irritated by it, and treated him with the casual kindness that one extends to a half-witted child. But Gregory did not regard him in that way at all ; and, although their relationship continued outwardly quite friendly, he watched the Export Manager's comings and goings like a lynx.

Foo had been acting as Gregory's servant for a week when, on their second Wednesday at sea, as was now his custom while his master was changing for dinner he brought him the nearest approach he could make to a cocktail. It was made of Californian white wine and fresh orange juice with a slice of a green lime. Setting it down on the fixed dressing-table, he left the cabin.

Having finished brushing his hair Gregory picked up the cocktail to drink it. He had already taken half a mouthful when he saw that a mosquito had alighted on the back of his hand. Setting the glass down quickly, he gave the insect a smack that killed it just as it stung him.

Next moment he felt a burning sensation in his chest. His eyes bulged and he gasped for air. From the mirror his own horribly distorted face grimaced at him. Clutching his chest, he reeled away towards the bed and fell upon it. As his sight dimmed and failed, as though he had suddenly been struck with blindness, one grim thought flashed through his mind.

Wittingly or unwittingly, the very man whom he had counted upon to help protect him if called upon to do so had brought him poison.

10

THE POISONED COCKTAIL

As Gregory squirmed upon the bed he knew that his only hope lay in getting rid of the poison he had swallowed. With a great effort he managed to sit up and push his finger down his throat. He was sick on the floor ; but that did not relieve the tearing pains in his chest, and his stomach now felt as if it were on fire.

Groaning he fell back again. As he had been sitting sideways on the bed his head came down with a hard thud against the wall of the cabin. What the poison had begun, the blow completed. He lost consciousness of his surroundings, although he still knew himself to be moaning and twisting in agony.

For how long he lay as though in a black pit, submerged under waves of pain, he had no idea. It was the sound of an exclamation which made him open his eyes. He could see again, but tears and sweat running into them partially obscured his vision. As through a mist he saw Wu-ming's face poised about eighteen inches above his own.

The sight of the Chinaman bending above him jerked his mind back into full consciousness. Gripped by renewed terror of death he stared upward. It flashed upon him that there could be only one explanation for Wu-ming's presence. He must have come to make sure that his victim was dead, and by taking away the cocktail glass remove the only evidence that he had been murdered. And now, finding that his enemy was still alive, but helpless, surely he would seize the opportunity to finish him off while he had him at his mercy.

Gregory's immediate impulse was to thrust up his hands, grasp Wu-ming's arms and, while grappling with him, shout for help; but he managed to check it. His throat was so parched that he doubted if he could do more than croak, and he was so exhausted from the effects of the poison that in a fight the odds must prove heavily against him. But he could feel some strength ebbing back into his limbs, and fear was making his brain work swiftly.

Frantically he wondered what means the jealousy-crazed Chinaman would use to kill him. It was very unlikely that so sophisticated a man would carry a knife; and, if he were, to use it would be to betray himself as the murderer. The same objection applied to strangulation, for it was certain that the marks on his victim's throat would be noticed and give away the fact that death had not been caused by a stroke or sudden seizure. Suffocation with a pillow would lead to blackening of the face, so also cast on him immediate suspicion. But there remained the poison. If he could manage to force his victim to swallow even another half mouthful, that would probably do the trick.

These thoughts raced through Gregory's mind in less than half a minute. During it he had remained absolutely rigid, and although he was not aware of it his staring eyes gave the impression that he was in a fit. Without speaking to him Wu-ming straightened up and turned away.

Gregory felt certain he was about to fetch the poison from the dressing-table. Gathering his strength he swung his legs off the bed and sat up. His head began to swim but, stretching out his hand, he grasped a heavy torch that lay on his bed-side shelf. At that moment the cabin door opened and Foo came in.

The sweat was streaming down Gregory's face and his mouth sagged open. It was possible that, believing him to be at dinner, Foo had come to tidy the cabin; but his appearance on the scene might have a very different explanation. Gregory's heart suddenly began to thud with even greater apprehension. It was Foo who had brought him the poisoned cocktail. If his young protégé had been suborned by Wu-ming and was his accomplice the game was up. He might have fought off Wu-ming alone, but in his present state he could not possibly prove a match for the two of them.

Foo's face showed blank surprise; but that might have been at finding Gregory still alive. On hearing Gregory move Wu-ming swung round and stared at him. His eyes were bloodshot, his face demoniac with pain, strain and fear. Suddenly he found his voice. It came half strangled at first then rose to a shout as he brandished the heavy torch:

'Stay where you are! I'll brain the first of you who tries to lay a hand on me!'

The cabin door was still open and his raised voice could have been heard by anyone passing along the deck outside. Wu-ming and Foo exchanged a swift glance of consternation, then the former said, 'He must have had some form of fit and gone out of his mind.'

'I'm not out of my mind!' Gregory cried angrily.

'Then why do you threaten us?' Wu-ming asked. 'It must be that a demon has got into you.'

Gregory glared at him. 'You know what's the matter with me, or you wouldn't be here.'

Wu-ming's expression remained blank and he shook his head. 'When you did not come in to dinner, we wondered what had happened to you; and I volunteered to find out. Since you will not let me help you, I will go and tell the others of the strange manner in which you have been afflicted.'

As he turned on his heel and left the cabin, Foo stepped forward again. He looked so genuinely distressed that Gregory now felt doubt of his complicity. It might be that he owed his life to Foo's timely arrival, as it had occurred well before he had recovered his power to shout for help. Yet it was Foo who had brought him the poison, and he knew how unscrupulous Orientals could be when striving to achieve some cherished design of their own. It was possible that during the past few days Wu-ming had been working secretly upon him, learned his story, and promised to have him put safely ashore when they reached China in return for his unquestioning obedience.

Gregory's previous experience of such matters had taught him that if Foo were guilty, he would be much more likely to give himself away if questioned now than later, when he had had an opportunity to concoct with Wu-ming a series of plausible answers; so he rallied his returning strength for the effort. Beckoning the young man over to him, he said:

'Give me your hand.'

Under the impression that Gregory wished to be helped to his feet, Foo at once made to obey, but suddenly found his outstretched fingers seized in an unexpected grip by which the backs of his knuckles lay beneath Gregory's thumb. With a swift motion Gregory jerked Foo's hand over and forced it down. Giving a squeal of pain he fell to his knees, his head thrown back, his body twisted sideways.

'Now!' said Gregory hoarsely. 'I want the truth; or I'll send you back to the stoke-hold.'

'Please, Sir! You're not yourself,' Foo gasped. 'Oh, you're hurting!'

'I've hardly started yet. I'll break every bone in your fingers unless you answer me properly. What was in that cocktail you brought me?'

'White wine and orange juice, with a slice of fresh lime.'

'What else?'

'Nothing else. Oh, let me go! No, nothing; I swear!'

'Where did you mix it?'

'In the pantry off the upper deck lounge.'

'Who else was in the pantry at the time?'

'The second steward and Mr. Kâo Hsüan's servant, P'ei. He too was mixing a drink for his master.'

'Who was in the lounge?'

'The chief engineer, the purser, two officers who were playing chess, and one of the young cadets.'

'No one else? Think now!'

'No, Sir. No one.'

'Did you walk straight through the lounge with the drink and bring it direct to me, or did you for any reason stop on the way?'

'I stopped once, Sir; but only for a moment.'

'Where, and why?'

'At the top of the upper deck companion-way. I almost ran into Mr. Wu-ming Loo there. He was on his knees looking for a little gold toothpick he had dropped. It was already getting dark and he asked me to help him find it before the light failed.'

'Ah!' muttered Gregory. "And what happened then?'

'I put my tray down on the deck and helped him to search. We found the toothpick almost at once; or rather he did.'

Gregory released his vice-like grip on Foo's fingers, let him get up, and said, 'Thank you. That's all I wish to know. I don't think you are in any way to blame for what happened.'

'You . . . you mean, Sir, that you won't send me back to the stoke-hold? That I may continue as your servant?'

'Yes,' Gregory nodded, wearily passing a hand over his eyes. The plan to kill him now appeared simplicity itself. Wu-ming need only have noticed that Foo brought him down a cocktail at the same hour every evening, then lain in wait outside the lounge. A servant could not possibly have refused his request to help him look for his toothpick, and in the failing light, while the man's back was turned, it would have been child's-play to slip the poison into the drink unobserved by him or anyone else.

Having given joyful expression to his relief at regaining his master's confidence, Foo slipped over to the dressing-table picked up the cocktail and, sniffing at it, asked, 'But why should you think this to have been the cause of your attack? It smells as usual and the glass is still nearly full; so you can have taken only a sip'

'Put that down!' said Gregory sharply. 'And leave it there. In no circumstances are you to take it away.'

At that moment a babble of voices sounded outside, and on Foo's opening the door, A-lu-te, Kâo, Captain Ah-moi and the ship's doctor all crowded into the little cabin.

As they bombarded Gregory with questions and expressions of sympathy, he did some quick thinking. There was no more chance of bringing home to Wu-ming this second attempt at murder than there had been the first; so to accuse him of it could result only in creating an incredibly awkward situation for all concerned. When their clamour had subsided a little, he raised a pale smile, and said:

'I'm afraid I made rather a fool of myself, just now. I've had a nasty turn, but it was my own fault. I meant to take a dose of ammoniated quinine to stave off a cold that I felt coming on ; but in the half-light I poured the dose from a small bottle of carbolic by mistake. Fortunately I didn't swallow much of it, but the pain was enough to drive me temporarily crazy. I'm over the worst now, though, so there's no need to worry about me.'

His explanation was readily accepted, but they continued to show much concern about him. Ah-moi offered to help his servant get him to bed, Kâo wished to fetch joss-sticks to fumigate the cabin against evil spirits, the doctor—who was of an older generation than Ho-Ping, and still had great faith in the ancient remedies of China—proposed to write out a prescription, burn it and mix the ashes with a soothing broth to be taken every two hours, while A-lu-te begged to be allowed to stay and nurse him through the night.

Gratefully but firmly he refused all these ministrations, insisting that he had everything he needed in the way of medicines, and that the kindest thing they could do was to leave him to recover in darkness and quiet.

When they had at last been persuaded to return to their interrupted dinner, he washed, drank a pint of hot water, then made himself sick again while Foo cleaned up and aired the cabin. With Foo's aid he undressed and, after filling the basin with cold water, freshened himself up by sluicing his head in it. Next he told Foo that he was to make no mention whatever of the cocktail to anyone, dismissed him for the night, and locked the door after him. Finally, he took two Carters and a luminol, put his gun and torch handy, got into his bunk and turned out the light.

His throat and stomach were still very sore, but the drug soon began to take effect. As he drifted off to sleep a grimly humorous thought came to him. Never before had it occurred to him to spare a mosquito, but he wished now that he had not killed the one that had settled on his hand ; for by doing so at that critical instant the insect had prevented him from drink-

170

ing down half the cocktail at one go, as was his usual custom, and thus undoubtedly saved his life.

He was woken in the morning by a gentle knocking, and, getting out of bed, let Foo in. To the young man's anxious enquiries he was able to reply truthfully that he had had an excellent night and now felt little the worse for his misadventure. But he added that he meant to stay in bed till lunch time, and that for breakfast he would have only a cup of clear soup or Bovril and some dry biscuits.

It was while Foo was absent, fetching this light meal, that Gregory noticed that the glass containing the rest of the poisoned cocktail had disappeared. Foo had been in the cabin for no more than two minutes and, in the full light of morning, it would have been impossible for him to have taken it away unobserved; so it must have been removed the previous evening when the cabin was full of people.

But by whom? Wu-ming had not returned with Gregory's other visitors, so it could not have been him. It occurred to Gregory then that while the others had crowded round his bed, blocking his view of the doorway and the cabin, Foo had remained deferentially in the background; so without being seen he could have snatched up the glass and slipped outside for long enough to toss it overboard. If he had, it could only mean that, after all, he was Wu-ming's secret accomplice.

As Gregory had already made up his mind that to accuse Wu-ming would be futile, the disappearance of the cocktail was of no great importance. Nevertheless it annoyed him, as he had meant to put it in a bottle and seal it up in Foo's presence, then make him sign a statement that he had witnessed the act; so that in the remote chance of fresh developments it could still be produced as a piece of definite evidence.

When Foo returned, Gregory said nothing about the cocktail, as he wanted a little more time to think things over. After breakfast he shaved and went along to have a bath. Then, as he was about to get back into bed, Foo raised the matter himself.

'Sir,' he said. 'Immediately I began to do the cabin I noticed that the cocktail was no longer on the dressing-table. Have you thrown it away, or put it somewhere? I ask only because you gave me strict orders not to touch it.'

171

Taking him by the shoulders, Gregory looked down straight into his eyes and said, 'No, but I noticed that it had gone while you were getting me my breakfast. If you did not take it away, who did?'

Foo's glance never wavered. 'I have no idea, but I swear to you, Sir, that I did not. You see, I understood the importance of leaving it there. Your explanation to your friends last night about the cause of your illness may have served for them, but not for me. It was drinking some of the cocktail that caused you such agony. The way you questioned me about it before they came in put that beyond doubt. Someone tried to kill you by putting poison in it.'

Gregory nodded. 'Yes; that is what happened. And to you there is no point in my pretending otherwise.'

Tears came into Foo's eyes and he said earnestly, 'It is terrible. I have not slept all night for worry. You must know, Sir, that I am devoted to you. How could I be anything else when I owe you so much? From now on I shall do my utmost to protect you. Whenever I bring you a drink in future it will be in a jug with two glasses, so that I can taste it first in your presence; and I intend to sleep on a mat outside your cabin door every night.'

With a smile, Gregory said, 'Thank you, Foo. I am quite satisfied now about your fidelity.'

The excessive caution which had become second nature to him warned him that Foo might be staging a bluff, but his life had depended on his judgment of men too often for him to be easily taken in, and he did not believe the young Chinaman capable of such a superb piece of acting. Taking his hands from Foo's shoulders, he stripped off his dressing-gown and got into bed.

'One thing seems to me certain, Sir,' Foo remarked as he folded the dressing-gown. 'Although we cannot prove it, the only person who could have put the poison in your cocktail is Mr. Wu-ming Loo.'

Owing to the warmth of the weather the cabin door was hooked back and its entrance had only the curtain drawn across it. Before Gregory had time to reply there came a knock on the door frame. With a swift uneasy glance at the curtain, he called, 'Come in.'

It was A-lu-te, accompanied by her maid Su-sen, who had come to inquire after him. As Gregory now spoke Chinese with considerable fluency and no other language was ever used at meals or in general conversation, they rarely spoke English except when alone together; so it was in Chinese that she anxiously addressed him, and that he assured her that he had really recovered sufficiently to get up, but was making his in-disposition an excuse for a lazy morning in bed.

Smiling with relief, she took the chair that Foo set for her; but the moment he had left the cabin, the smile disappeared from her face. Breaking into English, which Su-sen did not understand, she exclaimed in a low tense voice:

'It can't be true! That man of yours must be crazy!'

Her words made it clear enough that, as Gregory already feared, she had overheard Foo's last remark. To gain a moment's time, he replied blandly, ' I don't know what you're talking about.'

'I could hardly believe my ears, but I distinctly heard him say that Wu-ming put poison in your drink.'

'Perhaps your ears deceived you.'

'Gregory, stop fencing with me! A servant cannot be allowed to make such a terrible accusation and go unchallenged. Either he must show good cause for what he has said or be punished. But perhaps this horrible suspicion has something to do with the way poor Wu-ming says you threatened to brain him with a torch last night. Did you intentionally mislead us when you told us afterwards that you had swallowed carbolic by mis-take? What really happened? I insist on your telling me the truth.'

Her earnestness and excitement decided Gregory that she was liable to make serious trouble aboard unless she was given a good reason for keeping to herself what she had overheard, and he knew that she was much too intelligent to be fobbed off with a few uncoordinated lies, which were all he was cap-able of inventing on the spur of the moment; so he said:

'I wish I *could* tell you the truth. The trouble is that I don't

173

know it myself for certain. All I do know is that two attempts have been made to murder me.'

'Two attempts! But, in heaven's name, why have you never said anything about this?'

'For the simple reason that, although I have very definite suspicions about the identity of the person who is endeavouring to kill me, I have not one atom of proof. And to make an accusation without being able to prove it could result only in creating a most deplorable atmosphere of hate, distrust, lies and suspicion all round. That is why I have been keeping all this to myself, and must ask you to give me your word that you will do the same if I tell you about it.'

'Very well,' she said, after only a second's hesitation. 'I promise. But why should you suspect the unfortunate Wu-ming?'

'You have said it yourself. Just because he *is* unfortunate—unfortunate in loving you and finding it impossible to arouse in you the least sign of tenderness for himself.'

'Oh, Gregory! You are being absurd.'

'I am not. The classic formula for every murder investigation is to look for motive and opportunity. Wu-ming has had ample opportunities, and uncontrollable jealousy is one of the most common of all motives for murder. From the second he saw you that day in San Francisco, after you had dressed in your new clothes and been Americanized in a beauty parlour, he fell as flat for you as if he had been struck by an atom bomb. Within a few days he had changed from a pleasant, talkative, sophisticated young man of the world to a morose, silent goop who had so far forgotten his manners that he could not even keep his eyes from devouring you in public.'

'Of course he is in love with me; that is obvious. But I am not to blame for being unable to return his love.'

'I did not suggest that you were; but, as he sees it, you might if the circumstances were different.'

'You mean if I had not brought you with me from the island?'

'Yes.' On an impulse Gregory stretched out his hand to take A-lu-te's, but suddenly remembering Su-sen's silent presence in the corner, quickly withdrew it, as he went on, 'I owe you more than I can ever repay. Four months ago you most generously set yourself the task of restoring me to sanity, and you have succeeded in that. But to do so has necessitated your giving me your constant companionship.'

'You have already more than repaid the debt by opening a hundred new horizons to me.'

He smiled. 'I'm glad you feel that. We have certainly spent many happy hours together, and learned a lot from one another. But—let's face it—anyone having only a vague idea about the origin of our friendship might put a very different interpretation on the obvious pleasure we take in each other's company.'

'Even if I had never met you, it does not at all follow that I should have been in the least attracted to Wu-ming.'

'No, but the fact remains that after your transformation in San Francisco he suddenly realized that, in addition to your natural attractions, you personified a unique blend of the traditional East and sophisticated West; and for a man with his background that meant perfection.'

'It is true that he has said as much.'

'There you are, then. But he has had darned little chance to do more than whisper it once or twice, and I am the barrier that has prevented his doing so. That's why he has been driven so desperate that he is trying to get rid of me.'

'If you were my husband and he a lover to whom I had given some encouragement, I can imagine him contemplating such a crime; but not as things are. But tell me, what grounds have you for your extraordinary suspicions?'

For answer Gregory gave her an account of both attempts upon him; and, in order that she should not think him prejudiced, he went into every detail of his own speculations from the moment that the banana crates had crashed upon Tsai-Ping's head up to his noticing that the cocktail glass had disappeared that morning.

When he had done, she sat silent for a moment, then she said, 'Even if it is true that Foo met Wu-ming by the upper deck companion-way and set down your drink while helping him to look for his toothpick, there are no grounds whatever for supposing that he put poison in the glass while Foo had his

175

back turned. To me that looks like a red herring; and you say yourself that at first you suspected Foo of being Wu-ming's accomplice. If you put out of your mind for one moment this idea of yours that Wu-ming has been planning your murder, you will see that no one but Foo could have poisoned your drink. Instead of suspecting him to be only an accomplice, you should have realized that it must be he who both planned and carried out his attempt to kill you.'

'No,' Gregory shook his head. 'That won't hold water. He has no possible reason for wishing me dead. On the contrary; not only does he owe me a great deal but my death would result in his being sent back to slavery in the stoke-hold. If he were implicated at all it could only be because someone else had tempted him with the promise of a very considerable reward for his help. But I am convinced now that my suspicions of him were unjustified. Besides, how about the business with the banana crates? Foo could have had no hand in that.'

Again A-lu-te sat silent for a while, then her intelligent eyes narrowed a little as a new thought crossed her mind. 'When you were telling me about your speculations after Tsai-Ping's death, you mentioned that at one time you thought Quong-Yü might have been responsible.'

'Yes. If, through his grape-vine, he had learned of my association with Edgar C. Grace he might have thought that I was investigating some much more serious matter than Josephine's disappearance, and was using Kâo only as a stalking-horse to make certain of catching him at home. That would have been a motive for his trying to do me in before I could get at and cross-question him. But I discarded the theory as much too far fetched.'

'You must admit, though, that if he had a motive it would have been a simple matter for him, as a Tong boss, to order one of his hatchet-men to cut that rope. Whereas, in the very short time available, it would have been far from easy for an ordinary business man, like Wu-ming, to arrange an attempt on your life.'

'That is true; but where does Foo come into this?'

A-lu-te's eyes narrowed again. 'We know that Quong-Yü and Lin Wân co-operated in carrying Josephine off from the

United States. Let us suppose that they have some very strong reason for preventing anyone else getting hold of her. As you say yourself, Quong might have learned that the F.B.I. were behind you, and for that matter that you were helping us in our attempt to trace Josephine. If so, he would have realized that you were the only one of the four people coming to see him who really had the power to force his hand. Once he had eliminated you he would have had a good chance of stalling off his own compatriots. Tell me, does not that make sense?'

'Yes, it certainly does,' Gregory agreed. 'As a matter of fact it was one of my own first lines of thought; but where do we go from there?'

'Assuming I am right, on your first attempt to see Quong-Yü, Fate ordained that his thug should kill the wrong man; and on your second he had no chance to prevent you because you took him by surprise. We are already agreed that on being threatened by you he decided that things might be made too hot for him unless he told the truth; although no doubt he was largely influenced in that by the belief that we should give up our hunt rather than face a journey to Yen-an. Had you been in his place when he learned through his Tong members among the dock-workers that the yacht was being fuelled and provisioned for a ten-thousand mile journey, what would you have done?'

'Guessed that the hunt was still on,' replied Gregory promptly, 'then endeavoured to warn my pal Lin Wân that I had been forced to disclose Josephine's whereabouts, and that a bunch of people was setting out for China to attempt to get hold of her.'

'Exactly. And what do you think Lin Wân's reaction would be to such a warning?'

'He would curse Quong for having let him down and prepare a hot reception for us when we reached Yen-an.'

'Why should he wait till then?'

'True. He may try to make trouble for us directly he learns that we have landed in China.'

'That would be difficult, because he cannot possibly know for what part of China's immensely long coast we are making. But he might have wirelessed back to Quong instructing him to do his utmost to prevent the key members of our mission ever getting there.'

'Ah!' Gregory exclaimed with an admiring glance. 'Now I see how your mind has been working. You think Foo is one of Quong's hatchet-men and was smuggled aboard with orders to do me in. But why me? In the first instance I was a special case, because I was the link with the F.B.I.; but as soon as we left the States I once more became only an auxiliary. Your uncle is the head of the mission, and since Tsai-Ping's death Wu-ming has been the driving force behind it.'

'Regard the matter from Quong's point of view. Being acquainted with uncle Kâo he would appreciate that he is elderly, lazy and self-indulgent. He could know nothing of Wu-ming's change of spirit; and if he ordered a full inquiry into the way we spent our time while in San Francisco he would have learned that Wu-ming was neglecting his business to dance acquainted with Uncle Kâo he would appreciate that he is voyage only on my account. Whereas after his meeting with you he would have recognized that you were the brains of our party.'

'Thanks!' Gregory smiled. 'But what about that subtle brain of yours?'

She shrugged. 'I am only a woman, so he would write me off as of no importance. And he would be right to do so, for unaccompanied by a determined man I should be quite incapable of reaching Yen-an.'

'There is one assumption in your theory which I think invalidates it,' Gregory remarked after a moment. 'Except through neutral Legations, I doubt very much if anyone in the United States can now communicate by wireless with a private person in China. Quong may have sent a warning to Lin Wân by some under-cover route, but I'm quite certain he could never have got a message to the borders of Mongolia and received a reply to it before we sailed.'

'Yes, I suppose you are right about that,' A-lu-te admitted slowly. 'Still, if Quong has some big interest at stake in stopping us from reaching Josephine, he might have put Foo on board on his own initiative.'

'That is possible; but I don't believe it for one minute. In fact I'm sure that in all this you have been barking up the wrong tree from the beginning. After my talk with Foo this morning I am convinced that he is innocent.'

'How, then, can you explain the disappearance of the cocktail glass?'

'I can't; unless Wu-ming sneaked up behind you when you and the others came to see me. You were all crowded round my bed with your backs turned to the door so he could have slipped his arm past the curtain and picked it up off the dressing table with comparatively little risk of being caught.'

A-lu-te passed the point of her little pink tongue over her full lips before she said slowly, 'I should not be honest if I did not tell you that Wu-ming came with us when we left the saloon. But as you had threatened him he did not like to come into the cabin again, and waited outside to learn what we thought was wrong with you.'

'Then that settles it!' exclaimed Gregory, sitting up in bed. 'To my mind that lets Foo out entirely.'

'It does not to mine. It proves nothing, and I am convinced that Wu-ming is innocent.'

'In that case I am afraid we could argue the matter for hours without getting any further.'

'But we cannot leave things like this, otherwise another attack may be made upon you; and next time it may prove successful. The first precaution you must take is to get rid of Foo by sending him back to the stoke-hold.'

Gregory shook his head. 'That wouldn't help. In fact it might even make it easier to get me.'

'Why should you think that?'

'Because I shall stand a better chance of foiling another attack if I have a watch-dog; and this morning Foo volunteered for the job.'

A-lu-te clenched her small hands and cried, 'How can you even think of trusting this stowaway of whom we know nothing except that he brought you a drink with poison in it? You must be out of your mind!'

'I assure you I'm not. There is only one person out of his mind in this ship. That's Wu-ming, who has become so obsessed by you that his madness takes the form of wanting to murder me.'

'It is you who are obsessed by a prejudice that makes you blind to reason. You know well enough that I would not lose a wink of sleep if I never set eyes on Wu-ming again ; but since you will not accuse him and give him the chance to defend himself, in fairness I must speak for him. He is well-bred, well-educated and of a kind and gentle disposition. Violence is contrary to the very nature of such a person, and he has shown no signs whatever of madness.'

'He soon would though, given certain circumstances ; and, believe me, breeding and natural disposition count for nothing in psychological cases of this kind.'

With a slight frown, A-lu-te asked, 'What do you mean by "given certain circumstances"?'

'I mean if his obsession were sufficiently stimulated he would lose all control, and break out into a frenzy. For example, if he saw me entering your cabin at night I am sure he would force his way in and attempt to strangle me with his bare hands.'

For a moment A-lu-te considered this, then she said, 'Gregory, we cannot calmly ignore the fact that you are in great danger. Somehow we must find out who it is that menaces you. Even the risk you would run in an attack deliberately provoked would be less than that of waiting to be struck at again without warning. Do you agree?'

'Yes,' he replied, wondering what she was leading up to. 'It may sound rather boastful, but I'd back myself against most men in a scrimmage in the open.'

'Then I will tell you what I propose. Because I have at times shown impatience with Wu-ming, you must not think that I am not sorry for him. And now, I am most loath to cause him additional suffering by deliberately turning the knife in his wounded heart. But to do so seems the only way in which I can demonstrate to you that your suspicions of him are unfounded. Do you think you will be sufficiently recovered for us to put him to this test this evening?'

'Yes ; the sooner the better. I meant to get up for lunch anyhow.'

'Very well, then. After dinner I will give him real cause for jealousy. If you are right in your contention it will send him temporarily out of his mind, and he will offer you physical violence. But, if, as I anticipate, he shows only dignified distress, you must fulfil a promise that I ask of you now.'

'What do you wish me to promise?'

'That you will send Foo back to the stoke-hold.'

Gregory did some quick thinking. Such a test could not prove really conclusive either way. Wu-ming might still be guilty yet manage to keep his head. In that case the unfortunate Foo would have to be sacrificed. On the other hand, normal jealousy might drive Wu-ming to violence on this occasion without his ever having contemplated murder, and the case that A-lu-te had made out against Foo was unquestionably a strong one. All the same Gregory was still convinced that it was not Foo but Wu-ming who was trying to murder him, and if the latter did swallow the bait that would present an opportunity to put him out of action for quite a long time to come ; so he said:

'All right, I'll gamble my watch-dog against Wu-ming going berserk. Anyway it should provide us with a very interesting evening.'

11

THE PROVOCATION

AFTER A-lu-te had left Gregory, Ah-moi and the elderly doctor looked in to see him. The latter was much surprised to find that the sick man's treatment of himself had had such excellent results, but both congratulated him heartily on his recovery, then cracked the sort of jokes about his misadventure in which the Chinese unfailingly delight.

It was true enough, as they suggested, that the purge had probably done him more good than harm; as, now that the soreness in his throat and stomach had worn off, he felt as fit as ever he had been. He was by nature the lean type, and when young had held the belief that violent exercise was not only liable to strain the heart but often led to surplus fat later when hard games had to be given up. Occasional tennis, shooting, fencing, gardening and bouts of ju-jitsu had proved sufficient to keep his muscles in good trim, and he looked forward without the faintest misgiving to the night's encounter, should A-lu-te's promised provocation of Wu-ming produce one.

Lunch and the afternoon's routine of a nap, a little reading, then casual talks over the tiny tea cups with some of the officers passed off as usual. Foo, as he had himself suggested, acted as taster when presenting Gregory with his before-dinner cocktail, and over the meal A-lu-te exercised her wit with even more sparkle than was her wont, keeping her end of the table in roars of laughter. Only Gregory could guess that her bubbling chatter was largely due to suppressed excitement, and when they left the saloon he could hardly contain his curiosity to learn what means she would adopt to develop a situation.

As was their custom, with Wu-ming in attendance they retired to A-lu-te's canvas-walled sanctum in the stern; but nothing out of the ordinary was destined to happen there for some time to come, because Kâo joined them shortly afterwards. It happened that he was in a reminiscent mood and, after some general conversation, he settled down comfortably with his hands folded over his paunch to tell them of his gambling exploits, when he had taken time off from his job of Export Manager to pay visits to Deauville and Monte Carlo. On any other calm night, sitting there under the awning watching the phosphorescent wake of the ship fade away into the distance, Gregory and A-lu-te might have enjoyed listening to these tales of freak runs, lucky coups, and last-minute reversals of fortune; but as things were they could only suffer them in silence.

At length Kâo yawned prodigiously, declared himself ready for bed and asked if the others were coming. A-lu-te replied no ; she thought it would be nice to dance for a while first, and asked Gregory to put some records on her gramophone. There was nothing at all unusual in that, as since Gregory had taught her to dance in San Francisco they had kept it up with a turn or two on deck most nights when weather permitted.

Kâo wished them good night, they all stood up with the politeness of well-bred Chinese to bow him away, then Gregory started up the gramophone and took A-lu-te decorously in his arms. Again as usual at these sessions, Wu-ming settled himself a little more deeply in his chair to watch his beloved's every movement.

For three numbers, with the half-smile on her face that was habitual to her at these times, A-lu-te continued to dance sedately and, apparently, quite happily. Then, as the music stopped for the third time, she suddenly snatched herself from Gregory and rounded on Wu-ming.

Simulating anger long suppressed that had at last burst its bounds, she stormed at him, 'Why must you always sit there staring at us like that? Have you neither manners nor discretion? Out of pity I have borne with you for far too long! Are you so stupid that you cannot see when you are unwanted? Have we not made it plain enough that there are times when we wish to be alone? Get out of my sight! Go to bed! Go anywhere ; but leave us to amuse ourselves as we please!'

Gregory was filled with admiration for the act she had put on. He had feared that at the last moment she might feel squeamish about hurting Wu-ming's feelings, but she had gone the whole hog with a vengeance, and if Wu-ming failed to react there could be no putting it down to her having taken half measures. Without moving a muscle, but ready for anything, Gregory kept his eyes fixed on the Chinaman.

At A-lu-te's first onset, as much astonishment as any Celestial ever permits himself to show had appeared on Wu-ming's broad face. Then he slowly rose to his feet, bowed solemnly, and said in a half-strangled voice:

'This person was entirely unaware that his presence was unwelcome, and is deeply humiliated to realize his lack of perception. He had yet to learn that the sparrow may not delight his eyes by gazing on the bird of paradise without giving

183

offence. While hoping to receive pardon for his own short-comings, he also prays that the lady A-lu-te may never have cause to regret the deterioration in her manners which has resulted from her contact with the West.'

Bowing again, first to A-lu-te, then to Gregory, he turned and walked quietly away through the gap between the ship's rail and the end of the starboard screen.

Gregory let out a sharp breath. It was the perfect exit; a thing always to be remembered as an example of dignity maintained under great stress. He felt that their little plot had been cheap and unworthy; and it could not have failed more dismally to produce the results for which he had hoped.

Glancing at A-lu-te, he saw that two patches of rouge stood out on her high cheek bones, no longer blending harmoniously with the golden skin of her cheeks, and that even her lips had gone pale. Wu-ming's parting shot had been well-aimed, and must have hurt her cruelly. She was on the point of bursting into tears, and Gregory realized that he must do something to restore her morale without loss of a moment.

Stepping over to the gramophone, he quickly put on the record of one of her favourite tunes which fortunately lay handy, switched the machine on and, taking hold of her, swung her into a dance.

She did not resist, but her steps were automatic and lifeless. Gazing up at him with tears in her eyes, she murmured, 'How could I have done that?'

'You did it for my sake,' he told her, 'although I realize now that I never ought to have let you. Don't take what he said too badly. He knows as well as I do that at heart you are a sweet and gentle person, and would never have acted in that way of your own accord. When he has had time to think things over he'll be certain to decide that I have been nagging at you all through the voyage to get rid of him. And, anyhow, it seems you've proved your point.'

His rather specious argument appeared to afford her some consolation, as the tears ceased to well into her eyes, and after a moment she said, 'I shan't feel so badly at having lost face with him if I can regard it as the price of protecting you from Foo. You'll get rid of him now, won't you?'

'Yes,' he agreed, making an effort to keep the reluctance out of his voice. He knew that he could not possibly go back on his promise, nor, since she had carried out her part of their bargain so fully, had he any excuse for asking her to release him from it. She had made it unmistakably clear that her reason for wanting Wu-ming out of the way was so that she could be alone with him, and it struck him now that while Wu-ming had stigmatized her manners he had made no comment at all on the blatant implication of her outburst. Gregory wondered if his reticence had been due to a remarkably high degree of self-discipline, or if he had temporarily been so stunned by the violence of his dismissal that the moral aspect of the matter would not dawn upon him till later.

As the music stopped A-lu-te said, 'I don't think I want to dance any more.' But Gregory had no intention of allowing her to go to her cabin yet awhile, as he felt that if he could first cheer her up a little she would be much less likely to give way to a fit of remorse when she got there. Giving her a wicked little smile, he asked:

'Isn't it rather a pity to throw away an opportunity like this? It is a sure thing that Wu-ming won't go and tell anybody how we packed him off; not for the time being, anyhow. And as he has always spent the evenings with us, Su-sen and that dirty spy, P'ei, will be in bed by now; so we've a perfectly good excuse for not summoning one of them to act as chaperon. For once we might dance like a couple who are really enjoying themselves.'

A-lu-te knew what he meant. In the San Francisco hotels she had seen many couples tightly embraced moving as one body with cheek pressed to cheek, and had envied them their freedom to abandon themselves to the magic of the music in a way that was denied to her by the strictness of Chinese convention. The temptation was too much for her and she nodded.

Having changed the record, he took her firmly in his arms and laid his cheek against her smooth black hair. For the first time he could feel her heart beat, and for a few moments it raced a little at this unaccustomed contact, then it steadied and she gave herself up to the delight of the rhythm.

For over half an hour they danced together, speaking little,

185

but with a smoothness and enjoyment that they had never known before. Gregory was fairly satisfied that she had now got over the worst of her emotional upset, but he wanted, if possible, to send her off to bed in a really happy frame of mind. Ever since she had virtually adopted him, in the curiously mixed capacity of pseudo-slave-teacher-friend, he had deliberately refrained from paying her any compliments on her physical attractions, in order to avoid giving her any grounds for mistakingly supposing that he was falling in love with her. But now, knowing how much women appreciate such things, he thought he might pay her one without her putting any wrong construction on it. As the music stopped again, he said:

'You know, your hair feels as smooth as satin, and it smells heavenly.'

They still had their arms about one another, and turning her face up to his she replied with a smile, 'That is just the sort of nice thing one might have expected a Chinese to say. We attach so much more importance to a person's smell than you do in the West.' Her smile became mischievous as she added, 'Put your nose down next to mine, close your eyes and take a long deep breath through your nostrils.'

Returning her smile, he obeyed her, and found the sweet subtle odour that he drew in positively intoxicating. As he opened his eyes hers were laughing at him, and she said softly:

'There! That was a Chinese kiss.'

On an impulse begotten by that heady fragrance, he murmured, 'It was a new and lovely experience for me; but I still think our European kiss the more satisfying.'

Her languorous eyes went misty, and she offered him her half-parted lips. Gently he placed his mouth on hers then, gradually increasing the pressure, crushed her slender body to his own.

As he released her she gave a long happy sigh, and whispered, 'That was a new experience for me. Perhaps there are still a lot of things that we can teach one another.' Then, taking his hand, she turned to draw him down beside her on the nearby divan.

At that instant the silence was shattered by the sound of running feet. The noise was followed by a shout. Thrusting

A-lu-te behind him, Gregory swung round. Wu-ming, his face distorted by fury, was charging at him from the entrance to the lounge. Clutched with both hands above his head, he wielded one of the ship's big fire-fighting axes. For a moment it seemed that nothing could stop him from cleaving Gregory's skull from crown to chin.

There were still eight or ten feet between them; but Gregory could not jump back, or step aside. To have done so would have exposed A-lu-te. The push he had given her had sent her sprawling on the divan behind him. If he moved now the gleaming axe would come slicing down to inflict a dreadful wound on one of her knees or thighs. Instantly, he saw that his only chance lay in rushing in. By butting the Chinaman in the stomach he might halt him in mid career and send him over backwards.

With Gregory, in such a situation, to think was to act. Like a tennis player about to serve, he rose on the balls of his feet. For a second he remained poised, then, appearing to bow from the waist until his head was down to chest level, he suddenly launched himself forward. In an attempt to evade him, Wu-ming swerved while still coming on at full speed. That saved him from being rammed right on the solar plexus, but the top of Gregory's head caught him low down over his left ribs. The axe was already half way through an arc now ending at the base of Gregory's spine. Only the impact of head on ribs prevented the stroke going home. Its violence brought Wu-ming up short. His body twisted, causing the axe to turn sideways in mid-course. The weight of its steel head tore its wooden haft from his grasp. Staggering back, he let out a scream of rage as it hit the deck, slithered across it and, with a metallic clang, came to rest in the scuppers.

Gregory too had been brought up short. Raising his head, he drew back his clenched fist and slammed it into Wu-ming's stomach. With a loud grunt the Chinaman doubled up, then fell to his knees.

As he did so Foo came running round the corner of the screen. Shouting abuse he was about to fling himself on Wu-ming, but with a swift gesture Gregory checked him. During the past few awful seconds any help would have been welcome, but now he was completely master of the situation. Wu-ming was attempting to stagger to his feet; Gregory gave him time only to raise his head shoulder high, then hit him a smashing blow under the ear. He reeled over and hit the edge of a small table with his head. Sliding to the deck he lay there moaning.

Foo began to pant out an explanation of his presence. 'I was waiting about to see you safely to your cabin, Sir,' he gasped. 'Ten minutes or more ago I spotted him peering through the lacing between the screens. I knew from the music you must be dancing in here, but I didn't feel that I had the right to interfere with him watching you. I had to stay some way off, too, otherwise he would have guessed that I was keeping an eye on him. But when I saw him snatch the axe from the rack I came after him at top speed.'

'Thanks, Foo,' Gregory said, taking the will for the deed. 'Had things gone only a little differently you might have arrived in the nick of time to save me.'

With a happy grin, Foo asked, 'Shall I fetch one of the officers, Sir, to have him put in the clink?'

'No.' Gregory cast a glance at the still moaning Wu-ming. 'I mean to fix him myself. When I've done with him he won't give any more trouble. You needn't bother to wait up any longer, Foo; and you can leave us now.'

As soon as Foo had disappeared, Gregory seized Wu-ming by the arm, pulled him to his feet, and pushed him into one of the bamboo arm-chairs.

'Now!' he said, stepping back a couple of paces. 'What have you got to say for yourself?'

For a moment Wu-ming did not reply, then he struggled up from the chair, crossed his shaking hands over his middle, bowed and said in a hoarse voice, 'I have no excuse. None; except that something seemed to snap in my brain. I was watching you through the screens. I saw you . . . saw you kiss the lady A-lu-te. I endeavoured to restrain myself. For what seemed a long time I fought down a boiling of the blood within me. Perhaps it was for only a few minutes but it seemed as if my agony lasted for an hour. I forced myself to turn away. Then my eye lit upon the axe. My mind became a turmoil. I . . . I no longer knew what I was doing.'

'Well, well! Just think of that now.' Gregory's voice held a terrible biting sarcasm. 'And I suppose "something snapped in your brain", "the blood boiled within you", and "you no longer knew what you were doing", when you slipped the poison into my cocktail last night?'

For the second time that evening an expression of near astonishment appeared on Wu-ming's face, and he stammered, 'I . . . your cocktail! No, no. I know nothing of that.'

'You lying, murdering swine,' Gregory snarled. Then, with his clenched fist, he hit him a smashing blow right in the centre of his face.

Wu-ming's widely-spaced eyes opened to their fullest extent, as the bone of his pudgy nose crunched under the blow. With a howl of pain he fell back into the chair. The bamboos had scarcely creaked under the impact of his body before Gregory had seized him by the neck of his blouse, pulled him up, and hit him again.

Four times in quick succession Gregory lugged him to his feet then slammed him back, striking each time with savage, remorseless deliberation. His own knuckles were seeping blood from the force of his blows, but the Chinaman's face was streaming with it. Half his front teeth were loose, one of his eyes was bunged up and his jaw was broken. Between each blow he had given a yell for help, but his shouts were growing weaker when, from along the deck, the sound of running footsteps told that his cries had attracted attention.

Realizing that he must now finish matters quickly, Gregory hauled him to his feet again but, instead of striking him, grabbed his right wrist, spun him round, and twisted his arm up behind him. 'Perhaps,' he said, 'this will teach you not to have banana crates dropped on people's heads.' Then, exerting all his strength, he wrenched the arm upwards. Wu-ming let out a scream of agony, then there came the clear sharp sound of the bone snapping. With a final push Gregory sent the limp tortured body reeling back into the chair.

As he turned away he saw that A-lu-te was still sitting on the divan, but she had covered her face with her hands, and from between them there came a low moaning. Stooping towards her he said:

189

'I must apologize for giving such an exhibition of brutality in front of you. But I don't want to die just yet, and this was my one chance of putting my would-be murderer out of action.'

At that moment several people came pounding round the corner of the screen. Ah-moi was leading, closely followed by the officer of the watch and two sailors.

'What the hell is going on here?' bellowed the hefty Captain.

Gregory pointed first to the shuddering, groaning figure in the chair, then to the fireman's axe lying in the scuppers.

'He went off his head and tried to kill me. Apparently he took exception to my dancing with the lady A-lu-te; though why he should have done God alone knows, as we've danced together most nights since we first went ashore in San Francisco.'

The Captain bent over Wu-ming, and asked, 'Is what he said true?'

Still gasping with pain Wu-ming heaved himself up a little, and whispered, 'I . . . I attacked him, yes; but I did so to protect the lady A-lu-te's virtue.'

Taking a pace forward, Gregory snapped, 'Repeat that lie and I will throw you overboard.'

Ah-moi laid a large restraining hand on his shoulder and, turning to A-lu-te, said, 'Please give me your version of this most distressing affair.'

She had already taken her hands from her face. Large tears were running down her cheeks, but she replied in a perfectly controlled voice: 'It is true that Mr. Wu-ming Loo attacked Mr. Sallust with the axe, and it is quite untrue that Mr. Sallust was attempting to seduce me.'

The Captain made a sign to his officer. 'Have Mr. Wu-ming Loo put to bed, and send the doctor to him.' Then, having given a not unfriendly nod to Gregory, he bowed to A-lu-te and said in a voice that brooked no denial, 'The strain of witnessing this scene of violence must have quite exhausted you. Permit me to see you to your cabin.'

For the time being that was the end of the matter, and a few minutes later, although it was only just half-past ten, Gregory was getting ready to turn in. As he settled himself in bed, and relived his third narrow escape from death within three weeks, he thought, not for the first time, that it was better to be born lucky than rich. To have pu Wu-ming out of the game was a considerable relief ; but he was a little worried about the effect that this brutal treatment of his enemy might have had on the delicate susceptibilities of A-lu-te, and the possibility that a formal inquiry would be held, at which Wu-ming would insist, in his own defence, that he had actually caught her 'slave' in the act of kissing her.

It transpired that he need not have concerned himself on either count. Next morning A-lu-te greeted him as usual with a smile, and made no mention whatever of the previous evening's events. Apparently, with the practical philosophy of the Chinese, she had accepted the outcome of their plot as one of those passionate eruptions which occasionally disturb the river of life without preventing its flowing on. Captain Ah-moi's attitude was somewhat similar. Having sent for Gregory he said he regarded Wu-ming's outbreak as most regrettable, but that fortunately it had no ill results except to himself ; and that, since Gregory had already administered rough justice to his attacker, he hoped that he would spare all concerned further embarrassment by leaving matters as they stood.

Bearing in mind the facts that Ah-moi knew nothing whatever about the poisoned cocktail or the affair of the banana crates, but that he could not have failed to observe Wu-ming's morbid passion for A-lu-te, so had good grounds for believing him to have been the victim of a temporary aberration, the line the Captain took could not be considered as an attempt to evade his responsibilities. The suggestion that sleeping dogs should be allowed to lie could not have suited Gregory better, and by readily falling in with it he earned both Ah-moi's esteem for not bearing malice and his gratitude for being freed from having to give further time to the affair, as other matters of major importance were now calling for his attention.

It was their sixteenth day out of San Francisco ; so the yacht was now about to cross the major shipping lane that ran down from the great Japanese ports of Yokohama and Nagasaki to Singapore, and thence to Europe. While crossing the great wastes of the Pacific they had sighted less than half-a-dozen ships ; but now they might expect to encounter several during the course of a single day and, although they were still well outside any of the war zones, Captain Ah-moi evidently thought the time had come to take precautions against unwelcome questioning.

The first of these struck Gregory as a great piece of impudence, but he was in no situation to prevent it. As soon as their interview was over, Ah-moi asked him to come aft and there, with his own hands, he ran up the White Ensign. Turning to Gregory with a beaming face, he said:

'There! Previously when sailing in dangerous waters I have always flown the Stars and Stripes, but as I happened to have this in my collection of flags I thought it would be a nice compliment to you. It should prove just as effective and I am proud to sail under it, for your British sailors are the finest in the world.'

'I . . . er, appreciate the honour,' Gregory replied with a somewhat unhappy smile. 'But isn't it a bit risky? I mean, you might get into serious trouble if we happen to run into a British warship.'

'That is true, but very unlikely so far from both Hong Kong and Korea as we shall be during the next few days. And the risk is well worth running. You see, apart from her superstructure, this ship still has the lines of a destroyer, and the range of deck cabins might have been added to convert her into a survey or supply ship; so in the eyes of all but experts she will pass as an auxiliary of the Royal Navy. In consequence, should I refuse to disclose our business or destination in reply to signals, very few Captains would dare to hold us up.'

As this was just the sort of trick that, in similar circumstances, Gregory might himself have played, his disapproval gave place to a sneaking admiration; and, as the day progressed, he had ample opportunity further to admire the capabilities that Ah-moi displayed for blockade running. He ignored junks and other sailing vessels, but each time a smudge of smoke appeared on the horizon he promptly altered course. Once, when two steamers were sighted approaching one another, so that they would pass somewhere ahead of the yacht, he even turned her right round and ran back on his track for half an hour.

192

These numerous changes of course naturally slowed down the yacht's progress westwards, but by later afternoon they were approaching a group of tiny islets called the Tokaras about a hundred and thirty miles south of the southernmost tip of Japan. Just before sundown they made a landfall and altered course slightly to pass between two of them.

Meanwhile, as neither the outline of the ship, nor the flag she was flying, would be visible in the darkness, other precautions had been going forward against her being halted and boarded during the night. At Ah-moi's orders the portholes of all the deck cabins and the upper lounge had been screened, A-lu-te was informed that for the future she must not use her sanctum in the stern after dark, and even the navigation lights were not switched on ; so the yacht was totally blacked out.

Wu-ming had not emerged from his cabin all day and Gregory expected that, even if his injuries permitted him to get up, he would remain there for the rest of the voyage rather than expose himself to the loss of face inevitable as a result of his beating. The doctor was treating him with a fearsome mixture of magical formulae and herbal remedies ; so, although Gregory knew that the age-long experience the Chinese had had with herbs made many of their ointments valuable, he was not surprised to learn that his victim was still in very poor shape.

However, no open mention of Wu-ming was made over dinner ; and after it, as A-lu-te was to grace the upper deck lounge that night, some of the officers had got up a concert for her entertainment. Gregory was rather bored, as he had never been able to acquire an appreciation of Chinese music ; but out of politeness he sat through it till it ended at about half-past eleven, and after a little desultory conversation they all went down to turn in. The sky was overcast ; so it was very dark, and the ship was proceeding at only half speed through a calm sea. As they dispersed to their cabins and their chatter subsided, Gregory remembered afterwards noticing how almost unnaturally silent the ship became.

At the bridge end of the range of deck cabins there were two bathrooms. The one on the port side was reserved for the passengers and that on the starboard for the senior officers ; apart from Ah-moi, who had his own. It so happened that something had gone wrong that morning with the hot-water supply to the passengers' bathroom, and it was not until Gregory was about to go down to dinner that Foo told him that the repair had been completed ; so he had not had a bath that day. As the night was so sultry, and it had been very stuffy in the blacked-out lounge, he decided to freshen himself up with a dip before going to bed.

Gregory's cabin was at the extreme end of the port range and Wu-ming occupied the one next to him. As he passed it on his way to have his bath no sounds from it attracted his attention ; neither did he expect to hear any, as it was reasonable to suppose that by that hour the wretched man had been given a few pipes of opium and gone to sleep. The next three cabins were those of engineer officers, then came Kâo's, and lastly that of A-lu-te, who had been given the one next to the bathroom.

Having run a luke-warm bath, Gregory splashed about in it for a time then lay still while a variety of thoughts drifted through his mind. The sound of A-lu-te moving about next door came faintly to him, and he wondered a little uneasily if the kiss he had given her the previous night was going to upset their happy relationship. As was not unnatural in a virile man towards an unattached girl who was charming in both mind and body, and in whose company he had spent many weeks, he already felt attracted to her in a way that was not wholly platonic ; but Erika's death was still too near for him to be capable of falling in love with anybody. As far as A-lu-te was concerned, he felt that if she had really fallen for him she would have given some clear indication of it much sooner, but her ready response to his ill-considered impulse had shown that she was equally attracted to him. It looked therefore as if, given further encouragement, she might easily become seriously enamoured of him. That, he felt, would be most unfair to her, and, in view of Chinese convention should they be caught in a compromising situation, highly dangerous for them both. Obviously, therefore, he must watch his step, and, if she made any reference to what had occurred between them, even at the risk of temporarily hurting her, pass the matter off as a piece of fooling that had no significance.

Having taken this decision, he got out of the bath, and dried himself. He had just finished when he heard a shout. As he listened there came another and it sounded like a cry for help. Wriggling into his dressing-gown, he slipped on his shoes, pulled open the door and stepped out on deck.

Outside it was pitchblack, except for one bright streak of light some fifty feet away. As far as he could judge it came from Wu-ming's cabin. Hurrying towards it he saw that the door was wide open and its interior masked only by the curtain.

'Are you all right?' he called. There was no reply, so he jerked the curtain aside. Wu-ming's bed-clothes were tumbled on the floor, but he was not there.

Gregory was still grasping the curtain when a figure came running up out of the darkness. It was little Foo, and on seeing the cabin empty, he exclaimed:

'Then it was Mr. Wu-ming! I think he's thrown himself overboard.'

Two more figures appeared, coming from round the end of the range of cabins. They were Kâo and his man P'ei.

'Did you see what happened?' Gregory asked quickly.

'No,' Kâo wheezed, gasping to get his breath. 'P'ei was reading me to sleep. We heard a shout and ran out on deck. We thought it came from our side of the ship, but there was no one there. Then we ran across to the other, but there was no one there either.'

By this time shouts and the patter of running feet were coming from all directions. Two of the engineer officers came up behind Gregory and two sailors arriving from the opposite direction only just avoided cannoning into Kâo's broad back. One of the sailors cried:

'I told you it wasn't this side! The struggle I heard took place over to starboard.'

'Who was it called for help?' asked one of the engineers.

'It must have been Mr. Wu-ming Loo,' Gregory replied. 'We all know he wasn't himself, and his cabin's empty.'

'He's thrown himself overboard,' Foo said again. 'I feel sure I heard a splash just after those two cries.'

'What's all this? What's happening here?' boomed Ah-moi's rich voice, and the beam of a torch suddenly lit up the group.

It was Kâo who answered. 'No one seems to know for certain, but they say Wu-ming has jumped overboard.'

Turning, the Captain bellowed orders to the bridge for the ship to be put about and her lights switched on. Then he asked Kâo: 'Who says so?'

'He is not in his cabin,' said Gregory, 'and my man thinks he heard a splash.'

'I thought I did too, Sir,' P'ei now volunteered. 'As I was still fully dressed I was out of the cabin before Mr. Kâo Hsüan and ran on ahead of him. But I didn't see anyone.'

'Yes. I heard the splash distinctly, Sir,' one of the sailors put in. 'And before that there were two cries for help.'

'That's right,' added his mate. 'And there was a struggle.'

'How do you know?' Ah-moi asked sharply. 'You could not have seen anything, owing to the darkness.'

'I heard it, Sir. Me and my mate had just met in the stern, him coming from the port and me from the starboard. We'd been doing a round of the ship to see that no lights were showing, on orders from the Bosun. There was a trampling of feet. It was not like a man running, but a slithering sound, as if someone was being dragged across the deck.'

'That's so,' chimed in the third officer, who had just come round from the starboard side. 'I heard that sort of noise through the porthole of my cabin just after the cries had woken me. Then I heard a splash. That's why I ran aft instead of for'ard. I felt sure someone had gone overboard; so I raced to the stern and threw out a life-buoy.'

Muffled in a heavy coat the old doctor had now joined the group. In a calm voice he addressed Ah-moi. 'Captain; at night in such darkness sounds are often apt to be misleading. This evening when I visited Wu-ming his mind was much disturbed. I think the explanation of this tragedy is simple. He felt that after the humiliation he had suffered he could not face the future.'

'Then why did he cry out for help?' protested the engineer. 'I heard him do so distinctly.'

'Yes, yes!' chorused several of the others.

The look-out from the crow's-nest had just descended his ladder. He said gruffly, 'I heard the cries, Sir, and focused my

196

night glasses on to the deck. It was so dark down here that I couldn't see much, except the splash when he went over the side. But I got the impression a moment before that he was struggling with someone.'

'If you are right, this is no case of suicide,' said Ah-moi tersely. 'Somebody threw him over.'

'No!' exclaimed Kâo in a shocked voice. 'I cannot believe it! For taking his own life he had good cause; but who would wish to murder him?'

Slowly Ah-moi turned, looked hard at Gregory, and muttered, 'Last night . . .' He broke off there, but everyone present knew what had happened, and guessed his thought.

A pregnant silence fell. The ring of flat, broad Chinese faces about Gregory took on a new, menacing look, and he found himself the focus of a score of black, accusing eyes. All of them had found him already on the scene of the tragedy when they arrived. With a sudden sinking feeling in the pit of his stomach, he now recalled that the night before, in Ah-moi's presence, he had actually threatened to throw Wu-ming overboard. It was now as clear as if they had cried it aloud that they believed him to be Wu-ming's murderer; and he had no alibi.

12

THE CAPTIVE

IT was a very nasty situation. The atmosphere had suddenly become so hostile to Gregory, that for a moment he feared that the angry Chinese might close upon him and throw him overboard to join Wu-ming. But Ah-moi dissolved the group by giving a sharp order:

'All men on duty will return to their posts. Passengers, officers and servants are to go to the upper deck lounge and wait for me there.'

As they turned away Gregory saw A-lu-te on the fringe of the group. She had been there for some minutes and heard most of what had been said, but she did not speak to him. Up in the lounge he spent a most anxious twenty minutes. Everyone was clearly averse to discussing the tragedy further for the moment; so an awkward silence prevailed while the ship slowly circled on the chance that Wu-ming might be spotted. His weak condition and broken arm made it most unlikely that he had been able to keep himself afloat for more than a few minutes; so none of them was surprised when Ah-moi came in and announced that the attempt had been abandoned as hopeless.

The Captain sat down at one of the tables and questioned everyone in turn. When he came to Foo he asked what he had been doing on deck at that hour of the night; but Foo's explanation was quite adequate. He said that as he had nothing in common with the crew, and much disliked their crowded quarters, he had taken his sleeping mat up to a sheltered corner abaft the stern funnel; and Gregory confirmed that his servant had formed the regular habit of sleeping on deck.

Nothing fresh emerged from anything the others had to say and, with a stony stare at Gregory, Ah-moi summed matters up:

'At night in pitch darkness a wrong interpretation may easily be put upon sounds heard from a distance. Wu-ming admittedly had grounds for making away with himself, and the cries for help that were heard may, perhaps, have been made by him after he struck the water. But we cannot ignore these reports that a struggle took place and you, Mr. Sallust, were discovered within a few yards of the spot at which he must have gone overboard. The brutality with which you treated him last night showed the depths of your hatred for him; and even after it you threatened him with death. It is——'

Suddenly A-lu-te interrupted him. She spoke quietly but firmly. 'Honoured Sir. Permit me to inform you that there is no basis for speculating further on those lines. Mr. Sallust can

198

have had nothing to do with this. I too heard those cries for help, and at the moment they were uttered Mr. Sallust was with me in my cabin.'

In the shocked silence that followed one could have heard a pin drop. Her compatriots stared at her with fascinated horror. It was Gregory who first found his tongue and, determined to deny her statement whatever the cost to himself, he began:

'The lady A-lu-te is most generously——'

But Kâo cut him short and shouted him down. Turning on his niece, he cried furiously, 'Have you no shame, girl! Such a lapse from virtue even if confessed in private would call for the severest punishment. But to proclaim it publicly shows such abandon that I've a mind to turn you over to the stokers in the hold!'

A-lu-te was very pale; but she stood up, turned upon him with a withering glance, and declared firmly, 'Any shame that there is in this lies with my honourable uncle for entertaining such unworthy thoughts. Mr. Sallust told me he meant to have a bath. He had promised to lend me one of the books he bought while in San Francisco. When he came out of the bathroom I heard him pass my cabin; and as I did not feel like sleep, I called to him to bring me the book. He returned with it, opened the door of my cabin and handed it to me. He was on his way out when we heard Wu-ming's cries.'

Turning again, she bowed to Ah-moi and, a picture of injured innocence, walked with head held high out of the lounge.

There was a moment's awkward silence, but it was at once clear that no one present had the least doubt about the validity of her testimony. Ah-moi stood up, glanced round and said:

'What the lady A-lu-te has told us must remove from our minds all suspicions that any of us may have entertained about Mr. Sallust. And, as far as we know, no one else on board had any motive for desiring the death of Mr. Wu-ming Loo. I think we must now accept it that those who thought they heard sounds of a struggle were mistaken, and that he took his own life.'

Gregory had been of that opinion all along; but it was with very considerable relief that he went down to his cabin, as, had it not been for A-lu-te's lie, at best he must have remained a suspected murderer, which would have rendered his position in the ship next to intolerable.

The following morning, although the sea had become rather choppy, he went along with her to her stern lounge as usual, and as soon as they were seated, with Su-sen just out of ear-shot on the far side of the screen, he said in a low voice, 'I'm most terribly grateful for what you did last night. I need hardly assure you that I'm completely innocent of Wu-ming's death ; but things looked pretty black against me, and for a time I was afraid Ah-moi meant to take some action against me merely on suspicion.'

'I know you too well to believe you capable of so horrible a crime against a helpless man,' she answered slowly. 'That was why I lied to clear you. All the same, I am convinced that Wu-ming was murdered.'

'Whatever leads you to think that?'

'The sounds of a struggle were not accounted for.'

'In his weak and semi-delirious state he may have fallen on his way to the rail, then dragged himself to it before climbing over.'

'What about the sailor up in the crow's-nest? He said he thought he saw a struggle going on through his night glasses.'

'He must have imagined it. And Ah-moi was right last night when he wound up by saying that, apart from myself, no one had any motive for killing Wu-ming. Besides, if anyone had wanted to drag him out of his cabin and throw him overboard they would have waited until about three in the morning, when everybody but the watch would have been sound asleep.'

'Not necessarily. If someone had chanced to run into the murderer just after the deed, at that hour, it would have been very difficult for him to explain his presence in that part of the ship. As it was done while most of us were still awake there were half a dozen people on the scene within two minutes. That enabled the murderer to mingle with them and the explanation of his presence became as plausible as anyone else's.'

Not for the first time Gregory admired her capacity for sound reasoning. 'That's a point to you,' he admitted. 'But it doesn't mean a thing unless you can name someone who might have had a motive for killing him.'

'I am convinced that it was Foo,' she replied quietly.

'What ; my poor Foo again !' he laughed. 'Really, you seem to have quite a fixation about him. Next you'll be trying to persuade me that after all it was he who put the poison in my cocktail.'

'I'd wager my pearls against a string of false ones that he did.'

'D'you mean to tell me that in spite of the way our test of Wu-ming turned out you still believe him to have been innocent?'

'Yes. I went yesterday morning with Su-sen to inquire after him. At first he was most loath to allow me to enter his cabin ; but believing that sooner or later he would have to suffer the humiliation of coming face to face with me I thought it better that he should get it over as soon as possible, and while his injuries still made him an object for sympathy. You see, whatever he may have done he was driven to it by his passion for myself. In the eyes of a woman that excuses almost anything ; and I was greatly ashamed of having made his love for me the vehicle of his undoing. To restore his face I said that I had come to ask his pardon. We talked then for some time. His distress at having lost control of himself was very great, but, as he honestly believed that you were about to seduce me, understandable. Then he asked me to explain why you had accused him of putting poison in your cocktail. I told him, and he vowed that up till that moment he had not even known that you believed the cocktail to have been the cause of your illness. That led to my telling him about the banana crates. Again, he swore by his ancestors that your suspicions of him were entirely without foundation. His indignation at being thought capable of such crimes appeared so genuine that I could not help but believe him.'

After a moment, Gregory said, 'Knowing what a kind heart you have, I can quite understand how you felt about him, but I'm sure you let it influence your judgment. After all, having received your forgiveness about the last affair, was it likely that he would voluntarily blacken himself in your eyes by

201

making admissions about the earlier ones? In any case, he would not have dared to do so. For him to have done anything short of denying everything would have been virtually a confession that he murdered his uncle; and if you had passed that on to your uncle, when we got back to the island Mr. Wu-ming Loo would have been for the high-jump.'

A-lu-te shook her dark head. 'Your argument is a good one, but not good enough to make me alter my opinion. And if I am right it must have been Foo who attempted to poison you.'

'Hang it all, that doesn't make sense! Two nights ago when I was being attacked by Wu-ming, Foo came to my rescue.'

'No; since he was spying on Wu-ming he ought to have been able to prevent the attack taking place at all. As it was he waited, no doubt hoping that Wu-ming would kill you for him. It was not until Foo saw that you had disarmed Wu-ming that he disclosed his presence and cleverly gave the impression that he had rushed in to help you.'

'I think you are being unfair to Foo. The crisis occupied only a few seconds, and after he saw Wu-ming snatch the axe from the bracket he had quite a way to run.'

'Gregory, believe me!' A-lu-te leaned forward earnestly. 'It is Foo who is the evil genius on this ship. I am convinced that he is Quong-Yü's agent, and was put on board to wreck our chances of ever reaching Josephine. They got Tsai-Ping out of the way in San Francisco. Then, as the next most feared opponent to their plans, Foo tried to murder you. He failed, but seized the opportunity of Wu-ming's being incapable of defending himself to eliminate him. Next he will make another attempt on you, or perhaps on Uncle Kâo.'

'My dear, you really are letting your imagination run away with you. There is not one atom of proof to support your theory. On the other hand we proved conclusively that Wu-ming's jealousy of me had become such an obsession that he would have killed me if he could. Besides, Foo is such a little chap. He hasn't the strength to drag a struggling man out of his cabin, round the corner, across the deck, and chuck him overboard.'

'He might have gone into Wu-ming's cabin and stunned him

202

with a blow on the head. After that the physical effort would not have been beyond him.'

'If Wu-ming had been unconscious he could not have called for help.'

'He might have come round at the last moment.'

Gregory sighed. 'I'm sorry; but having come to know young Foo so well, and the mildness of his disposition, I simply cannot believe it. If you are really so set in your idea that Wu-ming was murdered, it would be more plausible to suggest that it was your uncle and P'ei who threw him overboard. Foo and I encountered them a moment after we had met; so they were already on the scene just as much as he was.'

'Uncle Kâo could have had no possible reason for murdering Wu-ming.'

'Exactly. And I don't suggest for one moment that he did. I don't believe anyone else did, either. He was obviously unhinged when he attacked me, and having made such a mess of things all round must have decided him to commit suicide.'

For some time longer they argued the matter without getting any further. A-lu-te again begged Gregory to get rid of Foo, but he felt that it would be most unjust to give in to her; so he stuck out against it. Yet two nights later another affair, pregnant with uncertainties and sinister possibilities, resulted in his having to do so.

During the two intervening days they zigzagged about the East China Sea making fair progress in a generally north-westerly direction; but the weather had at last turned against them, and it seemed as though Wu-ming's unhappy end had been the signal for both nature and circumstances to prevent Gregory and A-lu-te deriving further pleasure from the voyage.

In a private explanation with her uncle, although their code made it impossible for him to apologize to her, he tacitly admitted to having allowed righteous indignation at her admission to carry him away; but he insisted that for the future she should show greater circumspection in her dealings with Gregory, never spend more than a quarter of an hour alone with him, and in no circumstances whatever again allow him to enter her cabin. Added to this prohibition, driving rain and the discomforts inseparable from a high sea drove them from the stern lounge even in day-time; so, after their one talk following Wu-ming's death, they had little opportunity to exchange more than a few words, except in the presence of others.

On the second night of the storm they had both gone to bed early, leaving Kâo up in the lounge with the Chief Engineer, happily engaged in a game of spillikins played with beautifully engraved slithers of mother of pearl, upon the skilful handling of which they were making a succession of heavy side bets.

About an hour later a piercing scream rang out above the storm. It was followed by a bellow of rage and a spate of curses. Once more, a number of people, mostly in hastily-pulled-on dressing-gowns, ran out of their cabins and swiftly converged on the place from which the commotion was coming.

This time it was Kâo. On leaving the upper deck lounge he had pitched from top to bottom of the companion-way. Owing to his weight, as, in fact, the so-called companion-way was no more than a steep narrow ladder he might easily have broken his neck; but, fortunately, he had landed feet first and had sustained nothing worse than a sprained ankle. Foo was beside him and, although endeavouring to support him, was the object of his curses.

Their accounts of what had occurred were contradictory. Kâo said that just as he was about to set foot on the ladder the ship had given a lurch; so he had put out a hand to steady himself, but before he could grasp the side rail Foo had given him a swift push. Foo maintained that, seeing Kâo stumble, and fearing he was about to fall, he had grabbed at his arm in an attempt to save him.

That Foo had a right to be where he was at the time was indisputable, as it was customary for the personal servants to take turns in helping the steward on late duty to wash up the glasses and little tea-cups last thing at night. It had been his evening on, and having just completed his task he had followed Kâo out of the lounge. But that in no way mitigated Kâo's rage, or his belief that Foo had deliberately attempted to injure, or even kill, him.

Foo was escorted away under temporary arrest, and Kâo helped to his cabin; where Ah-moi, the Chief Engineer and Gregory joined him to hold another inquiry, while the Doctor was summoned to treat his injured ankle.

As was inevitable, the unsolved mystery of Wu-ming's death came up again. The fact that Foo had been among the first to appear out of the darkness near the scene of the tragedy now seemed to hold a new and sinister significance. Kâo was quick to link the two events together, and he and his companions began to seek a common motive which might lie behind both.

Gregory could not help wondering now if A-lu-te was not right in her belief that Foo was an agent of Quong-Yü's; yet he still found it next to impossible to believe that such a happy-natured, pleasant young fellow could be a professional assassin. In consequence he refrained from further prejudicing Foo's case by telling the others about the poisoned cocktail, or informing them of A-lu-te's theory.

Nevertheless, their deliberations led them to formulate a new theory which, in essentials, was not far from hers. They argued that as Foo was a young man of some education, about whose background they knew nothing, he might quite probably be a Communist; and that to reach Communist China might well have been his reason for stowing away, rather than the laudable one he had given of wanting to perform the rites at the tombs of his ancestors. During the early part of the voyage he could easily have picked up from members of the crew some garbled version of the mission on which they were engaged. Like all the other islanders, the crew had expected the Princess Josephine to return as their new Empress with Kâo after his first trip to San Francisco. It could hardly have been kept from the stewards, in snatches of overheard conversation, that they were still searching for her. Possibly Foo had misinterpreted the little he had learned and reached the conclusion that they meant to use the Princess as a figure-head for a counter-revolution in China. If so, and he was a Communist fanatic, that would account for his attempts to do away with the principal persons of the mission before it could land and begin operations against the so-called People's Republic.

Without Gregory being consulted, the discussion was terminated by Ah-moi's declaring that he intended to keep Foo in the cells until the yacht returned to the island and he could be dealt with there as had always been intended. Turning to Gregory he added that instead of Foo he could have Che-khi, who had originally been Tsai-Ping's servant, and until recently Wu-ming's, to look after him. They then wished Kâo peaceful sleep and left him to sniff up the scented blue smoke of the joss-sticks that the Doctor had lit to protect him against further calamity.

A-lu-te was already sound asleep at the time of her uncle's fall and, owing to the boisterousness of the wind, had not been roused by the commotion that followed it; so she knew nothing of the matter till she was told of it by Gregory and two officers with whom he was sitting, when she entered the lounge next morning. When she learned of Ah-moi's decision to keep Foo locked up indefinitely, she gave Gregory a quick look which showed how heartily she endorsed the Captain's judgment; but she refrained from putting forward her own theory, that Quong-Yü had planted Foo on board.

With the coming of daylight the storm had eased; and now that they were in the middle of the East China Sea they no longer had occasion to pursue a zigzag course, as they had passed well beyond the great shipping lanes. Next day they again had to proceed with caution, as they were entering the arc followed by coastal traffic, and Gregory was amused to see that Ah-moi had substituted the Hammer and Sickle of the Soviet Union for the White Ensign; but they met with no misadventure. On leaving their cabins the following morning —their twenty-first out from San Francisco—they saw the yacht had at last arrived off the coast of China.

It was far from an inviting prospect, as not a single house or tree broke the low, desolate coastline; but that suited their purpose. By eleven o'clock the ship was moving slowly up a broad estuary about seven miles wide, and Ah-moi summoned his passengers to the bridge to show them on a chart the place to which he had brought them.

They were entering the old mouth of the Hwang-ho, which lies about two hundred miles north of Shanghai, and from which the nearest towns of any consequence, Haichow and Hwaianfu, are a good fifty miles distant. Until just over a hundred years ago the lower reaches of the mighty two thousand five hundred mile long river had flowed through the province of Kiang-Su to issue there, but in 1852 a terrible flood had caused it to burst its banks just below the city of Kai-feng. Causing appalling devastation, it had taken a new course so that it had since poured into the sea hundreds of miles further north, on the far side of the great Shan-Tung peninsula.

As Ah-moi explained, the lower reaches of the old river were no longer navigable; so all commercial activities on it had died and its once prosperous towns had dwindled to villages. But it still carried off the local rains, and in some stretches it had been converted into a canal; so boats could proceed up it to the city of Kai-feng, near which it joined the true river. From there they could proceed onward by boat to the city of Tung-kwan, from which they would have to finish their journey by caravan.

The two stages of the water journey were of about three hundred and fifty and two hundred and fifty miles respectively; so it would have been very much quicker to make for the nearest railway and take a series of trains to Tung-kwan; but that would mean having frequently to show papers, and a constant risk of being detained by some Communist official who proved unbribable, whereas the junks and sampans that frequented the great waterways were so numerous that their occupants were rarely questioned.

Kâo agreed that precautions against interference must take precedence over speed, then Ah-moi went on to outline his further plans for them. His Second Officer and Third Engineer had both made two voyages to China since the Communists had seized power there in 1949; so they knew something of the new regime. He proposed that they should proceed in the launch up river to the nearest town, Antung-Ku, which lay about sixty miles inland; that there they should try to buy suitable papers, and in any case hire a motor sampan which they would bring back with them; and that they should then accompany the mission to assist in any further negotiations which might prove necessary on the journey.

To the first part of these proposals Kâo readily gave his consent, but he rejected absolutely the idea of the two officers coming with them. He pointed out that with A-lu-te, Gregory and himself, together with their three servants, the passenger capacity of an ordinary sampan would be fully occupied, and damnably uncomfortable, without quite unnecessary crowding for such a long and tedious journey. He added tersely that having travelled the world on his own for twenty-five years he needed no young men to make his arrangements for him ; so Ah-moi did not press his suggestion further.

By midday, with many careful soundings, the yacht had nosed her way into a creek flanked by miles of desolate marshes, and dropped anchor. Soon afterwards the launch set off on its way up river, and everyone else settled down to the three or four days wait which must elapse before it could be expected to return.

Gregory, meanwhile, had been feeling a growing concern for Foo. The more he thrashed the matter over in his mind, the more convinced he became that the young man was the victim of unfortunate coincidence which had twice brought him on the scene at the time of happenings that could not be satisfactorily explained. In this Gregory knew that he was to some extent swayed by Foo's pleasant manner and, apparently, open nature, but his conclusion had a basis of strictly practical analysis. A-lu-te's theory rested on Quong-Yü's having put Foo aboard. Surely it was inconceivable that the aged and wily Tong boss should have chosen for such desperate work a youngster scarcely out of his teens. The theory of the others rested on Foo's being a Communist. Even if he were, and that was his real reason for wanting to get to China, surely it was highly improbable that single-handed he would pit himself against a whole ship-full of political enemies? Finally, in either case, if his object were to prevent the mission reaching China, why should he risk his neck by attempting to murder a few individuals, when he could have stopped the ship by going below and, not once but several times, sabotaged her engines? It did not make sense.

And there was another point that weighed with Gregory. If he had not caused Foo to be moved from the stoke-hold in the first place, the youth would never have had the same opportunities to commit the crimes of which he was now suspected. That, Gregory felt, made him more than ever responsible for ensuring that Foo should not suffer unjustly. Lastly, he had decided from the beginning that, by hook or by crook, he would see to it that Foo got ashore when they reached China. It was one thing for a man of his age, while in the depths of despair, to accept the idea of having his memory obliterated; but quite another to stand by and see a young and promising individual turned against his will into a clod-hopper.

By the evening of their first day, lying in the mouth of the Hwang-ho, he had definitely made up his mind that Foo must be given the benefit of the doubt. To plead for his release, let alone for permission for him to land, was obviously futile; but, with his long experience in such matters, Gregory did not think he would find any great difficulty in freeing him.

Towards two o'clock in the morning he left his cabin. The ship was again blacked out. As she was at anchor there was no one on the bridge, and he had already ascertained that the only people he was likely to encounter were one of the two look-out men who had been stationed at the stem and stern of the vessel.

From several strolls round the lower decks that he had made during the voyage, he knew that the cells lay under the crew's sleeping quarters in the fo'c'sle. Going down the 'midship's companion-way he walked softly for'ard. No one was about, and when he reached the dimly-lit passage in which the cells lay he switched on his torch. He felt certain that, except in the event of a mutiny having occurred, the keys would, for convenience sake, be kept somewhere handy; and after flashing his torch for a few minutes along the bulkheads and girders, he found them hanging on a nail driven into the side of a short ladder that led upwards.

Taking them, he moved quietly back to the double row of cells and listened at each door in turn until he detected a faint snoring. At first he knocked very gently, then a little louder, until he heard the sounds of movement and Foo called out from behind the steel panel:

'What is it? Who is there?'

'Speak lower!' Gregory warned him quickly. 'Can you swim?'

'Yes, Sir!' came the excited reply.

'Good. Now listen carefully to everything I say. We are lying in the old mouth of the Hwang-ho. The duty officer is in his cabin and there is no one on the bridge; but there are look-outs posted fore and aft. Your best chance of getting away without being spotted is to tie a rope to the rail just abaft the bridge and lower yourself by it, so that you don't make a splash going into the water; then swim ashore as quietly as possible. Go over the starboard side and you will have only about two hundred yards to swim. You have two hours to go before the watch is changed, and nobody is likely to be moving about till then; so take your time. It never pays to rush this sort of thing. I am now going to unlock the door; but you are to count a thousand slowly—one hundred for each of your fingers and thumbs—before you leave this cell, so that I can get back to my cabin before you start. Is that all clear?'

'Yes, Sir! Yes! May Heaven bless you!'

Having tried two keys Gregory found the right one and un-locked the door. Then, softly calling, 'Good luck, Foo!' he turned away. But on reaching the short ladder he paused again, took a small label from his pocket and tied it to the bunch of keys before replacing them on their nail. Grinning broadly to himself he glided from shadow to shadow, as stealthily as he had come, back to his cabin. He had prepared the label before-hand, hoping that, if he could use it, his ruse might not only fox people but provide him with a little quiet fun. On it in red ink he had carefully drawn the Hammer and Sickle of the Soviets.

He was not disappointed. The following morning there was the very devil of a to-do. Foo's escape was regarded as a serious enough matter, but the fact that a label bearing the Com-munist symbol had been attached to the cell keys threw Cap-tain Ah-moi and his officers into a ferment. The Bosun, whose reliability none of them doubted, had been present when Foo was handed his 'evening rice' and locked up again for the night. Therefore, what possible explanation could fit the facts, other than that there was a Communist on board who had released Foo and then had the audacity to sign his exploit. Yet, as none of the crew was ever allowed ashore in foreign parts, how could the vile doctrines of Communism ever have penetrated to them? Foo had served in the stoke-hold for so short a time that he could have had little opportunity to contaminate any of the stokers. Could P'ei or Che-khi be the culprit? Had one of them become contaminated with the pernicious heresy while running errands for their masters in San Francisco?

Following ancient Chinese usage, Ah-moi had them, the look-out and half a dozen other people dragged before him on their knees with their hands tied behind their backs, and hurled terrible threats at them; but all to no avail. Even A-lu-te, who might possibly have suspected Gregory, was entirely deceived by the red herring; so except to him, the affair remained yet one more unsolved mystery.

On the fourth evening after the departure of the launch it returned. The Second Officer had secured a sampan but had brought it down only to the head of the estuary; so that when the passengers embarked its crew should not see the yacht from which they had come. The Engineer had also satisfactorily executed the commission Ah-moi had given him, as for a thousand dollars he had managed to buy a collection of papers. There were identity cards, travel permits and letters of introduction. Some were genuine, others forged, and they applied to over a score of different people; but owing to the illiteracy of most minor officials it was felt that, short of a very unlucky break, they would serve their purpose.

Since 1950 Mao Tse-Tung's government had expelled nearly all the Americans and Europeans, other than Russians, who had been living in China; so it had been agreed that Gregory should make himself less conspicuous by yellowing his face with saffron and wearing Chinese clothes. Then among the papers they had the luck to find two which had belonged to a Polish journalist. Both were out of date, but he decided that, while still adopting Chinese costume, it would be well worth carrying them as a precaution against being pulled in for a serious interrogation at which he could no longer maintain the fiction that he was a Chinaman.

Again, as a precaution against appearing conspicuous, they had decided to leave behind all rich garments, and go clad in

211

the padded coats generally worn by middle-class Chinese. This had made it easy for Su-sen to sew into their linings numerous wads of dollar currency and, against an emergency, several little packets of small diamonds.

Captain Ah-moi was anxious to get away from such dangerous waters as soon as possible ; so next morning he already had steam up. His plan was to run down to the Philippines and re-coal there, then cruise in the open Pacific for a month or more at low speed to save fuel, returning to the old mouth of the Hwang-ho at the end of the ninth week ; as it was not thought that they could accomplish their journey and get back in less than that time. If their sampan was not in the creek, he meant to sail again and cruise in the middle of the East China Sea, putting in afterwards once a week until either they appeared or sent him news of themselves.

Having said good-bye to him and his officers they went aboard the launch, which ran them up the estuary to the sampan. Its Captain was a rugged little man named Mai-lee-long and he had a crew of two. Their baggage was soon stowed ; then, after a final farewell to the Second Officer and the cadets who manned the launch, the sampan headed slowly up river.

Now that Gregory had a chance to see the cramped quarters in which they would have to live for the next three weeks, he felt that Kâo's rejection of Ah-moi's offer to send two of his officers with them had been very sensible. The sampan was one of the larger kind and, except that it was long, narrow and flat bottomed, somewhat resembled a little junk ; but it had only three small passenger cabins ; two in the stern and one in the bow. All had two-tier bunks ; so A-lu-te doubled up with Su-sen in one of those at the stern, Kâo had the other, and Gregory the one in the prow. As there was hardly room in it to swing a cat and its ceiling was so low that he could not stand upright in it, he was extremely glad that he was not called on to share it with one of the yacht's officers or, more unpleasant still, with Wu-ming, as he would probably have had to do had that unhappy gentleman still been alive.

Just forward of the after-cabins there was one fairly spacious day cabin which was raised on a half-deck. It was roofed over with bent bamboos and open at the ends, so resembled a short tunnel. Forward of it was the long open hold, normally used for cargo, and now turned over to the crew and servants who would sleep there on their mats. Aft of A-lu-te's cabin lay the galley, and aft of Kâo's a compartment in which the motor engine chugged noisily and the Captain slept.

While lying in the estuary they had sighted only a few fishing boats, but as they progressed up river these gradually became more numerous. Every few miles they now came upon a collection of rickety bamboo huts that passed for a village, and the one at which they tied up for their first night in the sampan was typical of the rest. Its poverty and squalor were indescribable. There were no solid buildings of any kind, but the lean-to's were crowded with half-naked humanity and a number of pitifully thin animals. With gaunt faces and hungry eyes the villagers stared at them, evidently quite unused to seeing even moderately prosperous travellers, while the children cried to them for alms in falsetto voices, begging even the scraps of garbage from the galley.

Late the following evening they reached Antung-Ku. As they approached they took it for no more than a larger village, until they came near enough to see that some of the buildings in its centre had two stories, and that the huddle of bamboo, tile and corrugated iron roofs, all seeming to run together with no space for streets between, covered the best part of a square mile.

Dusk was falling as they tied up alongside another sampan, which in turn was tied to a third moored to one of the tumble-down wharves. Anxious to see something of the homeland of her race, A-lu-te begged that they might go ashore, but Kâo would not hear of it till morning; so by the light of an oil lamp they whiled away a couple of hours playing one of the complicated versions of Chinese dominoes. Then they wished one another good night and went to their cabins.

Having spent some time in China between the two wars, Gregory was well aware that part of the price the traveller must pay for enjoying its colourful beauties is the waging of unceasing war against almost every form of bug that has ever plagued mankind; so before leaving San Francisco he had equipped himself with a good stock of insecticides. On stepping

213

down into the hold he saw that, gathered round a charcoal brazier, the sailors and the two servants were still talking together in low voices.

His new man Che-khi was a sedate dried-up individual, well on in middle-age, and in appearance vaguely like his original master; but, while he had no doubt suited the Mandarin, Gregory found him far from satisfactory. He was not lazy, but slow, forgetful and inclined to be unobliging; so, pausing beside him, Gregory asked if he had remembered to flit his cabin.

The man admitted that he had not, and gave as his reason that he had lent the sprayer that morning to Su-sen to do the cabin she shared with her mistress. Having told him to go and get it from her, Gregory continued on his way forward and climbed up on to the little fore-deck. From it rose a short foremast, a small hand capstan, piled sails and, surrounded by various other gear, the raised hatch that led below. As he scrambled over the sails he caught sight of a figure crouching in the shadows. Thinking it that of a thief who had just come up from his cabin, he sprang forward and seized the intruder by the shoulders. His captive made no effort to spring up or get away, but said in a swift whisper:

'It's Foo, Sir. Please! You're hurting me!'

Relaxing his grip, Gregory asked in a low voice, 'What the devil are you doing here?'

'I wanted to let you know that I got ashore safely, and to thank you,' Foo murmured in reply.

Gregory frowned. 'That was a most foolhardy thing to do. If one of the others had caught you, Mr. Kâo Hsüan might not have been able to send you back, but he would have had you beaten to within an inch of your life.'

'I had to chance that, Sir. It took me three days to walk here, but on the last day I saw the launch going down river with this sampan and I felt sure it was to pick you up. I've been haunting the waterfront ever since, on the look-out for its return. You see I've no money. The Bosun took my savings before they threw me in the cells. I've had to beg to keep myself alive, and I'm starving. I . . . I was hoping that you might add to your great kindness by letting me have a little money.'

214

Without a second thought Gregory took from his pocket one of the wads of notes he had been given when Kâo was distributing their funds among them. Peeling off five ten dollar bills he slipped them into Foo's hand, and said:

'That ought to keep you going for quite a time.'

'Oh, thank you!' Foo exclaimed gratefully. 'I shall now be able to afford a lodging, buy decent clothes, and get a good job. If you are staying here for long, Sir, I may be able to repay you.'

'I thought . . .' Gregory began, and had meant to continue, "that you wanted to reach the village where your parents died. Now you have money why delay in going there?" But at that moment he heard footsteps approaching along the hold; so, instead, he said hastily:

'No, we set off on our long journey up to Tung-kwan to-morrow. Quick now! Someone's coming! Make yourself scarce!'

Foo did not wait for a second warning but rose, sprang on to the prow of the neighbouring sampan, and disappeared in its shadows. Gregory went down to his cabin and a minute later Che-khi joined him there.

While he started to undress, his servant now conscientiously sprayed every corner of the small apartment with the flit gun. Then when he had done Gregory handed him a tin of powder and said:

'Scatter some of that down the sides of the bunk, and put some inside the bed as well.'

Obediently Che-khi carried out the first part of the order, then he drew back the bed-clothes. A three-foot-long bamboo snake was lying coiled up there. Instantly, with a horrible hissing noise it reared up to strike.

13

DEATH IN A BED
AND LOVE IN A TREE-TOP

A s Gregory had elected to use the upper bunk, the snake in it had reared up level with his face. In the poky little cabin there was scarcely room to turn round ; so he was as near to it as Che-khi. Owing to the low ceiling the heads of both were bent, and turned towards it. In their cramped position there was no possibility of grabbing up some weighty object to smash down upon it, or of springing away.

The venomous-looking brute was brown in colour fading to a yellowish hue where its belly showed as it raised itself to strike. Its eyes were small points of black that glittered brightly, reflecting the light of the oil lamp. Its forked tongue flickered with lightning speed, and its flattish ugly head swayed from side to side.

Gregory, aware that the reptile's brain was smaller than a rabbit's, knew that, without discrimination, it would strike at the first moving thing within its range of vision. Feeling behind him, he clutched the padded coat he had just taken off meaning to swing it up in front of the snake. Before he could do so Che-khi lost his nerve. With a high-pitched scream he turned to fly. Instantly the snake's head darted forward and it fixed its fangs in his neck.

Taking a chance, Gregory dropped the coat and seized the snake a few inches below its head. The force of its bite was already spent, so it was easy to drag it from the reeling China-man ; but its jaws opened wide, its tongue flickered madly, and, like a length of electrified steel wire, it thrashed about in violent efforts to snap home its poison-filled teeth into Gregory's arm.

Fortunately he still had his heavy Chinese boots on. Hold-ing its head well away from him, he lowered it towards the floor and, as its writhing body whipped from side to side upon the boards, he stamped upon it with first one foot then the other, until its vertebrae were broken in half-a-dozen places and, half pulped, it at last lay still.

Che-khi, meanwhile, had collapsed across the floor, and lay there groaning. Pulling him aside Gregory ran up the few steps to the deck and shouted for help. P'ei, Mai-lee-long, and the two coolies who made up the crew hurried to his assistance.

Between them they got the stricken man up into the air. The sampan captain squeezed as much poison from the wound as he could, then declared that Che-khi must be got swiftly to a doctor, and that he knew of one who lived no great distance away. As in cases of snake bite it is most important to keep the victim's heart going and in no circumstances allow him to fall asleep, they first forced a good measure of rice spirit down his throat ; then, instead of carrying him, they took him by the arms and dragged him, stumbling, across the intervening sampans on to the wharf. Gregory approved their treatment ; but, as the bite was in Che-khi's neck, and so near the brain, he had no great hopes of his surviving it. Very thoughtfully and greatly depressed, he went to bed.

His judgment of men had rarely been at fault, but he now felt that in Foo's case it had. Foo's having been on the spot only a few minutes before a snake had been found in his bed was one coincidence too many. Snakes always sought warm places in which to sleep and now that September had come the nights were beginning to get chilly ; so it was just possible that the deadly visitor had found its own way under the coverings of the bunk ; but the odds seemed all upon its having been deliberately secreted there.

For a long time Gregory puzzled unhappily over the affair, and he still could not hit upon any logical reason why Foo should want to kill him. Either theory, that he was Quong-Yü's agent or a Communist fanatic, might be correct, but neither was really convincing ; and to continue his attempts after all that Gregory had done for him displayed an ingratitude of such baseness that it was hardly conceivable. The only explanation seemed to be that, although he appeared to be perfectly sane, he was actually a madman.

In the morning Gregory said nothing to Kâo or A-lu-te of his having run into Foo on the sampan the previous night ; for to have done so would have necessitated his having either to invent a reason given him by Foo for being on the sampan or disclose the fact that it was he who had enabled Foo to escape from the yacht. But, of course, they had both heard about the snake being found in Gregory's bunk ; and, as soon as they had eaten, the three of them went ashore, with P'ei as guide, to the doctor's house to inquire after Che-khi.

They were distressed, but not surprised, to learn that he had died shortly after having been brought in. Kâo left enough money for him to be given a respectable burial, and in a chastened mood they enquired their way to the market to buy food for the day's journey.

Behind the screen of sampan masts, wharfs, and dwellings on stilts that fringed the waterfront, there were no squares or open spaces. The town was a warren of twisting lanes with the buildings on either side so close together that, even in midday, the sun could not penetrate to the garbage-littered cobbles. Men, women and children swarmed along them like locusts in a bean field. Most of them still wore old-fashioned blue cotton tunics and baggy trousers, and went bare-headed ; but in the better part of the town quite a number of women had taken to skirts and blouses, and more of the men were wearing shoddy cloth suits with flat European style caps. Here and there a more elderly man was dressed like Kâo and Gregory, in a long padded coat, and a round woollen skull-cap surmounted with a pom-pom. Shouting children darted through the throng in all directions, some clad only in a rice sack with holes in it for arms and legs, others stark naked. The smell was indescribable ; a mixture of garlic, ginger, cinnamon, sweat and still more unpleasant things, as old and young alike freely relieved themselves in any odd corner whenever they felt so inclined.

The shops in the main bazaar were little more than cupboards ; and although they were crammed with articles for sale the entire stock in most of them could have been bought for less than fifty pounds. Such was the poverty of the place that nothing seemed too worn or broken to be worth a few *cash,* and among a collection of junk on one old man's stall Gregory noticed carefully laid out a dozen rusty nails. About all the booths, however, there was one thing in common. Every one of them had prominently displayed posters bearing portraits of Mao and Chou En-lai. That was enough to show how strong the Communist hold had become upon the country; but the only other evidence of it they saw was two policemen clad in ill-fitting khaki jackets and with red stars on their peaked caps.

The purchase of the food did not take long, and by half-past nine they were back aboard the sampan, which soon afterwards set off up river. As they were leaving the town behind, they passed several boats with long poles protruding from their sides, upon each of which were perched several large birds. When Gregory enquired about them, Kâo told him that the birds were tame cormorants used by the boatmen for fishing. At a signal the birds dived noiselessly into the water and snapped up a fish, gulping it down into their pouches; but they were prevented from swallowing it by a leather strap round their throats, so the fisherman was afterwards able to make them disgorge their catch. Kâo went on to say that fish was the poor man's meat in China, so that at the season of the floods they even stocked their paddy-fields with them; and that it was also such a favourite food with the rich that over fifty varieties of carp alone had been bred, while of all kinds there were enough for anyone to eat a different sort every day for a year.

As their journey progressed, Gregory was to be thankful for that, as fresh meat was not easy to obtain in the villages where they tied up for the night, and the quantity of tinned goods they had been able to bring with them from the yacht was limited.

Their progress seemed maddeningly slow, as the sampan rarely covered more than thirty miles a day, and at times their irritation at its lethargic pace was increased by the motor breaking down or their running on to a mud bank. The monotony of the scenery added to the wearisomeness of the journey as there was rarely anything of interest to look at. Sometimes the river was as wide as a lake, with only a lane of rotting poles to mark the channel through the treacherous shallows; at others it became hardly more than a stream winding through a broad depression between distant slopes of higher ground which had been its banks in the days of its greatness. At times it dwindled to a useless trickle; but from point to point, by-passing these stretches, canals had been cut in a straight line to link up its navigable waters. Yet whatever the state of the river the scene beyond its banks remained much the same.

Despite the apparent bareness of the landscape, it was never deserted. Scores, and sometimes hundreds, of China's teeming millions who drew a meagre living from her soil were always to be seen. Some in flat straw hats tending their rice fields; others with a yard-square net suspended from four curved sticks attached to a pole, patiently dipping from the river bank for enough small fishes to make a meal; others again ploughing with lean cattle, or, as a family group, dragging the plough themselves. Occasionally a two or three-tiered pagoda could be seen on the horizon, or, nearer to, a circular thatched open-sided erection like a summer house, in the shade of which a bullock was moving slowly round and round, drawing water up to irrigate a field.

The waterway too never stretched emptily ahead. There was always another sampan in sight or a few crudely-made punts and rowing boats, many of the latter with owners who could not afford proper oars, so propelled themselves with two stout stakes to the ends of which they had tied short lengths of board from an old packing-case. And every mile or so there was another village, each indistinguishable from the last, a festering sore under the still scorching autumn sun, with its quota of wrinkled crones grown old before their time, old men whose ribs stood out like curved bars under the taut yellow skin, cripples with sickeningly-distorted limbs, and children whose eyes were crawling with flies.

For six days the sampan wound its way bewilderingly round a series of bends that led south, west and north, but actually made a great arc ending in a fairly straight course somewhat north of westward; and on their seventh day out from Antung-Ku they came to Su-chow, where they went ashore on another shopping expedition.

Like most Chinese cities it had suffered sadly from brutal bombings by the Japanese, who had brought more havoc there in a few days than the sackings of a hundred Chinese War Lords had done in fifty centuries. Most of its modern buildings and many of its ancient ones had been destroyed, and during the years of war and strife that followed there had not been the resources to rebuild them; but as a once-flourishing city of the 'fu' rank it had a large railway station, and several good streets. Along them trams were running and lorries honked their way through hordes of cyclists and pedestrians, while occasionally a car, occupied by one or more khaki-clad officials was to be seen.

Here, in the city centre, there was ample evidence of the new regime. From nearly all the brick and concrete buildings fluttered the five-starred flag of the People's Republic; the big gold star in its centre representing the Communist Party, the four smaller ones the workers, peasants and—typical of the Chinese mentality but hardly in keeping with that of Karl Marx—the bourgeoisie and 'patriotic' capitalists, respectively. Huge posters carrying propaganda slogans by the so-called 'Liberators' occupied nine-tenths of the hoardings, and at nearly every street corner stood a khaki figure armed with a revolver. As the place seethed with life there was no great risk of the shopping party being singled out and asked to show their papers; but, all the same, they made their purchase of a new supply of tinned goods, and got away from the main streets as soon as possible.

In the meaner parts of the city little evidence of bombing remained. The flimsy houses had burnt like tinder and wherever a shower of incendiaries had fallen whole districts had been consumed by roaring sheets of flame. The loss of life had been appalling, but the rapidity with which the Chinese breed had soon restored the numbers of the population; and as most of the houses had only paper-covered walls of bamboo or rice-straw, the devastated areas had resumed their age-old appearance within a few months.

While passing down one street they had to stand aside to let a funeral procession go by. It was preceded by men carrying gaudy banners of all shapes and sizes; then came the score of professional mourners in white, bearing, by long poles on their shoulders, a lacquered and gilded casket as large as a small room, with a sacred crane on top to fly away with the dead man's soul; and lastly, among the crowd of wailing people who followed it, were two youths almost buried under stacks of imitation paper money, which would be burnt so that the deceased might be rich in heaven.

As A-lu-te wished to see more of the city, but was already tired because she had not walked any distance for so long, they hired a sedan-chair for her, and continued their explorations. The result was disappointing, for it was almost impossible to tell one section from another. One human ant-heap merged imperceptibly into the next. In every narrow bazaar the merchants were haggling with their customers over little cups of tea, or doing complicated sums on beads of a generations-old abacus. Blind beggars tapped their way along, poor wretches grovelled on the ground displaying their revolting sores as they whined for alms, and human scarecrows patiently turned over the contents of the dustbins, hoping to come upon some edible morsel, or a broken crock that they might piece together and sell.

Now and then a soothsayer called to them from his booth to come and have their fortunes told ; or a usurer, with hundreds of copper *cash* strung on strings dangling from his neck, and great wads of People's Republic dollar bills—which could be bought by the thousand for a £1 note—eyed them speculatively. In nearly every place where alleys intersected and the buildings were more than twenty feet apart a juggler, conjurer or pair of acrobats was performing ; and the poor but generous crowd laughing or amazed at their antics, gave their mites willingly to support these free-lance entertainers. Vendors carrying trays of sweet-meats, little cakes or roast peanuts pushed their way hither and thither, crying their wares ; and occasionally, followed by a servant, a lady passed, wearing a jewel made from gleaming kingfisher feathers in her hair.

This, Gregory felt, with the benighted villages, the paddy fields, and the teeming life on the great rivers, was China as it had existed for five thousand years ; and it seemed that the Communists had done no more than scratch the surface of it.

That afternoon they continued on their way. Five days later they reached the town of Lan-yi, where the old bed of the river meets its parent stream. Next morning they passed north of the city of Kai-feng, but as it lay a few miles from the bank they saw nothing of it except the waterfront through which most of

ach was just large enough to hold a couple, and they
ogether on the nearest.

silence fell, during which Gregory suddenly remem-
e he had seen a similar tree-tops restaurant. He had
nly once, in the days of his hectic youth. It was a
sort outside Paris, and he had been taken there by
tist's model who had been delightfully pagan in her
 recalled now that the restaurant itself had private
airs, and was the type of *maison* to which, in those
chmen took their mistresses on Sundays; so it was
 which to entertain a respectable young lady. With
ghts in mind he began to wonder if he had not been
 in bringing A-lu-te up to the secluded retreat.

rned to look at her he saw that she was regarding
a puzzled, slightly anxious smile, and she asked:
ou suggest coming up here? Do you not wish to
waters of my mouth?'

 invitation that would have tempted any man, and
used it would obviously have hurt her cruelly. Con-
he felt, must now take care of themselves; but she
hild and he hoped that if he kept his love making
 side, she would not take it too seriously.

s were promptly and completely shattered. After
ng kiss she gave a sigh of happiness and whispered,
d you love me; for I have long made up my mind
 perfectly suited to enter on marriage.'

was a past-master at concealing his emotions in a
 managed to hide his consternation, and threw out
le doubt which could not offend her. Kissing her
d earnestly: 'My beautiful A-lu-te, I should be the
men, but for one thing. It breaks my heart to admit
ust face the fact; I am much too old for you.'

a low laugh. 'Nonsense, dear one! Age matters
inese girls are often given in marriage to men old
e their fathers, and learn to love them. In our case
ve to learn, because our minds are so wonderfully
ady. For that reason alone I would still wish to
 your hair was white. As it is I count myself truly

its commerce passed. A veritable forest of sampan masts hid the shore, and hundreds of small boats plied their way to and fro. On many of them whole families lived and died, having no other home. Their children learned to swim before they could even walk, and scores of them splashed round the sampan shouting for *cash* to be thrown into the water so that they might dive for the little coins.

Now that they were truly on the mighty Yellow River, it was far broader, so that at times its banks almost disappeared in the distance; but in many places it was still very shallow; and on several occasions they had to engage a score of sweating coolies to drag the boat with tow ropes through the turgid yellow waters of low rapids.

Another eight days and they at last reached Tung-kwan, where their water journey ended; so Kâo paid Mai-lee-long off, adding a very generous tip to the amount on his promising to keep his own mouth, and those of his crew, shut about the place at which he had picked up his passengers.

During the past week the paddy fields had been left behind and the villages gradually grown more infrequent. The country had become more undulating with ranges of hills in the distance, and the rich black earth had given way to brown dusty soil. In the town, too, although it was obviously a product of the same civilization, they saw marked differences as soon as they landed.

There were the same poverty-stricken Chinese families living twelve in a single unfurnished room, old men smoking three-foot-long pipes, itinerant musicians with flutes and guitars, children with rickets or bald patches on their heads where the hair had fallen out, and coolies carrying huge burdens by means of shoulder poles; but the tempo of the town was slower than of those further east. It had suffered little damage in the wars and its streets were wider. Down them, with slowly swaying humps, clopped strings of laden camels, and shaggy-haired ponies with big panniers at their sides. Here, there were very few Chinese wearing European dress, whereas among the passers-by there was quite a number of yellow-robed Buddhist priests and fur-clad Mongolians.

The ancient hostelry to which they went had a glazed tile

roof with up-curved corners and glaring dragons to drive off evil spirits ; but fundamentally it had a marked similarity to the great English inns of coaching days. It was two-storied and built round a big courtyard in which caravans assembled and departed, while behind its main block lay a large enclosed garden that, although dusty, had a number of fine trees growing in it. A balcony ran right round the upper storey and Kâo secured rooms for them opening out on to it at the back. They were sparsely furnished, each having only a cot and a primitive-looking wash-stand ; but the outlook was pleasant, and with the bedding, etc., they had brought themselves, they soon made them reasonably comfortable.

They had hardly got settled when the landlord sent a servant up to tell them that an official was below asking to see them. So far, having mingled inconspicuously with the broad stream of life that never ceased to pulse on the great water highway had saved them from being called on to produce their papers ; and they thought it the most evil luck that, after reaching almost the outskirts of China, they must now face the risk of being questioned. But there was no alternative ; so, in considerable trepidation, they went downstairs.

The official was a lean, bespectacled young man dressed in the khaki uniform that the Communists affected. With the ill-grace of one whose head has been turned by the grant of power beyond his mental capacity, he abruptly demanded their papers.

Kâo produced the papers of his party, but with a cunning that showed his ability as a negotiator, did not at once hand them over. Instead he complimented the young man on his smart appearance and said how much credit officials of his type did to the regime. He then went on to speak of their journey, implying that they had come from Nan-king, and casually referring by name to several well-known Communist leaders as if they were his personal friends. He then held out the papers in a bunch as though they were of little importance.

As soon as the young official began to sort them out they saw with relief that his degree of literacy was distinctly on the low side ; so in a fatherly manner, Kâo set about helping him. The descriptions on the permits to travel bore only a vague resemblance to the travellers, and some of the dates on them

had been not very skilfully altere
had a ready answer for everyth
anxious twenty minutes, the Cor
satisfied. It was now in order fo
for his trouble in coming to see
handsome side without being su
no difficulty about issuing them
Yen-an. That done, he solemnl
great relief, they returned to th

After sleeping through the hot
out to arrange for his party to j
him. Gregory then suggested to
a walk in the garden. As Su-sen
cony which overlooked it, mei
clothes, her presence there cou
sufficient chaperonage in the eve
edly ; so A-lu-te smilingly agree

Under the trees near the inn
where guests could take their r
hour of the afternoon they were
people, and the far end of the
the sampan the whole party ha
that Gregory and A-lu-te had ne
or more of their fellow traveller
they spoke only of how long th
likely to take and ways in which
able discomforts. It was not un
the garden that, glancing up, C
the great trees there had solid
with small tables on them, so
refreshments up among their le
had a short ladder propped aga

'These human birds' nests a
go up and see if this one is co

A-lu-te hesitated only for a
The roughly-circular platform
feet in diameter, so there was
for seats two small bamboo se
wedged between pairs of

branches
sat down

A shor
bered wh
visited it
summer
a pretty
morals.
rooms up
days, Fre
no place
these tho
rather ra

As he
him with
'Why did
drink the

It was
to have re
sequences
was not
on the lig

His ho
their first
'I am so g
that we a

Gregor
crisis ; so
only a su
hand he s
happiest o
it, but we

She gav
nothing.
enough to
I do not h
attuned al
marry you

fortunate that you can give me joy with your body as well as your mind.'

After her declaration there could be no question of finding a pretext for getting her down from the tree before giving her another foretaste of the joys she visualized ; so Gregory again took her in his arms. His reluctance to do so had been based solely upon fears that her liking for him might develop into a passion ; but now that control of the situation had become temporarily beyond him, he no longer hesitated to take full delight in her sweet breath, soft lips and scented hair.

Presently they began to talk in low voices, and she praised the restraint he had shown in taking no risk which might have compromised her during their long journey from the coast. By vowing that he had hardly slept from the thought of her being so near yet inaccessible, he brought happy blushes to her cheeks ; but, even as he spoke, he began uneasily to wonder what line of conduct she would expect him to pursue now that, willy-nilly, she had made him her betrothed. Loath as he was to commit himself still more deeply, he felt that he must ask:

'What about your uncle? Would you like me to request a formal interview with him?'

She shook her head. 'No. Our circumstances are so unusual that he could not give his consent to our engagement. It is better that he should remain in ignorance about our feelings ; otherwise he might think it his duty to my father to take special measures against our even talking together. We must be more circumspect than ever and possess our hearts in patience. All will be well in time, and I will bear you many fine sons.'

In spite of this generous promise, Gregory was by no means sorry to learn that she wished to keep their engagement secret. He estimated that the best part of two months must elapse before they could get back to the island, and in that time much might happen. It seemed highly probable, too, that old Sze Hsüan would have the strongest objections to his most cherished daughter marrying a ship-wrecked foreigner. After a moment, he said:

'Our circumstances certainly are ususual; and not very happy ones as far as your father is concerned. Naturally he must be expecting you to marry someone who is in the running

227

as a future Mandarin. I'm afraid he'll be far from pleased to learn that you wish to throw yourself away on a person of no consequence.'

A-lu-te smiled up into his face. 'You are quite wrong there. My father is a philosopher. He is both wise and kind. He knows that I have long outgrown the possibility of becoming a suitable wife to one of the young men of the Seven Families. Yet his fundamental belief in the *yin* and *yang* cannot have failed to make him aware that no woman is complete until she marries. That consideration will, I am sure, weigh with him beyond all else. And there is yet more to it. Normally, among us, when a girl marries she bids farewell to her family and becomes as much a member of her husband's as if she had been born into it. But you have no family. So I believe that in you I will bring my father the son he has so long desired.'

On that score there was obviously no more to be said. Gregory could not help feeling rather like a young man of Victorian times who, having kissed an attractive girl in a conservatory, afterwards found himself compelled to propose, simply because in her innocence she would have felt outraged if he had failed to make an honest woman of her. A-lu-te had laid no snare for him ; but clearly, in spite of her superficial Western culture, the tradition of her race and caste had, after their one physical contact on the yacht, established it in her mind that there could be only one satisfactory outcome to their association.

He wondered how he would have felt had he been twenty years younger, and decided that the thoughts of spending the rest of his life in the island would have driven him in revolt. But now there were considerable attractions in the idea. What more could a man of his age ask of the Gods than to spend the remainder of his days in comfort, security and delightful surroundings with a young, beautiful and unusually intelligent wife? Both mental and physical attraction having already drawn them together, time might well quicken his heart again to something much more vital than a fondness for her. That his instinct, in endeavouring to avoid anything in the nature of an affaire with her, had been right he was now more than ever convinced. But marriage was another matter. He knew that he would never love any woman again as he had loved Erika ; but he could give more to A-lu-te than any man who, in her peculiar circumstances, she was likely to meet, and himself be the happier for it. Even the idea of marrying again was going to take a lot of getting used to, so he was glad that plenty of time lay between the tree-top and the altar ; but for another hour he dallied very happily with his charming fiancée.

Kâo did not return until just before the evening meal. Over it, he told them that he had hired porters, tents, camp-kit, ponies and three good camels with palanquins ; one for A-lu-te, one for Su-sen and a third in the hope that the Princess would be returning with them. From Tung-kwan, at irregular intervals, caravans set out for all the principal trading places of central Asia, some of which were over two-thousand miles distant ; but Yen-an being the capital of the neighbouring province, caravans went up to it three times a week, and, as luck would have it, one was leaving at dawn next day.

When they had finished their meal, Gregory took A-lu-te out on to the front balcony, and they stood for a while over the main entrance of the great caravanserai watching the animated scene in the big courtyard below. The caravan with which they were to leave was already assembling there. Camels and ponies were being picketed for the night, bales of merchandise were being stacked ready for loading, and fires were being lit round which the drivers would doss down near their animals.

Suddenly Gregory leaned forward. He thought he had caught sight of Foo ; but the slim figure was some distance off and the scene was lit only by the afterglow of sunset, so the light was deceptive. For a second Gregory was on the point of dashing down to make certain ; but, even as he moved, the figure hurried towards the gateway and, mingling with the crowd became lost in it.

On thinking the matter over, he realized that it had been no more than a momentary glimpse of an upturned face that he had caught ; and, as a European, he still found it difficult to tell one Chinaman from another when they were some way away from him. Besides, he had left Foo in Antung-Ku. If the ex-stowaway had been following them to pursue some inexplicable vendetta, why should he have wasted so many opportunities in the twenty nights that the sampan had been tied up near the wharves of towns and villages? Deciding that he must have been mistaken, Gregory made no mention of the matter to A-lu-te; and, as they had to make a very early start in the morning, they went to bed soon afterwards.

They were called well before dawn and dressed by candle-light, putting on the special top clothes that Kâo had bought them for the journey. These consisted of long cloaks with big hoods which could be drawn right over the head as a protection against wind and driving sand. After a 'first rice' of stew and noodles they went out to the courtyard. It was then it occurred to Gregory that he had not seen P'ei since the previous after-noon, and he asked Kâo what had become of him.

'If one is prepared to travel hard one can make journeys such as this much more swiftly than with a caravan,' Kâo replied. 'I dispatched P'ei with a guide on fast ponies yester-day to Mr. Lin Wân, to hand him a letter of greeting and inform him that we are on our way to Yen-an.'

'Isn't it rather a pity to have warned him of our approach?' Gregory asked after a moment. 'He may prove unwilling to give the Princess up, and if we have to make an attempt to rescue her we should have had a much better chance if we had spent a few days in the city spying out the lay of the land beforehand.'

Kâo gave him a mildly pitying look and said quietly, 'Mr. Lin Wân does not live in the city, but in a great house some way outside it. Moreover he is the richest merchant in all Shansi, and has many retainers. No attempt to remove the Princess from his keeping against his will could possibly suc-ceed; so put such ideas out of your mind. Either she will accompany us on our return with his and her own consent, or not at all. That is why our best hopes lie in submitting our wishes to him without deceit or delay.'

'No doubt you're right.' Gregory's lips twitched in a cynical little smile. 'I wouldn't play it that way personally; but this isn't my party.'

Twenty minutes later they were on their way, Gregory and Kâo mounted on strong shaggy ponies, and A-lu-te and Su-sen cking uncomfortably in small sedan-chair-like boxes perched on the backs of camels. The caravan was made up of over a hundred people and nearly twice that number of animals. The majority of the beasts were laden with merchandise ; but there were several other palanquins occupied by women or elderly men, and other travellers, most of whom were riding on ponies. The remainder of the people were either poor Chinese or the Mongolian pony and camel men. These trudged along on foot and, although the sun was still hot at midday, were mostly clad in goat-skin garments and shaggy fur hats with big ear flaps, that they wore pulled down low to protect their faces from windburn.

Their way lay roughly north-westward and for the most part along the valley of the Lo-ho River. It was an unnavigable tributary of the Hwang-ho, picturesque enough, but rapid and frequently strewn with great boulders against which the swift current churned angrily. Now and then streams running into it necessitated their making a detour through low rugged sandstone hills. Even near the river cultivated areas were infrequent, and generally the track ran through sandy wastes. Although the days were warm the nights were cold, and every evening a chill wind blew from the west, driving the sand into every crevice of their clothing until the round goat-skin tents were pitched and they could crawl into their shelter.

Here, in remote Shansi, despite the fact that it was from this very province that the 'Liberators' had launched their first campaign for the conquest of China, it was said that the Communist writ no longer ran. Soon they were to have evidence to the contrary ; but, from the untroubled state of the rich monasteries, no one would have supposed that the atheist creed had managed to establish its grip.

The villages were poor places, mud-walled and teeming with lice ; but they were not crowded to suffocation in the same way as those in Eastern China, and the peasants who occupied them seemed to be a more healthy and independent race. Yet the caravan rarely made longer than a half-hour's halt at any of them, and usually pushed on until it reached a monastery before pitching camp for the night.

Generally these huge rambling buildings, with their many

courts and pavilions, were set on hill-tops, and in the quiet e‑
nings Gregory greatly enjoyed walking in their public par‑
with A-lu-te. The yellow-robed Buddhist monks, with their
great feathered hats resembling the helmets of the ancient
Greeks, never failed to give them a dignified salutation, and
there was a wonderful atmosphere of peace in the airy stone-
flagged courts from which other courts or splendid views could
always be seen through long carved lattice windows. Gregory
was not greatly given to prayer, except in desperate emergen-
cies, but when the big gongs boomed out, and the temple bells
chimed musically on the evening air, he felt a new understanding of these men who could surrender all worldly ambitions
to live out their lives in secluded communion with the infinite.

It was on their fourth day out from Tung-kwan that trouble
began to brew in the caravan. Kâo told Gregory about it with
an uneasy look. In spite of his oriental clothes, his saffron-yel-
lowed face, and the fact that he returned the briefest possible
answers when any stranger addressed him, they had smelt him
out for a 'Longnose', as they termed all Whites. In times past
that would not have mattered, as white travellers in these remote
parts were either missionaries who miraculously healed the
sick, or mad people who wished to explore profitless deserts and
paid lavishly for guides and porters to accompany them. But
during the last decade things had greatly altered. For many
generations the Chinese had regarded the Japanese 'monkey-
men' as the incarnation of all greed, spurious culture, and evil ;
and now, owing to intensive propaganda, they had come to
couple the 'Longnoses' with the Japs as destroyers of their
country.

On the fifth evening antagonism against Gregory had reached
a point at which the drivers refused to tether his mule or fetch
his tent when camp was made for the night in the vast outer
courtyard of another monastery. Grimly, he set about doing
these tasks himself, while Kâo and A-lu-te stood by, disturbed
and worried but unable by either request or threats to make
the men alter their minds.

Next day the track left the side of the turgid, rock-strewn
river and turned away to wind up into a range of barren, sun-
scorched hills. About eleven o'clock they halted in a desolate

gorge to prepare their midday meal, and after they had eaten it the trouble came to a head. The master of the caravan called a mass meeting of his personnel, and it was decided that a strike should be called if Gregory persisted in continuing with them.

No protest on his behalf appeared likely from the other travellers, as most of them were eyeing him with open hostility. Kâo's curses and A-lu-te's tears proved equally unavailing with the drivers; so Gregory now had to face the fact that he was to be left behind. The prospect was very far from being a pleasant one for, although he felt confident he could find shelter and hospitality in one of the monasteries, he by no means relished the thought of losing touch with his friends and finding himself stranded on the borders of central Asia.

But matters did not end there. Worse was to come. One of the camel men picked up a stone and threw it at him. Another followed suit. Kâo promptly ran for cover, but A-lu-te remained at Gregory's side and the second stone hit her on the shoulder. Knowing that it was only himself they meant to harm, he swiftly sidled away from her and took refuge, as far as he could, behind a small rock.

Getting out the pistol that he had always carried on him, he clicked a bullet up into its chamber. A wave of intense anger surged through him, as it flashed into his mind that to be stoned to death by a crowd of abysmally ignorant Mongolians, for a reason that they were incapable of fully comprehending themselves, was, of all things, the most pointless, futile, stupid way to die. As he had plenty of bullets he was fully determined to take as many of his moronic attackers as possible with him.

A hail of stones came over the low rock. He waited for another, and the second after it had come raised both his head and gun; yet he refrained from pressing the trigger. He saw that a small, insignificant-looking little man, whom he had hardly noticed during their four days' journey, had stepped forward from among the travellers, and was addressing the caravan crew.

Raising his voice to a high falsetto, the little man screamed abuse and threats at them. Gregory just listened in amazement, then a broad grin spread over his face. In his wildest dreams it would never have occurred to him that he might ever owe his

233

life to a Communist ; but it seemed that was what was about to happen.

Drawing some papers from under his voluminous cloak the little man waved them in the air, shouting that whoever disobeyed him would do so at their peril. He declared himself to be a 'Liberator' with power to dispense death or rewards, and told them that for the honour of the new regime caravans must be conducted in a law-abiding manner. The 'Longnose' he said, had paid to travel with them to Yen-an, so must be allowed to continue his journey unmolested. If he were not obeyed he would call them to account when they reached the city, and deprive them of their livelihood by having their permits to travel cancelled for good.

Sheepishly the drivers edged away, and the master of the caravan kow-towed to him. Five minutes later they were prodding the camels up from their squatting positions in preparation for moving onward. While they did so Gregory went up to his rescuer to thank him.

The Communist was half a head shorter than Gregory, but, under his big cloak, appeared to be a broad-shouldered man. Gregory guessed him to be middle-aged but it was almost impossible to tell, as his chin was buried in his neck-band, he was wearing thick tortoise-shell rimmed glasses against glare, and the shaggy fur of his hat came right down, concealing as much of his face as does the bearskin of a Guard's officer.

His reply to Gregory's thanks was brief. He simply said in his high-pitched voice, 'My colleague in Tung-kwan told me that you were a Russian Comrade, so it was my duty to protect you. I apologize for the ignorance of these men, but the Chinese People's Republic is still a young one.' Then, with a quick clenched-fist salute, he turned away.

Gregory could only assume that the young official who had inspected their papers believed that as Poland lay behind the Iron Curtain, Poles could now be considered as Russians. Realizing the danger that might lie in further conversation with his Communist protector, he made no attempt to continue it, but returned the salute and went off to saddle his pony.

For three more days they moved wearily on at pedestrian

234

pace, then they crossed a range of low hills and saw the city of Yen-an in the distance. But Kâo and his party did not continue on towards it. A few miles to the west of the city there rose a steep hill crowned by an irregular group of buildings that had the appearance of another Buddhist monastery. Pointing at it with his riding switch Kâo cried:

'There is the great House of Lin. From the descriptions of it that I have heard I cannot be mistaken.'

Accompanied by their personal camel-men and porters, they left the caravan, and after a further hour were ascending the slope towards the many-roofed residence. As they approached, a sentinel on a watch-tower blew three long blasts on a great horn. A few minutes later a pair of huge gates was thrown open and a little crowd of armed men appeared in the entrance.

At last they had reached their journey's end. From the Island where Time Stands Still they had come over ten thousand miles in their search for the lost Princess. Since they had set out three people had died unexpectedly and horribly; and Gregory had had five narrow escapes from death. Even his steady heart quickened, as he wondered if they would find the Princess there, and what new perils they might bring upon themselves by bearding the merchant prince who had carried her off to this feudal baron's castle known as the great House of Lin.

14

THE MERCHANT PRINCE'S STORY

I T soon became clear that, whatever attitude Lin Wân might adopt when tackled about Josephine, he had no intention of turning away his old acquaintance Kâo Hsüan. A small procession emerged from the gate to meet them. It was mainly composed of fierce-looking men with sten-guns slung at their sides, but now banging drums and cymbals, while at their head walked the obviously peaceable figure of a young man in tennis flannels, closely followed by P'ei.

Kâo and Gregory were riding a short distance ahead of their party, and as soon as they got to within speaking distance of the young man, he called a smiling welcome to them ; adding that he was Lin Tû-lai the third son of Lin Wân and had been sent to conduct them to his father.

As Tû-lai led them through the tall gates, Gregory saw that the mansion was even larger than he had thought it from a distance. The gates opened on to a main courtyard as big as that of a mediaeval castle and in some ways resembling one ; for it was as busy as a fair. In lean-tos along its walls animals of half a dozen kinds were being groomed or fed, several cooks were tending cauldrons over open fires, carts were being unloaded, servants hurried hither and thither, and tradesmen of all kinds were plying their crafts in odd corners. While beyond three of its sides rose a jumble of curved roofs and pagodas, showing that the great House of Lin contained numerous smaller courts and as many buildings as an English village.

A-lu-te was helped down from her palanquin and presented to Tû-lai, who then took his guests through a succession of airy corridors to a small court with a charming little pavilion at each of its sides, where servants were waiting to attend upon them. When their baggage had been brought he left them to clean themselves up after their journey and an hour later returned, now clad in a beautifully-embroidered Chinese robe, to escort them through more corridors to an apartment splendidly furnished with silks, lacquer, porcelain and jade. At its far end, in a big chair the back of which was gilded and inlaid with lapis lazuli to represent a peacock's tail, sat Lin Wân ; and beside him on a chair made in the semblance of the more humble peahen, sat an elderly woman whom he introduced at his principal wife, the lady Fan-ti.

The merchant prince was bald, which made him look older than Kâo although actually he was about the same age, and he had a cast in his right eye ; otherwise he was a fine-looking man, whose height and strong nose showed him to be of noble Manchu descent. He welcomed them most graciously, inquired how they had fared on their journey, and expressed the hope that their stay with him would be a long one. Kâo made no mention of the object of their visit, neither did Lin Wân enquire concerning it ; but it soon became obvious that he knew about the island. Later Gregory learned that his father had been invited to join the migration when the secret colony was formed ; and, although he had decided against it, he, and since his death Wân himself, had acted in many commercial matters for the Council in collaboration with its buyers of raw materials and export managers.

After an hour's courteous interchange of platitudes, Madame Fan-ti proposed to take A-lu-te to the women's apartments and install her there. But Lin Wân smoothly interposed. He said that the lady A-lu-te having travelled so far in the company of men was obviously unused to being segregated and would find the chatter of a lot of provincial females irksome. He was sure she would prefer to have the freedom of the house, and while remaining in the vicinity of her uncle could be equally well attended in the court of guests. A-lu-te thanked them both and, as tactfully as she could, intimated that she would prefer the latter arrangement. Tû-lai then took them back to the little pavilions, and they found that, having observed the lightness of the baggage with which they travelled, he had very thoughtfully ordered a variety of beautiful garments to be laid out for their use.

Splendidly clad and heavily scented they rejoined the Lins to eat what was modestly termed 'evening rice', but actually consisted of spiced duck, sharks' fins, peaches in clove syrup, sucking pig served with li-chees and a score of other delicacies. When the bowls had been removed Lin Wân suggested that Kâo might like to smoke a pipe with him while his son provided more suitable entertainments for their younger guests. Having received A-lu-te's assurance that she had everything she might need in her pavilion, Madame Fan-ti retired, and Tû-lai took his charges to his own apartments.

As the tennis flannels he had been wearing in the morning had hinted might prove the case, the rooms he occupied were strikingly different from his father's. Except for their latticed windows and outlook on a fountain court they might have been the flat of a rich bachelor in Paris, where, as it transpired, he had finished his education.

Like his father he was tall and had a well-formed nose in a thinnish aristocratic face. His mouth was firm and his teeth good, but he spoke with a pronounced lisp as the result of a malformed palate. Gregory put him down as about twenty-eight and wondered if having been sent to Europe had turned him into a rich playboy, but he soon had ample evidence that Tû-lai was neither lazy nor a fool.

He was obviously delighted to have visitors who could appreciate his personal possessions and, having installed them in comfortable arm-chairs with cigarettes and French liqueurs, he began eagerly to show them his collections of books, coloured prints, and records. As he talked it emerged that it was only by chance that he happened to be at home, as for several years past he had spent most of his time travelling in connection with his father's business. He was the third of five brothers, all of whom controlled various aspects of it, and his speciality was purchasing modern equipment for their ships and offices, which frequently took him to the United States and sometimes to Europe.

Gregory was interested to learn that the wealth of the House of Lin had originally been built up by caravans trading deep into the heart of Asia, and in the Middle Ages to such distant places as India, Persia and Arabia. It was only during the past century that they had extended their operations to shipping,

238

and they still maintained a large caravan trade with Russia as far west as the Caucasus.

Most of Tû-lai's books were in French; and when A-lu-te confessed that she did not understand that language, he said with a gay smile, 'Then you must stay here long enough for me to teach you. Other than Chinese it is the only language really suited to make love in.' Then he asked her about her taste in music.

She replied at some length upon the Chinese masters, but again confessed that she had not yet learned to appreciate the Western classics, and preferred the light music of Vienna and American jazz.

With the back of his hand he contemptuously flicked a large radio and said, 'I would turn that on for you, but for every tune we should have to put up with a quarter-of-an-hour's lying propaganda.' As an afterthought, he added, 'Do you dance, perhaps? If so I will put some records on the gramophone.'

A-lu-te said there was nothing she would like better; so for the next hour or so the two men took it in turns to dance with her. Then Tû-lai found some English books for them to read and escorted them back to their pavilions.

Next morning Madame Fan-ti sent Tû-lai, who was not her son but the child of Lin Wân by another wife, to say that if they would like to make a tour of the house she would be honoured to act as their guide. Naturally they accepted, and half an hour later Tû-lai returned with her to collect them.

Since her marriage, at the age of fifteen, she had never been further than into the city of Yen-an, so her acquaintance with the world was very limited; but on Chinese art she was most knowledgeable. One long suite of rooms was rarely used, but many a museum would have been envious of its contents. In some cases even the rich hangings were several centuries old and all the skill of long-dead craftsmen who lived only for beauty had gone into screens and cabinets, great china jars, graceful vases, and tiny scent bottles carved from a dozen different semi-precious stones.

When they had admired the collections, Madame Fan-ti took them to see the fine views from each side of the house;

and the last of these, which was by far the finest, she showed them through the long lattice grilles that shut off her own domain from the rest of the house. In the foreground lay an open space planted with flowering shrubs, and having in its centre an artificial pond round which a dozen or more women were sewing, idling or playing with children. At the far end of the court, which was built up into the steep hillside, two long undulating stone serpents with jaws locked where they met formed a balustrade. Beyond it one could see for many miles to blue hills in the distance.

But Gregory gave only a cursory glance at the view as his eye had fallen on a quite exceptionally lovely young girl who was sitting some distance from the other women and only about twelve feet on the far side of the lattice. She was smiling happily as she fed some pouter pigeons, and when she glanced up he saw that her nose was flattened, but her eyes were enormous, her face heart-shaped, her mouth a rich cupid's bow, and her golden skin flawless. He judged her to be about eighteen, but she might have been older if her childish appearance could be attributed to natural smallness and fine bones. A-lu-te had also noticed her, and asked Madame Fan-ti:

'Is that lovely little creature your daughter, or a wife of one of Mr. Lin Wân's sons?'

Their hostess smiled. 'She is neither, but I hope that I may soon be able to call her daughter. Poor child, she is well-born but her parents were no longer in a position to provide for her ; so we have taken her under our protection. As our dear Tû-lai had the misfortune to lose his wife last year from an intermittent fever, we are still hoping that he may come to regard this charming child as a suitable consolation.'

Tû-lai frowned, looked at his feet, and muttered awkwardly, 'Dear aunt, I am deeply touched by your good intentions, and I am far too sensible of my duty ever to disregard a command from my honoured father ; but I would greatly prefer to make my own choice of a new wife.'

Kâo had already half turned away towards the big court, which was next on their list for a visit, but he nodded sagely.

'In these days, Madame, one must get used to young people following their own inclinations.'

'You are right,' Madame Fan-ti agreed, as he stood aside for her to precede him. 'And we would never force the girl upon him. But it is of no great consequence. When one of his brothers sees this melting dew-drop he will laugh for joy to think that Tû-lai has been foolish enough to leave her for him.'

By the time they had watched the blacksmiths, the potters, the saddlers, the weavers, the joiners, the laundrymen, and others at their work, the booming of a great gong called them to the midday rice.

After it, Lin Wân courteously dismissed his wife and son, then took his guests to a smaller room, furnished in a mixture of the oriental and occidental, that he used for business. When they were all seated he glanced at A-lu-te and Gregory, and said:

'My honoured friend, Mr. Kâo Hsüan, has already spoken to me upon the matter which has brought you to me half across the world. Since he has told me of your deep interest in it, I felt that you would also like to hear the detailed account I promised him of the events which took place last May in San Francisco, as far as I am aware of them.'

As they bowed their thanks, he went on: 'The Prince who took the name of Joseph Août was a strange man. For a whim —and what else is a woman but a whim—he threw away his birthright; and after a great struggle succeeded in establishing himself as a common artisan in the United States. In that, and his readiness to embrace those revolutionary ideas which have since brought such calamity upon the world, we can regard him only as a madman. Nevertheless, he had great personal charm and in the days of our youth, before politics divided us, we were good friends.

For many years I lost sight of him altogether. In fact, I never saw him again after he went to America. But it so happened that I was in San Francisco at the time of his death. A friend of mine, a Mr. Tung-ho Ting, had been to his funeral and, after it, chanced to ask me if I had ever known him. As I had, I felt impelled to call on his widow and offer her my condolences. That was how I came to know Madame Août and her daughter.

'No one had ever questioned Madame Août's original suitability as a wife to a Prince of the Imperial House. It was the way in which she had left her parents and publicly degraded herself, after their arrival in Saigon as refugees, which later placed her outside the pale as far as any respectable marriage was concerned. Yet when I made her acquaintance years afterwards in San Francisco, I was able to understand, if not condone, the young Prince's having abandoned all standards of right conduct on her account. Not only must she have been very beautiful as a girl, but she had great natural dignity, and a charm that few people would have found it possible to resist. I was so struck by her modesty and intelligence that before my formal call was over I decided to offer to take her and her small daughter back to China, and receive them into my house.

'She refused my offer because it had been her husband's wish that the child should be brought up as a citizen of the United States. But the good impression she had made upon me remained; and afterwards, whenever my affairs took me to San Francisco, I called upon her to enquire after her welfare.

'The last time I did so was on May the 17th. I found her in a great state of agitation and after a while succeeded in persuading her to unburden herself to me. A few days earlier an emissary of General Chang Kai-shek had come to see her, and after showing his credentials had placed before her a proposition. It seems that the Generalissimo had conceived the idea of strengthening his Nationalist government by securing the public allegiance to it of the legitimate heir to the Imperial Throne. He offered Madame Août a handsome pension if she and her daughter would accompany his emissary back to Formosa, and make their home there.'

'It is strange that Madame Août told me nothing of this,' Kâo put in with a puzzled frown. 'When I saw her she did not appear to be worried about anything, or even give the impression that she contemplated a change in her placid life.'

Lin Wân turned towards him and asked, 'Did you not tell me last night that it was on the 13th that you called on her?'

Kâo nodded. 'I think that was the date; but I could not say for certain now if it was the fourth or fifth day before her death.'

'In either case she could not have told you about it, for the good reason that she had not been approached by the Generalissimo's emissary. I should have made it clear that her murder took place only three days after he came to see her.'

'Murder!' exclaimed A-lu-te.

'Yes,' Lin Wân replied quietly. 'I have good grounds for believing her to have been murdered. And, alas, that I am to some extent responsible for that. But let us go back to my talk with her.

'She told me that she was greatly tempted to accept the Generalissimo's invitation, as it offered a better future for her daughter than she could provide herself. But the previous day —that is the day after the emissary called—she had had a most unnerving shock. While out shopping she was stopped in the street by a man. He told her that he represented the Communist government of China, and that they knew of the offer that had been made to her. He added that if she refused it no harm would come to her, but if she accepted it, it would mean death for herself and her daughter.

'As she had already made up her mind to accept, she was naturally extremely perturbed by this threat, and sought my advice. The Generalissimo, as you will be aware, started his career as a Communist; so persons like myself have little faith in him and have always been averse to giving him our support. Therefore, in this instance, I was not influenced by any wish to further his plans. But it seemed to me that Madame Août was justified in her belief that a removal to Formosa would give the young Princess the rightful status that she had too long been denied; and that since we were in the United States the Communists were most unlikely to run the risks insep-arable from committing murder there. It was on these grounds that I advised Madame Août to ignore their threats, and wished her happiness in the new prospects which were opening for her.

'What happened after I left her we can only conjecture. It is more than probable that she rang up the Generalissimo's emissary and informed him of her decision to accept his pro-

243

posals; and that there was then a leak. In the agencies of a country divided against itself such leakages are only too common. It may have been only coincidence that Madame Août was knocked down the following morning by a car which did not stop, and which the police have been unable to trace; but I have the unhappy conviction that my judgment was at fault and the Communists carried out the first part of their threat.

'Immediately I heard what had happened I became greatly concerned for the safety of the Princess, and felt myself personally responsible for her. To secure police protection for her would have entailed a full inquiry in which, frankly, I did not wish to become implicated. It would also have meant a delay that, in view of the swiftness with which I believed the Communists already to have struck, I was not prepared to accept. Moreover, in affairs in which Chinese are involved, there are better ways of ensuring that satisfactory action is taken, if one is powerful enough to set them in motion. I went at once to Mr. Quong-Yü and instructed him to have the Princess brought on board my ship.

'That night, by means of a written conversation, I discussed her situation with her. I found her both straightforward and intelligent. Her mother had told her both of the Generalissimo's offer and of the way in which she had been threatened. Like myself, the Princess was convinced that the Communists had murdered her mother, and was then in terror for her own life. I renewed the offer that I had made her mother several years before, of giving her a home here at Yen-an, and she gladly accepted.'

As Lin Wân came to the end of his story, his listeners automatically ran over it again in their minds; and, except for a few very minor points, it seemed to explain perfectly the events that had puzzled them for so long. It was A-lu-te who enquired:

'Did she say nothing to you of a law student with whom she was in love?'

Lin Wân's bald forehead creased in a frown. 'I seem to remember her saying something about a young man to whom she regretted not having been able to say good-bye. But she did not seem to be particularly upset about that.'

'We were surprised to find, though,' Gregory remarked, 'that she neither returned to the flat for her clothes, nor sent someone for them.'

With a shrug, Lin Wân replied, 'To have allowed her to go ashore during the three days before the ship sailed would have been to have risked her being killed. As for sending for her things, they were of little value and but a bagatelle once she had become the ward of a rich man like myself.'

His reference to his great wealth stirred another query in Gregory's mind. How was it, if he had had such friendly feelings towards Madame Août, that, after her refusal of his invitation to make her home in Yen-an, he had allowed her to continue living in near poverty, instead of making some provision for her and the little Princess about whose future he professed later to have shown considerable concern? And yet another thought. Surely Lin Wân would have given Quong-Yü his reasons for wishing to have Josephine abducted. Why had Quong-Yü made no mention of Lin Wân's fears for the girl and his belief that her mother had been murdered?

Both were questions which Lin Wân could not be asked, and both no doubt had adequate explanations. A minute later it became a waste of time even to consider them further, for Lin Wân was speaking again, and he said:

'Having made myself this elevated young person's protector, I brought her here, and as long as she wishes to stay under my roof she is most welcome. But this evening I will present you to her, and should she wish to leave here with you she is perfectly at liberty to do so.'

Kâo bowed his thanks, A-lu-te clapped her hands with excitement, and Gregory smothered a sigh of relief. The long trail to find the Princess had been so beset with difficulties and dangers that he had been quite prepared for Lin Wân to conclude his story by saying that she had been removed from his care in mysterious circumstances, or had, after all, decided to accept the Generalissimo's proposals and gone to Formosa. That she was really there, somewhere quite nearby in another room of the great house, and free if she wished to return with them, seemed almost an anti-climax.

None the less, when a few hours later, after another rich
245

meal, Lin Wân and Madame Fan-ti led them towards the Princess Josephine's apartments, Gregory admitted to himself that the moment of actually coming face to face with her would be one of the most exciting he had known for a very long time.

15

A LADY IN DISTRESS

THE room into which Madame Fan-ti showed them was not a large one, but it was a lovely setting for a young and beautiful woman. Its walls were covered with yellow silk—not the muddy Imperial yellow but a bright golden colour—which had just here and there a butterfly embroidered upon it. The carpet was of a paler gold with a broad edging and intricate lozenges in blue. The furniture was light in design, and on its larger surfaces there was engraved a pattern of branches with inlaid chips of mother of pearl to represent almond blossom.

It was evident that the Princess had been prepared for her visitors, as she was dressed and bejewelled with considerable richness ; but no doubt Madame Fan-ti had advised her that this first interview with them might prove easier if she laid no special stress on her royalty, for she received them informally seated on the edge of a dragon-headed day-bed.

Nevertheless, Kâo and A-lu-te at once went down on their knees and, performing the ancient *k'o-t'ou*, knocked their heads three times on the floor at her feet. With a pretty gesture she smilingly signed to them first to rise then to be seated in chairs near her.

Gregory had remained with the Lins in the background, and contented himself with a deep bow ; but she quickly signalled to them all to be seated. She was, he thought, undoubtedly a good-looking girl, but she appeared somewhat older than he had expected. Her face, also, had something slightly un-Chinese about it and, had he seen her without knowing her history, he would have put her down as one of those quarter-caste Eurasians who are often made more lovely in European eyes from having a proportion of white blood. But the explanation of these small differences from the mental picture he had created of her was not far to seek. Obviously the financial strain that she had shared with her mother while living in America had aged her a little beyond her twenty years, and her Manchu descent accounted for her good nose and the lack of fullness in her lips.

Kâo had already launched into an account of the island from which they had come, and the origin of its colonization. As she encouraged him with understanding nods from time to time, he continued for about half an hour, and wound up with the reason why they had come so far to find her.

When he had finished she looked inquiringly at Lin Wân, and he said gravely, 'Illustrious lady, this is a weighty decision for one of your tender years to be called on to make. Your Imperial blood carries with it certain obligations. If, in normal times, it fell to your lot to ascend the throne of our ancient Empire, there could be no excuse for your attempting to resist the divine command. But this is a matter of inclination rather than duty. Should you feel yourself capable of filling the unusual and exalted position that is offered you, your doing so will bring happiness to a considerable number of excellent people; so you would be wrong to refuse it. On the other hand, should you be troubled by grave doubts of your fitness to reign over this island kingdom, and prefer to continue to accept, as long as it is available, the few amenities of my humble home, no blame whatever can attach to your refusal of this offer.'

Gregory felt that Lin Wân could not have put the matter more fairly, and he awaited the Princess's reply with the greatest interest.

Picking up a brush from a writing set on a small table con-

247

veniently near her, she laboriously drew some characters on a long slip of paper, then handed it to Kâo.

For a moment he regarded it with a puzzled frown, then Lin Wân looked over his shoulder, smiled and said, 'I notice an improvement ; but I fear the Princess has not yet learned to draw our complicated characters very clearly. Naturally, she has no difficulty in understanding the spoken word ; but, you see, to transmit Chinese by the sign language used by the dumb is extremely laborious. As Madame Août's second tongue was French they always used that when together, and when other people were present the Princess wrote her replies to them in that language. Fortunately I am well acquainted with French myself ; so since she became my ward she has also used it to write her replies to me, and I think it would be as well if, for a time at least, she did so with you.'

Having followed their conversation with an anxious look, Josephine picked up a fountain pen and another piece of paper ; and began to write on it in a large sprawling hand.

She was still writing when Kâo muttered unhappily, 'This is most unfortunate. I have never learnt French, and know only the few phrases I picked up during business trips to Paris and while on holidays in France.' Turning to A-lu-te he added, 'You do not speak French either, do you?'

She shook her head. 'No, uncle. I can neither speak nor read it.'

Seeing the look of distress that had come over Josephine's face, Gregory came to the rescue and addressed her in French:

'Your Highness will perceive that I speak French fluently. Should you decide to return with us to the island, during the journey I should be honoured to act as your interpreter.'

Her expression immediately brightened, and for a moment it seemed as though she was about to speak, but she made only a little throaty noise. Then she finished what she was writing and handed the slip to Gregory.

The message was ill-spelt and ungrammatical, which told him that she could never have learnt French properly ; but he suddenly remembered that her affliction had debarred her from going to school, so she must have picked it up colloquially from her mother. However, her meaning was quite clear, and he gave a free rendering of it in Chinese for the benefit of Kâo and A-lu-te.

'The Princess writes that she is most sensible of the high honour that you propose for her; but she is deeply indebted to Mr. Lin Wân for having saved her from the Communists, and has become very attached to him and his wife; so she would be loath to leave them. She asks that you should give her time to think the matter over.'

Kâo replied to her by explaining the danger in which the yacht lay of being forcibly requisitioned by the Communists each time she entered Chinese waters. The journey from the coast had taken somewhat longer than they had anticipated, so thirty-one days had already elapsed since they had left her. That meant that they would miss her on her first return to the old mouth of the Hwang-ho, and could hope to catch her on her second return, a week later, only if they started back within the next two or three days.

In answer to this the Princess drew a few simple strokes which embodied the meaning, 'Sunset tomorrow.'

Assured now of receiving her decision as soon as it was reasonably possible to expect it, Kâo became much more cheerful, and talked to her for some time of the beauties of the island, its riches, and the secure, orderly, peaceful life led by its people.

Scribbling on her block in French, she asked a number of questions about it, and wrote a pretty compliment to A-lu-te upon the unusual colour of her golden eyes; all of which were translated by either Lin Wân or Gregory. Then, as this somewhat difficult conversation began to flag, Madame Fan-ti said that Josephine must be tired from so much excitement. On this excuse they wished her good night and bowed themselves from her room.

Outside the women's quarters they found Tû-lai patiently waiting for them. As it was still early A-lu-te and Gregory accepted his eager invitation to spend an hour in his apartments before going to bed. On arriving there, he at once went over to put on the gramophone; but A-lu-te disappointed his hopes of dancing with her, as she declared that tonight her mind was so full of the Princess that she preferred to talk.

She was much worried by the thought that not understanding French was going to add greatly to the difficulty of her proving a satisfactory lady-in-waiting if the Princess decided to return with them. But Gregory told her not to worry too much about that, as Josephine had never even had a maid of her own until a few months ago ; and that having been brought up in the United States she must at least be able to write simple replies in English. They agreed that she had a pleasant personality, and that her manners, while lacking the finesse of a high-born Chinese, were as good as could be expected from a young woman with an affliction that had debarred her from any social life, even in San Francisco.

Tû-lai took little part in the conversation, and appeared somewhat unwilling to discuss the Princess ; but when A-lu-te asked him if he thought she would accept the invitation to become Empress, he replied with considerable feeling:

'She will be a fool if she doesn't! Your island sounds a paradise. How I wish that my grandfather had gone there with yours, and that we Lins now made an eighth to your Seven Families.'

'If we had, intermarriage would probably have made you my cousin,' she smiled.

The quick glance he gave her suggested that he would have liked to aim at a closer relationship ; so she looked hastily away and hurried on. 'All the same, I can't agree with you that the Princess would be a fool not to accept. Of course, such a position must be tempting to any woman's vanity ; but, unless she is far more clever than she appears to be, the amount of power she could wield would be very limited. Then, although the island may sound a paradise, women are still looked upon only as play-things there, and being confined to it for life is a big price to pay for the security it offers. She is obviously happy here, and there are few pleasures or luxuries with which we could provide her that she does not already enjoy. So, to my mind, she has nothing to gain by leaving all this for a new life among strangers.'

'Ah! But you have forgotten one thing.' Tû-lai waved a hand towards the costly appointments of his room. 'How long will all this last?'

250

'You mean that the Communists are gradually strengthening their hold on China,' Gregory asked, 'and in time will even grip such remote districts as this?'

Tû-lai gave a bitter smile. 'It is no longer a question of "in time". They have already done so.'

Gregory raised an eyebrow. 'You surprise me. We saw very little of them, even in the densely populated provinces further east.'

'That was because you came by the river and spent only a few hours in one or two of the towns. Even so, you were extraordinarily lucky not to have run into more of them than you did.'

'They don't seem to have made any great impression on the country.'

'Believe me, they have; although you would not have realized it, because you wisely refrained from talking to people, and did not look below the surface. The devastation caused by years of war and lack of resources has prevented them ____ing out their grandiose plans for creating a new ____ made very skilful use of such assets as

____h to realize that China's ____ation mark. Formerly, ____ families were left with ____o the next. For them it ____e rice they had put aside ____t was starvation from ____overnment buys all ____o one starves ____ what that ____ in

one, and China's agricultural areas cover hundreds of thousands of square miles. Those families who have not yet been given motor ploughs have at least seen them, and are working like devils for a government that promises that all shall be given them in a not-far-distant future.'

'Then it seems that the Communists are bringing great good to China,' A-lu-te put in.

'Up to a point, yes,' Tû-lai replied. 'But we shall have to pay for it later, when all culture and freedom of thought has been destroyed, and the Communist ideology forced upon our whole people. To bring that about they are spending vast sums on education, and every teacher in every school is a Communist. Their propaganda too is most skilfully directed and pervades every walk if life. And no one any longer dares to argue against the stream of lies they pour forth, because China is already a Police State, with spies everywhere. We know that they have several of them in this house; but it would be as much as our lives are worth to attempt to expel them.'

'Why then,' Gregory asked, 'if they are alread

do they allow you to go on living her

countries they have never hesi

their riches.'

Tû-lai shrugged agai

Russia, behind which

know that we run our

could do themselves. W

their agents, and face i

pretence that we a

They would gai

they alread

ar

a...
many y...
from carrying...
China ; but they have li...
they have.'

'In what way?' Gregory asked.

'For one, they have been wise enoug...
billions have always been near the starv...
after a bad harvest thousands of poor...
insufficient rice to see them through...
became a terrible temptation to eat th...
for seed, and many of them did. The resu...
which thousands died annually. Now, the g...
the rice, and stores enough of it to ensure that n...
and everyone has sufficient for fresh sowings. Think...
means to the peasants who have lived for many generations...
fear of an untimely death. In addition, the Communists have
given the first priority in industry to the manufacture and
import of agricultural machinery, to further better the peasants' lot. You must anyhow have seen some of the new ploughs
and tractors during your journey.'

'We saw a few,' Gregory agreed, 'just near the towns.'

Tû-lai shrugged. 'A few years ago you would not have seen

...eady so powerful,
...re in such luxury? In other
...ated to strip wealthy people of

...n. 'Our caravans still do a big trade with
... lies centuries of experience; and they
... ships much more efficiently than they
...Ve are already reduced to the status of
...is saved on both sides by a hypocritical
...re enthusiastic supporters of the regime.
...n little by turning us into a State concern as
...ay take the lion's share of our profits. No doubt there
...plenty of fanatical Marxists among them who would like
to rob us of everything we possess and kill us; but the big
shots know that to do so would be to kill one of the few
remaining geese in China that still lay golden eggs, and that
if such geese are not allowed to retain comfortable nests to
lay in they refuse to go on laying. That is why, to all appearances, we continue living here as in the past, and there is no
outward sign that they hold a sword above our heads.'

'I had naturally assumed that you had to make it worth

their while to let you carry on; but I had no idea that they allowed you to remain here only on sufferance,' Gregory said thoughtfully. 'Since that is the case, though, it amazes me that they still permit you to keep armed retainers.'

'They have to, for the protection of our caravans,' came the quick reply. 'Even the Soviets have not succeded in putting down brigandage in their sparsely-populated Asiatic territories. But the men are no longer sworn to obey us. Some of the older ones are still loyal; but if a Communist official arrived with an order for our arrest the majority of them would not hesitate to carry it out. And that might happen any time. I do not think it will for a year or two yet, but sooner or later they will decide that they have infiltrated enough of their people into our business to run it. In China, as you must know, only very rarely is anyone made bankrupt. Even before the time of the Great Sage, it was a well-established tradition that no man should smash another's rice bowl. But these people do it without compunction. One day they will descend on us without warning and fill our mouths with the salt of ruin.'

A-lu-te sighed. 'How terrible to live always under such a threat. I understand now why you think the Princess would be a fool not to come with us. But why don't you sell everything while you have the chance, and go to America?'

He looked at her, and then for a long moment at Gregory, before replying. 'I am sure I can trust you both. That is what we hope to do. At least, as far as it is possible. For many months we have been gradually disposing of certain assets and smuggling the proceeds out of the country. But it is an extremely difficult thing to do on a large scale without being caught. For example, we dare not sell or remove more than a small portion of the priceless treasures in this house. The spies among the servants are too stupid to learn much about our affairs; but they would notice if many of the most valuable pieces disappeared, and would report it. That would be quite enough to give away our intentions.'

'Then all those lovely things must pass out of the possession of your family,' said A-lu-te sadly.

'Yes,' he nodded. 'And once we are gone these Communist

253

swine will loot even the graves of our ancestors for the jewels that were buried with them.'

After a moment he added on a lighter note, 'Still, if we don't leave things too long, we shall get out with our lives and enough money not to have to beg for our rice; so perhaps instead of going to the United States I will ask permission to come to live in your island.'

'Having been out in the wide world for so long, I fear you would find little to hold your interest there,' said A-lu-te demurely.

He gave her a meaning smile. 'In certain circumstances I should be perfectly content to remain there for the rest of my life; but it would be an added advantage if one could some-times travel again. As I am quite a good business man perhaps your Council would give me a job in their export department —on the understanding, of course, that if I were married I could take my wife on my travels with me.'

'You will have to come there pretty soon then, or you will find the position filled.' Gregory launched the *double entendre* for fun, but added smoothly, 'I mean, we recently lost our Export Manager, but as soon as we inform the Council of his death they are certain to appoint someone in his place.'

In view of their conversation Gregory was not particularly surprised the following morning to see in the main courtyard the cloaked and fur-hatted Communist who had saved him from being stoned on the way up from Tung-kwan. He was talking to one of the cooks as Gregory passed through the great yard with A-lu-te and Tû-lai on their way to see a squash-racquets court that the latter had had built. Pointing out the Communist, Gregory told the story; but they were some way away from the squat figure and Tû-lai did not bother to give it a second glance, merely remarking:

'Perhaps he belongs to their headquarters in Yen-an, or has been sent into the province to collect funds, most of which he will keep himself. There are now many of these small-fry who gain an easy living by terrorizing the defenceless; but we should know it already if he meant any harm to us.'

Tû-lai had trained several young men to play squash with him; and Gregory was secretly amused to see that, although of time for reading, and apart from light French novels, she doesn't seem to have ever looked inside a book. Still, I am the only person in the party who can lighten the tedium of the journey for her, so you mustn't take it badly if I seem to be neglecting you. And, after all, you seem to be filling in your time very pleasantly with Tû-lai.'

'Yes, I find him a most agreeable companion,' she admitted calmly. 'As things have turned out it was very fortunate for me that he came with us.'

As Gregory felt affection, rather than love, for her, the way in which she was flirting with Tû-lai had not caused him to become jealous; but she had certainly given him grounds enough, and it occurred to him that she might feel hurt if he failed to show it; so he said with sudden asperity:

'I've a damned good mind to take that young man behind the rocks and punch his head. I will, too, if you don't stop encouraging him every time he makes eyes at you.'

Evidently delighted by his reaction, A-lu-te laughed, but said demurely, 'That would be both unkind and unfair. You cannot blame him for trying to poach on your preserves since he does not know that I am engaged to you.'

Gregory gave an angry snort. 'That's the infuriating part of this whole situation. If only we could tell everybody that you are my fiancée, I'd have a decent excuse for neglecting Josephine to spend more time with you, and he would have to keep to himself the pretty speeches he makes you.'

She shrugged. 'To disclose our secret before we get back to the island might lead to Kâo's refusing to allow you to travel further with us; and that would be terrible. So it seems we must put up with things as they are. At all events, even if Josephine's mind is as dumb as her mouth she is a most luscious creature, and I'm sure you must derive a lot of consolation from constantly looking at her.'

'Not as much as you seem to from being looked at by Tû-lai.'

'I think you very ungenerous,' she replied with a little sigh of self-pity. 'It is natural that a woman should enjoy admiration, and especially so when it comes from such an attractive young man. It makes me quite sad to think that he will be leaving us so soon.'

two of them showed great ability, all of them lost by handsome margins to their master in the games he had arranged to play as an entertainment for A-lu-te.

That evening, soon after sunset, Lin Wân informed them that Josephine had decided to accept the throne of the island; so they all went to pay her their respects and wish her a happy reign. She received their homage very prettily, but was called on to pay for it by an early lesson demonstrating the way in which a sovereign's personal wishes have frequently to be sacrificed for the common good.

She asked for a week in which to say her good-byes and make her preparations for the journey, but Kâo again deferentially pointed out that even a day's delay might jeopardize the safety of the yacht and its crew; so she had to agree to leaving after midday rice the following day. On other points, too, she had to give way to Kâo's polite insistence. He told her that, as on their journey to the coast they must give the impression that they were ordinary middle-class people, the quantity of baggage she took should not exceed by much the modest amount A-lu-te had brought with her; and that as A-lu-te's maid could serve them both, the limited cabin space in a sampan was the strongest of reasons for her giving up any idea that she should be accompanied by a personal maid of her own.

Madame Fan-ti invited her to join them for evening rice but she excused herself on the plea that as she must leave next day she had too much to do; so after Lin Wân had sent for sweet champagne, and they had drunk her health in it, they adjourned to the meal without her.

Afterwards, A-lu-te and Gregory again spent the rest of the evening in Tû-lai's rooms. He appeared most upset because they were leaving so soon; so both of them did their best to cheer him up—A-lu-te by flirting with him openly, and Gregory by asking her to dance with him only twice—so that their host could make the most of the opportunity to *jazz a l'* *America* which, he said, he had never before been able to enjoy so far from western civilization.

But they were by no means as near seeing the last of him as they had supposed, for the following morning he appeared dressed in travelling clothes, and announced his intention of escorting them as far as Tung-kwan. Apart from the pleasure his lively company was likely to give them, they were glad because it would make the lonely roads safer. With Kâo's hired men their little party would have included only seven males, whereas Tû-lai proposed to take with him six of the Lin caravan guards ; and the addition meant a total train of some thirty riding and baggage animals, the sight of which at a distance was enough to scare off foot-pads or small bands of marauders.

It was not until they were just about to set out that Gregory noticed that P'ei was once more absent from the party, and he asked Kâo what had become of him.

Kâo replied that, much to his annoyance, his servant had fallen sick the previous night, owing to something he had eaten, and was now in a state of complete exhaustion from a grievous colic. To delay their departure until he recovered was out of the question, but Kâo had left him ample money and Lin Wân had promised to furnish him with papers stating that he was one of his people ; so it was to be hoped that he would catch them up somewhere between Tung-kwan and Su-chow.

Lin Wân and the Lady Fan-ti came out to the great gate to see them off, and, after the exchange of elaborate farewells, they started on their long journey to the coast. Their pace was restricted to the steady plodding of the camels ; but even so, this smaller caravan was able to move faster than the big one with which they had come, and they covered fourteen miles before sundown brought them to a halt for the night.

The evening wind from the west had arisen as usual, and they had to keep their hoods well over their heads and faces to prevent the driving sand from getting into their hair and eyes ; but they managed to find a fairly sheltered place to camp under the lee of a cliff. On the way up A-lu-te had shared her tent with Su-sen, and now expected to have to accommodate Josephine in it also ; but the Lins had provided her with one for herself, while Tû-lai had one of his own, so they were not unduly crowded.

While their meal was being cooked they sat round the fire, and they remained there for some time after they had eaten. The difficulty of conversing with Josephine now became more apparent than ever, as, although she could listen to all that was

said, and convey understanding by gestures, she could make no contribution to the talk except by scribbling on pieces of paper, and her writing had to be deciphered by the light of a torch.

After a time, as Gregory was the only member of the party who could interpret her phonetically-spelt French, a tendency arose for them to exchange ideas without reference to the others. Kâo had been smoking a pipe of opium, so fell into a doze, and Tû-lai needed no urging to develop a private conversation with A-lu-te.

That first evening proved a fair sample of what became almost a customary pairing off in the days that followed. Gregory would have much preferred to spend his time talking to A-lu-te, as he found Josephine's mentality extremely limited, and there were even times when she appeared too stupid to write intelligent replies to quite straightforward questions. About her life in San Francisco she would say little, except that she had been unhappy there, and he got very tired of always talking about the island, which was the only subject that seemed to interest her. Yet she was so isolated from everyone else that he felt too sorry for her to ignore her signals and join the others, when at every halt she beckoned to him to come and sit by her side.

For all Kâo's easy-going jollity, he continued to perform his self-imposed duty of chaperon very conscientiously, there could be no question of either of the ladies wander[ing] away out of the glow of the nightly camp fires with Greg[ory] or Tû-lai ; but on the fourth evening while camp was b[eing] pitched, A-lu-te and Gregory chanced to be standing a[part] apart, out of ear-shot of the others, and she took the oc[casion] to say to him a little petulantly :

'You must find the Princess very charming to devote [so much] of your time to her.'

'On the contrary,' he replied. 'I find her a colossal [bore. Her] mother may have been beautiful, but her brain must [have been] about the size of a pea, judging from the little she [gave her] daughter. The girl is a positive ignoramus. Of cour[se it is] understandable that her knowledge of the worl[d is] limited, but she must have had more than the

'I had forgotten that,' Gregory lied, feeling that having shown his concern he might now make a generous gesture. 'If we continue at the rate we have been going we shall reach Tung-kwan in another three days. He really is a very nice fellow, and has been most kind to us; so I will try not to mind your amusing yourself with him for the little time remaining to you.'

As it turned out, Tû-lai had to leave them earlier than they expected and in most unhappy circumstances. They were moving well, and covering about twenty-five miles a day as against twenty on their outward journey; so by noon on the sixth day, they were emerging from the barren uplands into a sparsely-cultivated area, and had only about thirty more miles to go. It was while they were packing up after their midday halt that a fast pony rider, trailing a spare mount on a long lead, came galloping up to them. Throwing himself off his sweating pony he flung himself at Tû-lai's feet and lay there wailing. When they raised him up he gasped out that his Lord, the mighty Lin Wân, was dead.

The news threw the camp into consternation, and everyone crowded round the exhausted messenger pressing him for particulars; but he could tell them little. He knew only that on the third morning after their departure his master had been found dead in a room where he often worked late at night, and it was said that he had died of a stroke. He had been dispatched post-haste to overtake the young Lord, so that he might return as swiftly as possible to perform the ceremonies.

Tû-lai burst into tears. Kâo and the three women wept with him, while the camel-men, porters and guards joined in the lamentations with a prodigious wailing. But the bereaved young man soon pulled himself together sufficiently to take a tearful farewell of them, and set off home. With him he took spare ponies, but only one of the guards, leaving the others under the orders of a man named Chou to continue to the caravan's destination, protecting by their presence, the lady he was obviously so loath to leave.

Still much subdued by the tragedy that had overtaken their friend, they reached Tung-kwan late the following afternoon. Kâo paid off the men he had hired for the journey, and gave

259

a handsome present to Chou for distribution among the guards who meant to camp in the big courtyard of the inn for the night, then set off back to Yen-an at dawn the following morning.

At the inn they again succeeded in getting rooms on the garden side of the building, and shortly after their baggage had been taken up they were told, as before, that a Communist official demanded to see them. This time they went downstairs without any feeling of anxiety. Lin Wân's commercial activities being recognized by the government, his accredited agents were allowed to travel freely in any part of China, and he had furnished them with authentic papers, corresponding where it had seemed advisable with the false ones they had held before.

The young man slowly thumbed these over, peered at them through his glasses, and listened to further flattering remarks from Kâo on the smartness of his appearance. Then he said he was satisfied, received another tip, stamped the papers and took his departure.

Kâo decided that it was now too late to go out and try to find a reliable sampan captain to take them down the river ; so they had their evening meal early, and after it the four of them played mahjong until bed time. As they were leaving the table to go upstairs, and Gregory stood aside to let Josephine pass, she swiftly palmed a piece of paper into his hand. When he got to his room he opened and read it. On it in her colloquial French she had written, 'I must see you alone. Please come to my room when all are asleep.'

Unhappily he stared at it, wondering what her summons to a secret rendezvous in her bedroom portended. She was, as A-lu-te had not failed to remark, a luscious creature, and she had an appearance of ripe womanhood beyond her twenty years ; although that was not particularly surprising in an Oriental. On the journey south she had taken no pains to conceal the fact that she liked him, and experience had taught him that the less women had in their heads the more thought they gave to the sensual desires of their bodies. The fact of being dumb could make no difference whatever to her being subject to such natural urges, and it might well be that having been rigorously secluded from men for so long she had become obsessed with the idea of taking a lover at the first opportunity. If that was the idea, he had no desire at all to play such a role, and to have to tell her so could only result in an awkward and humiliating scene.

On the other hand, since Tû-lai had left them she had suddenly become depressed and nervy. Before making his formal farewell to her, the young Chinaman had taken her aside and said something to her in a low voice. Gregory had thought nothing of it at the time, but now the recollection of them regarding one another with intense seriousness for a moment came back to him, and he wondered if whatever had passed between them was the cause of the drop in her spirits for the past day and a half. Women's quarters in the east were, he knew, far from impregnable; so it was possible that in secret Tû-lai had been her lover, and she had been upset by his sudden departure. But that did not seem plausible for several reasons. From the beginning he had shown little interest in her future. On the journey she had hardly given him a glance. And anyhow she had known that she would see the last of him in another two days. Yet there could be no doubt that for the past thirty-six hours her past cheerfulness had deserted her.

After much thought, Gregory decided to risk the possibility of having to reject unwelcome advances from her, on the chance that she was a prey to some real worry about which she wished to consult him privately.

The lives of most people in Tung-kwan were still governed by the rising and setting of the sun; so their midnight really was the middle of the night, and even late revellers sought their beds well before that hour. By then the inn was completely silent, so Gregory had no reason to fear that anyone was still about. Opening his door he moved quietly out on to the balcony. There was no moon, but enough starlight for him to see that the whole length of it was empty. Next to his own room, on the right, lay Kâo's, beyond it was Josephine's, and beyond that on the corner of the house the one occupied by A-lu-te.

On such midnight forays Gregory never tensed his body and went on tiptoe, but allowed himself to go slack, and as he advanced each foot in turn just let it descend gently by its own weight. Without making a sound he passed Kâo's room and reached Josephine's door. The small squares in the lattice of the windows were covered with an opaque material, and through it came a faint light. Regarding the terms of her invitation as a permission to enter without knocking, he took the handle of the door in a firm grasp and turned it. At a slight pressure the door opened. Josephine was opposite it, sitting up in bed with a solitary thick yellow candle burning in a saucer on the floor beside her.

As Gregory stepped into the room she jumped out of bed. He had hardly closed the door behind him before she flung herself on her knees, clutched him round the legs and gasped:

'Monsieur! Help me, I beg! Only you can save me!'

For a second he stared down into her distraught face. Then it flashed upon him that she had spoken. She was not dumb! Therefore she was not the Princess.

16

THE MIDNIGHT RENDEZVOUS

LIKE an aircraft that has been boosted by a rocket take-off, Gregory's brain leapt from ticking over to hurtling speed. Lin Wân had cheated Kâo. But why? Had Tû-lai known? Probably he had. If so, as he was a decent fellow that would account for his reluctance to talk about or have anything to do with the fake Josephine: Who was she? Anyhow he ought to have realized days ago that she *was* a fake.

That she had habitually used French with her mother was plausible, but not that she did not understand English. In spite of the retired life she led, having been brought up in the United States the real Josephine must at least have known

262

enough to give orders to the daily woman. This girl had pulled the wool over his eyes by making him assume that she used French only because she found it easier.

And her lack of education! He must have softening of the brain not to have smelt a rat about her. The Chinese set great store by learning, and those who had settled in America no longer considered it to be necessary only in men. Even in straitened circumstances a girl of good class, like Josephine, would certainly have been taught history and geography, given good books to read and listened intelligently to talks on the radio. No wonder this girl was reluctant to give her ideas of life in San Francisco; the odds were that she had never been there. Her appearance, too, should have been a give-away. Believing her to be twenty they had accepted her as that, but any unprejudiced observer would have put her down as twenty-four or twenty-five.

Angry at the way they had allowed themselves to be tricked, and himself—as he had had better opportunities of finding her out—to an even more humiliating extent than the others, he snapped:

'What's the meaning of this?'

Ignoring his question, she continued to cling to his knees and implore him to save her.

'Save you from what?' he asked impatiently.

'From them! Oh, take me away from here! Take me away!'

Her last words rose to a high-pitched note.

'For God's sake keep your voice down!' he whispered, fearing that it might arouse A-lu-te or Kâo and that one of them would come in to see what was the matter. Then, pushing the girl away from him, he told her to get back into bed.

Instead of obeying she remained squatting on her heels staring up at him, her big eyes limpid with unshed tears and her bare arms held out appealingly. 'Please!' she whimpered. 'Have mercy! Only you can save me!'

'Speak lower!' he urged her. 'Save you from what?'

'They mean to kill me.'

'Who?'

'Chou, and the rest of the old Lord's retainers.'

263

'Why should you think that?'

'The young Lord, Tû-lai, told me so.'

'What have Chou and the others against you?'

'Nothing. It must be that they have been ordered to get the money back.'

'What money?'

'The money I was paid to impersonate the Princess.'

'Tû-lai knew about this, then?'

'Yes. But he must have thought it wrong that the old Lord should go back on his bargain. Before he left us he warned me, and urged me to escape at the first opportunity. But alone, how can I? I should——'

Gregory cut her short with a gesture. 'Before we go into that, let's try to get things straight. First of all, who are you?'

'I am Shih-niang, a singing girl of Canton,' she gabbled out. 'The old Lord bought me two years ago. My mother was half French. Girls like myself are given only one form of education. That is why I can barely write the simplest Chinese characters. It was my being able to speak French that gave the old Lord the idea that I could carry out this imposture. At first I refused. The thought of having to act as though I was dumb for the rest of my life seemed terrible. He dangled the temptation of becoming an Empress before me. He said that no one would suspect me if I made increasing noises until I could pretend that my voice was coming back. But I was frightened—frightened that I should be found out by the people of the island, and that they would kill me. As I still refused, he offered me ten thousand American dollars to play the part for three weeks. He said that would be long enough for his purpose. Then when we got near the coast I could run away. With my freedom and ten thousand dollars I could have made a fine marriage. So . . . so then I agreed.'

Breaking off, she jumped up, ran to her bed and drew from beneath the pillow a small silk satchel. Hastily pulling back its flap she showed it to Gregory. It was crammed with fifty and hundred dollar bills. Holding it out to him she cried:

'See! Here is the money! Take it, but get me away. All my life I have been protected. Nearer the coast I could have managed somehow. I'd have slipped away at dawn and got on a train. But here, and at night, I dare not go alone. I should be robbed and sold into a brothel long before I reached Canton.'

He shook his head. 'No. I don't want your money.'

'Please!' she implored him. 'To whom can I turn? The Lord Kâo and Lady A-lu-te would be furious if I confessed my imposture to them. For a girl like me they would care nothing. They would have me thrown out naked into the street. But you are just a man of their household, and so quite different. This money is a fortune. On it we could run away and live together happily for years. You *must* take me! You *must*! How can you be so heartless as to refuse?'

Again she had raised her voice and Gregory endeavoured to cut her short with a swift, 'Hush! Stop talking, and let me think a minute.'

Misinterpreting his meaning, she hurried on, but in a lower tone, 'I will be obedient and make you happy. I swear I will! I was well taught, and my limbs are strong and supple. I know the seventy caresses, and have practised the forty-one ways of attaining complete enjoyment. I can sing French songs, as well as Chinese ; and at the Feast of Lanterns I will hire five other girls to assist me in making for you the wheel of love.'

Suddenly she threw the satchel containing the money on the bed behind her, raised her two hands to the low-necked frill of her night-dress, and ripped it down the centre. It slid to the floor. Standing naked before him, she cried:

'Look! Am I not beautiful? Men have paid sums which would keep their families for a month to spend a single night in my company. But I am yours for as long as you wish, if only you will save me.'

Without shoes she stood about five feet high, so was moderately tall. She had a graceful neck set on broad shoulders and her hips too were broad, but neither gave an impression of heaviness, owing to their good proportions and her long shapely legs. Her breasts were full, round and firm ; her skin had the texture of satin, and her lovely golden body had not a single blemish on it. Gregory could well believe that she had paid high dividends to the Canton tea-house from which Lin Wân had bought her.

'Listen,' he said. But he got no further. A sound came of the door to the balcony being opened. He saw Shih-niang's eyes open wide, then dilate with terror. The thought flashed into his mind that it must be Lin Wân's men come to rob and kill her. Instinctively, fearing to be knocked on the head from behind, he ducked. As he did so a knife streaked over his shoulder. It caught Shih-niang in the side of the neck. She gave a high-pitched screech that ended in a groan, and fell back on the bed.

As Gregory swung round, the door was already being pulled to. He caught only a glimpse of a fluttering robe that might have belonged to anyone ; then it slammed shut. For a second he hesitated whether to give chase or go to the assistance of the stricken girl. The thought that, as she had been pierced in the neck, her life might hang on a matter of minutes decided him.

Running to the bed, he bent over her. Blood had gushed from the wound. Her head lay in a pool of it, and it was dripping down on to the floor. One glance was enough. Nothing could be done for her. The blade had severed her jugular vein. She was already unconscious, and no attempt to staunch the bleeding could now prevent her death.

Gregory's glance fell on the satchel she had flung down before tearing off her night-dress. Chou and his men could not have forgotten it, as it was for it that one of them had killed her. It looked as if on finding Gregory in her room they had lost their heads. Their leader must have had his knife ready, so thrown it, then panicked. But there were five of them, and they might come back for the money at any moment. Meaning to run from the room and raise an alarm, Gregory grabbed it up, so that they should not get it if they returned while he was absent. As he did so, some of the notes fell out on to the floor. His back was still turned to the door as he heard it open a second time. Swivelling round he saw that A-lu-te stood framed in the darkness of the doorway.

He was between the candle and the top half of the bed, so the deep band of shadow he threw hid Shih-niang's head and bloody throat. From where A-lu-te was standing she could see clearly only Shih-niang's dangling legs, the lower half of her naked body, and that it was Gregory who had been bending over her.

'So it *is* you!' she exclaimed, her voice vibrant with fury. 'From your recent conduct, when I heard someone talking in here I thought it must be. At least you might have had the decency to refrain from an attempt upon her in a place where I could hear you.'

Making an impatient gesture, Gregory was just about to cut her short, when a horrible gurgling came from behind him. It was Shih-niang's death rattle. It was the sort of noise that a dumb girl might have made during such a scene ; so although she had made no attempt to sit up and pull the bed-clothes over herself, A-lu-te assumed her to be fully conscious. Her golden eyes darkening with anger, she continued to storm at Gregory :

'Are you not ashamed! As for her, from the first she has shown more the characteristics of a gutter-wench than of a Princess. After this betrayal of what she owes to her position, I would rather die than serve her. And what will Kâo have to say about this pretty plot of yours to establish yourself as our future Empress's lover? You have——'

'For God's sake shut up!' Gregory broke in, at last checking her tirade. 'The girl is dead!'

As he spoke he took a pace forward. At the same moment a bulkier form appeared in the doorway behind A-lu-te's. It was Kâo, and now that the candle-light shone upon Shih-niang's gaping mouth and staring eyes, he took the whole scene in at a glance. Evidently he had caught A-lu-te's last words, for, pushing her aside, he thrust out an accusing hand at Gregory, and cried :

'Not her lover ; her murderer!'

Since Shih-niang's scream as the knife pierced her throat, barely two minutes had elapsed. A-lu-te had been first on the scene as she had already been awakened by Shih-niang's desperate pleading ; but the cry had roused a number of other people who had rooms opening on to the long balcony. Kâo had hardly arrived when several other men came crowding up behind him, demanding to know what was happening.

Gregory still clutched the satchel bulging with notes. Kâo's arm dropped, pointing at the notes scattered on the floor, and he shouted:

'He has killed her! He killed her for her money! We must seize him!'

Instantly Gregory saw that he was in as desperate a situation as could possibly be imagined. Shih-niang was dead. There was no one who could confirm the fact that she had been attempting to bribe him to run away with her; no proof that she believed Lin Wân's men to be plotting her death. He had even destroyed her message asking him to come to her room. There was no reason he could offer for being there. If he allowed himself to be seized, no amount of swearing to the truth on his part would be accepted as proof of his innocence. There was only one thing to do. He must fight his way out and make a bolt for it.

That swift decision taken, he stepped back towards the main door of the room, which led out into a corridor. Thrusting a hand behind him he found the door knob. It turned but would not give. Assuming that he would come to her by way of the balcony, Shih-niang must have shot the bolt of the door to the passage. He dared not take his eyes from the hostile faces now glaring at him from less than two yards distance. With frantically fumbling fingers he found the bolt, but was given no chance to draw it back. As his fingers closed round it, one of the men from a neighbouring room launched himself upon him.

With a kick that would have done credit to a ballet dancer, Gregory landed the toe of his right shoe under the man's chin. He was brought up short, his head snapped back, and he dropped to the floor like a sack of coals. While the man was still falling Gregory sprang past him. His chance of getting the door behind him open had gone, and he knew that his only hope now lay in seizing the initiative. Slamming his right fist into one man's face, he hit another with his left a glancing blow on the ear. The first went down with a howl, the second reeled away, but had already drawn his knife and came at him again from the side. Swerving, he seized his attacker's wrist, threw himself flat against him and kneed him in the groin.

268

The poor wretch gave a scream of agony, dropped his knife and doubled up.

Terrified at the sight of the havoc wrought by this human tornado in a few seconds, two less courageous visitors flattened themselves against the wall of the narrow room. Except for Kâo, whose portly form still blocked the door, the way was now clear. This was no time to argue, so Gregory gave him a swift jab in his fat stomach, thrust him aside, and ran out on to the balcony.

A-lu-te had stepped back there after Kâo had pushed past her into the room. But she had seen, as he had, the awful spectacle of Shih-niang, a dark streak of blood across her throat beneath her thrown-back chin, making her appear as though she had been decapitated. At the sight A-lu-te had screamed with horror, and on seeing Gregory dash through the doorway she screamed again.

But no further outcry was needed to rouse the caravanserai. Shouts, cries and the sound of running feet were coming from both inside and outside it. Shadowy figures were running towards Gregory from the far end of the balcony. For a second he thought of scrambling over it and jumping down into the garden; but it was a twelve foot drop. The risk of a broken ankle was too great. With such a handicap he would never get away. Only one line of possible escape was left open. There was no one on the short length of balcony outside A-lu-te's room; and beyond it was the corner of the building.

Kâo, half doubled up, with his hands pressed to his paunch, was groaning in the doorway of Shih-niang's room. Before Gregory had time to move, someone pushed past Kâo and darted at him. As the man ran out, Gregory side stepped, then, holding his open hand rigid, brought the side of it down like an executioner's axe on the back of the man's neck. The force of the blow, added to his own impetus, sent him crashing into the rustic railing of the balcony. It gave way under his weight. With a terrified cry, he hurtled head foremost into the garden.

The group of men running along the balcony were already within twenty feet. Swerving away, he raced past A-lu-te's room. At the corner of the building he cast a glance over his shoulder to assess his chances. With a gasp of surprise and thankfulness he saw that A-lu-te had thrown herself in front of his pursuers, in an attempt to bar their advance. He knew that the respite she had gained him could be only momentary, but even the grant of time to draw breath was incredibly welcome.

There was no one on the balcony along the side of the building, but he saw that thirty feet from the corner further advance along it was blocked by a solid wooden partition. Again, it seemed that his only hope lay in risking a drop to the ground.

Then a new thought sprang to his mind. In Europe the long range of rooms at the back of the inn would have been regarded as attics. Like a series of peaks and valleys each had its separate roof with a ridge sloping down to gutters. Inside, at their apex, the rooms were not more than eight feet high and their side walls were barely six. The corresponding slopes outside were little more than the thickness of the tiles higher. The gutter of the end roof near which he stood actually came down to a level with the top of his head.

Grasping the gutter with both hands, and praying that it would not break under his weight, he heaved himself up. After a frantic struggle he succeeded in getting one knee on it, then the other. Clutching at the sloping tiles he hoisted himself on to them, and swiftly spread himself like a starfish, to lessen the risk of any separate tile clattering down through the pull his wriggling exerted upon it.

To his immense relief they held, but he was still supporting himself by his toes in the gutter, and he felt that he dared not try to climb higher for the moment, in case his full weight brought both the ancient tiles and himself slithering down on to the balcony like an avalanche.

It was an extremely precarious position, but he knew that he must now gamble on the fact that when making an excited search for anyone, people rarely look upward. Flattened against the tiles as he was, if he remained quite still there was a good chance that his pursuers, finding this dead-end of the balcony empty, would assume that he must have jumped down into the garden.

With a heavy trampling of feet they came pounding round

the corner, and slowed to a halt just beneath him. As far as he could judge from their voices there were about six of them. Holding his breath, he waited. Panting from their exertions they gasped exclamations to one another.

'He's got away!' 'He must have jumped over!' 'There's no one there!' 'He couldn't have without breaking a leg.' 'Where else can he have gone?' 'He may have crawled into the patch of shadow beneath us.' 'Quick! Let's get down stairs and see!'

With the mentality of the herd they turned and ran back the way they had come. The sound of their pounding feet died away in the distance. Gregory drew in a deep breath. He was safe for the next few minutes, and must make the best possible use of them.

To have dropped down on to the balcony again would have been the height of rashness. An excited clamour was still coming from the long stretch of it; so any second another batch of men might come round the corner. On the other hand he feared that if he remained where he was much longer the ancient gutter which was bearing most of his weight would give way. To be safe on the roof for any length of time he knew that he ought to get into one of the valleys between its gables. The nearest lay between Shih-niang's room and A-lu-te's, and as he was lying on the outer slope of the latter, to reach it meant climbing over the ridge that cut the sky-line about six feet ahead of him.

That sky-line was the trouble. Even if the tiles held as he clambered up to the ridge, anyone glancing up from below could not have failed to spot him, in the starlight, as he crossed it. He decided that the risk was too great. But there was another possibility that might give him slightly better cover than he had at the moment, and enable him to take the strain off the gutter. Like most Chinese buildings that are over a hundred years old, the roof came down at each corner in a graceful saddle that terminated in an upturned sabre tooth. By working his way along to within a few feet of this curved corner ridge, he could lie in the bend it made and gain concealment on one side from its ornamentation.

It lay only about ten feet off to his right. Gingerly he eased himself towards it until the slope lessened and he no longer had to cling on to the tiles. For a few minutes he rested there, thinking only of the narrowness of his escape and wondering if his luck would hold; then he began anxiously to consider his next move.

For the time being he could not do better than remain where he was, but as soon as the tumult had died down he must take advantage of the remaining hours of darkness to get well away from the inn; otherwise the odds would once again be all on his being caught, and he had no illusions about what would happen then. Life in China had always been cheap. The Chinese had never developed the system of defence by solicitors and barristers, or the technicalities of legal procedure that often delay trials in the civilization of the West. He would be hauled before a magistrate, condemned to death for Shih-niang's murder and summarily executed.

Yet, somehow, before he made his attempt to get away, he felt that he must try to see A-lu-te. To her he owed even his temporary safety; for, had not she thrown herself in front of his pursuers and gained him a few moments' grace, he would already have been captured. To her, too, he owed the recovery of a balanced mind and the fact that he was now able to take pleasure again in the normal joys of living. As the result of their intimacy during the past six months she had filled an unforgettable place in his life, and this ghastly business that had occurred barely ten minutes ago meant that, after tonight, it was most unlikely that he would ever see her again.

He did not think she would accept the idea that he had murdered Shih-niang for her money, but would more probably decide that he had made an attempt upon the girl and, finding her unwilling, had threatened her with the knife; with the result that, owing to her continued resistance, she had been wounded in the ensuing struggle. It was at least probable that A-lu-te was thinking on some such lines. Anyway, in view of all that they had been to one another, he did not wish her memory of him to be embittered by the belief that he was really such an unscrupulous blackguard as to try to force a dumb girl, or that he had even contemplated being unfaithful to her.

Besides, she and Kâo had come ten thousand miles in their

272

search for the Princess; so he owed it to them to let them know that the dead girl had been a fake, and that not only had Lin Wân cheated them, but that it was his men who had murdered her.

At that, it struck him that had several men been involved he must surely have heard, if not their approach, at least the noise they made in their hasty retreat. From the second Shih-niang had reeled away with the knife in her throat, he had given only one swift thought to her attacker, then run to her aid; but now he had an opportunity to go over the event again, he felt certain that no sounds of confusion, such as a little crowd would have made, had reached him after the door was shut.

Again, as A-lu-te left her room she might have failed to notice one dark figure moving away at the far end of the balcony, but a group could not have escaped her attention; and, as it was the middle of the night would have suggested to her that something unusual was afoot. Yet obviously, on entering Shih-niang's room, no thought of possible robbery or violence had been in her mind. She had assumed that while everyone was sleeping he had been making love to Josephine. It looked then as if either Chou, or one of his men, alone had undertaken the job of closing Shih-niang's mouth for good and getting Lin Wân's money back.

Another thought followed: Lin Wân was immensely rich. Whatever his object, he had succeeded in tricking them, but only because Shih-niang had agreed to help him; so why rob the poor girl afterwards? Ten thousand dollars was a big sum to her but could mean little to a great merchant prince. It was difficult to believe that anyone in his position would be capable of such meanness.

Gregory then recalled that when he had been questioning Shih-niang about why anyone should want to kill her, she had said 'It *must be* that they have been ordered to get the money back.' That meant she had only been guessing. Perhaps, then, she had no certain knowledge at all about the threat that over-hung her.

When Tû-lai had parted from them he had stepped aside with her only for a moment, so could have had time to

273

whisper no more than a single sentence. Could he have simply said 'There is a plot to kill you; escape at the first opportunity'? If so, had she jumped to the conclusion that he was referring to his father's men, whereas the threat to her that he had in mind came from quite a different quarter? For that there was some support in the probability that only one person had crept up, outside her room, as, if it had been Chou, he would surely have brought at least one companion to keep watch while he did the deed.

Yet who else could have desired her death? Could A-lu-te have knifed her out of jealousy? That would not have been beyond the bounds of possibility if she had caught her lover in the act of betraying her. But such crimes are not premeditated, and this one had been; otherwise how could Tû-lai have warned Shih-niang of her danger? No, the idea was fantastic. And, apart from jealousy, neither A-lu-te nor Kâo could possibly have had any motive for making away with the woman they believed to be the Princess. Therefore it could not have been of them that Tû-lai was thinking.

One other possibility occurred to Gregory. Could Tû-lai have been referring to the Communists? He had told them that there were Communist spies among the scores of people who inhabited Lin Wân's great house. Had they discovered that the Princess was living there, but had had no means of identifying her until they got wind of the fact that Kâo had come to fetch her away? If so, and Lin Wân had counter-spies who informed him what the Communists found out, he might have learned that they meant to murder Josephine as soon as they could after she had left his protection. That would account for his having substituted Shih-niang for her. As Shih-niang had placed it beyond dispute that Tû-lai was aware of the substitution, it was fair to suppose that he also knew the reason for it, and that would account for the compassionate warning he had given her.

At last Gregory felt that he had a really plausible theory. Yet he was far from content with it. The whole thing rested on a Communist agent having followed them from the House of Lin. If one had, and the People's Republic wished to eliminate the Princess, why had they not simply arrested the woman they believed to be her soon after she arrived in Tung-kwang? Why take the unorthodox and pointless step of having her murdered?

Again, while Lin Wân might have been justified in pulling a fast one over the Communists, that could hardly apply to his old friend Kâo. Surely he would have told Kâo what he feared. Then, perhaps, they might have planned the substitution to draw the Communists' fire, while arranging for the real Josephine to be sent by another route so that, in due course, she could join Kâo in Su-chow or somewhere near the coast.

But that had not been the way of things. Otherwise Kâo would have been expecting Shih-niang to be murdered and known who her murderers were; in which case he would not have accused Gregory of murdering her for her money.

The sound of voices was still coming from beyond the corner ridge beside which Gregory lay, and he knew that he might pay for it with his life if he made another move before things had finally settled down. All he could do at present was to cling there and, by continuing to puzzle over Shih-niang's death, try to keep his mind off the extremely unpleasant death he would suffer himself if he were caught.

17

ON THE RUN

FOR the best part of an hour Gregory continued to badger his wits over the puzzle; but he got no further. In the rooms below him there had been a lot of coming and going, but at last it had ceased and for some time past quiet had reigned again.

All the same, he knew that he was very far from being out of the wood, and that the least false step might arouse another hue and cry after him ; but, for the time being, he at least had one thing in his favour. In China a criminal must be prepared to face summary justice *if he is caught,* but against that he has some compensation in the fact that police investigations are both dilatory and rudimentary. Their efficiency, at all times dubious, is also in direct relation to the importance of the person who appeals to the authorities, and what the police are likely to get out of the case.

The last thing Kâo would want was an investigation by the Communists ; so it was quite certain that he would not have called the police in, and, as the pseudo-Princess had been travelling incognito, it was very unlikely that anyone else would have either. To all but her own party Shih-niang was just a girl who had been killed by a robber, so nothing to get in the least excited about once it was known that the robber had escaped and the gory details of her end had been discussed. Even if someone had fetched the police, there would have been no business of taking photographs and finger-prints, or a medical examination of the body. A solitary policeman would have listened to what the people present had to say, asked for a description of Gregory, thrown a sheet over the corpse, and departed.

Yet there was just a possibility that someone had remained on watch, or that Kâo, furious at having, as he supposed, lost the Princess he had taken such pains to find, was still tossing wakefully in his bed. In consequence, Gregory considered it too risky to get down on to the balcony ; but, during his long wait, he had thought of a way by which he might get a word with A-lu-te without either calling her out or entering her room.

With his finger tips he began gently to prise up one of the old curved tiles. Below it he knew that he would find only lath and plaster and, by carefully scraping the plaster away, he hoped to make a small hole in the ceiling. If the noise disturbed her she would not take alarm, as in such old buildings rats were often to be heard scurrying about among the rafters, and when the hole was made he would be able to call down to her through it.

Alas for his hopes. He got the first tile off all right, but his doing so loosened two more above it. One of them began to slide. They were eighteen inches square and thick, heavy things. He had meant to prop the one he had taken off against the corner ridge, but before he had a chance to lodge it safely he was forced to use his free hand to grab another. The third came down abreast the second. Thrusting out an elbow he made a desperate effort to check its progress. It hovered for a second against his bent arm, then slithered away. In a final attempt to prevent it crashing on to the balcony below, he stuck out his foot. The move was fatal. It upset his precarious balance. With both hands full he had no chance to clutch for a fresh hold. Next moment his feet were over the edge, his knees scraped against the gutter and nothing could save him.

By the mercy of Providence, none of the other tiles followed him down, otherwise one of them might easily have killed him. As it was he landed feet first on the balcony, the tiles he was holding in his hands were jerked from him to crash on the boards, and he staggered backwards into the rustic wood railing. Under his weight it gave like a matchwood, and again he was hurtling downwards.

The second drop was more than twice as far as the first, but a lucky chance saved him from serious injury. While falling he managed to grab one part of the rail that had snapped behind him. His clutch on it tore its fixed end from the post to which it was nailed, but the pull needed to drag it free checked the speed of his fall considerably. Moreover it jerked him upright, so he again came down on his feet; although he remained on them only for a second before pitching sideways to roll over and over with most of the breath driven out of his body.

No sooner had he picked himself up, than he heard shouts coming from above. Evidently a number of people had not yet got soundly to sleep again after the first alarm, and the noise of his fall had brought some of them out on to the balcony almost immediately. As he was round at the side of the building he could not see them, but he could hear them calling to one another.

While he fought to get his breath back, he had to decide which way to turn. To his right lay the garden, to his left a passage which led to the street. He was tempted to take the latter, but it was fringed with lean-tos which might be servants' quarters. A second later his surmise was verified. Doors opened and several men ran out. His decision was taken for him ; it had to be the garden.

As he swerved away, one of them saw him and let out a yell. They were only about thirty yards distant, so he had not much of a start. The moment he appeared in the open space at the back of the house excited cries went up from the people on the balcony. Someone threw something at him, but it sailed over his head. Darting between the chairs and tables he reached the shelter of the trees. The starlight could not penetrate through their heavy foliage, so it was very dark under them. As he ran on and the trees grew thicker he had to peer ahead from fear of running into one of the trunks. Instinctively he slowed his pace a little, but a moment afterwards he was alarmed by the impression that his pursuers were gaining on him.

He thanked God that ever since landing from the yacht he had been carrying his pistol. The attack on him in Shih-niang's room had come so swiftly that he had had no time to draw it. Thrusting a hand under his jacket he made sure that he could do so easily. He did not want to use it now, but he would rather than allow himself to be overpowered in a mêlée. In his mind there was no doubt at all that, if he were caught, in a few hours' time he would find himself being strangled by the public executioner—and that seemed to him no proper way for an English gentleman to die.

Another minute and he knew that he must be nearing the bottom of the garden. When he reached it he would either have to turn and fight or attempt to dodge the men who were after him. Deciding that his chances would be better if he started to dodge now, he swerved to the left, ran on for a dozen yards, then stumbled against something that stood out from one of the big trees. Recovering his balance, he realized that he had run into the foot of a short ladder, and that the tree it leant against must be one of those with a table and seats up in its fork.

Deliberately to limit his freedom of movement was to take

278

a big chance; but, in the circumstances, he thought it should prove worth it. Swiftly ascending the ladder, he pulled it up after him and wedged it among the branches. By groping about he found a small settee. Carefully lowering himself onto it, he strove to check the rasp of his breathing, and drew out his gun. He knew that if he were discovered up there things were going to be extremely awkward; even shooting might not disperse the human pack long enough for him to get down and away with a good fresh start. Concentrating now on his sense of hearing, he tried to fathom what his enemies were doing by the sounds they made.

At first they had raced on past the place where he had taken a sharp turn. But soon they must have reached the wall and, seeing no figure against the skyline climbing over it, returned on their tracks. At a slower pace they came pattering back, arguing loudly over whereabouts in the garden they could have lost their quarry. They were met by a group of inn guests who had come down from the balcony and followed them through the trees. To Gregory's consternation he could see that some of them were flashing torches. Calling advice and directions to one another, the little crowd scattered and began to hunt among the trees, apparently believing him to be lurking behind one of them; but, to his relief, it did not occur to any of those who came near him to flash their torches upward.

For half an hour the search went on; then Gregory overheard a dispute that took place not far from him. One of the servants who had started the chase was insisting to some other men that the murderer had had ample time to climb over the wall before they reached it. His opinion was finally accepted and, apparently, the belief that Gregory must have got away was now becoming general; for the sounds of searching decreased, and soon afterwards there was once more silence in the garden.

From the position of the tree and the way in which the little settee was wedged between two of its branches, Gregory would have been prepared to bet that chance had brought him to the very one on which he had cuddled A-lu-te two and a half weeks before; but he felt now that sitting on it was as near to her as he was ever likely to get again. The thought depressed him greatly ; but to have made any further attempt to see her that night would have been absolute madness, and he knew that if he meant to make really certain of still being alive next time the sun set, he must be out of Tung-kwan soon after it rose.

Presumably she and Kâo would still make for the old mouth of the Hwang-ho ; but there could be no question of his rejoining them further along their route, owing to the fact that he could not possibly prove to them that he had not ruined their mission by murdering the object of it. Because A-lu-te had, on the spur of the moment, saved him from capture, it did not at all follow that, with a calmer mind, she would be willing to condone what she believed to be his crime ; while it seemed quite certain that Kâo would prove hostile to the point of endeavouring to bring about his death.

There was, of course, the matter of his being A-lu-te's bondsman, and her having made herself responsible to the Council for his returning to the island with her ; but it had been agreed that no blame should attach to her should unforeseen circumstances, arising in the course of the mission, cause their separation, and so render it impossible for her to carry out her pact.

This, therefore, was the parting of their ways. One question only remained. Which was *his* way?

Much the shortest way home—as the crow flies—was through Mongolia, Soviet Russia and one of the Iron Curtain countries into Western Europe. But—quite apart from being no crow—Gregory had a very healthy respect for the M.V.D. He had pitted his wits against the Soviet secret police before, and was prepared to do so again, if it was in the interests of his country, but not just to save himself a few weeks' extra travel.

The other alternative routes to safety lay north-east, through the Korean battle-front ; south, to the troubled zones above the Malay peninsular ; or south-east, to Hong Kong. All entailed a difficult, tedious and dangerous journey ; but of the three Hong Kong seemed much the best bet, and from there he would have no trouble at all in securing transport back to 'England, Home and Beauty'.

As the old phrase entered his mind, he sighed. England was forever England, but his Home was empty now, and the Beauty that had been the mainspring of his existence he would never see again.

For the first time it occurred to him that the unfortunate Shih-niang's death might also be a tragedy for himself. A-lu-te was a lovely person and, while he had now had ample evidence that she was capable of passion, there was no doubt that her mind was mainly dominated by her intellect ; so he did not think she would have asked of him more than he could give. Life could have been very pleasant married to such an exceptional woman, who combined in herself most of the best qualities of the East and West, in that enchanted Island where Time Stands Still. Whereas now, the future loomed tasteless, unsettled and desperately empty.

Feeling that he must allow at least an hour to elapse for things to settle down again before he left his hiding place, he began once more to speculate on what might really lie behind the night's events.

Although his theory that the Communists had killed Shih-niang did not altogether fit the facts as they appeared to him, he was still inclined to favour it. The thought turned his mind to Foo. It was now over six weeks since, on the night the snake had been put in his bunk, he had seen that mysterious young man ; so, unless the face he had glimpsed in the courtyard of the inn really had been Foo's, there was no reason to suppose that he had followed them all the way from Antung-Ku. But what about the Communist who had been with the caravan, and later had appeared in the great courtyard of the House of Lin?

Thinking of them both it occurred to Gregory that there was a certain resemblance between them, and he wondered that it had not struck him before. It was no more than that they were the same height and that there was a similarity in their way of walking. The garments worn by caravan travellers—long cloaks, great hats of shaggy fur pulled down over their ears, and hoods against the sand which covered their heads and faces most of the time—lent themselves perfectly to disguise. And, in addition, the little man with the caravan had worn thick-lensed spectacles.

It was just conceivable that it had been Foo, skilfully camouflaged to conceal the fact that he was still on their trail; but the idea did not really hold water. Reluctantly but definitely Gregory had decided that it must have been Foo who had put the snake in his bunk. If so, it was he too who had poisoned the cocktail, thrown Wu-ming overboard and pushed Kâo off the top of the ladder in the hope that he would break his neck. Why, then, if in secret he had been doing his utmost to sabotage the mission and had made two attempts on Gregory's life, should he have saved him from being stoned on the way up to Yen-an? That just did not make sense; so they must be different people.

There were other snags, too, about the theory that the Communists were responsible for Shih-niang's death. Why hadn't they just pulled her in on any trumped-up charge and liquidated her at their leisure? Again, if Lin Wân had known their intentions and, with Kâo's knowledge, deliberately planted her as a scapegoat, why, when she had taken the expected rap, had Kâo, without even bothering to inquire into what had happened, immediately accused Gregory of having killed her?

It seemed much more probable that Lin Wân had been playing a lone hand, and that Kâo knew nothing of the substitution. But wait! That was impossible, because Kâo had met the real Josephine in San Francisco.

Berating himself that such an important point should have escaped him for so long although the past two hours had been anything but ideal for quiet reasoning—Gregory sought to relate the whole picture to this new and definite fact that had so suddenly emerged from his cogitations.

Yet a moment later he was back where he had started. It was not a definite fact at all; no more than an assumption. Kâo had called on Madame Août in San Francisco, but he had never said or indicated in any way that her daughter had been present at their meeting. There was not one atom of proof that he had ever seen her.

That being so, the theory which remained by far the most plausible was that, for some purpose of his own, Lin Wân had palmed Kâo off with a fake, and, having done so, had had a good reason for wanting to get rid of the fake as soon as it could be done without suspicion attaching to himself. But for what reason? Surely not just to get back a few thousand dollars?

Suddenly Gregory got it. Lin Wân had been afraid that Shih-niang would not be able to keep up the pretence of being dumb, even for three weeks. If her mouth could be closed before she gave the game away, he would be in the clear for good and all. Kâo and A-lu-te would return to the island and report that they had found the Princess Josephine, but on the way back she had been murdered, and that would be the end of the matter.

Another thought: Tû-lai had been in the plot but had not approved it. He had known that Shih-niang had been secretly condemned to death by his father, but, out of compassion, he had warned her of her danger. There could be more to it than that, though. Perhaps he had felt repugnance at the idea of being on the spot when the deed was done. If so he could have arranged before leaving for a courier to overtake him before they reached Tung-Kwan, with an urgent message necessitating his immediate return. It would have had to be something of considerable gravity. What more suitable than that his father had suddenly died? Kâo's party would return to their island and not learn that the message was a lie until many months or, perhaps, years later. If that was the set-up old Lin Wân was still alive.

As Gregory's mind revved over, he was more than ever intrigued by these riddles:

Why had Lin Wân substituted Shih-niang for Josephine?

Had Kâo been aware that she was a fake?

Was Lin Wân still alive?

If so, what were his intentions with regard to the real Princess?

Was she still at the House of Lin?

If not, what had become of her?

Suddenly it occurred to him that to solve this extraordinary conundrum would be much more fun than sitting drinking gin-slings in the club at Hong Kong while waiting for a passage home.

Swiftly he began to tot up his assets and liabilities. On the one hand he was dressed as a Chinaman and now spoke colloquial Chinese with considerable fluency; he had papers which would keep him out of trouble with the Communists; he was armed and had plenty of money. On the other, he was now friendless and wanted for murder.

He had not much doubt, given reasonable luck, of his ability to get away from Tung-kwan without being caught, and of reaching Hong Kong safely; but to take on the powerful Lin Wân single-handed was a very different matter.

All the same, for a moment he contemplated the kick he would get out of a complete triumph—if he could find the Princess, take her to the Island where everybody would suppose her to be dead, clear himself in the eyes of the delighted A-lu-te, and earn her smiling gratitude.

That, he realized, with a sudden access of sobriety, was far too much to hope for; but he might at least get at the truth for his own satisfaction.

To do so he would have to return to the House of Lin, for it was there that the heart of the secret lay. How could he manage to get there? Wanted for Shih-niang's killing as he was, he could not possibly go openly into the great yard of the inn and bargain with a caravan master to take him up there in a day or two's time. He had got to be out of Tung-kwan an hour or two after dawn. But wait; there was a way.

It would be damnably risky, and the approach to it needed a lot of thinking out. Yet with luck and nerve he might pull it off. Even if he succeeded in reaching Lin Wân's great house again, the moment he entered it he would now be putting his head into the lion's mouth. But he had already taken his decision. Unless his old subtle skill in handling men had failed him, by the light of dawn he would once more be on his way to find the lost Princess.

18

THE ARM-PIT OF THE TORTOISE

SHIH-NIANG'S murder had occurred shortly after midnight. For an hour Gregory had lain hidden on the roof of the great caravanserai, the second hue and cry after him had continued for over half an hour, and for another hour he had remained up in the tree contemplating the grim uncertainties of the future ; so it was now a little past three in the morning.

As the date was October the 11th, dawn was still a good way off ; but he wanted to be out of Tung-kwan by first light if possible and, even if everything went well, time must be allowed for various preparations before departure. A try for an early start also meant that if things went wrong, yet he had the luck to escape a third time, he would still have an hour or two of darkness in which to get out of the town on his own. On these considerations, he decided that without further delay he would put his plan into execution.

It was based on the opening of a short story that he had read many years before and always considered to be one of the best in the English language. *Honours Easy* was its title, and it was by that brilliant editor of the *Manchester Guardian,* C. E. Montague. Its hero, when living abroad as a small boy, was given by his foreign nurse a tortoise. She told him that it was a useful pet, because it ate cockroaches. He promptly captured a cockroach and set it before the tortoise, like an early Christian in front of a lion. While the tortoise thought, the cockroach acted. Realizing its peril, it leapt for cover under the tortoise's shell and saved itself by taking refuge in its enemy's arm-pit. Gregory now intended to make a practical use of that admirable example—although he realized that there was always the unpleasant possibility that, in this case, the tortoise might think quickly and he would end up crushed between its jaws.

Lowering the ladder he came down out of the tree. Having checked his pistol again, he put it in his outer right-hand pocket so that without showing it he could cover anyone and, if necessary, shoot them through his coat ; then he cautiously went forward.

When he reached the edge of the trees he was relieved to see that no lights showed at the back of the inn. Skirting the last of the tables to his left, he made for the corner below A-lu-te's room, and entered the dark passage in which lay the servants' quarters. No sign of life came from the lean-tos there and, taking his time so as to make a minimum of noise, he walked quietly past them. He was heading for the great courtyard and thought that he might have to go out into the street then enter it by its main gate ; but just beyond the last of the lean-tos, he saw to his right the dim outline of a low, doorless arch in the wall of the inn. Turning into it, he found that it was the entrance to a low passage which ran through the building, enabling the servants to go to and fro without actually entering it. A moment later he emerged in the courtyard.

By getting so far without discovery he had got over his first fence, as had he been spotted on his way there by anyone who had participated in the hunt for him earlier that night, they would have challenged him as possibly being the murderer ; but now he was temporarily safe. The great courtyard had upwards of a hundred people in it and scores of animals. In the semi-darkness he could make out, on all sides, lines of hobbled ponies, squatting camels, stacks of merchandise, and low bivvies under which porters and drivers were sleeping round dying fires. Now that he could mingle with them, any of them who were awake would take him only for one of themselves.

Going boldly forward, he zigzagged his way between the drowsing beasts and goat-skin shelters towards the right hand side of the courtyard near its gate, as it was there that Lin Wân's men had made their little camp. It was so similar to the others that in the faint starlight it was by no means easy to pick out ; but, knowing roughly its location, he managed to identify it by counting the number of men and animals.

Chou and his four companions lay huddled in their bivvie, one side of which they had left open so as to get the benefit of the fire they had built outside it. As they were swathed like mummies in their furs and blankets it was impossible to tell which of them was which, and all of them were sound asleep.

Halting beside them Gregory looked towards the gate. The way to it was clear, and he took some comfort from the fact that it was only about fifteen yards distant. If things went wrong, as Chou and his men would still be half bemused by sleep he reckoned that he would stand a fair chance of getting through it before they could lay hands on their weapons and aim them at him. His uncertainty about how much Chou knew of Lin Wân's affairs made the step he was on the point of taking a most desperate gamble; but if it came off the reward would be high, so he was now determined to take it. Stooping down, he shook the nearest man awake, and whispered:

'Are you Chou?'

The man poked his head up from under his coverings and muttered incoherently: then, on Gregory's repeating his question, he rolled over, thrust out a hand, prodded his neighbour into wakefulness and, rolling back again, fell asleep. As the second man growled out a curse and sat up Gregory kicked the remnants of the fire into a blaze. Turning back he looked down into a round lined face that might have been any age between forty and seventy, and have belonged to any of the older men lying asleep nearby; but the light given by a flickering flame was enough for Gregory to make out a heavy scar on the lower lip, which removed any doubt about the man being Chou.

Putting his right hand in his pocket he closed it round the butt of his automatic, so that if the need arose he had only to squeeze the trigger. Being now firmly of the opinion that Lin Wân had ordered Chou to close Shih-niang's mouth, and fearing that Chou might seize this chance to pin the murder on him, he was fully prepared to shoot the Chinaman at the first sign of hostility. But he hoped first to intrigue and then to bluff him. Leaning forward, he said in a low voice:

'We cannot now afford to wait till dawn. You must get ready to start as soon as possible.'

Chou had been sleeping in his goat-skin cap, and his small dark eyes peered up through its shaggy fur like those of a Skye terrier. After a moment, he said: 'Why do you wake me in the middle of the night, Lord?'

Gregory took his finger off the trigger of his gun. Chou had recognized him and, although he did not know that he was covered with a pistol, had not made the slightest move to spring up, or rouse the courtyard by crying out that here was the murderer. That was another obstacle surmounted, and such a potentially dangerous one that it might prove the Becher's Brook of the whole operation. But there were plenty of nasty hazards yet to be faced before the completion of the course. Keeping himself tensed, ready to meet the first sign of trouble, Gregory quietly repeated what he had said.

'But why should we lose two hours' sleep to start now?' Chou asked.

'Because I must get away before everyone wakes up,' Gregory replied.

'Are you, then, coming with us?'

'Of course!' Gregory made his voice sound impatient. 'That was settled when the old Lord decided on the roles that all of us should play here.'

'I know nothing of this,' Chou said in a puzzled voice.

'Do you mean to say that the young Lord, Tû-lai, did not tell you before he left us that I should be returning with you to the House of Lin?'

Chou shook his head. 'He said nothing of that to me.'

'Then his distress and the hurry of his departure must have caused him to forget. Anyhow, that was the arrangement. Had I been able to secure the precious thing unsuspected we could have left at dawn; but I was chased, and for the past three hours have been in hiding. That is why we must get away before everyone wakes up and I am recognized.'

'Forgive me, Lord, but I do not understand,' Chou muttered.

Gregory wondered anxiously if he meant that he did not understand his words or their meaning. Between themselves such men as Chou spoke a patois unintelligible to others, and their Mandarin Chinese was even less fluent than Gregory's. Using the simplest expressions possible, he said:

'The Lord Lin Wân desired a precious thing and charged

me to get it for him. It was expected that the killing of the woman would lead to much confusion and——'

'Ah!' Chou interrupted. 'We were aroused about midnight by much shouting, and learned that in the inn a girl had had her throat cut by a robber.'

'Is that all you knew of it?' Gregory asked, and he could not altogether keep a shade of doubt out of his voice.

'Yes, Lord!' replied the Chinaman in a tone of surprise. 'What else should we know?'

Now, Gregory was again on extremely dangerous ground. Believing that Chou was responside for Shih-niang's death, he had visualized two possibilities. The first was that being aware that he, Gregory, was suspect, the Chinaman would seize on the opportunity further to divert suspicion from himself by raising a new alarm and endeavouring to get him captured. The second was that, if he posed as an accessory before the crime, Chou would believe that they had both been acting on secret instructions given them by Lin Wân, and so be bluffed into admitting to it.

The first possibility had been the immediate risk he had had to run in rousing Chou; and, having escaped it, to bring about the latter situation was the thing for which he had since been angling. But, if the Chinaman's spontaneous reaction could be taken at its face value, he had had no hand in Shih-niang's murder. Should that be so it destroyed the whole basis of the conception on which Gregory had been working.

That any of Chou's companions could have done the job without his knowledge seemed most unlikely; yet if neither he, nor one of them, had killed the girl, who the devil had? There was, of course, the possibility that even to someone presenting themselves as an accomplice Chou thought it safer to pretend complete innocence. That seemed the only possible explanation.

Staring down at the dark inscrutable face, lit only faintly by the still flickering fire, Gregory wondered what line to take now. Then, it suddenly came to him that whether Chou admitted his guilt or not, or even should he really be innocent, made no material difference to the plan conceived in the tree fork. He was Lin Wân's servant; therefore if he could be convinced that Gregory was obeying Lin Wân's orders he might still be induced to play the role that Gregory had planned for him. The question was how much, how little, and exactly what to say.

Gregory had already spoken of the 'killing of the woman'; but neither he nor Chou had so far given any indication who the woman was. If Chou were covering up he would know that she was Shih-niang, or anyhow the girl who for the past week they had all referred to as the Princess Josephine; so nothing must be said which with his secret knowledge he would know to be a lie. Yet that reference to a killing could not just be left in the air; as, if he *was* innocent, he would naturally expect to be told more about it.

Gregory's first impulse was to endeavour to skim over it with a few ambiguous remarks; but, on second thoughts, he decided that he would stand a better chance of winning Chou to his purpose if he spoke out with apparent honesty. Having stood silent for a moment while thinking furiously, he launched a slightly amended version of his original plan by saying:

'The woman who died tonight was she whom we knew as the Princess. It is not for me to enquire who killed her. I know only that her death was ordered. My part was to secure the precious thing with which the Lord Kâo Hsüan had entrusted her, during the confusion resulting from her murder. See, here it is.'

As he spoke he drew from an inner pocket his British passport, and showed it to Chou. He did not open it but held it down at knee level so that the firelight showed the dull gold of the Royal Coat of Arms stamped on its cover. Putting it back in his pocket he went on:

'I was with her when the killer came, ready to do my part. I did it, as you see, and got the precious thing. But then matters went wrong. The lady A-lu-te and her uncle arrived upon the scene. Instead of believing that, like themselves, I had been brought to the room by the woman's death cry, they thought it was I who killed her. I got away and have been hiding in the garden until I felt it safe to come to you.'

Chou's expression gave no indication of his thoughts. Un-winking he continued to gaze up at Gregory in silence for a full minute, then he said, 'Neither the old Lord nor the young Lord spoke to me of you. I know nothing of all this.'

At this frigid declaration Gregory was aware of a slight sinking feeling in the pit of his stomach. Unless he could bluff Chou into co-operating, his situation was going to be even more dangerous than it had been when he entered the court-yard. By having presented himself as an accessory to Shih-niang's murder, he had once more laid himself open to the risk that Chou—if he really were innocent—might suddenly decide to arouse the whole place against him. To plead for Chou's help would, he felt certain, be taken as a sign of weak-ness ; so he took a bold line and said with some sharpness:

'I did not say that you knew anything about the woman's death ; but you will if you remain here till morning. Whoever killed her left their knife behind and——'

Chou stiffened, tapped his belt, and cut in aggressively, 'I have mine here.'

'What if you have!' Gregory rapped back. 'Men have been known to carry two knives before now. But that is beside the point. What matters is that in the morning the police will come. There will be a full inquiry. If you are not well away from the town you will be hauled back and questioned.'

'Why should that worry me, Lord? I have nothing to fear.'

'Oh, yes, you have! Do you not understand that when the Lord Kâo Hsüan finds that the precious thing he entrusted to the dead woman is not among her possessions, he will realize that it has been stolen by the orders of the Lord Lin Wân? How can he help doing so when he knows how greatly the old Lord desired it? And what then? He has no idea that I am secretly in the service of the House of Lin, so suspicion will be lifted from me. Instead it will fall on you and your companions.'

Much to Gregory's relief he saw that Chou was beginning to look uncomfortable, so he pressed home his point. 'You know what devils the police can be to poor men when they are accused by a rich lord like Kâo Hsüan. They will flog you all to within an inch of your lives. Whether one of you killed the girl or not you will confess to it, rather than endure further torment. Then they will hand you over to the executioner to be strangled.'

Suddenly flaring into anger Chou burst out, 'It is you who should be strangled! I have no doubt now that to get the precious thing you killed the Princess yourself.'

The bitter accusation again seemed to attest Chou's innocence, and it momentarily disconcerted Gregory. But now was no time to puzzle further over that. The implied threat had brought them back once more to the flash-point of danger at which Chou might make a grab at him and begin to yell that he had caught the murderer.

Slipping his hand into his pocket, Gregory again grasped his gun. With an effort he managed to keep his voice low and steady as he took up the challenge and sought to turn it to his purpose.

'No. I did not kill her. But if I had, what of it? I should have done so only in order to carry out the wishes of your Lord.'

'Why should I believe that? You have given me no proof that you are in his service.'

'Is it not plain? Should I be here if I were not?'

'Perhaps; since you are seeking to make use of me to get away.'

Mentally Gregory winced as this keen shaft of truth went straight to the mark. He was beginning to fear now that the shrewd, tough little half-Mongolian caravan guard would get the better of him; but he had so much at stake that he risked a desperate throw, and asked:

'If your Lord had ordered you and your four men to take me as a prisoner from here to the House of Lin, do you think that during the journey I should be able to outwit or overcome the five of you and escape?'

For the first time the suggestion of a smile showed on Chou's round, wrinkled face. 'No,' he said decisively. 'It has been plain to us from the beginning that you are both a Long-nose and a townsman. By night you might trick us and get away; but we would catch you again before you had gone five miles. Once clear of Tung-kwan, I would stake my life on getting you to the House of Lin.'

'Very well then. Consider me as your prisoner. If I try to escape you can shoot me. I ask only that you should take me to your Lord. Surely that is proof enough that I am in his service.'

Chou did not reply. He sat there in silence, now staring at the ground; evidently still undecided whether to do as Gregory asked or to refuse and, perhaps, make some fateful move which would summon a crowd of a hundred men bent on administering rough justice.

The night was chilly, but Gregory's anxiety was so great that little beads of perspiration were breaking out on his forehead. With his right hand still on his hidden gun he made his final bid. Kneeling down, he put his left hand on Chou's shoulder, gave him a slight shake, and said:

'Listen, Chou. By doing as I ask you have nothing to lose and everything to gain. If you stay here you are going to be in bad trouble in the morning. Even if you get away later, but arrive at the House of Lin without me, your Lord is going to give you hell for leaving me behind. I have the precious thing —the thick paper with the gold designs on it—which will give him the power to humble his enemies. Take me to him so that I can hand it over and he will give you a handsome reward. Come! We have no time to waste! Wake your men and tell them to saddle the ponies.'

Chou's little dark eyes had narrowed to slits, but he nodded. 'If my Lord ordered the Princess's death so that you might take from her the precious thing, his anger would be great if I prevent it reaching him. If he did not, then when we come to him he will have you impaled upon a stake and afterwards throw your body to the vultures. We have talked enough. It shall be as you wish.'

As what Gregory had termed 'the precious thing' was no more than a slim booklet containing his photograph and a record of his more recent travels up to the past April, it could be of no possible use to the master of the House of Lin; so he had no cause at all to be elated by Chou's forecast of the situation in which he would find himself on reaching the house. Nevertheless, he had at last emerged victorious from their long wrangle, and that was all that mattered for the moment. Suppressing a sigh of relief, he stood up.

Chou, too, got to his feet and began to wake his companions. As they roused, one glance at the still bright stars in the dark vault overhead was enough to tell them that dawn was still a long way off. In loud angry voices they began to curse him, and ask what the devil possessed him to have got them up in the middle of the night.

On tenterhooks, Gregory had to stand there, fearing that at any moment the noise they were making might arouse a score of other men sleeping nearby, and that a general argument would follow, during which the reason for Chou's decision to make an early start would come out, with the result that he would yet find himself surrounded by a hostile throng.

In gutteral phrases of dialect, Chou stilled the clamour made by his fellows, and with surly looks they went about their preparations for departure. But others in the vicinity stretched out round dying fires were now stirring and calling questions; so Gregory knew that he was not yet in the straight.

He passed the next twenty minutes in an agony of apprehension; but, one by one, their more wakeful neighbours, whose curiosity had been aroused, accepted Chou's trumped-up explanations and again dropped off to sleep. The ponies were given a few gulps of water from leather buckets, then saddled or loaded with their panniers containing tents and provisions; the camel that had brought Shih-niang down to Tung-kwan was prodded up on to its legs, and the little caravan was ready to start.

Mounting the pony that had been saddled for him, Gregory trotted it up beside Chou's, and together they led the short procession out of the courtyard. Half an hour later they had left the last straggling houses on the outskirts of Tung-kwan behind, with dawn still a good hour away.

Gregory knew that he had much reason to be thankful; but, all the same, he was beginning to wonder if during the past hour he had not behaved like a crazy fool. He had pulled off an incredibly difficult coup, and was now safe in the arm-pit of the tortoise, but how the devil he was ever going to get out of it again he had not the faintest idea.

19

"THERE IS MANY A SLIP..."

THE little caravan had not been on its way for many hours before it was quite clear to Gregory that, unless he took some definite action, he was in for a most unpleasant journey ; and, infinitely worse, might not even live to reach the end of it.

Having already spent a week in the company of Chou and his villainous-looking crew on the way down from Yen-an, he had had ample opportunity to take their measure. These small, tough pony-riders all had a good dash of Mongolian blood and differed little in essentials from the hordes of wild tribesmen with which Genghis Khan had overrun four-fifths of the known world in the thirteenth century. Mentally they were primitive and, for the most part, lived only in the moment. They were greedy, ruthless, cruel and boastful, but brave, gay and open-handed. With reckless enthusiasm they would fling themselves into any violent sport, and, although they were quick to anger, their general attitude to life was that of happy children, for they chattered incessantly and laughed immoderately at the most infantile jokes. It was the unnatural lack of chatter and laughter among them now that so greatly perturbed Gregory.

The surly looks they had given him on setting out had been readily accounted for by his having caused them to lose two

295

hours' sleep; but after the first hour of the journey, during which they had carried on a heated argument in their own dialect, all five of them had fallen into a sullen silence. To Gregory's own efforts at conversation Chou replied only in monosyllables, while the others openly showed their hostility by pretending not to understand him, and even refusing to meet his glance.

The prospect of six or seven days in such uncongenial company was far from pleasant; but the matter which really agitated Gregory's mind was the memory of the attempt to stone him to death on his first journey up to Yen-an. That had been made by a more numerous band of ruffians but of very similar type; and these five had firearms. Once they were well out into the wilds, Gregory could see nothing to prevent their doing him in, if they felt so inclined, and for a much better reason than the mere fact that he happened to be a Longnose.

To induce Chou to let him accompany them back to the house of Lin he had had to provide a suitable excuse for wanting to return there. For that, the story he had invented about the 'precious thing', and having been commissioned to secure it for Lin Wân, had served admirably; but it was now a potential source of danger.

The minds of these primitive men were still steeped in magic and superstition. Had the 'precious thing' he had displayed to Chou been some fabulous jewel, that would have been the end of the matter. It would never have entered their heads to rob him of a thing which they could neither use nor dispose of to advantage in this remote and poverty-stricken province. But his British passport was a very different matter. Since it was a paper engraved with strange symbols, and the Lord Lin set a high enough value on it to have a Princess murdered in order to secure it for himself, to them it could only be some form of talisman which conferred great magical powers on its possessor.

It was therefore, Gregory now felt, a highly dubious asset. On the one hand, as they knew him to be carrying it they might be too scared of its possible powers to attempt anything against him. On the other, the temptation to gain such a prize might easily lead one of them to creep upon him in the night and murder him for it.

Obviously something had to be done to change their attitude and win, if not their friendship, at least their wholesome respect. The first item on the programme was to show he was armed; so he began to keep his eyes open for a suitable opportunity to produce his automatic and, if possible, use it with good effect. Having prepared it for an instant draw he rode on a little way ahead of the column and, after about twenty minutes, saw his chance.

At his approach a small flight of duck rose from a pond near the track and winged away towards the river. As he was a crack shot with a pistol there was just a chance that he might bring one down, but if he missed he would still have shown his gun, which was really all that mattered. Taking careful aim just ahead of the last bird in the flight he loosed off at it. His luck could not have been better. The bullet severed the bird's neck and it came hurtling earthwards.

With spontaneous cries of delight two of the men who were not leading strings of animals galloped forward in a race to retrieve it. Pocketing his gun Gregory produced a U.S. dollar bill and held it out to the winner. The man gave him a look of surprise but took it eagerly. Then, as he returned to his companions they all began to chatter.

While Gregory was tying the dead duck on to his saddle, Chou came up beside him, and said with open admiration, 'That was a fine shot, Lord. Few men could bring down a bird at that distance with a pistol.'

Gregory shrugged. 'From my youth I have been what you would call a soldier of fortune; so arms are my trade, and several times I have owed my life to being able to draw a pistol quickly.' Then, with a glance behind him he added, 'It is good to hear the men talking again. Why have they been so silent all the morning?'

Chou gave him an uncomfortable look. 'All of us admired the poor dumb Princess, Lord; and how can we help but believe that it was you who killed her. If it were done by the orders of the Lord our master, it is not for us to question the act ; but as men we cannot be expected to approve the killing of a defenceless woman.'

His answer was more or less what Gregory had expected, and it gave him the opening to say, 'I robbed her after she was dead, Chou, but I swear by your gods and mine that I did not kill her. Please tell your men that. And now, will you in turn swear to me that you had no hand in her death?'

'Yes. I swear it, And I can vouch too, for the innocence of my men. None of them could have left our camp-fire before midnight without my knowing.'

'In that case it must have been done by an agent of the Lord Lin's living in Tung-kwan, to whom he sent secret instructions. Perhaps we shall learn the truth when we arrive at Yen-an. Anyhow, until we get there let us accept one another's word that we were not responsible for this horrible business, and say no more about it.'

To that Chou nodded assent. Then, after a glance at the sun, which, as it was nearly nine o'clock, was now well up, he pointed downhill towards a stream some half a mile ahead that ran into the river, and said :

'As we started so early it is time for a long halt. That looks a good place so we will eat our rice there.'

Seeing another opportunity to get things on a better footing Gregory replied, 'Good ; then let us cheer the party up. I'll take the lead animals and all of you shall race to it. To the first man to water his pony at the stream I will give a prize of five U.S. dollars.'

Chou's face broke into a grin, and on his shouting the offer to his companions it was received with acclamation. A few minutes later the five men were lined up. Gregory fired his pistol in the air and in a cloud of dust they thundered off down the slope.

When he joined them with the two strings of animals, and duly handed over the prize, he felt that he was making good progress ; but the men had still not regained their natural cheerfulness and he wanted to get them laughing ; so he resorted to another stratagem.

As they set about preparing the meal he went behind a nearby rock and took his trousers down. After crouching there for a few minutes he rejoined them and began to lend a hand. Suddenly he let out a yell and clutched himself between the legs. They all stopped what they were doing and turned to stare at him, as he treated them to a delightful piece of pantomime. With a look of agony on his face he proceeded to slap himself about the crutch, shout, run up and down, jump about, and swear lustily. Having seen him go behind the rock they naturally assumed that while his trousers were down a centipede or a stinging ant had got into his clothes and was now making a meal off him.

It was just the sort of happening to appeal to their sense of humour. All five of them pointed at him, jabbered to each other and went into fits of laughter. Clapping their hands, and slapping their thighs in imitation of his frantic gestures, they laughed till they cried; and as he finally ran off behind the rocks to debag himself again and pretend to rid himself of his tormentor the whole valley was ringing with their mirth. The episode kept them merry all through the meal, and when they set off after it their gloom of the morning had been dissipated.

Soon afterwards they came to a fair-sized village, where Gregory managed to buy some toilet articles and other oddments, to replace things he had been compelled to abandon in Tung-kwan, and in addition a hooded cloak, fur hat and blankets.

By three o'clock in the afternoon they had already put in a longer day than usual, so they camped for the night in the courtyard of a small ruined temple. After they had eaten, as the men were not yet sleepy and Gregory knew that one of their favourite sports was wrestling, he suggested that they should have a series of matches, for which he would give prizes. They needed no second invitation but with ready shouts ran to collect stones for drawing lots, their system being that the two who drew the largest and smallest stones out of a hat should lead off in the first bout.

All of them were strong and agile but Gregory had no doubt that he could master any of them individually, and he had led them into the contest with a definite purpose. He had no intention of wrestling himself, but when the tournament was over he went up to the winner, gave him his prize, then in three swift moves threw him over his arched back.

There was a roar of applause, except for the man he had thrown, who picked himself up and came at him like a panther. But Gregory had expected that and, without ever allowing him to get a hold, tripped or flung him again and again in a succession of judo passes. When he had tired the man he told him to stop, and that he should have an extra five dollars for the falls he had taken. As he paid his panting antagonist he told them all that his ability to get the better of a stronger man was not due to any magic, but simply to a special form of training that anyone could learn. Then, to their delight, he spent the next half-hour teaching them the elementary principles of ju-jitsu.

By the time he tucked himself up in his blankets it was thirty-six hours since he had slept, the past night had been one of great strain and the day one of mental as well as physical effort, so he felt desperately tired ; but he had the considerable comfort of believing that he could now go to sleep without fear of being woken with a knife in his ribs. The additional tax he had put on his wits and muscles during the past eight hours had proved well worth while, as the five potential enemies with whom he had set out before dawn had been converted into admiring friends, and he had every reason to think that they would continue so for the rest of the journey.

In that he proved right ; the only things that marred his enjoyment of the five days that followed were the wind-borne dust of the daily trek, the cold of the nights, and intermittent bouts of anxiety about the tricky situation in which he would find himself when he arrived.

Considering the simple mentalities of Chou and his men, their reaction to Shih-niang's death could not possibly be put down to a cleverly conceived piece of acting ; so Gregory was now fully convinced that they had had nothing to do with it. The conclusion threw him back on the theory that the Communists were at the bottom of it, as the only other plausible one he had been able to evolve ; but to accept it left numerous blanks in the picture which he could not even rough in by the wildest guessing.

More than once, as he puzzled over it, he wished that he was one of those really clever people about whom one reads in detective fiction. If he had had a lisp and a head like an egg, or been a kindly old gentleman who went about sniffing everything, or a spinster who rarely left her arm-chair and her knitting, or the remarkable blind chap who just felt the things that ham-handed police superintendents brought to him, no doubt he would have had the solution to all the mysteries—from the falling of the banana crates on Tsai-Ping's head up to the knifing of Shih-niang—in a flash. Any of them would have said:

'My poor fellow, you have allowed that fat, jolly Kâo to pull the wool over your eyes all along. He may appear lazy but he is not, and he wants to be King of the Island. Moreover he is the one person who has had the opportunity to commit all these crimes.' And they would have proceeded to give six chapters on how he did them. Then, just as one was about to run off and get a warrant out for Kâo's arrest, they would give a gentle chuckle—or knock back five fingers of neat Rye—and, in the manner of the late Peter Cheyney, proceed to demolish the whole of their own theory. Having established the innocence of the happy-go-lucky Kâo on all counts, they would conclude:

'In all crimes *cherchez la femme*. Surely you learnt that in your kindergarten. You have allowed love to bemuse you, dear boy. The charming A-lu-te is by far the most intelligent woman in the Island, and she aspires to become another Empress Yehonala. To eliminate her only possible rival was her real reason for getting herself made a member of the mission. Her big mistake was to take you with her. If she hadn't she would never have been let in for that awful journey right into the heart of China. Of course, up to nearly the end of your stay in San Francisco she thought of you as only a harmless gigolo ; but the moment you called in the F.B.I. she realized what a danger her dear, honest, not very intelligent Gregory might be to her plans, and decided that he must be eliminated. To begin with, naturally, she made the even more stupid Wu-ming her tool ; but as he failed to do you in, even with a hatchet, and looked like giving her away, she and her maid Su-sen chucked him overboard. As the poor chap was

301

half dead already they had only to give him a rap on the head and drag him a few yards. The snake in your bunk was a typical woman's trick. Nine out of ten murderesses go for poison in one form or another. As for knifing Shih-niang, I expect she rather enjoyed that. After all she seems to have been quite fond of you, and it must have rather annoyed her to find you petting another young woman with no clothes on.'

At the conclusion of such day-dreams as these Gregory was apt to sigh. He knew as many different ways of killing people as Shih-niang had known of making love, and he was prepared to put any of them into practice against the enemies of Britain at any time, but detection had never been his line. To have worked it all out in a deck-chair, with a long cool drink to hand, while listening to the humming of the bees in the fragrance of a Surrey garden, would have been enchanting; but such joys were not for him. Since he was determined to know the truth, he must jog along on his pony the many weary dusty miles to Yen-an, and, when he got there, once more stick out his neck.

Shortly before midday on the sixth day after they had left Tung-kwan, they came over the last ridge and up through the last valley to the great House of Lin. As they approached, the man in the watch-tower sounded his trumpet, the gates were opened and a number of the armed retainers appeared at the entrance of the courtyard; but this time no figure in white flannels hurried out to greet them.

As they passed through the gates Gregory saw that the bustle and activity inside them was no less than it had been when he had left there thirteen days before. Then, within a few minutes of dismounting, he had the answer to one of his riddles. His tentative assumption that Tû-lai might have arranged for a false message to be sent to himself, so as to avoid being at hand when his father's order for the killing of Shih-niang was carried out, had no foundation. As reported by the messenger, Lin Wân had died of a heart attack on the night of October the 5th.

Gregory had received nothing but kindness from the old merchant prince; but, the circumstances being as they were, he could not help feeling relief that it was the son, and not the father, with whom he would have to deal. A servant at once took the news of his arrival to his master, and returning, led him through to the room that Lin Wân had used as an office. Tû-lai, clad in European clothes, was seated at the big desk engaged in sorting out a mass of papers.

As Gregory came in he stood up, gave him a sad but friendly smile, and said: 'It is a great surprise to see you again so soon; but you are very welcome. Please sit down. Can I offer you some refreshment?'

'Thanks.' Gregory smiled. 'I could do with a long drink to wash the dust out of my throat—a Gin-sling or something of that kind.'

Tû-lai lisped an order to the servant who had shown Gregory in, then turned back to him. 'If we were in my own room I would mix you one myself. But I have had to move in here because my father was a man of many secrets, and for the past week I have been trying to master his affairs.'

As Gregory sat down, he noticed on a side table near the desk an opium pipe with a beautifully carved jade holder. Following the Chinese custom, that however important one's business one should never enter upon it before a few exchanges having little significance have been made, he remarked:

'Surely that is Kâo's pipe. It is such a lovely thing that I've often admired it. I'm sure it must be.'

'If it is he must have forgotten it,' Tû-lai replied. 'While you were staying in the house he and my father smoked a few pipes in here together every evening. But don't let's stand on ceremony. Tell me what brings you here? I trust that your return does not mean that any misfortune has overtaken the lady A-lu-te?'

Gregory's face at once became grave. 'No. When I last saw her, six nights ago, she was in excellent health. But the same cannot be said for the other young woman who accompanied us to Tung-kwan.'

'You mean the singing girl, Shih-niang?'

'Of course.'

Tû-lai nodded. 'From what you say I infer that she is dead.'

'Yes; murdered.'

303

'I feared that unlucky fate would overtake her.'

'Unfortunately she left it too late to act upon your warning.'

'So you knew about that?'

'She told me of it herself; but only a few moments before she was killed. I wonder, though, that since you felt sufficient qualms about the matter to warn her of her danger, you stopped short of taking some step which would have saved the poor girl's life.'

With a shrug, Tû-lai spread out his hands. 'Mr. Sallust, having spent some time in China, you must be aware that the one thing a dutiful son can never bring himself to do is interfere in the affairs of his father.'

'I grant you that; but had she taken your warning in time you would have done so. While you were about it, why not have gone the whole hog?'

'Normally I should have done nothing at all. To be frank I disapproved most strongly of the whole affair; but it was not my business. As things were, I had just been overwhelmed by the news of my father's death. I was in a highly emotional state, and feeling compassion for the girl I acted on impulse. You must forgive me, though, if I fail to understand your attitude, as you must have taken part in her murder.'

'I!' exclaimed Gregory aghast. 'Whatever makes you think that? Everything points to her having been killed by an agent of your father's.'

'My father had nothing to do with it.'

'Oh, come! It was his singing-girl who was passed off as the Princess, and you have just said that you did not like to interfere because it was his affair. You knew that her death had been decreed, and to suggest now that he did not does not make sense.'

'You misunderstand me. He knew, of course, what was planned; but the idea of drowning her was not his, and none of his people was to play any part in it.'

'Drowning her?'

'Yes. It was decided that one night when you were going down the river she should be put overboard from the sampan and held under until she was dead. Did she not die that way?'

'No. We had not started on the river journey.'

'Of course. How stupid of me. Had you done so, you would not have had time to get back here so soon; but my father's funeral ceremonies have caused me to lose count of the days. Drowning was chosen for her because afterwards there would have been nothing to show that she had not fallen in by accident. Since she was not drowned, how did she die?'

'She was knifed in her room at the inn.'

'Did you catch her trying to get away; or was that owing to some change of plan at the last moment?'

'I had no more to do with it than you had,' Gregory replied tersely.

Tû-lai gave him a sceptical look. 'You seem to have forgotten your admission of a few moments back, that you were with her when she was killed.'

'I did not actually say that, although it was so. Nevertheless I had no part in planning her death and I was unable to prevent it.'

At that moment the servant entered with the Gin-sling. Gregory took a long drink, and as the man left the room Tû-lai said: 'Anyhow I can hardly suppose that you have come all the way back here to reproach me for not having prevented Shih-niang's murder. What reason led you to return?'

Gregory had given much thought to the reply he should make to this question, and had decided to attempt a colossal bluff; so he said quietly, 'Kâo sent me back to collect the real Princess.'

'Really!' Tû-lai raised his eyebrows. 'I find that rather surprising. Still, you can have her with pleasure—providing you've brought the money.'

With a slight quickening of the heart, Gregory remarked, 'She is still here, then.'

'Certainly. Why should you have supposed that I had sent her away during the past fortnight?'

'To be honest, I didn't know for certain that she was here when I was here before,' Gregory confessed. 'In fact, although I ought to have tumbled to it from the beginning I didn't realize that Shih-niang was a fake until she told me so herself on our reaching Tung-kwan.'

Tû-lai's face suddenly broke into a boyish grin. 'Well, just fancy that! I naturally assumed you were in the plot. No wonder you were taken by surprise when she was murdered. I apologize for having disbelieved you. Anyhow, if you've brought the cash you can take Josephine away whenever you like.'

With some hesitation Gregory produced Shih-niang's satchel and, laying it on the desk, said, 'I take it this is the money that you refer to?'

Emptying out the satchel, Tû-lai gave the notes it had contained a few flicks with his fingers, then he frowned at Gregory and asked, 'What sort of joke is this?'

Gregory shrugged. 'Personally I don't think there is much of a joke about it. That is the money your father paid Shih-niang to impersonate Josephine. The poor girl died under the impression that it was to get it back that your father had arranged for her to be killed. As I dropped some of the notes it is a bit short of the original ten thousand dollars; but of course I'll make it up out of the money I have on me.'

'Do you really think this paltry sum is what I meant by money?'

'I'm afraid I'm very much at sea in this whole business,' Gregory admitted. 'You say your father had no hand in Shih-niang's death; but your mention of money made me think that perhaps, after all, he had; although I have thought all along that he was not the sort of man who would either go back on a bargain or kill one of his own concubines for a fist full of dollar bills.'

'And you were right. The sum which Kâo agreed to pay my father for the Princess was half-a-million dollars!'

'I see. So you are holding her to ransom?'

Tû-lai smiled. 'My father was a very able business man, and he preferred to use business terms. No doubt he would have said that this payment was to reimburse him for the expenses to which he had been put in connection with the Princess. But, if you wish, I have no objection to speaking of it as her ransom. "A rose by any other name . . ." you know. However, the thing which does concern me is—can I hope that you are now about to produce this handsome contribution to the maintenance of the House of Lin? or is it that, knowing

306

my father to be dead and believing me to have only scant knowledge of his affairs. Kâo Hsüan sent you back here in the hope that you might succeed in putting a fast one over on me?'

Gregory smiled back. 'You can rule out any hope of the half-million dollars.'

'I feared as much,' Tü-lai remarked amiably. 'As Kâo had no means of raising such a sum before he arrived here, I did not see how he could possibly have managed to do so in the past week. I may take it, then, that my father's dear old friend conceived the charming idea of sending you to try your hand at cheating the poor orphan?'

'No ; that's not right either.' Gregory paused for a moment, then leaned forward a little. 'Look ; d'you mind if we start again from the beginning. It's clear to me now that I arrived here with a lot of misconceptions about your father and yourself. On that account I have not been altogether honest with you. And, of course, it's obvious that you have quite a wrong idea of the part that I have played in this affair. Let's be frank with one another and put all our cards on the table.'

Tû-lai gave a slightly ironical bow. 'Permit me to observe that, so far, I have told no lies to you.'

'I didn't suggest you had,' Gregory replied with a disarming smile. 'I was simply apologizing for my own lapses. All the same, there must be a lot that I know about this set-up that you don't, and vice versa. Are you willing to come clean with me if I come clean with you?'

'Why not? The affair intrigues me greatly, and there are still many things about it that I don't understand. As you are my guest I will offer you the privilege of speaking first.'

As Gregory acknowledged the courtesy he had a slightly uneasy feeling. Perhaps it was his imagination but he thought he had detected a slightly sinister inflection on the word 'guest'. In this great house, all the inmates of which were virtually Tû-lai's slaves, and which lay the best part of a month's journey from the nearest British Consulate, what was there to stop the word 'guest' being converted into 'prisoner'?

But he had known the risk he would have to run when he had decided to return to it ; so he proceeded to give a truthful account of the way in which Shih-niang had met her end, and of how, by displaying his British passport, he had bluffed Chou into covering his escape from Tung-kwan. Then he said:

'So, you see, I was lying to you when I told you that Kâo had sent me to collect the real Princess. I came back to try to get hold of her on my own account; but I had no idea that you were holding her to ransom, and I had no intention of trying to make money out of the business if I succeeded.'

Tû-lai nodded. 'You interest me more than ever. Do go on. If you are not after money, what did you hope to gain by obtaining possession of Josephine?'

'Nothing; except a certain personal satisfaction. After these many months of unsuccessful search for her, and the people of the Island having been told that she was dead, I should have got a big thrill from taking her back there and presenting her to the lady A-lu-te.'

'A-lu-te.' Tû-lai repeated with a little sigh. 'And what part do you think that lovely lady has played in all this?'

'No part at all, except to pursue the search for the Princess with all the vigour of which she is capable. It was she who was largely responsible for badgering her lazy uncle into coming to China, when he would have preferred to give up the hunt before we left San Francisco. I am convinced that she had no idea at all that your father had foisted a fake Princess on us, or the least suspicion that the girl was to be murdered.'

'I am glad you believe that, for I am also convinced that she would never have stooped to soil her hands with this dirty business.'

For a moment they were silent, then Gregory said, 'Now it is your turn. So far, I have learned only three things from our talk. Namely that the Princess is here; that you are asking half a million dollars' ransom for her; and that your father and Kâo entered into a conspiracy in which Shih-niang was to be passed off as Josephine, and afterwards murdered. What else can you tell me?'

'I'm afraid you will find my contribution somewhat disappointing,' Tû-lai replied thoughtfully. 'You see, for most of the year I am away from home and I was not here when my father returned from his last trip to America. Had I been, no doubt he would have told me the Princess's history then, and why he had brought her back with him. As it was I did not even know of her existence until about five weeks ago, and I had been home for several days before I learned of her presence here. That same afternoon the lady Fan-ti took me to the women's quarters and presented me to her; then, a few evenings later, it was suggested that she would make a charming wife for me.'

Suddenly there flashed back into Gregory's mind the morning on which Madame Fan-ti had taken A-lu-te, Kâo and himself to see the view through the lattices to the women's court. Recalling it to Tû-lai, he said:

'If you remember, Madame Fan-ti mentioned that you lost your first wife last year, and said that it was time you took another. Then she pointed out a most lovely little person and told us that your father did not wish to press you but hoped that you would take her as a new wife. Was she the Princess Josephine?'

Tû-lai nodded. 'Yes; and I recall thinking at the time that my father ought to have warned the lady Fan-ti not to take A-lu-te to the women's court, in case she stumbled on the truth. That, of course, was why he opposed her being installed there when she first arrived. The lady Fan-ti was not told of the deception it was intended to practise until later, and that morning visit might have ruined everything. At the sight of Josephine Kâo became as nervous as a cat, and, if you remember, did his best to hurry us all away.'

'Then he had seen her before, in San Francisco?'

'Oh, yes; from various things I heard him say to my father I feel sure he must have. Anyhow, as I was telling you, they wanted me to marry her; but, lovely as she is, I felt most reluctant to take a dumb girl for a wife; so I stalled about it. A fortnight later we learned that your party was on its way here. My father called me into his office, and it was only then that I learnt a certain amount about this business.

'He was in a high good humour, as he thought that Kâo was bringing him half a million dollars; and as I had shown reluctance to become affianced to the Princess, he knew that it

309

would be no hardship to me if she was disposed of elsewhere. He explained that he would never have suggested the marriage if he had thought Kâo would pay up; and that this was the outcome of a highly-speculative venture that he had entered into when last in San Francisco, without really expecting it to come off. He had never before spoken to me about your Island, and I had known of it only as a customer on our books entered as Mr. Six, with agency addresses in several cities; but he told me its history, charging me to keep it a close secret, and about how its Council wished to make Josephine its Empress. He also told me how he had come to know the Août's in San Francisco and of the narrow life they led there. Beyond that he said very little, except that when Kâo arrived I was to say nothing to him or any of his people about the money side of the affair.'

'Did he give no indication of what had led to his becoming involved in the first place?' Gregory asked.

Tû-lai shook his handsome head. 'No, and it was not for me to question him. I was very fond of my father, and it would ill-become me to besmirch his reputation now that he is dead. But in fairness I should tell you that he would go to almost any lengths to increase his great fortune. Although he did not actually say so, I gathered the impression that when Kâo first went to San Francisco to collect Josephine, my father learned of his intentions and forestalled him, with the idea that the Council would pay a big sum to get her back. I think, too, that he was quite capable of cheating Kâo out of his half million if he had seen a way to do so.'

'Do you mean that he had already conceived the idea of substituting Shih-niang for Josephine before we arrived?'

'I do not say that; although the precautions he took that the lady A-lu-te should not meet the real Princess seem to suggest it. But, of course, if he did have some such idea it must have gone up in smoke as soon as he realized that Kâo already knew Josephine by sight.'

'Yet the substitution took place all the same.'

'Yes. It was on the day after your arrival that my father told me Kâo was in no position to pay up after all, but they were considering a scheme by which we still might get the half-million in the long run. As it would have been quite contrary to his principles to let Kâo take Josephine away simply on trust, I thought perhaps he was toying with the idea of letting him do so providing that he left the lady A-lu-te behind as a hostage. Naturally I should have been all in favour of that, but I was barking up the wrong tree. The following morning he told me that it had been decided that Shih-niang should play the part of the Princess ; and that I must show her every sign of respect until we saw the last of her, because it was of the utmost importance that the lady A-lu-te should not suspect the deception which it was proposed to practise. How it was thought that the fraud would enable Kâo to raise half a million dollars, I have no idea ; but, once again, it was not for me to question my father. That's pretty well all I know about the matter.'

'You have said nothing yet about that part of the plan which required that Shih-niang should be killed.'

Tû-lai shrugged. 'I have said nothing because I know nothing. You will recall that while you were here I spent my evenings entertaining the lady A-lu-te and yourself ; so I was not present at any of the deliberations between my father and Kâo. But on the last night of your stay, after you had gone to bed, I came in here to ask my father's permission to accompany your caravan down to Tung-kwan. He agreed at once ; and it was then that he remarked to me:

' "For a girl of limited accomplishments Shih-niang gave an excellent performance, and I am really quite distressed at the thought of having to sacrifice her."

'I took it that he meant that by giving her to Kâo he was adding to his liability in the venture by the considerable amount of money that she represented ; but he went on:

' "It is necessary that she should die, and her death appear to be an accident ; so I have had to agree that a few nights after they leave Tung-kwan in a sampan she should be held under water until she drowns. I wish matters could have been arranged otherwise, but there seems no alternative if this affair is to be carried through to a satisfactory conclusion."

'As he used the word "they", and I knew that the lady A-lu-te was kept in the dark about the whole business, I jumped to the conclusion that it was you whom, in his mind, he was coupling with Kâo. That is why, at the beginning of our talk, I was under the impression that you had been in Kâo's confidence from the beginning, and that you had arranged Shih-niang's murder between you. '

'In the circumstances I can hardly blame you for that,' Gregory said with a wry smile. 'And, of course, when you warned Shih-niang you had myself as well as Kâo in mind?'

'Yes. Somehow it never occurred to me that a big, cheerful, lazy man like Kâo would take on that sort of unpleasant task himself.'

'Nor me,' Gregory agreed, 'although, of course, he may have hired some thug to do it for him.'

For a moment they were silent, and Gregory did some quick thinking. There was at least a possibility that Tû-lai was lying. As an affectionate son he might be throwing all the blame on Kâo with the object of protecting his father's memory. Yet it seemed highly improbable that he had invented the whole story. One point that had emerged quite early in their talk could be taken as proof that he had not. He had readily ad-mitted that the Princess was there in the house, and offered to hand her over on the payment of half a million dollars ; so there could be no doubt that he had been telling the truth about how Lin Wân had demanded the sum for her from Kâo. Therefore, there could also be little doubt that Kâo had decided that some advantage to himself was to be gained by accepting Shih-niang as a substitute. But what that advantage could be remained a mystery ; as did what had really hap-pened in Tung-kwan, and how far, if at all, Kâo had been responsible for the girl's death.

Finishing his drink, Gregory set down the glass and asked : 'Have you no idea at all what object your father and Kâo had in getting Shih-niang to play the part of Josephine?'

'None,' Tû-lai replied. 'Unless it was as a temporary mea-sure, adopted to prevent the lady A-lu-te making trouble about leaving here without the Princess.'

'Yes ; I thought of that. But it seems hardly likely. I see no reason why Kâo should not have explained to her that half a

312

million dollars' ransom was required, and that he hadn't got it.'

'True. Perhaps, though, it was a temporary measure designed to give Kâo time to raise the money; and it was intended to send the real Princess on to him as soon as he had paid up.'

'That is certainly possible. But, if so, why should the carrying out of the plan have necessitated Shih-niang's death? And, more inexplicable still, why should it have been decided to kill her long before Kâo could get to a place where he had any chance of raising the money? Even if it had been regarded as essential to prevent her from revealing the secret of her temporary imposture after her usefulness had ceased, that does not make sense.'

'I agree. It is quite impossible to formulate any plausible theory on the limited information we have at present. Still, there is a chance that I may come across something among my father's papers which will throw more light on the matter.'

Gregory sat forward eagerly. 'Do you really think so?'

'Yes. My father was a very secretive man but also a very methodical one. He made careful notes of all his transactions and in addition kept several diaries dealing with various aspects of his affairs.' Tû-lai paused and waved a hand towards the stacks of papers on his desk and several shelves of files locked behind a grille at the far end of the room, and added, 'But you can see for yourself that it will take me weeks to go through them all.'

'Yes; it looks like a long job,' Gregory agreed. 'And I suppose in the meantime you would not consider allowing me to take Josephine away, unless I could produce half a million dollars.'

Tû-lai smiled. 'I fear my honoured father would turn in his newly-made grave if I accepted much less for her; but I am open to an offer.'

'You think, though, that I am in no position to make you one,' Gregory smiled back.

If you were telling the truth when you said you did not know that my father was holding the Princess to ransom until I told you of it this morning, I should find it surprising to learn that you arrived here carrying a small fortune on you.'

313

'I am not. But say I were, and I handed the half-million over, what would its real value be to you?'

'I don't quite understand what you are driving at,' Tû-lai replied with a puzzled frown.

'I mean, in view of what you told A-lu-te and myself about the Communists, and the way in which they now check up on all your financial transactions, what could you manage to keep for yourself out of such a sum?'

'Oh, I see! Well, the answer to that is that as I should not be disposing of a tangible asset in exchange for it, I should be under no necessity to declare it. But, of course, to be of any real value I should have to get it out of the country. Smuggling currency is both difficult and expensive, and there is in addition always the risk that an agent may be caught, which means the complete loss of the consignment he is carrying. I suppose I should have to consider myself lucky if I could get anything over two hundred thousand dollars of it safely banked outside China.'

'You must add to your liabilities the possibility of one of these smuggling operations being traced back to you. If that happened it would probably cost you the best part of what you had left to buy yourself off from being put in a Communist jail. I think you'll agree that to be relieved of any such risk, and the worry inseparable from conducting such an operation, would be worth another hundred thousand.'

'I suppose it would. But I still don't see where this discussion is leading us.'

'Simply to this. I am in no position to make you a concrete offer of any kind. But I know people who I am certain would empower me to do so if I were able to get in touch with them. As it is I can only ask you to accept my word for that, and rely on their goodwill. You are a representative of one of the oldest families in China, and one which was invited to settle in the Island when it was first colonized. Let me take Josephine back there and come with us yourself. If, out of gratitude, the Council does not vote you a hundred thousand dollars' worth of real estate, with a pleasant house, servants and all the rest of it, I'll eat my hat.'

314

'*Mon Dieu!*' Tû-lai smacked his fist down on his desk and sprang to his feet. 'This is a terrific idea! Terrific!'

Gregory also stood up, and, grinning at him, said, 'Can I take it the deal is on, then?'

'Of course it is on!' exclaimed Tû-lai, shaking him warmly by the hand. 'Nothing could suit me better. What a laugh we shall have at having got the best of that fat fool Kâo! And I shall see the enchanting lady A-lu-te again.'

That factor, as an inescapable commitment implicit in the offer, had not escaped Gregory, and it was the one thing which had caused him to hesitate before making it. He was uneasily conscious that to invite such a likeable rival to settle in the Island might well prove against his own interests. Yet unaided it would have been very difficult for him to get back there; whereas Tû-lai, having a fleet of ships at his disposal, could get him there with comparative ease. And Tû-lai held the Princess, without whom he would have been running his head into a noose if he returned at all. On balance, he felt that he might well leave the future to take care of itself, and that by returning to the House of Lin he had achieved a remarkable triumph.

As these thoughts were coursing through his mind Tû-lai said, 'Come ; it is long past lunch-time. Our fascinating talk has led me to forget my duties as a host, and you must be famished. After we have eaten I will take you to the women's quarters and present you to the real Princess.'

They fed in Tû-lai's own apartments and over an excellent meal, cooked by a French-trained chef, he talked excitedly of their plans, asking Gregory all sorts of questions about the Island, and speculating on how soon he could wind up his father's affairs so that they could set off there. When coffee was served he sent a servant to request Madame Fan-ti's permission for them to wait upon her, and as soon as her consent was brought, they walked through several long airy corridors to her suite.

They found her sitting in her boudoir with her hands crossed idly in her lap, and dressed in the pure white of deep mourning. It was evident that although eleven days had elapsed since her husband's death, she had not yet recovered

315

from the shock and, owing to the depth of her grief, was still hardly conscious of the world around her.

Having apologized for disturbing her, Tû-lai said, 'Dear Aunt, you will remember Mr. Sallust. He has returned from Tung-kwan and I am anxious to present him to the real Princess Josephine without delay. May I have your permission to send for her, in order that I may do so?'

'Josephine,' murmured the elderly lady in a grief-stricken and slightly bewildered voice. 'Josephine; our little Princess. But have they not told you about her?'

'Told me what, dear Aunt?'

'I should have done so myself; but these last days I . . . I . . .' Two large tears rolled from the corners of her once beautiful eyes and ran down her withered cheeks.

'Pray calm yourself,' begged Tû-lai, 'and tell us what has happened to her. Is she ill?'

Madame Fan-ti sadly shook her head. 'No; but two nights ago the poor child was abducted. A Communist agent got into the women's quarters and stole her away.'

20

THE GREAT MAN-HUNT

GREGORY had been tempted to return to the House of Lin by the possibility that there he might fathom the mystery that surrounded the Princess Josephine; but for his chances of being able to take her back to the Island he would not have given a row of beans.

As he had seen it, Shih-niang's substitution for her had suggested that she was either dead or—if she ever had been an inmate of the great House of Lin at all—no longer there. If she were there, and old Lin Wân was still alive, to get her out of his clutches would prove about as difficult as getting gold out of the Bank of England. If he were dead there was no reason to suppose that his son would be any more ready to hand her over. Lastly, even could he be persuaded or tricked into doing so, there remained the almost insoluble problem of getting her across the Pacific to an island which was not served by any regular means of transport.

Within a little over an hour of Gregory's arrival all these doubts and difficulties had been miraculously resolved. The girl was said to be there, Lin Wân was dead, and by skilful negotiation Gregory had achieved the seemingly impossible. Tû-lai had become his eager ally, and was already planning a triumphant arrival at the Island in one of the Lin ships. Yet now, just as Gregory was beginning fully to savour the sweets of success, Madame Fan-ti's revelation that Josephine had been abducted turned them to dust and ashes in his mouth.

If anything could have added to his anger and frustration it was her statement that Josephine had been carried off by a Communist agent. After his talk with Tû-lai it had at least seemed clear that Kâo had either killed Shih-niang himself or employed someone else to do so. That he had planned her death was beyond dispute, but his plan had been to drown her one night after they had left Tung-kwan by river. As she had been knifed before they left, Kâo, after all, might have had nothing to do with it. As the Communists had actually kidnapped Josephine, it now appeared obvious that they had been involved in the affair from the beginning; so it might be that another of their agents had forestalled Kâo and, believing Shih-niang to be the real Princess, killed her before he had a chance to do so himself.

There was yet another possibility. Had Kâo a tie-up with the Communists? Knowing himself to be unable to get the best of Lin Wân on his own, had he bought their help, or entered into some sort of deal with them? Perhaps he had got them to rid him of Shih-niang, and Josephine was now being taken south by them to join them either in Tung-kwan or some city further east. Without the government knowing anything about the matter, Kâo might have made it worth while for the local Communist boss in Tung-kwan to put his bravos on the job, in the same way that Lin Wân had employed Quong-Yü to have Josephine kidnapped in San Francisco. A bribe of say, ten thousand dollars might quite well have been sufficient to secure such co-operation; and for Kâo, at that price, it would have been dirt cheap compared with having to try to raise half a million for Lin Wân.

While these new speculations were coursing swiftly through Gregory's mind, Madame Fan-ti was blaming herself to Tû-lai for having neglected to report Josephine's disappearance to him. He assured her that in her state of grief such an oversight was readily understandable, and, having obtained the poor lady's permission to question all her women, they left her.

Tû-lai explained to Gregory that although the women of the head of the house, and of his brothers and sons, continued to occupy a separate portion of it, which in the old days had been the seraglio, for the past twenty-five years or more they had no longer been kept strictly in purdah. The custom of employing eunuchs to guard them had gradually fallen into disuse after China became a Republic, and instead elderly concubines or old nurses had been made responsible for the good behaviour of the younger ones.

The wives, whose honour was never doubted, were free to go about as they pleased and the unmarried girls, although always accompanied by a duenna, were allowed a fair degree of liberty, which included receiving visits from approved males and making occasional visits to the bazaars in the nearby city. In the case of the latter, as the duennas were not always above taking bribes, this had now and then led to clandestine love affairs; but if discovered, lapses of that kind resulted in all concerned receiving heavy punishment.

In consequence, while such intrigues were rare, a resourceful man might have pretended to have fallen in love with Josephine after seeing her about and, by lavish payments to one or more of the old women, secured help to get in to her after everyone had gone to sleep. Then, with a free field and the night before him, he might either have used some trick to induce her to come away with him, or, as she could not cry out, forced her to do so.

For the best part of two hours Tû-lai questioned a succession of Josephine's companions, duennas and servants. None of them would admit to having had any part in the affair. The belief that the Communist agent who had arrived shortly after the Lord Kâo Hsüan's party, was at the bottom of it was based on the fact that on several occasions when she had passed through the great courtyard he had respectfully handed her bunches of flowers. A snivelling old woman begged forgiveness for having allowed him to do so, and said that, as the poor dumb girl could not even exchange a word with him, she had felt there could be no harm in letting her enjoy these tributes of admiration.

It emerged that no doors had been forced or, apparently, been treacherously opened from within; but a rope had been lowered to the ground from the balustrade of the women's court and left dangling there. As the tall wall below the terrace had a slightly inward slope, with the aid of a rope it would not have been difficult to scale it; so it looked as if someone inside had lowered the rope and that was the way the man had got in. On the other hand, he might have been let in, and brought it with him coiled round his waist under his outer garment. In any case, there could be little doubt that was the way they left; thus evading the possibility of being challenged when making their way out through the great courtyard.

It was that which favoured the theory of an abduction rather than an elopement. An enamoured couple could have slipped through the gates soon after they were opened at dawn with little risk of discovery, whereas to drag even a dumb girl that far, and through them, unwillingly, without someone intervening, would have been next to impossible; but to have rendered her unconscious then lowered her over the wall would have been easy.

The only pieces of concrete information gained from the inquiry were that no man other than the Communist agent had manifested any interest in Josephine; that from his description he was undoubtedly the same man as the Communist who had come up with the caravan from Tung-kwan; and that some quite valuable pieces of jewellery that Lin Wân and Madame Fan-ti had given Josephine since she had been living in their house had disappeared with her.

Tû-lai ordered three women whom he considered had been lax in their duties to be locked up on a diet of unhusked rice and water until further notice, then retired to his own apartments with Gregory for a council of war.

The prospect of securing a property in the Island had so captured his imagination that he was now determined to do his utmost to get Josephine back, even if it meant coming into conflict with the government. That this might be so was certainly to be feared as, having discussed the idea that Kâo had possibly employed a local Communist boss to get hold of Josephine for him, they dismissed it.

Tempting as it was to adopt such a theory it had to be ruled out owing to Lin Wân's account of what had occurred in San Francisco. He had said that the Communists there had threatened both Madame Août and her daughter with death if they accepted General Chiang Kai-shek's invitation to go to Formosa, and that Madame Août had been murdered because she had ignored their warning. That meant they had been after Josephine ever since.

Gregory filled in the gap for Tû-lai by giving him a résumé of the puzzling events which had taken place during the journey from San Francisco to Antung-Ku. Of them, they decided, there could be only one explanation. Having lost trace of Josephine after her mother's death, the Communists had kept the Aoûts' apartment under observation in case she returned to it. On learning about the inquiries Tsai-Ping was making of everyone in the block, they had had him followed to the yacht; then smuggled Foo on board so that if the mission succeeded in tracing Josephine it would lead him to her. Either under instructions, or because he was a fanatical Marxist, he had endeavoured to liquidate the most potentially dangerous personalities of the mission well before they could reach their objective. At Antung-Ku, the first Chinese town they had entered, it seemed probable that he had passed on such information as he had obtained and been relieved of his task. There was, however, the possibility that still sticking to the trail that might lead to Josephine, he had disguised himself at Tung-kwan in the shapeless garments worn by caravan travellers, come on to the great House of Lin, and, a fortnight later, succeeded in abducting her.

But, whether it was Foo, or some other Communist agent, who had carried off Josephine made little difference. Apparently the threat issued in San Francisco to kill her still stood, and it looked now as if two or more agents had been put on to hunt her down independently. If so, and one of them in Tung-kwan had killed Shih-niang in mistake for her, she could count herself lucky that the other had kidnapped her instead of stabbing her to death in her bed. It seemed probable that the man who had got hold of her had spared her temporarily only so that she might be taken before some higher authority, and questioned about matters connected with the House of Lin before she was dispatched. In any case, if there was still a chance of saving her, every moment counted ; so immediate action must be taken.

While Tû-lai changed into Chinese riding clothes he sent orders that every caravan guard available should be mustered ; then he and Gregory anxiously debated in which direction they should set off. Gregory thought it improbable that Josephine was being taken down to Tung-kwan as, if so, he should have passed her on the road the day before. A further factor was that the nearest Communist headquarters were in Yen-an, so it seemed more likely that she had been taken there.

In the great courtyard they found twenty-two strong pony riders assembled. From Tû-lai's enquiries about Josephine's disappearance they had already guessed what was in the wind ; so when he appeared they greeted him with excited shouts. As Gregory rode up into the lead beside Tû-lai, he glanced at his watch and saw that it was half past three ; then they cantered out of the gates like mediaeval nobles leaving a castle to go to war, with their wild retainers waving their weapons, uttering fierce cries and thundering along behind them.

The city of Yen-an was only a few miles away, and on crossing the next rise they could see its ancient mud walls in the distance. A quarter of an hour's hard riding brought them to a large open space in its centre, one side of which was occupied by a caravanserai very similar to the one in Tung-kwan. Having led his cavalcade into its spacious courtyard, Tû-lai gave orders to dismount and tie up the ponies. Then he called the men round him, gave them their instructions, and told them that they were to report back there in an hour.

As they dispersed he led Gregory through the building to a garden at its back. Like the inn at Tung-kwan it had a score of tables and sitting down at one of them he ordered hot wine to be brought. Turning to Gregory as the servant left them, he said:

'A drink will serve to pass the time. There is nothing we can do ourselves, and my men will make far better detectives than we should. All of them know our bird by sight; so if he is in the town they will soon ferret him out, and the warders at the prison are great gossips. Through them we'll learn if Josephine is in the women's cells—or if she has already been done in by these Communist swine.'

The hour of waiting seemed a long one, but at last it was over and they went out to the courtyard to hear the men's reports. The information they had gathered was reassuring but very puzzling.

Josephine was not in the prison, neither had any young woman remotely resembling her been brought in during the past forty hours. On the other hand there was ample evidence that the Communist agent they sought had been in the town the previous day.

The first report of his appearance was at the inn itself early in the morning. He had arrived on foot and in a very groggy condition. His story was that he had met with an accident and injured the back of his head. When his wound had been attended to and he had eaten a light meal he had wanted to leave again at once, but he was still so shaky that he had been persuaded to lie down for a few hours. Later he had asked the address of an honest merchant and gone out. On his return he had bought two riding ponies and hired two mounted men to accompany him. Then, at about two o'clock in the afternoon, they had set off, leaving the city by its north gate.

The merchant had been questioned, and said that he had bought from a man a short string of not very large, but well-matched, pearls for twenty-four thousand J.M.P. dollars, which, although only a little over thirty English pounds by the rate of exchange, was a sum with considerable purchasing power in those remote regions. As far as had been discovered the only other transactions entered into by the man while in Yen-an were the purchase of blankets, a haversack, a water-bottle and a heavy bludgeon; and he had neither visited the Communist headquarters nor made contact with any of his uniformed colleagues.

To make anything tangible of this account was most diffi-cult. The wound on the back of the head sounded as if the man had been attacked from behind, rather than had a fall; but, if so, by whom? It was, of course, possible that Josephine had seized an opportunity when his back was turned to her to strike him down, although such an act of resolution by a young girl who had led an exceptionally sheltered life seemed highly unlikely. And if she had, what then? Presumably he had lain unconscious for several hours, while she had made off with the ponies. But, if so, why had she not returned to the House of Lin?

Tû-lai suggested that as soon as the man had her clear of the house, he had set about killing her, and fear had lent her the strength to inflict the injury on him in her death struggle; but that did not explain why he had arrived in Yen-an on foot. Gregory favoured the idea that they had been set upon by robbers who, having beaten up the man, had made off with the girl and the ponies to their own village; but that did not explain why, on his arrival in Yen-an, he had not gone straight to the Communist headquarters for help to trace and recap-ture her, instead of to the inn. Why, too, he should have *hired* two companions, bought a spare mount, and ridden off to-wards the north defied their wildest speculation.

To their next move there was only one pointer. As the Com-munist had carried Josephine off he must know what had happened to her; therefore if they gave chase and could over-take him they should be able to squeeze the truth out of him. Before departing, in order to cover their respective theories, Tû-lai dispatched four men back the way they had come to search the defiles on either side of the road for Josephine's body, and a further six to the nearest villages round about to inquire of the headmen regarding the activities of robbers, and threaten with his dire displeasure any one of them who later might be proved to have had knowledge of Josephine's whereabouts without disclosing it. Soon after five o'clock, with the remaining twelve men of their escort shouting lustily once more, they galloped in a cloud of dust out of the north gate of Yen-an.

The track again led alongside a river; but now it was the little Yen-ho, a smaller tributary of the great Hwang-ho than that along the valley of which ran the greater part of the road from Tung-kwan. In long shallow stretches, broken here and there by foaming rapids, it meandered from its source in the north-west. The nearest township on it was An-sai, which lay something over twenty miles away.

As their ponies were still fresh they got there at half past seven, and in the afterglow of a marvellous sunset at once set about making their enquiries. Within ten minutes they learned that on the previous day the man they were after and his two companions had reached there about half past four, then, after halting for a meal, had pushed on up the valley. As the pursued had a lead of some twenty-six hours, the only hope of catching them up lay in riding for most of the night; so, having watered the ponies, they again took the road.

An hour and a half later the river had dwindled to a brook and they were within a few miles of its source. It was now fully dark and on rounding a sudden bend in the track Gregory would have ridden on, had not Tû-lai called on him to halt. Having known the region since boyhood the young Chinaman was aware that the road forked there. One of its branches ran west of north to the township of Tsing-pien, which lay about forty miles away, just inside the Great Wall; the other took a more westerly course through the township of Poa-an, then led up to Chwan-tsing, another town just inside the Great Wall, but thirty miles or more further off.

As it was impossible to tell which road their quarry had taken, it was decided that with Chou for guide, and five of the men, Gregory should head for Tsing-pien, while Tû-lai and the other six headed for Chwan-tsing. It was further agreed that on reaching their destinations, whichever of them had lost the track should turn along inside the Great Wall to rejoin the other, or one of the men who would be left behind with a message for him.

Soon after they parted the moon came up; so the going became easier, but by one in the morning it was well down in the sky. By then, since leaving Yen-an Gregory's party had covered over fifty miles, and tough as the ponies were, their flagging during the last hour was a clear indication that they should not be pressed much further.

It was now bitterly cold and they were not carrying camp equipment with them; so he kept the ponies going at a walk while looking about for some shelter for himself and his men. Two miles further on they came to a cliff face with two shallow caves in it. They offered scant comfort but would at least keep the frost off; which, as there was no brushwood about to make a fire, was a big consideration. Having tethered their ponies, the seven of them huddled up for warmth in the deepest of the caves, and got such uneasy sleep as they could until dawn.

An hour's ride in the morning brought them to a monastery, where they were able to get a hot meal; but inquiries there proved disappointing, as the men they were after had not stopped at it. By one o'clock they were within sight of Tsing-pien, but Gregory now had little hope of getting news of their quarry in the town, as they had questioned several groups of travellers going south, and people in the few hamlets through which they had passed, without result. His pessimism was justified. After another meal Chou and his men ranged the bazaars for the best part of two hours, but no one they questioned had seen a man answering the description of the one they sought.

Their reports could only mean that the fox had either gone to earth or taken the road followed by Tû-lai up to Chwan-tsing; so it was now for Gregory to get there as soon as possible. The town was between fifty and sixty miles away to the west, and as the ponies had already covered over ninety miles in less than twenty-four hours they needed at least a day's rest before they could again be put to any further strain.

In consequence, with Chou as his adviser, Gregory bought six fresh ponies, and arranged that one of the men should stay behind to take those they had ridden so hard, back to Yen-an by easy stages. They also bought blankets and provisions, and at five o'clock in the evening cantered out of Tsing-pien, intent on covering as much ground as they could before halting for the night.

From Tsing-pien they had already seen the Great Wall of China in the distance, and now their way lay alongside it. As the course it followed had been based on tactical considerations, it ran for the most part along a series of crests, undulating like a gargantuan stone serpent along them and, where they broke, dipping sharply into valleys at a new angle to rise to others.

By far the greater part of it still stood intact, rising on average twenty feet from the ground, and broad enough on top for two cars to be driven abreast along it, between its double edge of castellated battlements. As they trotted along for mile after mile, always within rifle shot of it, its immensity was brought home to Gregory. When his journey, equivalent to a hard day's ride, was done, he would still have seen only one-thirtieth part of it.

Begun over two hundred years before the birth of Christ, completed by the Han dynasty and, for most of its length, splendidly reinforced with stone by the Ming Emperors, it was the greatest human endeavour ever undertaken by man. The magnificent bridge spanning Sydney harbour, the sky-scrapers of New York, and even the Great Pyramid were childish efforts by comparison. Across hill and dale it ran for one and a half thousand miles ; in its structure were embodied fifteen thousand watch-towers and twenty-five thousand forts. To the south of it a vast fertile land had nurtured the greatest genuine civilization of all time ; to the north of it there still lay only limitless wastes of sand and a few scattered oases, sparsely populated by nomad tribes of barbarians.

After the sun had set they rode on again by the light of the moon ; but by ten o'clock they were so utterly weary that they had to call a halt, and doss down for the night in one of the watch-towers that still had its roof intact. During their evening ride they had covered nearly half the distance to Chwan-tsing; so they reached the town just before midday the following day.

At the principal inn of the place Gregory found Tû-lai waiting for them. As his party had had the longest side of the triangle to cover, and had not been able to change their ponies, they had got in only that morning. He was almost dropping with fatigue; but the hope that Gregory would arrive had kept him from going to bed, as he was positively bursting with news. Josephine had again appeared upon the scene and was only a few hours ahead of them.

Over a cup of hot wine Gregory listened enthralled to Tû-lai's story. On the first night they had pushed on as far as Poa-an, arrived there in the small hours of the morning. When they knocked up the inn, the servant who let them in had cursed roundly, as it was the second night in succession that he had been roused from his sleep to admit late-comers. A good tip quickly consoled him and induced him to reply readily to questions. His description of the previous night's travellers left no doubt that they were the Communist and his two companions. They had arrived a little after midnight and left soon after dawn.

It had been out of the question for Tû-lai to go further that night, but by taking two hours less sleep than his quarry he had reduced their lead by that much; and when he left Poa-an next morning they were exactly twenty-four hours ahead of him.

However, the day had proved a bitter disappointment. He had hoped to reach Chwan-tsing by the late afternoon, but his ponies, still jaded from the sixty-five miles they had done the preceding day, were no longer capable of such an effort. Within two hours of the start spells of trotting had to be abandoned, and during the afternoon, in spite of giving them frequent rests, he and his men had to dismount and lead them. In consequence, on reaching a small monastery about five o'clock, although they had covered only some forty miles of the fifty-five he had hoped to do, he had decided that they must take a long rest there.

During the day various people he had questioned en-route

had confirmed that he was still on the right scent and said that the party ahead were now also travelling slowly owing to the obvious tiredness of their ponies; so, in the hope of further decreasing their lead, he had ordered a fresh start for two o'clock in the morning.

That had proved a tactical error. The country through which they were passing was rough, sparsely wooded and mountainous. Despite that, as long as the moon was up they had made steady going, but soon after it set they had taken a wrong track which had eventually petered out, and had been unable to find their way back to the right one. For three bitterly cold and exhausting hours they had cast this way and that in the darkness, dragging their unwilling ponies by the bridles across shallow streams and up steep hillsides. Eventually they had called a halt on a piece of high ground but soon after, as dawn broke, their luck returned, for they saw the road winding through the valley below them.

With revived spirits they set off again towards Chwan-tsing, knowing that they now had only another eight miles or so to go. Then, after they had been on their way for half an hour, they saw the figure of a man lying at the road-side. As they approached he raised himself and called feebly to them. Dismounting, they had gone to him, propped him up against a rock and given him a drink of water. He had been very badly beaten up and left to die in a nearby gorge, where he had lain all night; but with the coming of morning he had managed to crawl as far as the track in the hope that some travellers would soon appear. It was while they were examining his injuries that his face had struck one of the men as familiar; then they had recognized him. Breaking off his narrative, Tû-lai asked:

'And who do you think he was?'

'Our old Communist friend in a different rig-out,' Gregory hazarded.

'No.' Tû-lai smiled. 'Kâo's servant P'ei!'

'Snakes alive!' Gregory exclaimed. 'I had forgotten all about him.'

'So had I. But that is not surprising, as I had never even spoken to him and hardly knew of his existence. Apparently when you all left with Shih-niang he was sick; so it was arranged that he should remain behind until he had recovered, then catch you up.'

'That's right; but that was a fortnight ago, and he had only eaten something that disagreed with him. Where has he been in the meantime?'

'Until four nights ago he was still living in the house. You know what that great courtyard of ours is like. People of all sorts are always coming and going there. On the flimsiest pretext anyone could scrounge a living from the open cooking fires for months without any particular notice being taken of them.'

'And what the devil was he doing up in this part of the world?'

'He was carrying off Josephine.'

'What! D'you mean that it was he, and not the Communist, who kidnapped her?'

'Not in the first place. P'ei played his cards very skilfully. He saw the other man presenting Josephine with bunches of flowers and making up to the old duennas; so he guessed what he was up to and let him do the dirty work for him. All he had to do was to keep his eyes skinned every night, and when he saw our bird tether some loaded ponies in a gully about half a mile from the house he simply hid nearby. When Josephine and her kidnapper appeared he slogged the chap on the back of the head and made off with her.'

'I see. That explains the state of the Communist the following morning and his actions afterwards. P'ei would not have known that he had Josephine's trinkets on him, and evidently did not bother to go through his pockets. By selling her pearls he was able to hire a couple of toughs and ponies to give chase. He was after P'ei while we were after him; and last night he suceeded in getting the girl back.'

'You've hit it.'

'I'm beginning to see daylight about Kâo now, too,' Gregory said thoughtfully.

'Are you?' Tû-lai raised his eyebrows. 'Then you are more clever than I am.'

'I mean, it seems obvious that P'ei only pretended to be ill

329

on Kâo's orders, and it was just an excuse so that he could be left behind to get hold of Josephine.'

'Yes, that part's plain sailing; but not the fact that Kâo gave him orders to kill her.'

'To kill her! In heaven's name, why?'

Tû-lai shrugged. 'I haven't an idea. In view of his negotiations with my father, it seems quite inexplicable, doesn't it? One can understand his trying to get her without paying up the half-million, but to kill her afterwards seems the act of a madman. Perhaps that is the explanation. His having planned to kill Shih-niang for no apparent reason was another piece of craziness. Perhaps he is a homicidal maniac.'

'No. There must have been a reason for that, because your father gave his consent to it.'

'True.'

'Besides, ruling out for a minute this statement of P'ei's, there is now an explanation for Kâo's intending to kill Shih-niang. If he was expecting P'ei to turn up with Josephine, he would not have wanted two Princesses on his hands, and may have thought it necessary to close Shih-niang's mouth about the part she had played.'

'That certainly could not have been the reason he gave my father for wanting to do away with her.'

'No; but he could have invented some other for your father's edification.'

'That's possible; although I can't see why he should have mentioned it to him at all. Still, as he did, that gives us one good hope of solving the mystery. I shall be very surprised if my father did not leave some entry about it in one of his secret diaries; and, for that matter, others about the whole affair from the beginning. As soon as we get home we'll hunt through them.'

Gregory nodded. 'From what you say they may give us a lot of data. I doubt, though, if they will tell us how the Communists got on to Shih-niang in Tung-kwan, and they certainly won't tell us why Kâo ordered P'ei to kill Josephine. About that—do you really think P'ei was speaking the truth?'

'I'm as certain of it as I can be of anything.'

'Why do you say that?'

'For the excellent reason that he had not carried out his orders. The girl is still alive. At least, she was about three hours ago.'

'That is certainly a bull point. What reason does 'P'ei give for having disobeyed his master?'

'Very sensibly, I think, he feared that when he had killed Josephine, to ensure that he never gave away the secret of her murder Kâo would kill him. So he decided that instead of doing what he had been told, and rejoining your party, he would settle down to spend an honourable old age in China. To do so he needed money, and he was shrewd enough to realize that little Josephine, simply as a piece of warm female flesh and blood, was quite a valuable bit of property. Assuming that as soon as her disappearance was discovered we should think he had taken her south to Tung-kwan and Kâo, he came north and was heading for the frontier. Here, in Chwan-tsing, he hoped to sell her for a tidy sum to the chieftain of one of the Mongolian tribes across the border.'

'I see. And what have you done with him?'

'I had him hanged from the nearest tree!'

'Damnation!' Gregory exclaimed, starting forward. 'There are scores of questions I would have liked to ask him. He might have thrown light on all sorts of queer happenings that took place on our journey. And with patience we might have got a lot more out of him about this extraordinary game that Kâo has been playing.'

Tû-lai waved a casual hand. 'Don't worry, I squeezed everything out of him that there was to squeeze before he died; and I mean that literally. At first he was very reluctant to talk, so I had my men lower a boulder weighing half a ton on to his stomach. As he was already suffering from internal injuries the effect must have been pretty painful and——'

'I'm not over-scrupulous myself,' Gregory interrupted, 'but you may spare me the murky details. The thing is, what else did you get out of him?'

'Nothing that is of any great importance.' Tû-lai gave a loud yawn. 'I'll answer any questions you may have later; but if I don't go and lie down now I shall fall asleep where I sit.'

331

'At least tell me where you believe the girl to be at the moment, and what you propose to do about her?'

With an apologetic smile, Tû-lai lisped, 'I am sorry. After the gruelling we had last night I am feeling dead beat; otherwise I should have gone in pursuit already. We came upon P'ei about half past seven this morning, and got in here at ten o'clock. On arriving I learnt that the Communist, Josephine and the two hired men had spent the night at this inn. They didn't leave till nearly nine o'clock, so I missed them only by a little over an hour. My men found out that on leaving the town they took the road south, which leads to the head of the Ma-tien river. About twenty miles from here it crosses the boundary into the province of Kansu, so it looks as if for some reason he is anxious to get out of Shensi; but the fact that they made such a late start shows that now he has got the girl back he no longer feels that there is any necessity to hurry.'

Tû-lai paused a moment, then went on, 'The nearest town of any size down the river is King-yang; but it is well over a hundred miles away, so we should be able easily to overtake them before they get there. As they can have no idea that they are being followed, and particularly now they have a woman riding with them, it is unlikely that they will cover more than twenty-five miles a day. I suggest that we should sell all the ponies and buy fresh ones, but not start until moonrise. That will give us a good six hours sleep and time for a meal before we leave. With fresh mounts, between nine o'clock and two in the morning we should have no difficulty in doing twenty miles. That is nearly as much as they will have done today. Then if we set off again at dawn we ought to catch them up by midday; or, at least, by the afternoon. Do you approve?'

With a nod, Gregory stood up. 'Yes. You get to bed at once. Chou and I will see to exchanging the ponies, and buying some more camp equipment in case we have to spend the dark hours of the night out in the open. I wish to God that you hadn't been in such a hurry to hang P'ei. Still, now it's done. it can't be helped.'

Giving another yawn, Tû-lai shook his head sleepily. 'After we had given him the rock to nurse, he would have died anyway before we could have got him here. And what does it matter as long as we get the girl?' Then he stumbled upstairs to the room which he had ordered to be prepared for him.

In accordance with their arrangement they started out soon after nine. The first part of the way was easy enough, and, even when they got into the rugged country in which the Ma-tien had its source, in the bright moonlight there was no danger of their losing the track. Since they had all had a good rest and were remounted, they could if they wished, have gone considerably more than the twenty miles before the moon set, but had they done so there was the danger that they might overshoot their quarry; so at about one o'clock they halted on the edge of a wood where there were plenty of fallen branches to keep a fire going, and made camp.

Next morning they cooked a meal at sun-up, and, filled with excitement, took the road again at a trot. Another ten miles brought them to the head of the river, and soon afterwards it developed into a narrow but swiftly flowing stream that every few hundred yards swirled between half-submerged rocks or hurtled in a cascade of foam over low waterfalls.

It was eleven o'clock, and they were beginning to look about for a suitable site to make their midday halt, when, on breasting a rise, they sighted their quarry moving at a walk through the valley below them.

Even at that distance Gregory had no difficulty in identifying the party ahead. The small male figure in the lead was the Communist, the even smaller figure beside him, wrapped in a hooded cloak, was the Princess Josephine. Behind them rode the two hired men, each leading a baggage pony. But he was not alone in his swift appraisal. At the same instant Tû-lai and his men had also realized that the chase was as good as over. With wild shouts, all twelve of them kicked their ponies into a gallop and careered off down the hill.

Cursing them for their impetuosity, Gregory followed. He was afraid now that, having been given such good warning, the party ahead might get away and succeed in hiding themselves in some cave or gulch of the fantastically broken ground, before they could be caught.

As his pony pounded down the slope he saw all four turn

their heads to look back. Evidently assuming that they were about to be set upon by brigands, they too broke into a gallop.

But their leadership was bad. Instead of turning off the track while they had the chance, and disappearing among the huge boulders that lay in the valley on its side away from the river, they cantered on up the opposite slope. By the time they reached its crest Tû-lai's leading men were up to within a quarter of a mile of them.

When Gregory in turn crossed the ridge he saw that Josephine and her companions were still sticking to the track and down in the next valley bottom. The man had her pony by the bridle and was forcing it to keep pace with his own. But she, evidently unused to riding, was swaying wildly in her saddle, and looked as if she might fall off at any moment.

The hired men had abandoned their led ponies, but, even so, had dropped behind. At the foot of the next slope Tû-lai's leading men came up with them. That gave the two riders ahead a short respite as, instead of galloping on, the Lin retainers stopped to mill round the hired men, pull them from their saddles, and make them prisoners.

Gregory was a good horseman, but he was not pressing his mount. He felt that as Tû-lai had tracked the Communist down this was his party. He considered it certain now that the quarry would be captured ; so he was quite content to take no part in the culmination of the chase, but watch it from well in the rear.

Down in the valley bottom the track led away from the river ; or rather went straight on, by-passing a great mound of rock that rose nearly a hundred feet in height on its river side, causing the torrent to make an abrupt bend round it. Half way up the slope Josephine's pony stumbled and nearly threw her. Pulling up, her companion tumbled off his mount and lifted her from the saddle. Leaving the ponies on the track they ran towards the rugged pile of stone and began to climb it.

Too much of a realist to hope that the enemy would get away, Gregory had enough of the British sporting spirit to feel sorry that the fox had been panicked into entering a trap which could so easily have been avoided by taking the opposite direction. Tû-lai had now only to spread his men out along the track where it formed a string of the river's bow and there could now be no escape for the fox. It was simply a matter of dismounting and scaling the rocks in a converging semi-circle until they got him.

As Gregory rode up to the foot of the mount, the Communist was two-thirds of the way up it, and still half dragging, half carrying the Princess up with him ; while Tû-lai and his men were rapidly closing in on them.

On its landward side the pile of rocks rose only about forty feet above the track, so Gregory decided that he might as well scale them and be in at the finish. Dismounting, he began the climb and listened to the shouts above him. By the time he was half way up, the quarry had reached a flat ledge roughly fifteen feet square, which formed the summit. Beyond it lay a sheer drop of a hundred feet to the boulder-strewn river.

Suddenly an awful thought entered Gregory's mind. What if the man had been inspired to take this course deliberately, with the idea of demanding that either he should be allowed to proceed freely with his prisoner or he would throw her over? Now, in frantic haste, stubbing his toes and barking his knees, Gregory began to scramble all-out for the top.

Tû-lai was carrying an automatic rifle. Gregory heard him shout, 'Now, you filthy Communist, we've got you! Put your hands up or I fire.'

With a final effort Gregory pushed past one of Tû-lai's men and thrust his head up over the ledge. The man they had hunted for three days and nights was standing only about ten feet away from him. He had lost his fur cap and was no longer wearing heavy horn-rimmed spectacles. He was, as Gregory had at times thought possible, young Foo.

At the same instant, Foo saw and recognized him. With surprise and elation dawning on his face, he cried:

'Mr. Sallust! You are sent by God to help us! I saved you from being stoned to death by the caravan men. I beg you to save us from these bandits now.'

Hauling himself over the lip of the platform, Gregory replied, 'They are not bandits, Foo, but the Lord Tû-lai and his retainers. Although you made a quixotic gesture in saving

335

me from the caravan men, you have many other things to answer for. And you stole this lady from the Lord Lin's house, so he has every right to reclaim her.'

Flinging an arm round the lovely flower-faced little person beside him, Foo cried, 'I will not have her taken from me! We would rather die together! For over two years we have loved one another desperately and we would rather jump to death over the precipice behind us than be separated.'

It was at that instant that a great light dawned in Gregory's mind. There was no reason whatever to suppose that Foo was a Communist or a murderer. He was the young law student of San Francisco, whose love letters had been found in Josephine's room.

21

A TRY FOR A THRONE

T E N days later Foo and Josephine were married with all the ancient rites and ceremonies in the great House of Lin.

At first Tû-lai had opposed an early marriage, because it might interfere with his own plans. He knew that the Council's original object in sending an invitation to Josephine to come to the island was that she should choose a husband from among seven candidates for her hand, each representing one of the Seven Families, and that her consort should be accepted as Emperor. For her to arrive there already married would invalidate this method of appointing a new ruler ; so Tû-lai foresaw that, instead of being welcomed and rewarded by the Council for producing her, he might be met with reproaches for causing them pointless embarrassment.

From the Ma-tien River they had made their way back by slow stages ; as Josephine, being unaccustomed to riding, had suffered severely from her five days on pony-back, so had to be carried in a hammock. During the journey Gregory and Tû-lai had on several occasions hotly debated the question of the marriage. It was Gregory who had finally made terms with Foo for his surrender ; and they had been to the effect that, while he was prepared to regard Josephine as Tû-lai's ward, their engagement was to be sanctioned, he was to retain his freedom, be given accommodation in the House of Lin, and permitted reasonable access to his fiancée.

At the time it had been clear that unless Foo had been granted the terms he demanded the young couple were quite prepared to commit suicide, and Gregory was determined to see that the bargain he had made with Foo should be kept. Tû-lai had not actually suggested going back on the agreement, but he had argued that no stipulation had been made about the length of the engagement, and that it would be time enough for the marriage to take place when they arrived in the Island

Gregory had quickly guessed the way Tû-lai's mind was working. He was hoping that once Josephine was in the Island the glamorous prospect of becoming the Empress of it would tempt her into breaking off her engagement to Foo ; so that he, Tû-lai, could after all reap the kudos of being responsible for the foundation of the new dynasty. To Gregory it seemed most unlikely that Josephine would give Foo up ; but, in any case, now that he once more regarded Foo as his own protégé, he did not mean to allow any risk of the young man's prospects being sabotaged.

In consequence, he had played on Tû-lai's sentiments, pointing out what desperate ordeals Foo had been through during four long months to win his love, and pleading that it would be most ungenerous to make him wait even a day longer than was necessary to enjoy the fruits of his stupendous effort.

Tû-lai was by nature of a kindly and romantic disposition ; so by the fourth day, when they reached the House of Lin, he had almost been won over, and Madame Fan-ti overcame his last flickers of resistance. Their arrival, and the extraordinary story they had to tell, roused that poor lady from her lethargic grief to a new animation. With brimming eyes she listened to Foo's account of Josephine's adventures and his own, then she took the young lovers to her heart and ordered immediate preparations for a wedding on a grand scale.

Foo's story was that he had not learned of Madame Août's death until two days after it had occurred. He had at once hurried to her apartment only to learn that Josephine had disappeared without leaving any address. Distraught with anxiety, he had made fruitless inquiries of everyone who might give him a clue as to where she had gone, and called day after day at the flat hoping that she would return or send for her things. When the yacht arrived in San Francisco on the first of July he was still calling there two or three times a week, so he soon learned that other people had started to make inquiries about her. It had been easy for him to trace back to the yacht those who were hunting for her, and as Tsai-Ping's persistent investigation among Madame Août's acquaintances had gone on for a month, it seemed to him that anyone so wealthy and determined must succeed in tracing Josephine in the long run. In consequence, when he saw the yacht being provisioned for a voyage, he determined to stow away aboard her, in the hope that her owners would eventually lead him to his beloved.

During the voyage he had not deceived Gregory about anything, except in giving a false name and saying that his reason for being on board was to get to China so that he might give his parents proper burial. After swimming ashore he had gone up to Antung-Ku, knowing that whoever landed from the yacht would have to pass through the town on their way into the interior. When the sampan had arrived he had gone aboard that night not only because he was penniless and hoped to borrow money from Gregory, but also to try to find out the sampan's destination. In both matters he had succeeded, as Gregory had told him that the party was going up to Tung-kwan.

He had got there by going overland, and on the way had had a stroke of luck. While in the city of Kai-feng, some minutes after a passenger beside whom he had been sitting in a bus had got out, he noticed that the man had dropped his wallet. By then Foo was getting very short of money, and was at his wits' end how to raise enough to complete his journey; so instead of handing the wallet to the conductor, he had stuffed it into his pocket. On examining this windfall he had found that the notes in it amounted only to a small sum, but it also contained the papers of a Communist agent. It was that which gave him the idea of posing as its owner.

To do so, had he been remaining in Kai-feng, would have been exceedingly dangerous; but since he was moving on he thought the risk of being caught worth running; for by presenting himself as an official he would be able to get free travel on the railways, and, by throwing his weight about in small inns, bluff frightened people into giving him free meals. With some of the money that he had left he had taken a third-class ticket on to Cheng-chaw, and there began his imposture.

By these means he had reached Tung-kwan a week ahead of the sampan, and had only to wait for it to turn up. To prevent himself being recognized he had adopted the thick-lensed spectacles and the voluminous garments of a traveller in those parts, then loitered about in the courtyard of the inn until he had overheard Kâo make his bargain with the caravan master. As there was no other way up to Yen-an, he had then shown his papers and joined the caravan himself.

On his third day in the House of Lin, he said, his heart had almost stopped beating; for after a hundred and thirty-seven days of separation, misery, and often near-despair, he had at last once more seen Josephine. Two days later he had again seen her cross the courtyard, and managed to give her a bunch of flowers he had ready with a note hidden in its centre. Next day, while receiving from him another bunch, she had passed him a reply. On paper bedewed with tears of happiness at knowing that her faithful lover had come seven thousand miles to find her, she gave him directions how to set about carrying her off. From that point they had managed to correspond daily, and she had smuggled him out a jewel to sell in Yen-an, so that he could buy ponies and have money with which to bribe one of the duennas to let him get in to her on the night that they had escaped.

When giving an account of their escape to Madame Fan-ti, Foo learned that three women were being punished either for negligence or on suspicion of having admitted him to the women's quarters; so he and Josephine begged clemency for them all, and this was granted.

Josephine's story was known to all of them, except for the first part of it which had occurred in San Francisco. Foo had already had it from her; so he retailed it, aided now and then by her in the deaf and dumb finger language that they used between them.

Her mother had told her nothing at all of the offer made by General Chiang Kai-shek to provide for them on a handsome scale if they would both go to Formosa, or of the threat from the Communists which had followed it. In consequence, her mother's death had come as a complete shock to her, and she had at first supposed it to have been caused by a genuine accident.

On leaving the hospital after her mother died, she had intended to go sraight to Foo, both to seek comfort in his tender regard for her and his counsel on what she had better do now she was left alone in the world; but a woman had way-laid her as she came out of the hospital. The woman had said that she represented a Chinese Insurance Company with whom Madame Août had had a policy, and that Josephine must come with her at once to the office to fill up certain forms, otherwise she might later have difficulty in claiming the money.

Madame Août had never told Josephine that she held a life insurance, but as her mother was inclined to be secretive about money matters, Josephine had assumed the woman's story to be true and accompanied her in a taxi down to Chinatown. On the way, the woman had explained that the company was run in connection with the biggest Tong fraternity in San Francisco, and that its president was a very busy man, but it was essential that Josephine should be interviewed by him personally; so she must not mind if she had to wait for some time before he could see her.

In Grant Avenue she had been taken up to the sixth floor of a big block and left in a waiting room at the back of the building. It was already late in the afternoon so she did not become really worried until about seven o'clock. For another hour she was put off with excuses, then told that the president's car had had a breakdown, but as a great favour would see her at his private house when he got home. By then she was a prey to grave misgivings, but the office appeared highly respectable and the people there seemed anxious only to help her. Eventually, soon after nine, she was taken by the woman and a polite young Chinaman down to a car, but instead of running them out to one of the residential districts it drew up a quarter of an hour later at a deserted wharf. As the door of the car was opened she tried to run away, but she could not cry out for help, and taking her firmly by the arms they practically carried her to a waiting motor launch. For the next twenty minutes she was almost overcome with terror, as her imagination conjured up all sorts of terrible things that might be about to happen to her ; but her fears were groundless. After being carried up a ship's ladder and taken down to a big day cabin richly furnished with Chinese antiques, to her immense relief she had found herself in the presence of Mr. Lin Wân, whom she knew as an old friend of her mother's.

Mr. Lin Wân had apologized profusely for the steps that had been taken to bring her there, and excused them on the grounds that in a time of such distress he had thought it unlikely that she would accept a simple invitation from one whom she could only regard as an acquaintance. He had gone on to break it to her that her mother had been murdered by Communists, and that knowing her to be threatened with the same fate, he had taken the liberty of having her kept safely out of the way until darkness had fallen and she could be brought to his ship without any risk of her enemies knowing where she had gone into hiding. He had then had her taken to a luxurious cabin by a stewardess, who gave her a sleeping draught.

Next day Mr. Lin Wân had stressed the extreme danger she would be in if she remained in San Francisco, and offered her a comfortable home in his wife's care if she liked to accompany him back to his house near Yen-an. He had not pressed her for an immediate answer, but suggested that she should take the day to think it over.

341

That evening, she had told him about Foo, and said that she would be glad to accept his offer of a home provided that Foo, if he were willing, should be allowed to accompany them to China. Mr. Lin Wân had at once agreed; so she had written a letter to Foo explaining the circumstances in which she found herself, and asking if, for love of her, he would sacrifice his career as a lawyer. To the letter she had had no reply; so she had sadly come to the conclusion that he put a higher value on his prospects as a citizen of the United States, than on herself. Two days later the ship had left San Francisco.

While at Yen-an, she said, she had received nothing but kindness, particularly from Madame Fan-ti and Mr. Lin Wân, to whom she could never be sufficiently grateful for having saved her; and now that her brave Foo had so clearly demonstrated his love, her cup of happiness was overflowing.

Foo, of course, had never received her letter; and, although Gregory kept the thought to himself, he had little doubt that the reason for that was because Lin Wân had never posted it. By this time, too, he was also extremely sceptical about Chiang Kai-shek's offer and the Communist threat. To him they looked remarkably like inventions by Lin Wân to induce Josephine to accompany him to China. But there was still no direct evidence of that, or what part, if any, Kâo had played in this extraordinary plot.

During the few days before the wedding, Gregory saw quite a lot of Josephine and came both to like and admire her greatly. In appearance, she was as unlike Shih-niang as a small gay delicately tinted butterfly is to a big richly-marked moth, and the difference in mentality between the two girls was still more strongly defined. As was only to be expected, having been sold into a brothel in her early teens, Shih-niang had been almost illiterate, whereas little Josephine was widely read in both the Chinese and European classics. Moreover, she was highly intelligent, possessed charming manners and had a good sense of humour. But the thing that impressed Gregory most about her was the remarkable way in which she overcome her terrible disability. Although she was incapable of uttering a word, by frequent small gestures and the constant change of expression on her lovely features she somehow succeeded in conveying the impression that she was actively participating in every conversation.

On her wedding day she looked positively radiant and everyone declared that they had never seen a more handsome couple than the bride and bridegroom. Both were apparelled in costly garments provided from the cedar store chests of the house and as they moved their elaborate head-dresses scintillated with the sparkle of scores of jewels. Yet, above all, it was their faces which attracted all eyes, for the ecstatic happiness which glowed upon them seemed heaven-inspired and a benediction on the spectators.

As they approached, Tû-lai whispered to Gregory, 'How right you were to insist on this ; I would have committed a crime had I endeavoured to prevent it.' But, all the same, he had no thought of abandoning his plans for taking them to the island.

From the morning of the wedding, for three whole days the great House of Lin was given over to revelry and feasting. After that, the newly-weds were to be allowed seven days' retreat in a pavilion set apart for them. At the end of the week, if Tû-lai's arrangements went as he expected they were to leave with Gregory and himself for Shanghai, where they would all board one of the family ships.

Of Tû-lai's elder brothers, one was in the United States and the other in hospital, in Pekin, recovering from an operation; so he had sent for the brother next in seniority to himself to come up from Shanghai and take over affairs at the family headquarters. In the meantime, he continued to spend several hours each day going through his father's papers.

Although he had already found three secret drawers in different bureaux, there had been nothing among their contents to throw further light on the conspiracy between Kâo and Lin Wân, and it was not until three days after the wedding celebrations were completed that the latter's secret diaries were discovered. They would not have been found then, had it not been for the arrival of Tû-lai's brother, who said he had an idea that their father had kept his most personal papers in a cache up in the ceiling. After an hour's fumbling among the elaborately-carved scroll-work they found a boss which when

343

pressed released a sliding panel, and on the woodwork all round it lay more piles of papers.

That evening Tû-lai took Gregory to the room and showed him the relevant entries in the diaries. They still left certain matters unexplained, but with the few more bits of information that Tû-lai had wrung from P'ei, and some admissions that Foo had got out of him after beating him up, they practically completed what now transpired to be an extraordinarily grim picture of ruthlessness and double-dealing.

After they had discussed the matter for some while, Gregory asked, 'How do you feel about going to the Island now?'

Tû-lai shrugged. 'I see no reason why this should make any difference to my plans. As Kâo's elder brother is still alive, he is not yet even a member of the Council ; so he still has a long way to go before he can achieve his ambitions. He is bound to meet with much opposition, and I may be able to help thwart them. Besides, I have a personal reason for wishing to go there.'

'There is a lot in what you say,' Gregory agreed, uneasily aware that Tû-lai's 'personal reason' was A-lu-te. 'And since you have the means of getting me there I shall certainly go with you. To some extent I am under an obligation to do so ; and now we know the game Kâo is playing, I intend to do my utmost to spike his guns. It was of Josephine that I was thinking. In the light of our new knowledge I don't think it would be right to take her.'

'I don't see why we shouldn't. We have known for the past fortnight, from P'ei's confession, that Kâo gave him orders to kill her. But her circumstances are now very different; and forewarned is forearmed, so she should be quite safe with her husband and ourselves to protect her.'

'That's true ; but is there any real point in taking her there now she is married?'

'As far as I am concerned, no. There is no longer any reason why the Council should reward me for doing so ; but I am quite prepared to buy a property there if they will let me. As far as Josephine is concerned, I feel that the risk to her is small and that she has everything to gain by going. She has no fortune of her own and Foo is in no position to support her. Life in either China or the United States must prove a hard struggle

344

for a young couple with no money, particularly in view of Josephine's disability. Whereas, since she is a daughter of the Imperial House, the Council are virtually bound to give her an honourable position, and there is still a possibility that they may yet decide to make her Empress.'

Gregory nodded. 'It is certainly a gamble I would take myself, were I in her shoes; although I've a feeling that you underestimate the risk. Anyhow, in fairness to them I think we ought to put all the cards on the table and let them decide for themselves.'

'To that I am quite agreeable,' Tû-lai replied. 'But the sooner we get there now the better our chance of upsetting Kâo's applecart; so we must ask them to decide without delay. In the circumstances, I feel we should be justified in breaking in on their blissful solitude and putting the matter to them tomorrow afternoon.'

Accordingly, the following day Foo and Josephine came to confer with Gregory and Tû-lai. Gregory did most of the talking, and, having explained to them the implications of the passages in Lin Wân's diaries, he summed the situation up by saying to Foo:

'So you see, it is now clear beyond dispute that Kâo Hsüan is an evil and dangerous man. The fact that Josephine is now married, of course, greatly lessens the risk that he will attempt anything further against her; but one must not count on that. It depends largely on how far he has progressed with his plans when we reach the island. As he presumably left Tung-kwan on October the 11th, he should get home about November the 18th. We shall be able to make the journey considerably faster, as Tû-lai can provide papers which will enable us to travel from Tung-kwan to Shanghai by rail. But even so, as it is November the 4th today, if we start in four days' time we can't hope to get there before the first week in December. That means that Kâo will have had at least a fortnight in which to play around. A fortnight is not very much for a man who has been developing a long-term policy; all the same, it may have been long enough for him to strengthen his position in some way which would give him temporary jurisdiction over us. I think that is the only real danger; and it would be asking a bit much of the

345

gods to expect to win a position of security and ease for life overnight, without taking some chances. Nevertheless, if you feel that you would prefer to shield Josephine from the least possibility of harm by remaining here, Tû-lai and I will perfectly understand, and not think any the less of you.'

Foo make a little bow. 'Thank you for putting the position so fairly.'

Then Josephine, who had been following the whole conversation with her usual animated glances, wrote rapidly on the tablet she always carried and handed it to Gregory.

She had written, 'May I ask what you think is the best we could expect if all went well?'

To that he replied: 'It is just possible that they might make you Empress; although I think that very improbable. You see, to be frank, I don't think they would accept you as their ruler now that you have a husband who is not of noble birth.'

'Oh, but I am!' Foo said quickly. 'As I told you on our way back here, my real name is Feng Yu-ch'un; and although I did not mention it at the time, my great grandfather was Captain of one of the Eight Banner Corps under the Great Empress Mother Yehonala.'

'That would certainly make a considerable difference to their regard for you,' Tû-lai remarked. 'I doubt if the Council would agree to anyone outside one of the Seven Families becoming Emperor; but your noble blood would make it possible for them to place Josephine on the throne with you as her Consort.'

'Yes; I think they might do that,' Gregory supplemented. 'Because, although they observe the outward forms of Old China, the island is actually a Limited Monarchy. The real power has always been retained by the Council.'

For a moment Foo remained silent, and evidently a prey to conflicting emotions, then he said, 'I am not ambitious for myself, and I would be quite content to work to support Josephine in a small house of our own; but her birth entitles her to expect much more, so it is a great temptation to attempt to secure for her at least a life of honourable ease on an allowance from the Council. Nevertheless, I will not make the attempt,

346

because I could not bring myself to expose her wantonly to danger of any kind.'

Josephine again wrote on her tablet. She handed it to Foo, and when he had read it, signed that he should pass it on to Gregory.

Taking the tablet Gregory saw that she had written, 'Beloved. Last spring the only remaining representatives of our ancient civilization invited me to accept their throne. It is my right that I should present myself to them, and offer to serve them in any capacity they may wish.'

With a slow smile Gregory stood up, took her hand, kissed it and murmured, 'Your Highness, the gods have always loved courage. In you I believe that I salute another Empress Yehonala.'

Tû-lai and Foo had also come to their feet. The strain of decision had now left the latter's face, and it had taken on a look of resolution as he exclaimed:

'So be it then! We will try for a throne!'

Four days later, with the blessings of Madame Fan-ti and all other members of the family, they left the great House of Lin. The journey down to the coast was uneventful, and although the weather was overcast for the first part of the voyage they encountered no storms. The only delay they met with was on approaching the Island, as its position was charted only approximately, and they had to cruise about for two days before they found it.

A little before three o'clock the ship dropped anchor outside the reef, opposite the forbidding cliffs through which a narrow canyon led to the harbour; and twenty minutes later the party was ready to go ashore. They had discussed at great length the procedure they should adopt on their arrival, and it had been mooted that they should take with them a bodyguard of armed sailors. But the idea had been ruled out; first because such a display of distrust and force might arouse the antagonism of the islanders; secondly because it seemed extremely unlikely that they would be offered violence; and thirdly because if they were, the whole ship's company would have been insufficient to have any hope of rescuing them. It was, however, agreed that the ship should lie off shore until further orders, in case their reception proved so unfriendly that they felt the only sensible thing to do was to sail away in her; and, as a precaution against any personal vendetta that might be launched by Kâo, all four members of the party carried loaded pistols concealed upon them.

In those fortunate latitudes, although it was December the 5th the sea was a deep blue, the sky cloudless and, as the ship's launch carried them ashore, the heady scent of tropical flowers was wafted to them on the balmy air.

When the launch entered the harbour they saw that quite a crowd had assembled along the wharf, as fishing junks had already reported the arrival of the ship. On their coming along-side, the majority of the watching crowd showed only curiosity, but several men ran forward and willingly assisted in securing the boat to a flight of stone steps. Jumping ashore first, Gregory ran up them to come face to face with a tall man, better dressed than the rest, who bowed courteously and said:

'Honourable Sir. Permit me to inform you that this island is a leper settlement, and that to land upon it is forbidden unless you or your ship's company are in distress.'

'I have been here before,' Gregory replied promptly. Then, with memories of the pompous individual who had daily strutted up and down the wharf, when he had been an inmate of the cage up on the hill opposite it, he asked, 'Where is the Harbour-Master?'

The tall man gave him a surprised look, and answered, 'I am the Harbour-Master. My predecessor had the misfortune to join his ancestors a week ago.'

Josephine, Foo and Tû-lai had meanwhile come up the steps and were now standing beside Gregory. In a loud voice, so that the crowd of fishermen and wharf-hands could hear, he cried:

'Then, most honourable Harbour-Master, this is a great day for you. My friends and I have brought you Her Imperial Highness the Princess Josephine, whose arrival was expected here early last summer.'

The Harbour-Master's eyes opened wide, a murmur of astonishment ran through the crowd, then it broke into loud cries of excitement and applause.

For a moment the new Harbour-Master remained dumbfounded ; then, with a deep bow to Josephine, he stammered, 'We . . . we believed Your Highness to . . . to be dead. I . . . I will send a runner immediately to inform the Council.'

'Thank you,' said Gregory. 'And I would be glad if he could also apprise the lady A-lu-te of our arrival.'

The man nodded, but an uneasy expression had appeared on his face, and he muttered with a thin-lipped, slightly apologetic smile, 'Her Imperial Highness must forgive me, but I have no accommodation down here in which it would be at all suitable for her to wait until a fitting reception can be arranged. The building up there on the hill, will, I fear, be considered by so illustrious a person a place of extreme squalor ; but at least it has been fitted up as a rest house for unexpected guests. Permit me to send for a chair, so that she may be carried up there.'

'By all means send for a chair,' Gregory replied promptly, 'but Her Imperial Highness will be quite happy to sit in it down here.'

With an acutely worried look, the Harbour-Master plucked at the sleeve of his jacket, drew him slightly aside, and whispered, 'We have been told on excellent authority that the Princess was murdered nearly two months ago. I do not know you, and I have only your word that this is her. Perhaps I am being extremely foolish, and shall have to pay for my attitude later. But it is a regulation that all strangers arriving here should be accommodated in the guest house. I must enforce it ; otherwise I may lose my position. Any trouble between my men and the crowd would be most regrettable. Please give me your assistance by allowing us to escort your party in an orderly manner up to the building on the hill.'

Gregory was loath to allow his friends and himself to be penned up in the cage, but he had visualized having to submit to it temporarily on landing as a definite possibility ; and, as they were armed, he felt that, if the necessity arose, they could always shoot their way out again ; so he said:

'Very well, then ; but send the runner off at once to let the Council know that the Princess is here.' Then he told the crew of the launch that they might take it back to the ship.

Murmuring his thanks, the Harbour-Master turned away and began to rap out sharp orders to some of his men. A few minutes later a sedan-chair was produced, Josephine got into it and, accompanied by the entire crowd, they went round the inland end of the harbour and up the steep winding path to the guest house.

Its keeper, old Chung, was still there. Recognizing Gregory at once he greeted him with surprise but obvious pleasure; then set about superintending the bestowal of the guests' baggage, which had been carried up by a score of coolies who had fought for a share in the job.

The Harbour-Master bowed himself away, and, as Gregory observed with satisfaction, made no move to lock the gate of the cage after him. A portion of the crowd accompanied him back down the path; but the greater part of it remained outside the cage, staring goggle-eyed through the wire at Josephine, who had seated herself in one of the bamboo arm-chairs on the terrace.

As soon as Chung had got rid of the volunteer porters, he had returned to his small kitchen to make tea for his visitors. Gregory joined him there and said:

'Well, Chung; how have things been going on the Island since I left it in June?'

'I had here the crew of a native canoe, that had been caught up in a storm and blown several hundred miles, soon after the yacht's departure,' Chung told him, 'but we got rid of them early in August. Since then we have had no excitements until the return of the yacht after her long voyage. She got back about a fortnight ago.'

'And since then?' Gregory prompted.

Chung frowned. 'There has been a happening which has caused everyone in the Island much grief.'

'Really,' said Gregory, disguising his swiftly aroused interest by giving his voice a sympathetic tone. 'I'm sorry to hear that. Tell me about it?'

Taking the boiling kettle off the stove, Chung replied, 'Eight days ago, to celebrate his return, the Lord Kâo Hsüan gave a banquet. There were sixty guests, and afterwards nine of them died; it was said from food poisoning. Among those who went to greet their ancestors were the Lord Kâo's brother, the Man-

350

darin Li-chia Sung, the Chief of Police, Dr. Ho-Ping and our old Harbour-Master.'

For a second, Gregory held his breath. Chung's words had instantly revealed to him that he and his friends had placed themselves in a highly dangerous situation. Before they set out he had felt certain that Kâo would not be content to wait events, but would take some further step to bring his plans nearer fruition as soon as possible after he got home. It would not have surprised Gregory at all to learn that A-lu-te's father had met with a fatal accident, and that Kâo had succeeded him on the Council. But that, in the brief space of a fortnight, a holocaust of this kind might have wrought such havoc among the ruling caste of the island was a possibility that had never entered his mind.

He had expected to have been met with the open enmity of Kâo as well as more subtle forms of attack ; but he had counted on getting a fair hearing from the Council, and the support of both the Chief of Police and his old friend Ho-Ping, whom he knew to be honest men of influence. By their removal the scales had been weighted enormously in Kâo's favour, and Gregory now had to face the grim thought that he was up against odds that might well prove too much for him.

After having said to Chung how distressed he was to learn of the tragedy, he left him, returned to the others, took Tû-lai aside, and told him what had happened. They discussed the possibility of getting Josephine back to the ship at once, but decided that for the time being it was out of the question. The news of her arrival was swiftly spreading all over the Island. More and more people were streaming up the hill to gaze through the wire at her with excited interest, and outside the cage there was now a crowd of two or three hundred. Friendly as the people appeared to be, Gregory and Tû-lai agreed that now the Princess, for whose reception such joyous preparations had been made six months before, had at last arrived, they would certainly not stand calmly by while she was taken down to the harbour and rowed away again to sea in one of the small boats.

The only course seemed to be to await events as though they had nothing to fear. Some comfort, at least, could be derived from the attitude of the crowd, as it was a guarantee that they could not be imprisoned for any length of time without trouble arising; and that no hole-in-the-corner method could be employed in dealing with them, as the people would expect the Princess to be received with honour, and would have to be given some explanation if she was not. For the rest, they could only pin their faith on their wits and weapons.

It was nearly five o'clock when they sighted a cavalcade approaching down the avenue of palms that led to the harbour. It consisted of a strong force of police, a great lacquered palanquin carried by twenty bearers, and a large sedan-chair. At the bottom of the hill Kâo was helped out of the palanquin and eased his bulk into the sedan; then six of his bearers hoisted its poles on their shoulders, and, streaming with sweat, carried him up the steep path.

At the gate of the cage he alighted, waved back three police officers who were with him, and entered it alone. He did not bow to Josephine, or return the bows of the three men with her, but walked straight up to them. Then, his heavy face black as thunder, he said to Gregory:

'You must be mad to have come back here!'

Feigning surprise, Gregory replied, 'I cannot think why you say that, Sir. Surely you do not still believe that I killed that poor girl in Tung-kwan. In any case, whatever you believe, it should already be plain to you that I have since been employing myself most faithfully in the interests of the Island.'

'You lying trickster!' Kâo snarled. 'Of course you killed her! And since you have returned you shall be made to pay for it.'

'In view of the service I have rendered to the Council, I had expected a better reception,' Gregory said with an injured air. 'I can only suppose that your mind is embittered by jealousy, owing to Tû-lai and myself having succeeded where you failed. It was he who is mainly responsible for bringing Her Imperial Highness here. Be good enough to allow him to present you to her.'

For a moment Kâo stared at Josephine, his mouth working with anger; then he sneered, 'She is no Princess! You know that well enough! You murdered the Princess yourself in

Tung-kwan. As for your companions, I see you have with you the little rat who tried to kill me on the yacht, and Lin Tû-lai. His being in this party shows him to be as big a rogue as his father. It is clear that this girl is your tool, and you have brought her here in the hope of foisting her upon us as our ruler. How you expected such an ill-conceived plot to succeed, I cannot think.'

Breaking off for a second, Kâo cast a quick glance over his shoulder at the silent, staring crowd; then he turned right round and cried loudly to them:

'This woman is no Princess! She is an impostor! These people are a gang of criminals, and they will be brought before the Council tomorrow morning. Now that I have been appointed its President, you may be sure that they will be made to pay in full for this wicked deception they have attempted to practise upon you.'

22

IN THE HOURS OF DARKNESS

Kâo had gone, leaving two police officers and half a dozen men at the guest house; so its inmates were now prisoners. However, they had not been deprived of their weapons, as no attempt had been made to search them. In fact, apart from locking the gate of the cage, placing a guard on it and installing themselves in the big common-room, the police had taken no steps to assert their authority.

Gregory took that as an indication that Kâo was not sufficiently sure of himself to order hands to be laid on them, at all events in the presence of the crowd. The greater part of it had received his announcement in puzzled silence. There was some hissing, but it had seemed to be directed as much at Kâo as at the 'criminals' he had denounced. It was, anyhow, clear that he was by no means popular, and Gregory formed the impression that if only Josephine could have addressed the people they would have taken her word rather than his. But, unfortunately, that was out of the question; and for any of her friends to have done so on her behalf would not have had the same effect.

As it was, she waved to them from time to time, and many of them, obviously bewitched by her loveliness, waved back. Some of the men, too, who had known Gregory, shouted friendly greetings to him. That heartened them considerably, as the eager interest shown in them might prove a valuable asset in protecting them from violence; but in other respects it did not lessen the danger of their situation, for now that Kâo had got himself appointed President of the Council his new powers must make him a truly formidable enemy.

Soon after Kâo's departure, Gregory returned to the galley. In the circumstances he thought it very unlikely that Kâo would attempt to poison them that night; but he did not mean to take any chances. Kâo had not even spoken to Chung, and Gregory believed the elderly guest-house cook to be entirely reliable, but there was just a possibility that one of the police might have been ordered to slip something into the food; so he remained there while their evening rice was cooked and supervised the serving of it.

On account of Josephine, Foo was naturally taking matters worse than the others, and was already almost in despair, but she had shown great courage, and Gregory and Tû-lai did their best to cheer him up by pretending a confidence in the outcome of events that they had small grounds for feeling. They all agreed that no one could have foreseen that Kâo would become such a power in the Island in so short a time; but they endeavoured to comfort one another with the thought that, as he could hardly yet have got firmly into the saddle, there must still be considerable opposition to him, and that with skill and determination it might be rallied to his undoing.

As darkness fell the crowd began to melt away, and when

only a few people were left staring in through the gate of the cage the senior police officer came up and presented himself to the prisoners. Courteously, but firmly, he told them that he had orders to lock them into their cubicles, and, as nothing was to be gained by offering resistance, they agreed to his doing so. Their minds were filled with uneasy speculations about what fate might hold in store for them next day ; but, putting on brave faces, they wished one another good night.

Gregory had taken for himself the cubicle into which he had been put after having been washed up as a cast-away, although it recalled for him most unhappy memories. It was there that it had been fully borne in upon him that he would never again behold his beloved Erika. The pain was gone now, and when he thought of her it was only to recall the many wonderful times they had had together, with thankfulness that they had been so blessed ; yet deep down he knew that he could never be completely consoled for her loss, and that if he found happiness again with A-lu-te it would be of an entirely different kind.

About A-lu-te he was extremely worried, as he had no idea how the new situation in the Island might have affected her. To him it seemed certain that the nine men who had died after Kâo's banquet had been deliberately poisoned by him, and A-lu-te's father had been one of them. She had been her father's darling and devoted to him ; so if she suspected that he had met his death through foul play it was very possible that she had accused her uncle. If she had, Kâo would have taken drastic steps to deal with her ; so she might no longer be free, or might even, perhaps, have become a victim of his ruthlessness.

Although Gregory had said nothing about it to the others, such thoughts had been causing him acute anxiety all the evening, and he had been awaiting the coming of night with great impatience, as it was not until everyone had gone to sleep that he could make an attempt to find out.

He had never given away how he had managed to escape from the cage before, so everyone had assumed that he really had made a colossal jump from the roof over the electric fence at its back ; and, on arriving there that afternoon, he

355

had been much amused to see that the fence had been heightened. That had been a considerable comfort to him, as it meant that his old escape route was still unsuspected.

For the best part of three hours after being locked in his cubicle he sat turning things over in his mind far from happily; then he tore the curtains into strips and made another hole in the ceiling. Having tied round his neck a thin parcel that he meant to give to A-lu-te, if he could find her, he scrambled up through the hole on to the roof. For some minutes he lay there listening, but no sounds broke the stillness; so he got to his feet and, with a stone tied in the end of a length of the curtain, proceeded to hook and haul down a branch of the tree that overhung the roof—just as he had done nearly eight months before. Ten minutes later he was cautiously making his way up the steep slope at the back of the cage.

On the far side of its crest he had once more to pass through the belt of semi-jungle in which disturbed parrakeets screeched, and small animals scuttled away in the undergrowth at his approach; but this time he had the comfort of knowing that it was not inhabited by poisonous snakes. Beyond it, a quarter of an hour's brisk walk brought him down to the two factories in which were faked the *objets d'art* that brought the Island its wealth.

It was now close on one o'clock in the morning, so no one was about; but, since a meeting might have proved calamitous, he took advantage of every patch of shadow as he advanced along the road and turned into the avenue of palms. As there was no moon he could not see the cluster of beautiful buildings down in the valley; but, against the starlit sky, the delicate outlines of the roofs of the few houses that he passed recalled to him the fairy-like loveliness of the hidden scene as he had first gazed upon it. After leaving the avenue, another ten minutes' walk brought him to the lake.

As he crossed the bridge he could feel his heart beating heavily. Upon what he would find, or fail to find, in the next few moments so much depended. If A-lu-te were not in her room, it would not only confirm his fears for her, but mean that his best hope of saving little Josephine, and the rest of them, would be gone. Increasing his pace he walked swiftly past a thick screen of bamboos. As he emerged on their far side he drew a quick breath of relief. The house was in darkness except for a dim light that came from A-lu-te's room; the curtains had not been drawn and she was in it.

After a cautious glance round to see that no one else was about, he crossed the grass. Before, he had been able to make out only her head; but now he could see that she was clad in mourning white and sitting motionless on her day-bed, apparently absorbed in thought and staring out of the french window. In a few rapid steps he reached and knocked upon it.

At the same moment she rose, grasped the handle of the screen door, and pulled it open. As they came face to face she gave him no welcome but, her eyes wide with apprehension, exclaimed:

'You must be mad to have come here!'

He smiled. 'Anyhow, it seems you were expecting me.'

'Tonight, yes. Knowing your boldness I felt certain that somehow you would manage to escape from the cage again. I meant that you must be off your head to return to the Island.'

'How could we possibly guess that Kâo would make himself master of the place in a fortnight?'

Backing a little way into the room, she asked, 'What difference could that make to you?'

'Surely you can see that for yourself,' he replied, following her in and pulling the door to behind him. 'If we could have got here earlier we might have spiked his guns. As it is we have landed ourselves in a damnably tight corner.'

'Your danger would have been as great whenever you arrived,' she said sharply. 'Everyone here would have been against you.'

'To start with, perhaps. But for your sake I was prepared to take that risk.'

'For my sake?'

'Yes. But you don't seem very pleased to see me.'

'I am not. For the past seven weeks I have been doing my utmost to forget you.'

His face hardened. He had expected that she might still be

357

worried and puzzled about what part he had played in Shih-niang's death, but it had never entered his mind that her reception of him would be completely frigid. Greatly upset and distressed by her attitude, he said nothing for a moment, then he snapped:

'If that's the way you feel, I wonder that you bothered to wait up for me tonight.'

'As I had plighted my troth to you, I felt it my duty to be here to see you if you came,' she replied coldly.

'Duty be damned!' he exclaimed, 'Curiosity, you mean! And by everyone's being against me, I take it now you include yourself. But if you have some of Kâo's braves waiting to pounce on me as I go out, you had better warn them that I am armed.'

A-lu-te drew herself up. 'I feel shame for you that you could harbour such a thought ; and it shows how little I really knew you. How could you possibly suppose that a woman like myself would ever betray a man she had loved—even if he had done murder?'

Gregory gave an angry sigh. 'So you still believe that! I'm sorry about what I said just now. I didn't mean it. You see, I've been under the impression that you would be hoping that I should turn up again if I could possibly find a way to clear myself ; and now that I have it's quite a shock and a bit humiliating to find that you have had so little faith in me.'

'It cannot be a worse shock than the one I sustained at Tung-kwan.'

'Perhaps not, but you intervened to save me then.'

'That was an impulse to which any woman in love might have been subject.'

'Still, I should have thought that on thinking matters over you would have given me the benefit of the doubt.'

'Why should I? Everything pointed to your having killed the Princess ; and if that were not enough I understand that you are now giving further proof of your roguery by attempting to foist a false Princess upon us.'

'Nothing of the kind!' he retorted angrily. 'The girl down at the guest house is the real Josephine. Even if you don't believe me, I should have thought the fact that Lin Tû-lai brought us both here would have been proof enough for you of that.'

'Is . . . is Tû-lai here too, then?' she stammered.

'Yes. Didn't you know?'

'I was told only that you had returned with a story that the Princess was not dead after all ; and that you had brought her here.'

'So I have! Think back for a moment to the other girl. You must remember how, although she was supposed to have been brought up in the United States, she understood no English ; how she could hardly write the simplest characters ; and how ignorant she was on practically every subject. It was she who was the fake, and we were all had for a lot of mugs—myself more so than anyone, as I was speaking French to her all the time and had more chance to find her out.'

A-lu-te gave a little gasp, and put a hand up to her mouth. 'Yes . . . Oh, yes ; there were many little things! But I don't understand. What does this mean?'

'It means that your Uncle Kâo is one of the biggest criminals unhung. He knew she was a fake all the time, and planned her death to serve his own ends.'

'Kâo!' she gasped again. 'If you are right, perhaps . . . perhaps other people are too. They have been whispering all sorts of terrible things about . . . about a banquet that he gave.'

'If they have been saying that he poisoned nine of his guests, including your father, I have no doubt they are right.'

Tears welled up into A-lu-te's golden eyes and she suddenly sat down on the day-bed. 'He . . . he has always been so kind, and . . . and so jolly,' she sobbed. 'I cannot believe it.'

Gregory had never seen her cry. Sitting down on the day-bed he put his arm about her shoulders and said gently, 'I'm afraid you've got to. I've no proof of that, but I have enough of other crimes he has committed with the same object to make it as good as certain. It was largely in the hope of preventing him from continuing with his devilish plans that I came back here. That I should have arrived too late to save your father and the others is a tragedy ; but I still mean to do my damnedest to unmask him.'

A-lu-te gulped back her tears. From loyalty to her uncle she had put out of her mind many half-formed suspicions of him, but now they all came crowding back, outweighing the single count of the situation in which she had last seen Gregory. With the conviction that she had held for the past ten weeks now shattered, she murmured unhappily, 'Please . . . please tell me what you have found out?'

He shook his head. 'I can't now. It's too long a story. But you will hear it all tomorrow. That is, if you can get yourself into the Chamber when we are brought before the Council. Anyhow, you will hear all about it soon afterwards; but as you have so many influential friends I am hoping that you could get yourself passed in dressed as one of the attendants.'

'Yes; I think I could do that,' she nodded. Then, as she thought again, she added swiftly, 'But you must not stand your trial. You must not! Now Kâo is the President of the Council you wouldn't have a chance. It is a certainty that he would overrule the others and have you condemned. You must escape. Now that you are free you must go down to the harbour and steal a boat. There will be no one to stop you at this hour, and you could row out in it to the ship that brought you. That is, if it has not sailed away already.'

'No; she is still there. But, even if I wanted to, I couldn't do that. I must return to the others.'

'Of course; how stupid of me. All this has made me temporarily half-witted. I was simply urging on you the course I meant to press you to take while I was sitting here waiting for you.'

'You intended then to do your best to make me save myself in any case?'

'Oh, how can you think otherwise? But can you not, even now, get Tû-lai out of the guest house and escape to this ship with him?'

'It's just possible I might, but that would still leave Foo and——'

'Foo?'

'Yes. He is the young student who was in love with Josephine in San Francisco. It was to try to trace her through us that he stowed away in the yacht.'

'Then it was not he who tried to murder you after all?'

'No; but if you think back a bit you'll see now who did.'

Anyhow, even if I could get him and Tû-lai out, my escape route would prove much too difficult for Josephine.'

'But it is you more than any of the others that Kâo has his knife into,' A-lu-te protested. 'I beg you to escape to the ship while you still have the chance. The others are in nothing like as much danger ; and when the people realize that it is the real Princess you have brought here they will protect her.'

Gregory shook his head. 'They won't be given a chance to realize it, as long as Kâo remains master of the situation ; and it is her blood much more than mine that he is after. We are all in this together, and I must sink or swim with the others. I still think we will manage to swim through, if you will give me your help.'

She hesitated a second, then she said, 'I'd do anything to help you escape ; but I must be fair to Uncle Kâo. I have only your word for all this, and no proof at all that he is not right in saying that you and some others came here with the intention of trying to get hold of the wealth of the Island for yourselves through fooling us into placing a false Princess on the throne.'

'All right, then.' Gregory smiled. 'I'll tell you something else. Josephine was married to Foo in the House of Lin five weeks ago, so she is no longer in a position to be married to a member of one of the Seven Families. In bringing her here we hoped for no more than that she should be allowed to settle with her husband in the Island, and that the Council would make her an allowance sufficient for them to maintain themselves in reasonable comfort. My own object in returning was to prevent Kâo from reaping the reward of his crimes, and to be with you again.'

A-lu-te nodded, and gave him a sad little smile. 'I see now how wrong I have been. You are, as I believed to begin with, a brave and faithful man. And it all fits in. Very well, then, what do you wish me to do?'

Gregory unwrapped the parcel that he had brought, showed her the thing it contained, and told her the use to which he wished her to put it. Then they discussed at some length the steps she should take in order to be in the Council Chamber when the prisoners were brought up for trial in a few hours' time.

When everything was settled, the anxiety of both of them about how things would go was too great for them to feel like love-making; but as they stood up she offered him her lips.

She, too, was now involved in a desperate gamble; but having convinced her of his honesty he knew that she would not have had things otherwise, and that he could count on her courage and loyalty. Before going out into the darkness, he took her in his arms and kissed her fondly. It was for the last time; but that he could not know.

23

THE DIARY OF LIN WÂN

As dawn broke over the Island where Time Stands Still, the four prisoners were roused by their guards, and as soon as they had dressed, Chung served them with 'first rice'. Gregory had got back without incident and, although he had had less than three hours' sleep, his wits were sufficiently about him for him to make the elderly cook eat a little from each of the bowls before leaving them on the table.

By half-past seven they had finished breakfast, and the senior police officer told them that he had orders to take them to the Palace. The sedan-chair in which Josephine had been carried up the hill was produced for her again, and with the others walking beside it they set off.

As soon as they got down to the harbour a small crowd began to gather and accompany them. Then, as they advanced up the avenue of palms, the crowd was swollen by people coming from all directions until, when they neared the Palace, the best part of a thousand men and women were marching along before and behind Josephine's sedan-chair.

The crowd neither hissed nor cheered, and it was clear that the emotion which had caused them to abandon their daily tasks was an intense curiosity. That the people were favourably inclined towards the prisoners, rather than hostile, was shown by the remarks that were made from time to time as they caught a glimpse of Josephine. The sight of her young and innocent beauty seemed to win all hearts, and once more Gregory felt how tragic it was that she could not speak to them. Even a few words from her as she left the sedan to walk up the steps in front of the Palace would, he felt certain, have been enough to start a revolution in her favour.

As they entered the building, the great court outside was packed to suffocation; but inside it there were only officials, and Gregory knew that by now most of them must be under Kâo's thumb. That Kâo was taking no chances they soon had evidence; for, on entering the second ante-room, a dozen policemen suddenly closed upon and seized them. In a minute their pistols were found and taken away; then they were allowed to go again. It was a move that Gregory had expected might happen before they left the guest house, so he accepted the loss philosophically. Their weapons would have been of value had they been attacked during the night, or in some place where they could quickly have taken cover, but to have drawn them here in the Palace could have led only to a bloody fracas in which they would have been overcome within a few minutes.

After a short wait, the great bronze doors, inlaid with mother of pearl, were thrown open and they were marched into the Council Chamber. Nothing had been altered there since that day in the preceding April, when Gregory had entered it before. Of the seven members of the Council four were the same; but Kâo now sat in the place of honour formerly occupied by his dead brother, up on the dais beside the empty pearl and lapis-lazuli throne. In Tsai-ping's old seat there sat a very young member of his family that Gregory knew only by sight. The other change was that Captain Ah-moi Sung had been elevated to the rank of Mandarin by the death of his aged father.

A-lu-te had told Gregory, only a few hours earlier, that the stalwart Captain had been among those invited to Kâo's banquet, but had been unable to attend owing to a temporary illness. Gregory thought it highly probable that Ah-moi owed his life to his indisposition, as he was just the type of forceful and honest personality that Kâo would have wished to get out of his way. To see him there comforted Gregory greatly, as he felt that Ah-moi would assure him of a fair hearing; and, although the bluff sailor did not smile at him as the prisoners were led in, he gave him a long, searching, not unfriendly look.

It was Kâo who opened the proceedings. Calmly and with no trace of the vindictiveness he had displayed the previous afternoon, he addressed his fellow Mandarins.

'Excellencies,' he said. 'Of the four persons brought before you only the principal criminal is known to you all. I refer to the man Sallust, who having been cast away on our Island last March, has repaid our hospitality by the basest possible treachery. The young man who calls himself Foo will be recognized by our colleague Ah-moi Sung as the Communist agent who stowed away in the yacht. Their male confederate is one Lin Tû-lai, the third son of Lin Wân of Yen-an. The woman is one of Lin Wân's concubines.

'As they and their histories are all known to me, I am able to reveal to you their many crimes, which have culminated in this childish but wicked attempt to gain wealth and position for themselves by placing an impostor on our throne. Therefore, you will require no other evidence to find them guilty.

'The history of our search for the Princess Josephine was given to you in great detail by myself, on my return a fortnight ago. The truth of that account has been vouched for by my niece, the lady A-lu-te, who was with me from the beginning to the end of my journey. For the greater part of it we were accompanied by my colleague Ah-moi Sung who, with his officers, will no doubt also have given you a true version of the most distressing happenings on our voyage. Therefore, all the circumstances will be fresh in your minds, and I need not take up your time by repetition of them.

'To come at once to the point. There has never been the least doubt in our minds that it was Sallust who murdered the Princess Josephine. My niece and I caught him red-handed. Where we were wrong was in assuming that he murdered her for the considerable sum of money she had with her. That was not his object ; but this present conspiracy reveals it to us. He killed her in order that he might make this attempt to place a woman of his own choosing on our throne. In the light of that revelation all the crimes that preceded the Princess's death are easily explained.

'While we were in San Francisco he must already have had this plot in mind, and to assist him in it he smuggled aboard the yacht the man Foo. It was, you will recall, Sallust who "discovered" Foo, or to be accurate persuaded our colleague Ah-moi Sung to have him transferred from the stoke-hold to the passenger accommodation, where he could more readily receive and act upon his villainous master's instructions.

'It will be obvious to you that for Sallust to succeed in his vile plot it was necessary for him to eliminate all the members of the mission ; as only then could he have returned to you, posing as the sole survivor of a chapter of accidents, and with a pseudo-Princess whose identity none of you would have been in a position to challenge.

'The accident, in San Francisco, which deprived us of our honourable colleague Tsai-Ping must have been regarded by Sallust as a piece of good fortune ; as it meant that he would have one less murder to carry out. But that was off-set by Mr. Wu-ming Loo's insisting on joining the mission ; and he had on one occasion before our arrival in San Francisco, met the Princess. As he knew her he was in a position to unmask an impostor, so that made it doubly necessary to eliminate him also.

'At the inquiry following Wu-ming's death it was Sallust who came under suspicion. Now that a motive for the killing has been established, we can have no doubt that it was he, with the aid of Foo, who threw the unfortunate Wu-ming overboard.

'We come now to Foo's attempt upon myself. To its miscarriage, I think both I and my niece owe our lives; for it resulted in our colleague Ah-moi Sung's having Foo locked up for the remainder of the voyage. Whether through lack of personal courage or out of caution, Sallust was, apparently, loath to proceed to further violence without the aid of his henchman. It is now obvious that it was he who enabled Foo to escape when we reached the old mouth of the Hwang-ho; but the accommodation in the sampan was too limited for him to be secreted on board. In consequence, the lady A-lu-te and myself arrived at the House of Lin in safety.

'At this point, it seems that Sallust decided that he must abandon his original project of producing a false Princess on his own, and keeping to himself all the benefits which might be expected from the imposture planned by him. In any case, it is now evident that while we were at the House of Lin he took Lin Tû-lai into his confidence, and that Lin Tû-lai agreed to become his confederate.

'Their announcement on their arrival here yesterday will have made clear to you the events that followed. Sallust accompanied us back to Tung-kwan and there cleared the way for a renewal of his ambitious schemes by murdering the Princess, while Lin Tû-lai brought this woman from his father's seraglio to the coast.

'No doubt they originally hoped to get ahead of me, establish her here, and discredit me upon my arrival; but it is probable that they met with delay in diverting one of the Lin ships from its normal business to bring them to the Island. That they should have arrived after me is fortunate, for that has made it easier for me to establish the truth and reveal to you their villainy.

'I have only one more thing to say. No ordinary punishment can fit the abominable crimes of which they are guilty. Sallust is the murderer of a Princess of the Imperial House, and the others are his accomplices. I demand that their sentence should be that which they would have received in the old China. The death of a thousand cuts, to be brought to a conclusion on the tenth day by slow strangulation.'

Kâo had twisted events into such a logical sequence that they had become a terrible indictment. He had made a far

366

stronger case than Gregory expected, and no sentence could be more appalling to contemplate than the one he had demanded. Everything now hung on whether Gregory would be able to get a hearing, and he saw at once that Kâo did not intend to allow him one; for he had already signed to the seven servants standing in the background to bring forward the opium pipes, so that the seven Mandarins might go through the formality of deliberation before pronouncing sentence.

Stepping forward, Gregory said loudly, 'Excellencies, I claim the right to speak in defence of my friends and myself.'

'Here, you have no rights,' Kâo replied sternly.

'By the laws of humanity every accused person has such a right,' Gregory protested.

'My colleagues know that I speak the truth, and that is enough,' Kâo thundered.

'It is not enough,' Gregory retorted. 'In this Island you claim to carry on a great civilization. The basis of all civilizations is the maintenance of justice. I will ask you a plain question. Does, or does not, this High Council consider itself a Court of Justice?'

'It does; and justice will be done here,' Kâo said firmly. 'I order you to be silent, so that we may deliberate and justice take its course.'

'There can be no justice where the accuser also acts as judge,' Gregory urged desperately. 'And that is what you propose to do.'

Kâo shrugged his great shoulders. 'On that I will give way to you. I will refrain from voting, and leave the passing of sentence on you with confidence to my colleagues.'

With a flicker of new hope Gregory looked at Ah-moi and cried, 'I know your Excellency for an honest man. Will you not support my contention that this court cannot administer true justice unless both sides are given a hearing?'

The big sea captain nodded, then glanced round his fellow Mandarins. 'He is right. Whatever lies he may tell in an endeavour to persuade us that he did not commit these crimes, it is proper that we should hear him.'

'It is a waste of time,' snapped Kâo.

But to the immense relief of the four prisoners, the others

signified their agreement with Ah-moi ; so, drawing a small, thick book from his pocket, Gregory bowed to the Council and began.

'Excellencies, I too will not weary you with needless repetitions about events already known to you ; but I have a big canvas to cover ; and I beg that, however unlikely some of the statements that I make may at first appear, you will hear me with patience to the end. Much that I am about to say is, I frankly admit, based only on assumption ; but, upon salient points, the evidence I propose to place before you is so incontestable that, when I have done, I am convinced that you will agree that no other explanation completes the picture.

'First, the basis of our defence is that it was not I but Kâo Hsüan who plotted to become the most influential and wealthy individual on your Island.'

'It is a lie,' Kâo growled.

Ignoring the interruption, Gregory went on, 'You will recall that for twenty-five years he was your Export Manager. During those years he lived a life of luxury in the great cities of Europe and America. No one who knows his disposition can doubt that he thoroughly enjoyed the many diversions they have to offer ; and that by comparison, on his retirement, he found the restricted life here lacking in all savour. He is moreover an inveterate gambler.

'I must now make an assumption for which I will later give ample grounds. After a short period of retirement he decided that the only way in which he could escape spending the rest of his life in boredom was by getting control of the Island and becoming its Dictator. That would have enabled him, at times, to leave his own nominees in authority here while making trips abroad again, during which he could have used the Island's resources for his gambling and other pleasures.'

'This is the most fantastic nonsense,' Kâo cut in. But one of the Mandarins laughed and said, 'All the same, it is most diverting. Let him go on.'

Gregory bowed to him and continued. 'With the death of your late Emperor, Kâo Hsüan saw his chance. Only the life of his brother stood between him and a seat on the Council. Once on it, he believed that with his powerful personality he

368

would be able to dominate it and get himself appointed its President. In support of my contention I ask you to consider what has actually happened since his return to the Island.'

The Mandarin who had laughed now looked away, and the faces of the others took on a new gravity.

Having paused to give due effect to his thrust, Gregory spoke again. 'Since the Emperor's sons had pre-deceased him, he had no heir; so, had things gone as Kâo Hsüan expected, he would have been under the necessity of doing no more than invite the only man who might block his way to power—the Mandarin Tsai-Ping—and his brother, to dinner.'

With a roar of rage Kâo sprang to his feet and bellowed, 'This is monstrous! I will not sit here and allow myself to be maligned! I demand that this malicious foolery be ended.'

It was now the young Mandarin of the Ping family who replied. Raising his voice against Kâo's, he cried, 'And I demand that the prisoner be heard to the end. It may be that he will give us a different version to yours of how my Uncle Tsai died, and tell us what it was that my honourable father ate at your banquet that you did not eat.'

With a grim smile, Gregory bowed to him. 'I shall come very shortly now to the matter of your honourable uncle's death. But first, as I was about to say, Kâo Hsüan's ambitious plans were unexpectedly upset. From fear that one of its members might harbour just such ambitions, the Council very wisely decided to invite Princess Josephine to come here and choose a husband from one of the Seven Families. That was a severe set-back for our conspirator, but it did not turn him from his purpose; and as a first step he got himself appointed as your ambassador to fetch the Princess and her mother to the Island.

'About his conduct when he arrived in San Francisco we must make another assumption—namely that he wanted to get in as long a session of gambling as possible before returning. In any case, instead of conveying your invitation to Madame Août at once, he did not even call on her until May the 13th; and then only to pay his respects, leaving any mention of the invitation till a later date. But it was on that day that Mr. Lin Wân enters the story, and I now intend to read you some extracts from his diary.'

'I protest!' Kâo's face had suddenly gone pale, but he came to his feet again. 'That diary may be a forgery! That account given in it may not be true! Lin Wân is dead, and no one but he could vouch for what is written there.'

'Enough!' rapped out Ah-moi. Then, turning his back on Kâo, he said to Gregory, 'Read these extracts to us.'

Opening the book, Gregory said, 'I shall read only extracts that are of interest to your Excellencies. The first concerns events on May the 13th.

' "Called on Madame Aôut to pay my respects. Her daughter a lovely little creature but should be married by now. Met there that old rogue Kâo Hsüan. He invited me to dine on his yacht two nights hence and play Fan-tan afterwards. I accepted."

'The next entry reads: "Dined on yacht and lost four-fifty dollars to Kâo at Fan-tan. This makes me angry, but I think I see a way to far more than repay myself. Being aware that I know all about their Island the officers of the yacht talked to me freely. They are full of excitement at their reason for being here. Kâo has been charged to take Josephine Aôut back to the Island so that she may be made its Empress. The Council of the Island is immensely rich. If I handle this with skill there should be more profit in it for me than I would make from a life-time of trading with them."

'The next entry reads: "Have seen Quong-Yü and arranged matters with him. To kidnap both women simultaneously would more than double the difficulties; and Quong insists that Madame Aôut cannot be left to furnish information to the police. In any case her presence here would cause me great embarrassment. Have regretfully decided that she must be eliminated. Quong is to send the girl aboard after dark. He stuck out for his price—a hundred thousand dollars—but she must be worth ten times that to Kâo and his friends."

'The next entry reads: "Madame Aôut dead and girl on board. She was naturally much frightened but entirely re-assured on seeing me. I invented a story about an invitation from Chiang Kai-shek, as a result of which Communists had killed her mother and now threaten her life. She has accepted my protection without question. Have instructed Quong-Yü

370

that, without revealing who has her, he is to act as my go-between with Kâo, and ask a million dollars for her ransom."

'The next entry reads: "Kâo refuses to negotiate. I cannot understand it."

'The next entry reads: "Kâo still refuses to negotiate. This is becoming awkward as I am due to sail the day after to-morrow, and I am a hundred thousand dollars out of pocket."

'The next entry reads: "Everything is settled. Not altogether satisfactory from my point of view, but it was quite impossible for me to foresee the turn matters would take. However, it is proving one of the most fascinating intrigues in which I have ever engaged. Yesterday, invited Kâo to dine last night and play return game of Fan-tan. After a dozen hands I admitted to having had the little Princess kidnapped. He was furious; but I only laughed and asked what she was really worth to him. He replied 'nothing' and from that I could not budge him. Then, after a while, feeling there must be more in this than met the eye, I drew a bow at a venture, and said, 'Very well, then. As she is such a lovely little thing, I will get my money's worth out of her as well as I can by keeping her to look at during my voyage to China; then I will find some means to send her to the Island—for nothing.' Immediately, he took alarm, and shortly afterwards admitted that while she was of no value to him alive she was worth a considerable sum to him dead. I insisted that before I would do a deal I must know the reason for that. He then had no option but to reveal the truth to me. It seems that he is already weary of his retirement and hankers after the flesh-pots of Europe. He maintains that in a few skilful moves he can make himself the Dictator of the Island, and from then on stay there or travel as he likes. But if the Princess ever reaches the Island and marries into one of its Seven Families, the creation of a new Emperor will place such ambitions forever beyond his reach. I should be most loath to order the killing of the child, but I asked him how much he would give me to do so. He replied by naming an absurd sum, and eventually I got him up to half a million. It then transpired that he had not got it. However, he should have that and more if he succeeds in becoming Dicta-tor. Before we parted it was agreed that I should give him six months in which to bring his plans to fruition, and meanwhile take the girl home with me. If by the end of that time he has not sent me the money I am to send the Princess to the Island. If he pays up I am to have her killed. Of course I shall not do so. She is much too lovely ; and it would be a fine distinction to have an Imperial Highness in the family. I shall marry her to one of my sons." '

Closing the diary, Gregory went on, 'So you see, Excellencies, the position in which Kâo Hsüan was placed. Had it not been for Lin Wân's intervention, we can hardly doubt what would have happened. Your ambitious President would, in due course, have received Madame Août and her daughter on the yacht, and he would have seen to it that Josephine met with a fatal accident during the voyage. Then, freed for good from her as a menace to his plans, he would have been able to proceed with them at his leisure. Even as things were, we may fairly assume that he intended to do so during the six months' grace Lin Wân had given him. But the Council decreed otherwise. They sent him back to search for the Princess.

'We now come to his second stay in San Francisco. Knowing the Princess to be by that time in China, and that Quong-Yü would not voluntarily reveal the criminal activities that took place six weeks before, he no doubt felt confident that the mission would have to return to the Island and confess failure. That would have been the case, had not Tsai-Ping asked me to go to Washington. The co-operation of the F.B.I. led us to Quong-Yü, but it became swiftly apparent to our conspirator that I was the only person who could exert pressure enough on the Tong boss to make him talk. Given those circumstances, I consider it a fair assumption that they got together and planned to kill me on the way to the Tong headquarters. I escaped death only by a miracle ; and instead of myself, it was the unfortunate Tsai-Ping on whose head Quong-Yü's hatchet-men let fall the banana crates.

'We may well suppose that Kâo Hsüan was pleased to see that capable and conscientious Mandarin safely removed from his path ; and in the larger picture things did not seem to be going badly for him. Quong-Yü's disclosure, that the Princess was seven thousand miles away in a remote part of China, gave him good grounds for suggesting that the hunt for her should be abandoned. But in that he was overruled by a combination of Mr. Wu-ming Loo, the lady A-lu-te and Captain Ah-moi Sung; so to save face he was compelled to agree to the mission's continuing to carry out its instructions.

'Now that we were bound for Yen-an he was under the necessity of getting rid of Wu-ming, in case he learned on our arrival there of the bargain that had been made with Lin Wân. Moreover, my handling of Quong-Yü must have caused him to realize that I, too, might prove a serious menace to his plans; so he decided that both of us must be eliminated at the earliest suitable opportunity.

'Having set his servant P'ei to spy on me, after we had been two weeks at sea he learned that it was my habit to have Foo bring me a cocktail every night when I was changing for dinner. One evening the cocktail brought to me contained poison. At the time I did poor Wu-ming the injustice of believing that it was he who had attempted to murder me; although Foo told me that P'ei had been in the pantry when he mixed the drink. Two months later, when Foo rescued the Princess from P'ei and beat him up, he forced him to talk. P'ei then confessed that his master, Kâo Hsüan, had ordered him to put poison in my cocktail.'

Ah-moi held up his hand. 'One minute! What is this about Foo rescuing the Princess from Kâo Hsüan's servant?'

Gregory cast a swift glance at Kâo, who, grey-faced and glowering, had now resigned himself to the role of silent on-looker; then he replied:

'We shall come to that in due course, Excellency. With your leave I will continue to take each event in its proper order. As I was about to say, I had the good fortune to escape your President's polite attention, but poor Wu-ming did not. After his attack on me he was in no state to defend himself, and again we have an admission by P'ei to Foo, that it was he and his master who threw Wu-ming overboard.

'In an endeavour to kill two birds with one stone, Kâo Hsüan did his best to cast suspicion for that crime on me; and things might have gone ill for me then, had not the lady A-lu-te generously provided me with an alibi.

'The removal of suspicion from myself tended to throw it upon the murderers, although I had not the sense to see that at the time; so my enemy's next move was a double-edged one aimed at diverting suspicion from himself and depriving me of my watch-dog, Foo, so that I might be more easily attacked. Two nights later, he took advantage of Foo's being at the top of a ladder with him to throw himself down it, then he accused Foo of having attempted to kill him. By his stratagem he succeeded in getting Foo locked up; but apparently he could find no opportunity to make a further attempt upon myself until we reached Antung-Ku.

'That it was P'ei who went ashore there from the sampan and procured a snake to put in my bunk on Kâo Hsüan's orders can rest only on assumption, as Foo, knowing nothing of that episode, did not question P'ei about it. I escaped, but Tsai-Ping's old servant, Che-khi, died of the snake's bite; and, in view of all that had gone before, who can doubt that Kâo Hsüan was also responsible for the agonizing death suffered by this innocent man.

'During our long journey up river I can only think that I owed my immunity from attack to the confined quarters of the sampan. My would-be murderer must have felt that should he again try to kill me while we were in it, and fail, he would have exposed his hand, and might become the victim of a reprisal. But after we left Tung-kwan, he made one final effort to eliminate me before we reached Yen-an. He suborned the master and men of the caravan with which we were travelling to stone me to death. Fortunately for me, Foo, who had joined the caravan in disguise, learned of the plot and succeeded in foiling it.'

Gregory paused and, opening the diary again, went on, 'I will now read you some further passages from the secret jottings set down by Lin Wân. Those which interest us start on September the 28th. On that day an entry reads:

'"A surprise this morning. There arrived here one P'ei, a servant of Kâo Hsüan, with a letter from his master. In it Kâo tells me that he is on his way up from Tung-kwan, to collect the little Princess. This is good news in one way but bad in another. The half-million dollars that he brings will be welcome; but had he sent them I had meant to keep them, and the Princess; at least until he had disgorged another half-million for her. But as he is coming for her himself I have not the face to go back on our bargain so must hand her over to him. I never expected that Kâo would find himself in a position to pay up so soon—if ever; so I had intended to marry the girl to Tû-lai. Fortunately he has shown some reluctance to take her for a wife, so he will be not greatly disappointed. Kâo asks me in his letter to make no mention of our bargain to any of those who are accompanying him. But I must now tell Tû-lai something of this matter, and at the same time warn him to keep it a close secret."

'The next entry is on the 30th, and reads: "A bitter disappointment. Kâo has arrived, with his niece and a well-mannered Englishman who is, apparently, an intimate friend of the family—but no half-million dollars. It seems that Kâo has not got far with his ambitious plans since we last met, but he still has great hopes of achieving them if I will aid him. We are to talk of this tomorrow."

'The next entry reads: "I have had talk with Kâo and I am wondering if I have let him get the best of me; but I think not. He certainly has a most subtle mind, and, knowing that I would not let him have the Princess unless he paid me for her, he produced a most ingenious plan. We are to find some girl who can temporarily be passed off as Her Highness. He will take this woman away with him, and as they go down river have her drowned—although her death will be made to appear an accident. He can then return to the Island and, with his niece for witness, state that the Princess lost her life on the way there. As there is no other candidate for the throne that the Council would be willing to accept, it will remain vacant and Kâo get his chance to become Dictator. Should he succeed he will be in a position to pay me for my help. Should he fail I can take the Princess to the Island myself and expose this cheat of his in having reported her to be dead. I am to find a girl suitable to undertake the imposture; but I put my price for carrying the whole matter through at a million dollars, and he agreed."

'The next entry reads: "I settled on the girl this morning. I
375

greatly regret having to sacrifice Shih-niang, but she is the only one in my seraglio at all suitable. She is, perhaps, a little old for the part, but she speaks French fluently and can write it fairly well ; and that was the language used by Madame Août. I spent most of the day bargaining with her and, when she at last agreed to do as I wished, coaching her in the role she is to play. This evening I took them to see her, and she passed her first test to the satisfaction of both Kâo and myself. The lady A-lu-te was completely taken in, also the Englishman ; and for this part of Kâo's plan to succeed that is all that matters. I have quite good hopes now that within the stipulated time I shall receive my million dollars. But whether I do or not, I still have no intention of ordering the little Princess to be killed. If Tû-lai continues to be fool enough to refuse her I shall marry her to one of my other sons." '

Again Gregory closed the diary, then he said, 'It remains only for me to give your Excellencies an outline of events after we left the House of Lin. Their main features are: First, our discovery that at no point had Communist agents been concerned in these happenings. That being so, we have no alternative but to assume that it was Kâo Hsüan himself who threw the knife over my shoulder at Shih-niang, on discovering that she had given her secret away to me. Secondly, that Kâo Hsüan, having learnt that Lin Wân contemplated double-crossing him by marrying the Princess to Tû-lai, left P'ei behind with orders to kill her. And thirdly, that P'ei, fearing that Kâo Hsüan would kill him to ensure his silence, decided to double-cross his master ; with the fortunate result that after he had abducted the Princess, Foo was able to rescue her from him.'

For a further ten minutes, Gregory gave details of these last moves that had preceded the departure of himself and his friends from China, then he said:

'I will conclude by calling your Excellencies' attention to the state in which we found things on our arrival here. We are told that a week ago Kâo Hsüan gave a banquet for sixty guests, and that nine of them afterwards died from food poisoning. Those who died were some of the most prominent men who might have been expected to stand between him and his ambitions. When you see him here today having so nearly achieved the status of a Dictator, can you believe that it was food poisoning?

'There rests the case of Her Imperial Highness the Princess Josephine, of myself and of my two friends. Kâo Hsüan has already surrendered his right to act as one of our judges, I accuse him of murder on a scale equalled only by the Borgias, and I leave your Excellencies to judge between us.'

For some time past a dull murmur from the crowd outside had penetrated to the Chamber. As Gregory ceased speaking, in the silence that followed it became much clearer. A police officer slipped in through a side door, closed it quickly behind him, looked anxiously at Kâo and said:

'It is the people, Excellency. They are becoming unruly. They are demanding that the Princess should be presented to them.'

Ah-moi answered for Kâo, 'Tell them to have patience. An announcement will be made to them shortly, when we have concluded our deliberations.' Then he signed to the servants to bring forward the opium pipes.

On first entering the Chamber, Gregory had seen that A-lu-te had succeeded in taking the place of one of the seven young women whose duty it was to keep the pipes instantly ready for smoking. She now advanced with the others and, bowing low before her uncle, offered him the beautiful jade pipe which he had left in Lin Wân's room.

For the past half-hour Kâo had been sitting hunched upon his stool, with all the life gone out of his usually cheerful face. Now, taking the pipe from his cushion, he gave her a sardonic smile and murmured:

'So you, too, are among my enemies?'

But he made no move to smoke the pipe. Instead, laying it aside, he stood up and said in a loud voice, 'As I am not sitting in judgment on this case, it would be wrong for me to join my colleagues in smoking a pipe of deliberation.'

The old scar above Gregory's left eyebrow showed white in a sudden frown. For a moment it seemed that by getting Kâo to forgo any part in judging the case he had sabotaged his own carefully laid plan.

377

But Kâo bowed to him and went on in a quieter tone, 'Nevertheless, Mr. Sallust, I congratulate you on your victory. A good General knows when he is defeated.'

As he spoke the last words he swiftly slipped something that he had just taken from his pocket into his mouth. Next moment he was seized with violent convulsions, and his great body fell with a crash from the dais to lie sprawled at the feet of his fellow Mandarins.

24

THE THREE WISHES OF GREGORY SALLUST

O n the following afternoon Gregory was walking with A-lu-te in her garden, and they were talking of the amazing scenes that had taken place the preceding day, after Kâo had committed suicide.

While the trial was going on, the crowd outside had swollen until it included nine-tenths of the population of the Island, and extended for nearly half-a-mile down the avenue of palms. The clamour of the people to see Josephine had grown so great that had they been refused rioting would have resulted ; so the six remaining Mandarins led her out on to the first-floor balcony of the Palace, and, being by then convinced that she was the real Princess, they did so willingly. She received a tremendous ovation, and it was over an hour before the people would let her go in.

Afterwards the Council had held an Extraordinary Session. During it the argument had been put forward that perhaps, after all, it was a good thing that she was already married, as had she married into one of the Seven Families that family

might have been unduly favoured with appointments and in
time come to regard itself as superior to the others. It was
also pointed out that although Foo was not of sufficient birth
to be acceptable as Emperor, he had high-caste Manchu-
warrior blood in his veins, so was not unfitted to assume the
role of Consort. In consequence, it had been decided that
Josephine should be made Empress, and that as Kâo had been
the last male of the Hsüan line, Foo should be appointed to
fill the vacant place as the Seventh Mandarin.

On the announcement of these decisions the population had
gone wild with excitement. The whole Island had been given
over to rejoicing, and the Mandarins had opened the reserve
store-houses to the people so that there might be feasting in
every home. Bonfires had been lit, thousands of fireworks let
off and the joyous celebrations gone on till dawn.

After Gregory and A-lu-te had talked of this happy outcome for a while, they fell into an uneasy silence. At length
she broke it by saying:

'There is something I have to ask you, but I don't know how
to put it.'

'Oh fire away,' he answered lightly. 'If we are to be married,
surely there is nothing you need be afraid to say to me.'

'If . . . ' she echoed. Then, after an awkward pause, she
added, 'That is just it. Do . . . do you really want to marry me
very much?'

His face was serious, but he smiled down at her. 'Before I
answer that, since it was you who brought the question up it
is only fair that you should tell me how you feel about it.'

Looking down at the ground, she murmured, 'I plighted my
troth to you, and I could not go back on that. So I am yours
if you wish it.'

'Of course I wish it—given certain circumstances,' he said
slowly. 'But it has always been accepted that the girl has the
right to change her mind. During the two months we have
been separated your feelings may have changed. If you no
longer love me, I should not wish it.'

With her eyes still cast down she nodded. 'It is that which
I felt you should know. You have so many wonderful qualities
that any woman would be proud to be your wife; and you are
379

the most delightful companion that anyone could have. But I know now that the feeling I have for you is not really love.'

'If that is so, you must love someone else.'

Again she nodded. 'Tû-lai. He does not know of our secret engagement, and last night he asked me to become his wife.'

'And what did you reply?'

'I said that I would give him his answer this evening.'

Gregory put his arm round her shoulders and gave her a little hug. 'Then I willingly release you from your promise to me. I have always felt that I was too old for you. He is the right age and a splendid fellow. I'm certain that he'll make you happy in a way that I could never do.'

'Oh thank you! Thank you!' she murmured, bursting into tears. 'I feel simply terrible about this. But . . . but I've been in love with Tû-lai ever since I met him.'

'There! There!' he comforted her. 'Dry your eyes, my pretty, and just think of me from now on only as a good friend. I'll do the traditional thing and act as god-father to your first baby.'

In a remarkably short time she stopped crying, and a few minutes later she said, 'One thing has been puzzling me a lot. Why did you make me go through that performance yesterday with Kâo's opium pipe?'

A slight frown appeared on his face; and instead of giving her an answer he asked, 'What was considered to be the worst crime in old China?'

'Patricide,' she replied without hesitation. 'But, as ancestor worshippers, for a man to kill his father was almost unheard of.'

'Was there not a crime still more heinous?'

After a moment's thought, she said, 'As the Emperor was the Great Father, to kill him would, of course, be infinitely worse.'

Gregory nodded. 'And am I not right in thinking that such a crime would have brought life-long, indelible disgrace on every member of a regicide's family?'

'Yes. Their shame would be so great that they would never be able to hold up their heads again.'

'I thought so. That is why I refrained from disclosing three

380

of Kâo's most terrible crimes. To take the last one first; there was one entry in Lin Wân's diary that I did not read out. He wrote it only an hour or so before he died. It was to the effect that, on leaving, Kâo had made him a present of a most beautiful opium pipe, and that he meant to smoke it that night.'

Gregory paused for a moment, then went on: 'Now we'll go back to the very beginning of Kâo's ruthless steps to remove everyone who stood between himself and Dictatorship. You will remember that towards the end of March both the Emperor's little sons were drowned. It was said that by some oversight the Imperial boatmen were not warned for duty that afternoon; so rather than disappoint the children the Harbour-Master had them taken out by two of his men. From the terrace of the cage I saw them go to their deaths. Their nurse was kidnapped, although I did not realize it at the time. We were told afterwards that she had taken her own life from remorse at having neglected her charges. Perhaps she did, but it is more probable that she was murdered. The little Princes were taken outside the reef contrary to orders, and I feel sure that the boat was overturned deliberately as the culmination of a clever plot stage-managed by the Harbour-Master on Kâo's instructions; then when the men who did the deed swam ashore they were promptly executed so that they could not talk. To close that episode for good, a week ago Kâo invited the Harbour-Master to his banquet, and had him poisoned, so that he could never talk either.'

Covering her eyes with her hand, A-lu-te murmured, 'Those poor little boys! How terrible! There seems to have been no end to Kâo's crimes.'

'I have yet to tell you of his most infamous coup,' Gregory said quietly. 'On the night of the Emperor's death Kâo was on duty as his gentleman-in-waiting. Kâo was the last person to see him alive, and the first person to enter his room, when the valet reported that he could get no reply to his knock, in the morning. The Emperor was thought to have died from a wasp sting on the tongue; but it was known to be his habit to smoke several pipes of opium before he went to sleep, and I'd bet my bottom dollar that the last pipe he smoked was Kâo's.

Perhaps Kâo had just made him a present of it, or it may be that he was already too fuddled with the fumes of the drug to notice that it was not his own when Kâo handed it to him. And, of course, the following morning Kâo was able to retrieve it before anyone saw the pipe and recognized it as his.'

A-lu-te looked slightly puzzled and asked, 'Do you mean that Kâo put poison in the opium?'

'No. It was the pipe that did the killing. Lin Wân was a much older man than the Emperor so he died much more quickly ; but, both of them died as the result of a type of seizure, and the symptoms being much the same struck me as curious. After P'ei's confessions we knew Kâo to be a murderer ; so on our return to the House of Lin, having found Kâo's beautiful pipe on Lin Wân's desk led me to examine it carefully. I found that concealed in the mouth-piece it had a strong steel pin, which could be set by a hidden spring to fly out and pierce the tongue or lips of anyone who smoked it. In each case before setting, of course, the pin was smeared with cyanide, or some other very rapid poison. Kâo knew that Lin Wân meant to double-cross him by marrying off Josephine to Tû-lai or one of his other sons. That he killed Lin Wân that way there can be no doubt at all ; so I think we can be pretty certain that he used the same method to murder the Emperor.'

After a moment A-lu-te looked up with fresh tears in her eyes and said, 'Then I have cause to be even more grateful to you than I knew. Had it become publicly known that I was the niece of a regicide, I would never have lived down such a disgrace.'

Gregory smiled at her. 'You must not thank me, but the gods who decided Kâo to take poison when he did, instead of fighting the case out to a finish. Had it not ended as it did, I might have been forced to disclose these other crimes in a final bid to save our lives. I was hoping that as he had left the pipe with Lin Wân, the sight of it would make him realize that I still had one last card up my sleeve. To my enormous relief, it did the trick ; and he threw his hand in.'

'Tell me just one more thing,' A-lu-te said, brushing her last tears away. 'It is about the three wishes that the Mandarins offered you yesterday, for the great service you had rendered